CW01499193

ACKNOWLEDGEMENTS

As always, thanks to Jill, Kath and Nanisa for reading and commenting, and for sorting out a colossal muddle of names. To Marsali Taylor, too, for Shetland sailing advice (of course!) and to all those who helped me in the Northern Isles once again, particularly the school bus driver and the Norwegian couple stuck in the church when the door handle fell off. You know the story.

Dramatis Personae

On the Sea Stag:
Kolbein, the skipper
Alfarin and Borgny, rather grand passengers
Thorgrim and Vigdis, not as grand as they think they are
Sibbi and Kjartan, kinsmen who make no pretence to grandeur at all
Gunnar, a refugee
Sundry clever slaves

Hjaltlanders:
Eyvind, lord of the hall at Gulbervig
Ivar, lord of the hall at Skalavagr
Thora and Svart, living at Gulbervig
The monks of St. Ninian's Isle and their neighbour, Thorir
Unnr and her family and neighbours at Dunrostar hofdi, always happy to take in guests

Orcadians:
Thorfinn Sigurdarson and his wife Ingibjorg
Ketil, his man, along with Skorri, Alf and Geirod (and his dog)
Sigrid, a woolworker, not working
Afi, a boat builder
Bolla, a maid

I

THIS, THOUGHT SIGRID grimly, was probably – almost certainly – a mistake. But it was too late now.

The coast of Rinansey was slipping away through the mist to the south, her last sight of Orkney. It had been a long time since she had last left these islands. What had driven her to do it this time?

This small trading ship was slow, slow on the waves and slow pottering along the coast and stopping wherever a bit of a deal could be done. She had bartered for a passage on it using a nice bit of woven braid she had made and had no particular customer for. She might have been better waiting: the boat she was pursuing was light and fast, and had no need to stop for a bargain. She might never catch up with Ketil Gunnarson and his crew.

'Can you not spin at sea?'

The old grandmother sitting opposite her had a sympathetic look, and was industriously picking at a sprang frame on her lap. She had made several bags on it since they had left the last calling place, working away with her long, gnarled nails. Sigrid wondered if she would have a use for them, or if she simply could not sit still and not be doing something. She knew the feeling.

'I can,' said Sigrid, 'and I would. But …' She held up her bandaged fingers.

'Oh, dear! Cooking fire?' asked the old woman, assuming

they were burns.

'Um, no,' said Sigrid. 'I slipped and fell on some rocks.' It was a version of the truth. 'I usually do a lot of woolwork. Tablet weaving, mostly.' She even had her weaving tablets and some wool with her, in case she was away from home so long that her fingers had healed enough for her to work. She needed to work. What was she going to do if they did not heal properly? Apart from her small farm, abandoned now to the boy Gnup to look after, she had no source of income other than her woolwork.

'Nice,' said the old woman. 'Widow, are you?'

'Yes.'

'Long?'

'A few years.'

'Twenty years, me,' said the other woman, with some pride. 'Died on a raid in Ireland, so they tell me. But my sons were grown by then and they came back safely, so they've looked after me. Going up to see one of them now – lives up in Hjaltland.'

'Oh? That's nice,' said Sigrid, trying to look interested. Hjaltland was the next stop, the next point north from Westray. If you didn't count Fritharey, anyway. From Hjaltland, she would find another ship – a faster one, if she could – that would take her to Nordvegr. Then down the coast, and round to the lands of the Danes. By then she just might have caught up with Ketil. What would he say to her when he saw her? He had asked her to come with him, but she had said no: she was sure he had not meant it. And then she had changed her mind, but he had already left. In his little ship he would not have sailed straight to Danmark, she was sure. That was a crossing for much larger vessels, and chancy even then.

The old woman was telling her about her son in Hjaltland.

'Nice little farm,' she was saying, as Sigrid paid attention again. 'And right by the beach, so lots of fish and shells. They eat more fish than we do. I tell him he's going to turn into a sea worm, the amount of fish he eats.'

Sigrid chuckled obediently.

'Have you been to Hjaltland before?' the woman asked.

'Only briefly,' said Sigrid. 'Only on the way to Orkney. A good while ago.' Ten years, she thought, or more. It had seemed to her at the time nothing out of the ordinary, a few bits broken off Nordvegr and tossed into the sea. Orkney was different, rich and green, a land of promise in the mist. Had it fulfilled the promise? Well … she was still there, was she not?

She decided that was a line of thought best abandoned.

'And is that your daughter with you?' she asked, nodding to the younger woman who had come on board with her companion. She would have been surprised if the old woman had denied it: they both had wide, sloping foreheads and large front teeth, and a lot to say.

'That's right.' The old woman paused in her plucking, and made a face. 'I envy you, you know, travelling on your own. Had you no one to come with you?'

'Not really, no.'

Helga had offered. Her neighbour Helga, shocked at Sigrid's plans to leave, had wildly told her she could not go alone and that Helga would abandon her husband and children to go too. Sigrid was touched, but she had mixed feelings. Sigrid was determined to catch up with Ketil, to get to Heithabyr, but Helga was easily distracted. A nice arm ring, an unusual pot, or a well-muscled chest, and she would forget all about Sigrid's plans, and then Sigrid would probably have to help her to extract herself from some new, unsuitable relationship or, alternatively, find space in her meagre luggage to carry Helga's purchases all the way to Danmark and back. So she had told Helga to stay at home, and had gone to find a boat on her own.

'I suppose she's helpful enough,' said the old woman, her eyes on her daughter. 'I mean, she carries things for me, makes sure I'm comfortable.' The woman did indeed look comfortable, seated on a thick sheepskin with a woollen rug around her, swaying easily with the movement of the ship. 'But she never stops talking. Look at that poor sailor, now: I'm sure his ears are worn out!'

Like mother, like daughter, thought Sigrid. But she was happy enough to sit and be talked at, as long as few responses were required. She was busy with her own thoughts.

Heithabyr. The trading town where she and Ketil, outsiders because their families were from Nordvegr, had been brought up as neighbours. The town she had left when her parents had died, from which she had travelled, very young, back to those relatives in Nordvegr who had brought her up, married her off, and waved her goodbye when she headed south with her husband. The town where

Ketil and his brothers had lived with their father Gunnar, a cupmaker. Ketil had travelled and was now Thorfinn's man, dealing with Thorfinn's problems. Thorfinn Sigurdarson was earl of – well, of quite a bit, really, including Orkney and Hjaltland, his allegiance distantly to King Harald in Nordvegr. One of Ketil's brothers had become a priest – a Christian priest – and headed to Rome, apparently. And Ketil's older brother, Njal, had taken over the business and stayed in Heithabyr, making his cups, marrying, and bringing up, if Sigrid remembered rightly, two small boys to follow him into the business. A business that was reportedly doing well, until King Harald and King Swein of Danmark had fallen out, and Harald had taken his fleet and his hird and harried the coast of Danmark, a harrying which had, according to the reports they had received only days ago, included the burning of the wooden town of Heithabyr.

Ketil had been told that Njal's wife and children were dead, and he was going to see if there was anything he could do to help. Thorfinn had given him his blessing. And Sigrid, because she was never wholly convinced that Ketil could manage anything complicated on his own, was following. And if it would be any faster to jump over the side and run across the waves, she would do it, she thought, her fingers twitching with impatience.

As it turned out, of course, the skipper did count Fritharey. The little island, the halfway point between the northern tip of Orkney and the southern tip of Hjaltland, had a population outnumbered by sheep and was only half-habitable. The wool, she remembered, was good, but she had nothing to buy it with: her savings were in the silver arm rings on her arms, tucked under her sleeves, and there were not nearly enough of them as it was. She stood on the shore, waiting for the skipper's negotiations to be finished – a deal involving wool, shellfish and some barrels, apparently – and stared up at the beacon on the hill, then around at the scattering of longhouses here on the lower south side of the little island. If Ketil had been here, there was no sign. If the wind had been good he might well have passed it by completely.

The wool was wrapped up in fleeces and the shellfish were poured into buckets on the ship, and the barrels, made of that rare commodity, good wood, were rolled ashore. The passengers and crew boarded again, hardly used to dry land, and the ship pushed off, painfully slowly. The island's rising coast crept past, and then they were out in open water again, sail up, oars in. The wind was reasonable, though Sigrid would have liked to see the sail bulging with something like a kindly tempest to speed them along. She hoped the repair to Ketil's ship was holding up. The thought that she might in fact have passed him, that disaster might have happened and he and his hird had sunk, could not be tolerated. He was ahead of her, and, with luck, she would catch up.

The southernmost tip of Hjaltland appeared just in time, almost at dusk. It reached out to them like a finger poking at something suspicious, a few lights at different points allowing the skipper to work out the shape of the land as they approached.

'We'll stop at Dunrostar hofdi,' said the skipper. 'That'll do us for the night.'

'Where after that?' asked Sigrid. She felt there was just enough light to go on for a while yet, into the evening, but forced herself to admit the skipper probably knew best. There would be skerries, no doubt, and other hazards.

'Up the west coast,' said the skipper with a grin. 'I have plenty of friends round the islands along the west - they would like a bit of wool or shellfish from Fritharey.'

Sigrid wondered how good his trading really was, or if he made more from the people who bought passages with him. Where, she thought, would her braid end up? Exchanged for a barrel or a bucket of whelk, or a rattle of hacksilver?

Once again, sail down and bound, they were passing on the strength of their oars between spikes of land, some shadowy headlands high above the waves, some pressed down like well-worked flatbreads. At last the lights on shore veered towards the lamps on the ship, and some of the crew leapt out into shallow water, hauling on ropes and helping the broad ship to beach safely, the keel crunching a path up the land. A couple of other small boats were there, dragged above the tideline, and she stood with her bag waiting for her turn to jump down on to what she could barely see but could already tell, from the sound, was a stony beach. The skipper came and helped her, mindful of her injured hands.

'There are houses just up there,' he said. 'See the people waiting to meet us? I come here often. We can stay the night on land.'

'That's my son's place, just over yonder,' said the old woman with the sprang frame, eagerly proprietorial. She was already on the beach, scrambling across the flattish stones, her daughter beside her still talking. 'He'll find space for us all, no doubt – it's a grand size of a house!'

A narrow, rising path took them up off the shore, the daughter helping her mother just ahead of Sigrid. There would be no going further tonight, certainly. She only hoped that the woman's poor son had not only space for all of them, but plenty of food to spare: she was starving.

II

'SO WHEN WE get there …' said Skorri, not for the first time. There had been delays: the dog had been sick, and Geirod had insisted they land and camp for the night.

'We do what needs to be done,' said Ketil, relatively patiently.

'But the town's been burned to the ground,' said Skorri. 'A wooden town. Like Bergvin. Burned.'

'So I've been told,' said Ketil. He had seen places burn – longhouses, sometimes halls. He knew what it would look like, what it would smell like.

'And your brother makes cups. Out of wood.'

'As I said, yes.' It was the family business – one at which he was no good at all, neither making nor selling. Sigrid would remind him of that.

Skorri made a puffing noise, as if to indicate that there was very little hope for this venture. Ketil thought he was probably right. But he had to see if there was anything he could do for his family, whatever was left of it. He thought for a moment about his other brother Thialfi, the priest. Had news of Heithabyr's destruction reached Rome? Did he know, too? A picture came to his mind of Thialfi making a slow journey north from Rome, overland, probably, to see what had happened. It would be strange, after all this time, if they met in Heithabyr. He had not seen Thialfi for years.

And Njal would be glad to see them both, anyway. If Njal

was still alive.

The sail was full, the little ship running nicely. Ketil had checked the repair he had had done at Birsay and was pleased with it. Skorri was steering, as much as was required, while the others sat by shipped oars: Alf, looking more like a skald than a soldier, the wind wistful in his hair, was idly scratching runes into a piece of soapstone, while Geirod, his yellow dog pressed against him, was working at the ends of two ropes, binding them together. Ketil watched the horizon to the north. A day's sailing to Hjaltland, then across to Bergvin – in the summer they could have done it overnight, but the autumn dusk settled earlier. They had friends in Bergvin and could stay there if need be. Then down the coast, and see if the Kings, Harald and Sweyn, had sorted out their differences, or if a more indirect route to Heithabyr might be advisable. They would get news in Bergvin.

'Do you think there's still fighting?' asked Alf, setting his stone down to clean off his knife. 'I could do with a bit of fighting.'

'Aye, there's been very little fighting now for a while,' Skorri agreed. 'I mean, we keep ourselves fit, but that's not the same as a good fight. Keeps the mind alert.'

'There was the fight between Bjorn and Einar's nephews,' Ketil reminded them, hoping that Skorri was wrong. He needed his men alert. 'That was not so long ago.'

'A mock fight,' said Skorri, dismissively.

'Mostly,' Alf conceded.

'At least on the Danish coast we might see a bit of action,' said Skorri. 'A bit of fun. We're getting stale.'

'Maybe, when we've done what has to be done in Heithabyr,' said Alf, 'we should go on east?'

'What, to Russland?' Skorri looked surprised. Not, Ketil noted, unpleasantly surprised.

'Or further,' said Alf. 'I'm sure there'd be some fighting down that way. I hear there are lots of little kingdoms and such – there's bound to be a few disagreements we could join in.'

'I don't want to go east,' said Geirod, making them jump. He was not one to voice his opinions too often. 'I want to go back to Birsay when we're done.'

'I'd have thought as long as you had your dog you'd be happy enough, Geirod,' said Skorri.

'Not if we go east.'

'You could go back to Birsay, and we could go on to … who knows where? Jorsalaheim itself?' said Alf, eyes lighting up at the romance of such an adventure. But Ketil found himself unusually disturbed at the thought of his hird breaking apart.

'Let's consider such things after we have dealt with Heithabyr,' he said firmly. 'One problem at a time.'

'And we haven't even got there yet,' said Skorri. 'Anything could happen.'

What happened was Gulbervig.

Gulbervig, at the curve of a kindly bay as round as a hole in the heel of your hose, was a popular spot for ships coming from the Norwegian coast to the islands, or waiting to leave for there.

They had made good time from Birsay, skimming quickly between the islands and, with a last stop on Rinansey for a bite to eat and extra fresh water, they had flitted north through dottings of seabirds and the swell of seals to reach Hjaltland in the early evening. There would be time to find a friendly host in Gulbervig, or to make camp for themselves by the shore if necessary. Ketil knew there was open land just beyond the settlement where, sheep permitting, they could be undisturbed. The ridge of the mainland rose above them, comfortingly steep, reminiscent of Nordvegr. Orkney, it seemed to Ketil, was far too flat and vulnerable, though he knew that people who understood farming thought it a much better land.

Alf saw to the ship while Ketil and Skorri raised the tent, and Geirod gathered driftwood for a fire, kindling it with grey lichen from rocks above the water line. The night was mild: they would be comfortable enough, with a hot meal inside them and all four of them, five with the dog, cosy under the wood and deerskin shelter. And tomorrow they would take the whale-path to Bergvin.

But the next day, in better light, Ketil saw that his was not the only ship visiting the settlement. A sizeable knar, broad and important-looking, was at the shore. They had not passed such a vessel on their way, so, he reasoned, it might have arrived late last night from Nordvegr.

'I'll go and see who it is,' he said. 'There may be news of

what's happening further south.'

He left Skorri and Geirod to clear up their camp, and took Alf with him for the short walk towards the gathering of longhouses, near to where the knar had landed. By contrast with last night there seemed to be plenty of people about: he could see women standing in doorways, spinning as they watched for anything interesting going on, children playing on the shore and around the smaller, local boats, men heading off to the more open land beyond – would they be harvesting? He was never very sure about farming – Sigrid would know. Around the knar stood a different set of people: the men, and both of the women, wore cowls, convenient for sailing, and they seemed aimless by comparison with the inhabitants. Perhaps there was a problem with the ship. Ketil and Alf made their way towards them, trying to pick out someone who could give them news.

'That might be the skipper,' murmured Alf, pointing to a neatly dressed, confident-looking man in a green cowl. The man was talking to a young woman, and the pair were laughing together.

'Maybe,' said Ketil. 'His boots don't look right. But we'll see.'

Two women, and – how many men? Half a dozen? Apart from them, the crew of the knar were clearly identifiable, through and through sailors with dark faces reddened by wind and salt. The others must be passengers.

'Who here is the skipper of this ship?' Ketil asked as he approached.

'That'd be me.' Not the man Alf had pointed out, but a short, tough individual with his fists on his hips. 'This is the Sea-Stag, just in last night from Bergvin. Who are you? Looking for a passage?'

'No, I'm –' But before he could go on, he felt Alf tap him on the arm, and at the same moment heard voices raised just beside them. He spun.

The confident-looking man had abandoned the young woman, and was facing a lad – perhaps a man? – and addressing him as loudly as if he were the crowd at a Thing. The other passengers watched. It was hard to gauge their thoughts.

'Listen here, Gunnar,' he announced. 'You're young and you'll learn. Don't go around accusing men – perfectly respectable men – of things when you can't possibly be right.'

'But I'm sure …' The lad's voice had broken, at least, but he sounded unsteady. 'I'm sure you took it.'

'And I can tell you that I never took it. What would I want with it? I have plenty of fine things of my own – why should I take yours?'

'You – you stole it!' Gunnar was shaking, clearly upset.

'Now, lad, I warned you!' said the other man. 'See, nobody here believes you! Look at them all – they just feel sorry for you, making a mistake like that! Now, just leave it be and I'll say nothing more.'

Ketil, who had seen the boy's hands, took a step forward, but he was too late. Gunnar threw a punch at the confident man, missing his jaw but brushing past his ear. The man, taken by surprise, staggered sideways, and Gunnar did his best to follow up with his other fist. This time, Ketil caught it before he could do any more. Gunnar squawked and struggled, then subsided. The confident man took two steps to recover his balance, and stood, panting.

'Did you see that?' he gasped. 'He hit me!'

'Barely,' said Ketil. He let go of Gunnar.

'You saw it. Everyone saw it, didn't you?' He turned to the other passengers. Some of them mumbled, and one, an older woman, said definitely:

'Oh, yes, he did! He hit you!'

The man nodded at her, and turned back to Ketil, reinforced.

'You had to step in and stop him! He hit me!'

'Enough,' said Ketil. He glared at the confident man and then at the boy. 'From both of you.'

'Who are you?' The question came from the skipper, with a different tone this time – suspicious, and not ready, Ketil thought, to meet someone else's authority.

'I'm Thorfinn's man – Earl Thorfinn Sigurdarson,' said Ketil. 'My name is Ketil Gunnarson.'

He heard a sudden intake of breath, and looked at the lad Gunnar.

'Ketil Gunnarson?' Gunnar repeated. Ketil frowned. Gunnar was not an uncommon name.

'Yes.'

'From Heithabyr? Brother of Njal Gunnarson?'

Ketil felt his heart begin to thud.

'Yes,' he said. 'That's me.'

'Then,' said the lad, 'I am your nephew. I am Gunnar Njalson.'

Ketil gaped, a hand out to grasp Gunnar's arm. The lad gave an uncertain smile, half-greeting, half-nerves.

'Gunnar?'

'Oh, well,' said Alf beside him, 'I suppose that means we're not going to Jorsalaheim.'

'I went to Nordvegr to find you,' said Gunnar, 'and at the court – I went to the King's court! I didn't see the King.'

'Just as well, coming from the Danes,' murmured Alf.

'But they said you were working for Thorfinn in Orkney, so that's where I was going.'

Ketil nodded. When he looked at the lad, he could see traces of his brother in him, traces of the little boy he had been when Ketil had last seen him. He had been fond of his nephews, but it had been so long.

'And – and Heithabyr?' he asked.

'Destroyed,' said Gunnar, shaking his head sadly. 'Father and Young Njal, they died. You won't know that Mother died last year, I suppose, so it was just me.'

'I'm sorry,' said Ketil. He had anticipated the news for so long that it was no great shock, only sorrow. 'Were you injured? Are you all right?'

'I was lucky,' said Gunnar, though his grey eyes clouded at the memory. 'Just lucky, Near the door. It was the smoke, see: they were hardly burned. I went back later, when it was cool enough – me and the neighbours, we all went together, and buried the dead.' He swallowed awkwardly. 'And I rescued a bag of cups from the shop, and I dug up the silver from our field. And there was a big arm ring amongst it with lumps of amber in it, and,' he drew breath, deep and fierce, 'and that man stole it!'

III

TOO MUCH THINKING on the boat, Sigrid thought, waking for the fourth or fifth time from an unsettling dream. Too many memories. This time she had been dreaming about her dead husband – dead in life, alive in the dream. It had not been a happy dream.

Thorsten had had his problems, she reflected, staring into the dark roof of the old woman's son's longhouse. Thorsten had been Einar's man, in the days when Einar and his men had raided all summer, leaving the women in charge of longhouses and farms, bringing back exotic treasures and wild tales to be told around the fire in the great hall on long winter evenings. And then Thorsten had been injured, his leg almost destroyed, and she found that raiding had been Thorsten's best way of using up his violence and filthy temper, until then. She had lost baby after baby in poverty and rage, until little Saebjorn had managed to live a year. A wild year, where Thorsten had attacked at least one man, had had to pay compensation for his death, had used up all their savings, and then – well, at the end his strange behaviour might have been the first signs of his illness that winter. He and Saebjorn, choking on the water in their lungs, dead within a week of each other. And Sigrid, brought up in Heithabyr, living around Thorfinn's court, believed in a God to whom one ought to make amends for the sins of the dead. So she had done her best: she had built a bridge, a plank of stone she had laboured over to fit it across a small stream near her longhouse, a recompense and a route for Thorsten to reach Heaven. For she had

13

loved him once, a long time ago, and besides, the thought of Thorsten still wandering, his soul not at rest, was frightening. It was bad enough to have him sitting grumpy in her dreams.

She turned over carefully, trying not to disturb the old woman and her daughter, who shared the bedspace. Actually, when she thought about it, the dreams might be the aftereffects of their supper. She had never eaten so many shellfish at one meal before – in the broth, wrapped in bread with cheese, poked into the fire and flicked out to be sliced from their shells and eaten on their own. She wondered how they would be served in the morning – in a beremeal porridge, perhaps? Still, she could not complain that she had been starved. The whole family and their guests ate extremely well. Even the cats looked enormous. If the crew stayed here too long, they would never all fit back in the boat.

It had been, on the whole, a pleasant evening, if she had not felt such a sense of urgency. The old woman she had met on the boat was clearly gently loved in the household and was welcomed with hugs and much exchange of gossip – for a while it was impossible for any of the others from the boat, standing about grinning foolishly at the spectacle, to make themselves heard, ask for shelter, take their seats by the fire and dry off their salty skin. Any fears Sigrid had had about food were unfounded: it was a large household and, from all she could see, a prosperous one, with family of all ages coming and going, talking and singing, children playing on the bed platform, women tending to the fire and stirring pots, and the man of the house, the old woman's son, seated in his high place like a lord, grinning at all about him.

Next to Sigrid, at the end of the longhouse nearest the door, there seemed to be the only quiet point in the place. A girl, younger than Gnup, she thought, hardly more than a child, was seated with some pieces of slate and a metal point, scratching marks on to the stone. Sigrid glanced over her arm, and her eyes widened in surprise. She was drawing, with some accuracy, a horse.

'That's very good,' she said, and the girl looked round at her in surprise, making a face that seemed to say she wanted to do better. But she said nothing.

'Unnr,' came a call from the host's wife, 'put that away. It's time to eat.' She cast a quick, apologetic smile at Sigrid. 'She's mute. She just spends all her time drawing.'

14

'Oh!' Sigrid found herself stiffening, wondering what to say to the girl. She had known people before who were deaf and dumb – but no, Unnr was not deaf. Strange how easy it was to make that assumption. The girl was piling two or three fragments of slates into a small bag with the metal point, and tying the pouch on to her belt, keeping it close. She nodded at Sigrid, as if confirming that she had done as she was told. Then she set to with her dinner as heartily as everyone else.

The others from the boat were enjoying their dinner, too, eating as if they had been three weeks at sea with no provisions. Sigrid wondered if the boatman had other hospitable places to stay along the coast as he went: some of the passengers almost looked as if they were on the journey for pure pleasure, seeing new places, making new friends. It was almost tempting to carry on with them and forget all her own concerns.

But she would not be going on in that boat, not if it were going west. Ketil would never have bothered going up the west coast of Hjaltland. He would be wanting somewhere to take a moment before making his journey east to Nordvegr. So she needed a boat to take her up the east coast, she imagined: if there was not one, she would have to walk.

She had asked their host the previous evening about paths along the coast, and he had assured her there would be a boat.

'It would take you days,' he said, discouragingly. 'Four at least, to walk.'

And Ketil would not be walking: he would be slipping past the neck of every voe in his smart little ship, finding the best point for departure. Her host had been definite about that, too.

'Gulbervig,' he said. 'See, you'd barely find it if you were walking. It's a bay up the coast. That's round about where ships come in from Bergvin. You're best on a boat.'

'If I can find one.'

'There's always boats,' said the man, nodding. 'If you can't find one, I'll take you myself. You'd be far quicker.'

'Any excuse to get in a boat,' confirmed his wife with a smile. 'Particularly if there's farming to be done.'

He grinned back.

'So whereabouts in Orkney are you from? I've been over there quite a few times.'

'I live near the Brough of Birsay,' said Sigrid. 'Near Thorfinn's hall? If you've heard of Einar Einarson …'

'Oh, I think I have. Tall, thin man. I thought I heard he had died?'

'He has. No clear heir, either.'

'Oh, aye. But Thorfinn will sort it out,' said the man. 'To his best advantage, no doubt. Tell me, do you know a man called Hrolf?'

'One of Einar's hird? Yes, I do. He's my neighbour.'

'Oh, aye. Yes, I've met Hrolf. Him and his wife. Helga, is that not her name?'

'That's the one,' said Sigrid, heart sinking.

And a smile came over the host's face.

'Oh, aye. I remember them.'

And his wife was no longer smiling. Huh, thought Sigrid. Even across the sea, Helga can still cause trouble.

Next morning she emerged from the longhouse to take a look about her. To be fair, this part of the mainland was as green as Orkney, though the land was steeper and around the longhouse the ground was hummocked and strangely shaped – not good for ploughing, but the sheep did not mind. They were on a broad headland, not very high, and close enough to the beach for all the gathering of shellfish to eat and seaweed to dry and cook them over. The air was fresh and cool, and inland Sigrid could see higher ground, cliffs over to her left swathed in mist, cliffs to the right over which she would have to find a way, if she were to walk north. She hoped there was a boat: she also hoped that her host would not have to sail it. She did not particularly want to spend a day or two listening to an account of Helga's charms, extensive as they were.

However, it seemed that their host's wife actually did want to hear about Helga, at some length. She pressed a cloth wrapped bundle of bread and cheese into Sigrid's hands, directed her to a neighbour's boat, and stalked back into the longhouse. Sigrid had barely taken two steps towards the neighbour when the shouting started. She moved faster, and almost collided with a slight figure that emerged from behind the longhouse. It was the girl she had seen last night, the daughter of the household. Unnr. She had a tight, anxious look about her.

'What's wrong, Unnr?' she asked, before she remembered

the girl was mute. She gave her head a quick shake, then jerked it back towards the longhouse, hunching her shoulders. 'You don't like listening to your parents quarrel?' she asked gently. The girl shook her head again, agreeing with her. Then she touched Sigrid's arm, took her pack, and carried it, leading the way, in the direction her mother had pointed out to Sigrid. Sigrid followed.

The neighbour was a large man with a rich golden beard down to his waist, but no hair on his head which he covered with a grubby nailbinding cap. His boat was tiny, with a sail Sigrid could have woven in half a day, yet the neighbour allowed Unnr to hop in after Sigrid, arranging her thin legs protectively around Sigrid's pack. All three of them sat with knees touching but dry feet – the boat was so light the neighbour had been able to shove it out on to the water and leap in in one quick movement. He was very helpful.

'We'll stop along the way. There are a few settlements likely to have had a lookout. Someone might have spotted your friend's boat going by. It sounds a fine boat. Likely someone will have seen it, eh, Unnr?'

Unnr nodded.

'Do you often just set off up the coast?' asked Sigrid, not minding which of them answered. Unnr shrugged, and the neighbour grinned.

'Oh, aye. Plenty to see and do, and a few fish to pick up along the way, eh?'

So they meandered up the coast, hailing folk from the water or skidding up on to beaches to find information.

'With four men and a yellow dog?' asked a boy around the middle of the day. He and Unnr and the neighbour shared Sigrid's bread and cheese, and the boy fetched water from a stream for them. 'Aye, that went past … let me think. The day before yesterday, maybe?'

'That sounds about right,' said Sigrid, any hopes that she might be catching up dashed. 'Oh, well, onwards.'

'I can't take you to Nordvegr,' said the neighbour, anxiously.

'No, I'm sure,' said Sigrid, alarmed at the thought of his tiny boat heading out across the sea. Steering out around some of the skerries had been worrying enough. She wondered how much longer it would take them to get to Gulbervig, and, her mind beginning to wander, she wondered who Gulba was. Strange to have a place named after a woman.

'But you'll find a boat in Gulbervig, no doubt,' said the neighbour. 'A bigger one.'

It would have been hard to find a smaller one, unless it was a child's toy. Sigrid smiled.

'I'm sure it will be fine. Something will come along.'

Fingering her silver arm rings through her sleeve, she hoped she was right. And that when it did, she would be able to afford it.

IV

'WELL, IF WE don't put it to the Thing, then you'll have to decide,' said the head man at the local hall. His name was Eyvind – good fortune and a good wind. Ketil was not sure it suited him. Normally a head man would be happy to pass a question like this on to the Althing, the general assembly, for a common decision. Eyvind seemed reluctant. 'You're Thorfinn's man. Is that why you carry a sword?' He regarded Ketil's sword with a mocking glance.

'I carry an axe, too,' said Ketil. He liked the feel of a sword, unusual though it was, but he could defend himself with anything. 'I'm an interested party,' he went on. 'Gunnar's my brother's son. And I'd like to think that you're Thorfinn's man, too – aren't you?'

The man looked as if he would like to wriggle, but was holding himself still. He glanced around the hall, pushing his thinning hair back. Older than Ketil, he had protruding front teeth but no chin, and sagging cheeks.

'Of course I am,' he said, after just slightly too long a pause. Ketil had the sense that he had been seeking someone's approval, but whose could he need? He was in charge here in Gulbervig.

'Do you know either of the men? Or anyone else from the ship?'

'The Sea-Stag,' put in the skipper, Kolbein. 'That's her name: the Sea-Stag.'

Ketil looked at him for a moment. The broad-beamed cargo ship looked solid enough, but if he had had to find a name for it himself it might have had something more to do with cows.

'He's here fairly regularly,' said Eyvind, now that Kolbein had his attention. 'Back and forth between here and Bergvin, you know?'

'Good trade,' said Kolbein with satisfaction. 'But this time I'm expanding my horizons – going down to Orkney, that's the plan.'

'Is it, indeed?' said Ketil. 'And –'

'Once I've finished here, aye? I've a deal to do in Skalavagr over the hill, once I can get away from here.' He gave a knowing smile, as if the deal was already to his advantage.

'That's good,' said Ketil, forced into more words than he would normally use just to stop Kolbein's flow of information. 'I'm delighted to hear it. I hope your deal is a success. Now, the others – do you know any of them, Eyvind?'

Eyvind looked about the hall, not strikingly impressed. There stood Gunnar, looking defiant but nervous, and not far from him the man he had struck, beside the woman who had come to his defence. The man was handsome, in a roughish way, and well-dressed without anything too fancy. He smiled at Ketil, ready to impress him if Ketil turned out to be important. The woman was stocky, with black hair scraped back on each side and bundled on top of her head to hang loosely behind: she was a married woman but had pulled off her headcloth when they entered the hall, and was now engaged in refolding it. Her face was weatherbeaten but her eyes were bright.

'This is Thorgrim,' she said, as Eyvind failed to identify them, 'from over the way. I'm his wife, Vigdis.' She flipped the headcloth over her head and tied it in place, then gave an unexpectedly pretty smile. 'There, that's better!'

'You won't know us,' said a man further down the hall. He stood near a torch, but angled so that his face was hard to see. The light showed greasy red hair cut short. 'No one knows us.'

'So who are you, then?' asked Ketil.

'I'm Sibbi, and this is my cousin Kjartan,' said the man. Kjartan was bulky, where Sibbi was small and wiry, but they shared a similar squashed nose. 'We're new around here,' Sibbi added, with a grin in his voice. 'Looking for work, maybe. We'll see how we find things.'

'Where are you from?' asked Eyvind, and Ketil could sense a hint of unease. Newcomers were not always good news.

'Inland from Bergvin.'

'Whose hird?'

'Man called Atli. Nothing much. Quiet place. Thought we'd like to see a bit more of the world, didn't we, Kjartan?'

'Aye,' said Kjartan. He seemed about to say more, but stopped. Eyvind, not entirely satisfied, looked on to see who else had come with the Sea-Stag. A couple stepped into the light, tall and finely dressed. Ketil had the impression that they had been waiting for the lesser folk to speak before they made themselves known.

'I am Alfarin Sweynson,' announced the man, in a voice used to being listened to. 'And this is my sister Borgny. We are on our way to the court of Earl Thorfinn Sigurdarson in Birsay.'

Are you, indeed? thought Ketil. He felt Eyvind look his way.

'From where?' Eyvind asked, when Ketil said nothing.

'The hall of Arinbjorn Egilsson, near Bergvin,' Alfarin announced. He spoke as if he expected to impress: Arinbjorn's hall seemed to be something to be proud of, yet there was a frown on Alfarin's face. Ketil was not sure he had heard of the man, but lords rise and fall. 'Needless to say we have no part in this – incident.'

His sister turned quickly to him, then looked away again. She was, Ketil thought, a very handsome woman, pale skinned, hazel eyes under narrow brows, high cheekbones and fine, mobile lips. She had pushed back the hood of the travelling cowl she wore, leaving her head bare and the light free to play on the elaborate braiding of her dark blonde hair. Usually only poor people wore cowls, but it was different at sea: they were practical and warm. Hers was a little more than that: Ketil reckoned it was made from very fine sealskin, with a pattern embroidered round about it in coloured wools. He wondered what Sigrid, with her sharp eye for woolwork, might say about it. But he was not here to think about Sigrid.

Eyvind had turned his gaze back to Gunnar.

'A Dane?' he was asking, suspiciously.

'Born of a Norwegian family, sir,' said Gunnar promptly. Ketil knew how he felt: he had spent his own childhood walking along the top of that narrow wall. And it was the Norwegian king who had seen Heithabyr destroyed, along with Gunnar's father and brother, yet he had gone to Nordvegr to seek Ketil. He would be safe in Orkney, though. Thorfinn was very nearly his own man.

'I see,' said Eyvind. 'And why did you punch this man ... what's your name, Thorgrim?'

'Thorgrim,' Thorgrim confirmed, talking over Gunnar's words.

'I believe he stole something of mine,' Gunnar managed to make himself heard. 'And he denied it, and he was rude and he provoked me.' Gunnar's lips pressed tight. He seemed aware that he had sounded rather prim. Ketil smiled inwardly: the boy was very young still.

'And did you?' Eyvind asked with a sigh. Everyone knew it was a pointless question.

'Of course I didn't,' said Thorgrim, drawing himself up straight. He was not a particularly tall man, but when he straightened he had some presence. Vigdis stood beside him, the ideal of respectability. 'Why on earth would I do that? I have wealth of my own without stealing another man's arm ring!'

'Look, I've known this man for years,' Kolbein, the skipper, decided to make his point. 'Never known him do anything dishonest. Wouldn't let him on my ship if I thought he was a thief. Not on the Sea-Stag.'

Thorgrim flashed him a look which was probably grateful.

'Where's your pack?' Eyvind asked reluctantly. 'You know we'll have to search it.'

'Of course,' said Thorgrim. 'I mean, I'm not keen on the idea, but if it will set this young man's mind at rest ...'

It quite clearly would not. Though Ketil could not offhand think of an opportunity Thorgrim might have had to hide Gunnar's arm ring, it was evidently not in his pack. There was a chance that Gunnar was mistaken, of course, but if the arm ring were not in Thorgrim's pack it would prove nothing, and Gunnar would not be satisfied.

Thorgrim brought his pack from the back of the hall, and laid it in silence before Eyvind, like some kind of solemn sacrifice. The two kinsmen, Sibbi and Kjartan, and the brother and sister, Alfarin and Borgny, stood without speaking: it seemed that no one knew either Thorgrim or Gunnar well enough to take sides. Kolbein, though, made some muttered remark about the search being a waste of time.

'He's obviously not taken it, and I could be halfway to Skalavagr by now,' he said. 'Getting my deal done.'

Eyvind gave him a weary look.

'Then you'd best search on his behalf,' he said. 'And Ketil, will one of your men search on behalf of Gunnar?'

Ketil nodded to Alf, who drifted across to the pack and smiled at Kolbein. Kolbein frowned in return: Alf never inspired confidence in tough men, not at first sight. Kolbein knelt by the pack and Alf joined him, facing each other so that Eyvind and the others could witness their search.

There was nothing out of the ordinary there. Spare clothing, both clean and dirty; a comb and a bowl and spoon, some bread and hard cheese, and a cloak for wearing on shore.

'What about his wife's pack?' Gunnar demanded, almost as soon as they had confirmed that Thorgrim's pack was empty of all valuables.

'Oh, must you?' asked Vigdis. 'But I suppose you must. Will you fetch it, dear?' she asked Thorgrim, and he went back to the gloom of the hall's darker end, and brought back another pack. Alf had delicately retied Thorgrim's belongings, and stooped once again to see to this pack. Again, he and Kolbein fingered their way, perhaps more gently, through clothes and utensils and a string of beads, with no bangle to be found.

'Looks like you were wrong,' said Eyvind to Gunnar, not unkindly.

'Up his sleeves?' Gunnar whispered, but Thorgrim pushed his sleeves up, one at a time, revealing a fine row of silver arm rings but none with the amber pieces in it that Gunnar had described. Gunnar's head sank.

'Well, a piece of silver in compensation, then,' said Eyvind. Gunnar heaved a weighty sigh, and fingered his own sleeves.

'How much?'

Eyvind seemed likely to take his time to decide. Ketil allowed himself a moment to take in more of the hall – nothing very grand, and the few local men lingering to watch looked neither fit nor bright. He heard quiet footsteps behind him in the darkness of the hall. He turned, not too quickly, shifting his attention from Eyvind and Gunnar. A man had come up almost to join them, cloaked, hair tousled by the wind, boots muddy, hands empty of weapons but eyes watchful. Ketil could barely see the man's face – not all the torches were lit – but decided he was not an immediate threat. Eyvind appeared not to have noticed him: was that because he was familiar, or because Eyvind's mind was distracted? As Thorfinn's man, always mindful of defence, Ketil wondered if Eyvind was not as alert as he might be. He shifted slightly, just in case he was wrong about the newcomer, making sure he could reach a knife smoothly.

Eyvind had reached a moderate decision about the price Gunnar had to pay to Thorgrim for insulting and assaulting him – after all, the assault had not amounted to much. Gunnar, who was clearly a law-abiding young man, slid off a thin round of silver and handed it to Eyvind. Eyvind weighed it in his hand, nodded, and held it out for Thorgrim. It was on Thorgrim's own arm in a flash. Ketil thought he heard a little sound from the newcomer – it was almost like a sigh.

It reflected, too, a relaxation of the tension in the hall. The matter was settled: the witnesses, such as they were, began to talk among themselves. Kolbein exchanged his cowl for a cloak from his pack, and made for the door, presumably to start his walk over to Skalavagr. Thorgrim, smiling, exchanged a few quiet words with his wife Vigdis and they gathered up their packs again, showing no urgency to leave, content with the outcome. Alfarin and his sister approached Eyvind, gravitating by nature to the most important person in the room. Sibbi and Kjartan looked about as if wondering when food might appear. Gunnar, his shoulders sagging, stood where he was. Ketil bent to say a word in Skorri's ear about watching the newcomer, and went over to his nephew.

'I'm sure he has it,' muttered Gunnar, without looking at either Ketil or Thorgrim. 'Positive.'

'No proof,' said Ketil shortly. 'Why are you so sure it was him?'

'He was the only one anywhere near my pack. It was at the front of the boat, where I could keep an eye on it. I went to talk to one of the sailors for a moment, and when I looked back Thorgrim was amongst the packs, and you couldn't see what he was doing because of the way he was standing – as if he was deliberately hiding what he was up to. I mean, even at the time I thought he was acting oddly. But it wasn't until we were gathering up our stuff and coming up to the beach that I thought I would take a good look. And the arm ring had gone. It was lovely, but more importantly – well, I don't have much left. And it was the most valuable thing I had.'

'And you're sure it couldn't just have fallen out?'

'Absolutely sure. It was wrapped in a sprang bag in a cloth bag, and tied up with string. All the other things were there, just not that.'

'In two bags and tied with string? Are you sure he would have had time to undo all that while you were talking to the sailor?'

Gunnar thought for a moment. The question had clearly not occurred to him before. Ketil watched him as he considered, impressed that he had not just jumped to the answer that supported his case.

'Yes, I think he would have, if he had been quick. I had checked the parcel before we boarded the Sea-Stag in Bergvin: if he had seen me doing that he would have known what to look for.'

'Why not just take the whole parcel? It would have been quicker.'

Gunnar's mind was quicker now.

'It would have been bulky: there are a couple of good cups in it, too, that I was keeping as examples to show people if – if I could start making cups again. I'm not as good as Father was, but I can make a nice cup.'

More than I ever could, thought Ketil. He could see his brother's eyes in Gunnar's long face, and when he talked of the cups he could see Njal's hands, too, working the wood. If Gunnar were half as good as Njal had been, he might well find a place to make a new life for himself. But what could have happened to the amber and silver arm ring?

He had barely begun to think about it, when the door of the hall banged open, and a dark, muscular man strode up to the front, straight towards Thorgrim.

'So you're back!' he growled. 'And if you're back, then where's my silver?'

V

AT DUSK THEY pulled into yet another voe, with yet another small settlement curled in at its end. Arrivals at dusk were becoming a habit, she thought. Before she could worry about where to stay, the bearded man told her that his sister was always ready to take in a guest. Her longhouse was not large, but she was indeed welcoming, showing Sigrid at once to a place by the fire, and handing her a cup of wonderfully spiced hot wine. Her elderly husband sat in pride of place in his chair, and a daughter, her husband not around, apparently, helped her with preparations for their guests. They too had seen a small boat pass a day or so ago – the daughter had noted the yellow dog and, she said, a handsome fair-haired man clearly in charge. Sigrid sniffed, but she was relieved, all the same, to know they had made it safely this far.

'I hope you don't mind,' said the woman, when all that was sorted out, 'but I haven't gathered any shellfish today. I have made chicken broth.'

Feeling she had had enough shellfish the day before to do her for a month, Sigrid beamed. She settled back, then grew restless again with no woolwork to do.

'Have you hurt your fingers?' asked the woman.

'I fell on some rocks,' said Sigrid. 'I make braids for a living, but …'

'Do you? Do you have any with you?'

So Sigrid brought out her braids, and by the time the broth

was ready, she had exchanged three of them, her best, for a slim silver arm ring and her night's lodging. And a bowl of hot water to wash the salt from her face and the parts of her hands she could reach.

There was not much conversation from the old man, who seemed to think she was his sister and kept asking her about her daughter. The wife hushed him apologetically, but Sigrid did not mind. Dinner was served early, and most of the talk around the fire was family news, interesting, no doubt, to the neighbour and his sister and their kin, but undramatic and soothingly dull to Sigrid. Unnr passed Sigrid a plate of flatbreads, then, pointing at the bandages on her fingers, offered by gestures to rip one up for her. She smiled and thanked her.

'It's awkward, rather than sore,' she said, and realised that that was true: the fingers were less painful than they had been. Maybe soon she would be able to thread her bone weaving tablets again.

'At least you haven't lost one,' said the widowed daughter with a grin. 'My husband had his ripped off, just here!' She pointed to the knuckle on the middle finger of her right hand.

'Yes, that would be more inconvenient,' Sigrid agreed. 'How did he lose it?'

'Caught in a rope on the boat,' said the woman, shrugging. 'He told me he hardly felt it till he got home. At least it was clean.'

'That's good.' Her own wounds had not been: it had taken quite a while to soak out the mud and grit. She winced at the memory. 'And presumably he can still sail.'

'Oh, yes. Don't know what I would do with him if he couldn't! He'd be at home getting under my feet.'

Like everyone she had met in Hjaltland, Sigrid thought. Never content with the land, always hopping into boats. Well, she would have to find one of them happy to take her across to Norway, for very little cost. In the morning they would press on to Gulbervig, presumably – unless they caught up unexpectedly with Ketil along the way – and she would make enquiries, but for tonight: well, two days on the water did not refresh her as much as it seemed to help the islanders, and last night had not been restful. She could feel her eyes closing, despite sensing the daughter's eagerness to chat next to her. She would have to make her excuses, or she would be asleep where she sat.

'You're from Orkney, then?' the woman asked. 'Whereabouts?'

'Buckquoy. Near Birsay,' said Sigrid, half-expecting the woman to ask her about Helga.

'Near Birsay! Ooh! Have you ever met Earl Thorfinn, then?'

Sigrid straightened a bit, taking her chance to make a good impression. You never knew where an opportunity for business might turn up.

'Oh, yes. I do a lot of woolwork for his wife, Ingibjorg. Braiding, wall hangings, that kind of thing.'

The woman looked gratifyingly admiring, then frowned.

'Ingibjorg? Isn't she kin to Kalf Arnason?'

Sigrid blinked, more awake now.

'Yes, Kalf is her cousin, I believe.'

'Have you met him?' The woman had lowered her voice, with a quick look round the company at the fire, as though one of them might stop her if they heard her. Sigrid thought back. She had not met Kalf, no. When Kalf had launched his attack at Kirkuvagr, his tricksy attempt to bring down Earl Thorfinn and seize his lands, he had not actually touched the shore: he had waited to see if his tricks had worked, and when his allies were overwhelmed in the little settlement, he turned his warships and fled. It was hardly much of an acquaintance.

'No, no, I haven't. He has not visited Earl Thorfinn since I lived there.' She kept her tone flat, as if she had barely heard of Kalf. She had thought him long gone, over to the west. Why was this woman asking about him?

'Oh, well,' said the woman. 'But imagine being at a court like that!' And for a while Sigrid was able to distract herself with a description of Earl Thorfinn's hall, and the adornments, and Ingibjorg's clothes, and the food, and the men, and the rest of the buildings in the settlement up on the Brough, the chapel and the sauna and all the things he was building and rebuilding. The woman sat with eyes wide, asking all kinds of questions, and Kalf was not mentioned again.

Sigrid slept much better that night, in a bedspace shared with the daughter and warmed with a hot stone, and there were no unsettling dreams. Whether that was thanks to the chicken broth, she was not wholly sure.

'Aren't you heading home again?' she asked Unnr next morning. The girl showed every sign of wanting to hop back into the tiny boat with her and the neighbour. 'I thought you were just out for the day.' Unnr made a face and shook her head, then patted the boat affectionately.

'She often comes up the coast with me,' said the neighbour, who was finishing an industrious combing of his long copper hair. Sigrid wondered where he had found a comb that tough, and wondered if she could get one for her own messy curls. Her headcloth was already firmly in place, her cowl over it for extra security. 'Anyway, you never know what you might see at Gulbervig. The road to Nordvegr! And if you take that, who knows where you might end up?'

Well, indeed, Sigrid thought. Who knows? It was not a happy thought.

Unnr and Sigrid hopped into the boat just as it touched the waves, and the neighbour bounced in after them, not quite upsetting the fragile craft. And off they went again, picking up a little wind in the sail this morning, working their way slowly north. Ahead of them, Sigrid could see only green tongues of land reaching out to them: she had no idea, from here, which were the arms of bays and which were separate islands, perhaps. She had been told there was a passage through the islands somewhere here, but it was impossible to discern it. She prayed that Ketil and his crew had gone to Gulbervig, and that there might be a delay before they set out for Bergvin, and that she had not fallen even further behind them in this tiny boat. But the weather looked fine, and Ketil was a confident sailor, and trusted his hird and his boat – surely he would be long gone by the time she reached Gulbervig?

The rain started then, soft at first, then solid, soaking into their clothing and dripping into everything on the boat. The neighbour drew in to another beach where they stopped and sheltered under a rock to eat their food, cold chicken and bread from the neighbour's sister, and some berries from the shore that they picked to sweeten their meal. The rain dropped relentlessly, and they sat in silence, until at last the neighbour said,

'I didn't realise you were from near Birsay.'

'Well, not originally. But that's where I live now.'

'Who was your husband?'

'Thorstein Erikson. Einar Einarson's man.'

The man nodded, staring out to sea, as far as one could see it through the rain.

'Einar's dead, isn't he?'

'Yes, he died not long ago.'

'Heirs?'

'None, now. Thorfinn will sort it out.'

'Thorfinn will sort it out,' the man repeated, still staring. Sigrid suddenly wondered if Thorfinn really would sort it out. She always just assumed that he would, that he would make the right decision, in the end, and all would be well. Much depended on finding a good replacement for Einar: Sigrid's own security on her little farm, the happiness of the people around her at Buckquoy, but most importantly the safety of the settlement on the Brough. Easily defended around its cliffs, Birsay relied on a competent lord at Einar's hall to protect the land side and the harbour. With Einar gone, what would happen if, say, Kalf came back and made another attack?

'Well, it doesn't look as if this rain's going to stop any time soon,' said the neighbour, and stood with a sigh. Unnr and Sigrid followed, picking their way back to the little boat. The man lifted one side and tipped it over, trying to spill out the puddles of rainwater, but it was still a soggy seat when they boarded again. Even the neighbour did not seem that keen on sailing much further.

'Will there be somewhere to stay at Gulbervig?' she asked, for want of something to break the sombre silence.

'Oh, aye,' said the neighbour. 'I mean, there's a hall, and all, but likely we'll stay at Thora's. She's a friend of my sister's – nice woman. I mean, it's her son's house, but he's not married yet so she's in charge.'

'How often are there ships to Nordvegr?'

The man shrugged.

'They come and they go, you see – it just depends. The weather, whatever. Trade.'

Of course, thought Sigrid. It was not as if he could tell her there would be two ships every Sunday. She was talking for the sake of talking. She hoped Thora would be welcoming. An unfamiliar hall might be much less cosy than someone's own home.

Thora was indeed welcoming. The fire was lit, the longhouse was warm, and in a very short time Sigrid was sitting comfortably in borrowed, wonderfully dry, clothes, with a cup of spiced wine in her hands and her hair loose. Thora sat with her, carefully replacing her sodden bandages. She was a woman it was easy to like on sight, with a warm smile and an air of knowing where everything was and willingness to share it.

'Where are you travelling to, then?' Thora asked as she worked. 'These are nearly healed, you know. But it must have been sore!'

'It was! I'm going to Nordvegr, probably.'

'Oh! That's a shame. There's no ship bound for there just now. There's a knar just come in from Bergvin, a couple of days ago, but it's heading on to Orkney, I think the skipper said. In any case, they're not going anywhere just now. They've been delayed.'

'Oh, yes?' Not that it was of much interest to Sigrid, but Thora clearly wanted to give her the local gossip.

'Yes! It's very sad, I suppose, but then we don't really know the people.'

'What's that, mother?' Her son appeared, black hair wet from a plunge in the water barrel. He rubbed his face with a cloth.

'What happened last night, Svart. I was just telling Sigrid it was very sad, though the man wasn't from these parts. You see, he was killed.'

VI

'AH, SVART,' SAID Eyvind, resigned, 'I might have known we could not have a dispute without you coming in. What is it now?'

The new man did indeed look as if he would be handy in a fight, and quite ready to join one.

'He stole my silver,' Svart said again, and though it was clear he was angry, he held himself well in check. It seemed to be an old complaint, but Gunnar was looking interested.

'I did not!' said Thorgrim at once. 'By Thor's beard, this is a place to avoid, if every man accuses newcomers of theft! Here,' he said, laying down his pack dramatically, 'It's already been searched, but search it again if you want to! Everyone here has already seen everything I own!'

'Ah, it'll be long gone,' said Svart dismissively. 'Or melted down and turned into something else. But I know it was you!'

'It was not! How could it have been me?'

'You saw me bury it! I knew I should have gone back later and shifted it again, but I was busy. Two days later I remembered, and went back, and it was gone!'

'Why did you not accuse him at the time?' asked Eyvind wearily. 'You know it's best to deal with these things straight away.'

'He was off at sea, wasn't he?' Svart snapped. 'He must have dug up my silver as soon as I was away, and then he came down here and got on a boat to Nordvegr, so they told me. What could I do then? I wasn't going to go after him there.'

Gunnar drew breath to speak, but Ketil laid a warning hand on his arm. There was no sense in allying himself with a local until they knew what the full situation was. Gunnar could find himself paying more compensation, and still not recovering the amber arm ring. But Thorgrim was right: two accusations of theft in one day looked distinctly suspicious.

'Ah, look at that rain!' The exclamation came from Kolbein, the skipper, who had turned back at first from departure to see what Svart had to say. Now he was staring out through the high double doorway of the hall, and beyond him all Ketil could see was silver-grey water, pouring down. 'No sense walking to Skalavagr in that. I'd be drowned.'

He sauntered back to the top of the hall again, and laid down his pack at his feet, pushing his cloak back. He took a seat on one of the long benches, leaning back against the table and stretching out his legs comfortably. Ketil caught a scowl on Sibbi's thin face, but his cousin Kjartan seemed unbothered.

'I suppose you're all staying here tonight,' said Eyvind, not exactly the welcoming host. 'I'll tell my wife.' He rose reluctantly from his high seat, and looked about him, as if wondering where his wife might be. She had certainly not put in an appearance for the unplanned adjudication.

Ketil exchanged glances with his men. They were all now gathered in there, comparing their tent with the sturdy hall, and thinking of the rain. No point in unnecessary suffering. Alf and Skorri nodded: they would be staying here. And anyway, Ketil felt a growing interest in Thorgrim and what he might have done with Gunnar's amber arm ring.

'What about me?' demanded Svart.

'You can stay here too, of course, if you don't want to go home,' said Eyvind with a shrug.

'No, I mean what about my silver? What about him?' He gestured to Thorgrim.

'I'm innocent!' snapped Thorgrim. 'Why does everyone keep accusing me of theft?'

'He's a good man!' chimed in Vigdis, his wife. 'Leave him alone!'

'Svart, come over here, son,' said Eyvind, stepping away

from his seat to lay a hand on Svart's shoulder. He had to reach up slightly to do it, but he guided Svart over to the side of the hall. Svart went unresisting, looking puzzled.

'What's he saying to him?' Gunnar muttered. 'Why's he defending Thorgrim? The man's clearly a thief.'

'Local matters,' Ketil murmured back. 'Leave it for now, Gunnar. There might be other ways of finding out. Come over here: we'll have a conversation of our own.' He drew the boy across to an empty bench, further from the fire. His men stayed where they were: Alf had drawn out a bone flute, and was trying a few cheerful notes, and Skorri seemed to be venturing into conversation with the two cousins, Sibbi and Kjartan. Skorri was a sociable soul. Ketil sat, and gestured Gunnar to join him.

'Tell me about your fellow travellers,' he said softly. 'Who talks together? Who avoids others? Have you known any of them for longer than just this journey?'

'No,' said Gunnar, 'I only met them at Bergvin. And it's not a long voyage, you know – though we had to wait a day for a good wind.' He paused, thinking. 'Well, Alfarin and his sister don't talk much to the rest of us. They're quite grand. But friendly enough, when they have to be.'

And going to visit Earl Thorfinn, which is interesting, Ketil remembered. Was Thorfinn expecting them?

'The rest of us all talked together,' Gunnar went on. 'Sibbi's quite funny, but Kjartan's nicer. I mean, Sibbi makes fun of people, says things that are sometimes a bit nasty, but always funny. Kjartan's sort of kind.'

'Did they know Thorgrim and Vigdis already?'

Gunnar scowled, trying to think. He was not really of an age where he would notice how other people fitted together.

'I don't think so. I mean, it wasn't obvious.'

'And Vigdis – is she always so devoted to her husband? Do they normally get on well?'

'I've never seen them argue.'

Ketil reflected that he had known more useful witnesses.

'What about Kolbein, the skipper? Did he talk much with his passengers?'

Gunnar nodded.

'Mostly about his ship, and how wonderful it is,' he said,

with half a grin. 'He tried talking to Alfarin and Borgny quite a bit, you know, making himself out to be important, trying to impress them. I don't think they took him very seriously – I mean, I don't think they really noticed him. Alfarin asked him questions, sometimes, about Hjaltland and Orkney, just the kind of things you would ask if you'd never been here before. I listened to learn a bit. But it wasn't much – just about the main harbours, the biggest settlements, how many warships Earl Thorfinn had – that kind of thing.'

Ketil's scalp prickled. As Thorfinn's man, he was not at all keen on men who came and asked about harbours and warships.

'And what kind of answers did Kolbein give him?'

'He didn't say much. Just sort of half-answers, as if he didn't really know. And some of the things I knew already, so I'm sure Alfarin did, too – I'd heard of Birsay, and Hamnavoe, and here, Gulbervig, when I was looking for you at Harald's court.' Gunnar stopped again, thinking back. 'And when it came to the warships, he gave Alfarin a very odd look – sort of suspicious – and said he had no idea, the number changed all the time.'

'That's an odd answer,' said Ketil. Ships could sink quite fast, but it took a long time to build one, and even longer to prepare the sails. Thorfinn's fleet was fairly stable. Was Kolbein equally wary about such queries?

Their conversation slid into Gunnar's story of his journey from Heithabyr to Harald's court to Bergvin to Hjaltland, as the rainy day drew on.

'You took on quite a journey,' said Ketil, surprised at Gunnar's initiative, but Gunnar shrugged.

'I had no relatives left but my uncles – I had to come looking,'

Eyvind's wife and her women appeared, tending to the fire, starting the process of making the evening meal, serving warm wine at last. Thorgrim and Vigdis had tried to talk with Alfarin and his sister, then given up and gone to settle next to Skorri and Alf, where the conversation seemed to thrive. Ketil watched them. Thorgrim and Vigdis gave the impression, setting aside all accusations, of a respectable couple. Yet two accusations seemed a very unhappy coincidence. He glanced round to see if Svart was still in the hall, but he had gone. So, too, as far as he could see, had the nameless man who had stepped into the shadows, watching Thorgrim. Thorgrim had attracted some local attention. It struck Ketil that he had spoken a little like the local men. Perhaps he had lived here himself – had he, in fact, come home here? If so, had he friends to whom he might have passed that amber arm ring?

The food was served, to Ketil's hird, to the ship's passengers and Kolbein, and to a few of Eyvind's own hird who had scuttled in out of the rain to warm themselves by the fire. Kolbein's crew were presumably provisioned on the ship. Alfarin and Borgny sat near Eyvind's high seat in the place of honour, and Ketil was invited to sit at his other side, as Thorfinn's representative. He preferred to be less exposed but it would have been insulting to refuse, so he relied on his men to take their places around the hall, habitually keeping an eye on everyone. Gunnar sat with Skorri. Geirod made sure his yellow dog was given a bone. Everything seemed almost boringly normal, a typical evening in a typical small hall, with unremarkable food and reasonable wine and beer. Eyvind's hird included a couple of older men, fighting days long past, who regaled them with well-practised stories of dubious origin, and Kolbein told tales of voyages on his precious Sea Stag. Thorgrim and Vigdis kept quiet, probably wisely. Alfarin and Borgny applauded politely at the end of each tale or song, but did not join in. And Ketil, his scalp still prickling, watched.

'Here, try some of this,' said Eyvind, leaning towards Ketil confidingly. He tipped a small blue-black jar, round like a ball, over Ketil's wine cup. 'Spiced honey – the best!'

Ketil thanked him politely. He was not a great drinker, and preferred his wine less sweet, but Eyvind seemed very proud of the honey. He sipped, and made an appreciative sound. Eyvind nodded, delighted, and kept watching him so that he had to finish the whole cup. He promised himself he would touch no more, longing for a draught of clean water to wash away the sticky sweetness.

By the time the food was gone and the men were concentrating on drinking, Svart had reappeared, soaking, sliding in at the back of the hall to take a seat and a cup of beer near Geirod. They nodded to each other, but Ketil did not see either of them speak. Ketil wondered how far away he lived, to make it worth a soaking just to come into the hall. His was not the only wet head, though: it was that time of the evening when every guest had to decide how long they could go before they would have to make a dash outside to relieve themselves, and by now some were less steady on their feet. Ketil was finding it hard to keep track of who was where, and was annoyed to find he was feeling the effects of that one cup of wine. He decided to wait until someone else reasonably sober could show him the way to the privy. He noticed Thorgrim getting to his feet, a hand on Vigdis's shoulder, and thought he looked both steady and confident. He set down his own cup, nodded to Eyvind, and followed. He stumbled, and righted himself with an effort.

Outside a few torches spat in the rain, though the downpour seemed to have eased a little. Ketil tried to watch Thorgrim's direction but kept back, mostly because the wall of the hall was worryingly unsteady. He stopped, clutching at it, and tried to concentrate on the nearest torch. It burned green and blue – that could not be right. But then everything seemed to be glowing green. He wondered if he was green, too – he felt peculiar, anyway. Voices came and went around him, making no sense. His head was burning, aching, spinning. He had no idea if it was the hall still next to him or not. Whatever it was, it supported him as he pressed his forehead against the stone, and vomited liberally.

There, whatever it was that would sort it out, he told himself. He did feel a little steadier. He could hear the sea. The privy must be somewhere over here, then. And to his amazement, he found it.

The broad bay, the boats on the shore, the rest of the little settlement, all were invisible as Ketil made his way back. As he approached the wall of the hall, though, he heard voices, and stopped at once, almost in control of his legs. His mouth tasted vile.

The voices were low, and the first was a woman's, light and breathy.

'No, no, I cannot.'

'Grant me a moment only. Please, my lady: I'm bewitched, and only you have the power to release me.'

Ketil blinked, wondering that any woman could fall for honeyed words like these. That voice … not wholly familiar, but a recent acquaintance. Thorgrim. But my lady?

'No, I cannot. I must not, Thorgrim. I am betrothed.'

'A political marriage, no doubt?' came Thorgrim's

wheedling tones. 'A man you do not love?'

'That's … beside the point,' said the woman. 'He is a very important man. And very powerful – if he found out –'

'He wouldn't find out, not from me – and who else would know?' Thorgrim was persistent, anyway. And the woman – surely that must be Borgny? Ketil did not think he had heard her speak, but the tone fitted. He was pleased with himself for reasoning that far. He hoped they would go soon – he was not sure how much longer he could stand upright. 'Anyway, who is this powerful man?'

'It is Bjorn Einarson,' said Borgny, a hint of pride in her voice. 'A favourite of King Harald, and by now, I believe, the lord of an important hall in Orkney. I go to join him there.'

Ketil caught his breath. There was something wrong there – but what was it? His head had begun to lurch again.

'An important man indeed, my lady,' said Thorgrim, impressed. 'But still …'

'No, Thorgrim, no. I cannot.'

A note of panic had entered her voice. Ketil thought it was time to step in.

'Good evening,' he said, slightly too loudly. 'Are we all heading back to the hall?'

But he had overestimated himself. His own sudden movement had knocked him off his balance. He toppled between them, bent over and vomited again, causing them both to spring apart, away from him.

'Are you all right?' Borgny asked, surprisingly kindly.

'Too much to drink,' said Thorgrim, not without sympathy. 'He'll be better out here. You go on inside, my lady,' he added solicitously, as if he were going to watch over Ketil. But Ketil stumbled after Borgny, and they all entered the hall again, Ketil easing himself back into his seat with a hand to every pillar as he passed it. One of the serving women, seeing him, gave him a clean cloth to wipe his face, and a cup of ale, well used to such cases. Ketil wanted to tell her he had had only one cup of wine, but the words seemed difficult to manage.

And now mercifully people were beginning to find spaces for themselves by the side of the hall, unrolling packs of bedding, tucking themselves into their cloaks. The torches were extinguished, leaving the dwindling fire as the only light. Eyvind and his household retreated to their longhouse, leaving their guests to sleep, and to continue their occasional excursions to the midden.

Ketil slept lightly, near where he had sat for the evening, tumbled about by dreams he could not quite catch. What woke him he was not sure, but he could see the grey light of dawn around the edges of the great doors. He sat up, and at once regretted it.

And at that moment, he heard a scream.

VII

'KILLED? YOU MEAN no one has taken responsibility for it?' asked Sigrid. If someone had owned up and explained why they had killed someone, and paid the fine, it would hardly be called murder.

'Oh no, no, not killed by someone,' said Thora happily. Whoever it had been, he clearly meant nothing to her. 'I mean he died, probably in an accident.'

'But it was someone off the ship from Nordvegr?' Sigrid could not help making sure: Ketil was the kind who could get himself into all kinds of difficulties, unsupervised. And there would be no point in trying to follow him any further, she told herself, if he had got himself killed. She could turn around and go home. Couldn't she?

'That's right, yes,' said Thora, unaware of Sigrid's thoughts. 'A merchant, apparently.'

'Do you know what he looked like?' Sigrid pressed on, ignoring the anxious beating of her heart. Ketil had pretended to be a trader before, but surely he would have had no need to do so now?

'Middle height, dark hair,' said Svart shortly. Sigrid's heart skipped and settled. Ketil could never be described as middle height, even if he had somehow darkened his white-blond hair. How annoying, she told herself: she would still have to find him.

Though a fatal accident … Ketil attracted trouble wherever he went. Perhaps she could catch up with him, after all.

'Tell me,' she said, 'has a small boat arrived here recently, with four men in it from Orkney? Four men and a yellow dog?'

'You mean Thorfinn's man?' asked Svart. 'Ketil Gunnarson, they call him?'

'That's right, that's him.'

'Yes: they're at the hall.'

'They're still here? They haven't sailed for Nordvegr?'

Svart looked at her in surprise.

'No word of them going to Nordvegr. They're at the hall, the four of them – and the dog.' He gave a little, snorting laugh, with no humour in it. 'They were trying to work out what happened.'

Sigrid's heart was very unreliable this evening. Now it was dancing along, almost making her hiccup. It would be the thought of Ketil and his men trying to solve the mystery without her help, of course. They had always needed her before. Even Thorfinn recognised that. She suddenly longed to dash out of this cosy longhouse and find her way to the hall, to see what was going on. But that would not do: Unnr and the neighbour were here by the fire, Thora had the dinner nearly made, and Svart seemed to know something of what had happened: she could start asking questions here, and not run foolishly into an unfamiliar hall when they would doubtless be halfway through their own evening meal there, and probably drunk already. No, she would stay here – for now.

'So what happened?' she asked.

Svart shrugged.

'The fellow was staying in the hall, and they found him this morning outside. It looked as if he'd fallen on some rocks in the dark.'

'Who was he?'

Svart shrugged again, and if Sigrid had not been looking straight at him she might have missed his quick glance at his mother. Thora was scooping flatbreads off the hot stones in the hearth.

'Some merchant. He'd come off the boat from Bergvin. He'd … he'd had an argument with one of his fellow passengers, or they thought they would rob him. Something like that. So I suppose that kind of thing, with a death afterwards, that would interest Thorfinn's man.'

Sigrid pressed her lips together, thinking.

'Was the merchant travelling alone? Had he friends with

him?'

'A wife,' said Svart. 'That's all.'

'Were there other passengers apart from them?'

'Oh, aye,' said Svart. 'A fine-looking woman with her brother, very grand, and a couple of fellows looking for work. I think they were all intending to go on to Orkney. Oh, and a young fellow, too – don't know what he was doing, but I think he was heading south and all.'

'It's Kolbein's boat, isn't it?' asked Thora, handing Sigrid a bowl of stew and a flatbread with care, mindful of her injuries. Sigrid breathed in the wonderful aroma. 'The Sea Stag?'

'That's right,' said Svart. 'He crosses back and forth a lot.' He took a breath, as though he were not accustomed to much talking but had decided to take a chance. 'Doesn't often go down to Orkney, though. He must just have decided since all his passengers were going there he might as well try a change. He'll trade anywhere, that man, anyway, and if he could make a bit more out of the passengers, too, that would suit him well.'

'He usually goes over to Skalavagr while he's here,' Thora remarked, having served everyone else. Unnr and the neighbour were tucking in eagerly, their flatbreads nearly gone. They seemed unconcerned by accidental deaths, though Unnr was watching Svart carefully. 'Is he not away over there?'

'He was waiting for the rain to stop,' Svart replied. 'And now he's stuck, because Ketil won't let anyone leave until he's found out more about what happened.'

'Very sensible,' said Thora. 'And you know this Ketil, then, do you not, Sigrid?'

'Yes, and his hird,' said Sigrid. 'Ketil does a lot for Thorfinn, so he's around the court a good deal.' She did not mention their shared childhood in Heithabyr. 'His men are good company,' she added. She had to admit she was quite fond of Skorri, Alf and even Geirod – well, of his dog, anyway.

'Are you around the court too, then?' asked Thora, curious.

'Yes, quite a bit,' said Sigrid. 'I help Ingibjorg with woolwork – and of course if there's any big feast we all go to serve the food and drink.'

'Oh, yes, of course,' said Thora, and sighed. 'It's the same here. I'd rather stay by my own hearth than lug great jugs of ale and plates of bread around while all the men get drunk.'

'Who's the lord here?' Sigrid asked. She would need some local information.

'Eyvind Thorson,' said Thora, rolling her eyes a little. 'His wife's all right, but it's not the most exciting place to be. Eyvind's an odd one, anyway.'

'Odd? In what way?' Sigrid smiled sympathetically, as if to convey that she would be happy to share her own experience of odd lords. Einar, she supposed, had been a bit strange. 'Our old one learned to read Latin!'

'Ha! Nothing that interesting,' said Thora with a grin. 'Latin? What did he need to do that for?'

'He just wanted to,' said Sigrid, not very sure of the answer herself. 'So Eyvind's not a scholar, then?'

'Not him, no. But he thinks he's clever, doesn't he, Svart?'

'I suppose,' said Svart. Sigrid wondered how good the conversation was here when there were no guests. Svart did not seem to contribute a lot.

'He likes to plot, you know, trying to play off his men against each other. But he's not as good at it as he thinks: it's so easy to see through him, and the men just laugh behind his back, don't they, Svart?'

'Aye, well, sometimes, right enough,' said Svart. 'Sometimes ...'

Thora gave him a sharp look.

'What's wrong, Svart?'

Svart shifted on the low bench, staring into the fire, but Sigrid could see the tension in his shoulders. Unnr and Thora watched intensely, and even the neighbour set down his spoon for a moment, rubbing broth from his beard with the back of his hand. Svart's gaze flickered around them, almost meeting his mother's eye, then down to the glowing fire again.

'I said something stupid,' he said. 'And now they think I killed him.'

'That you killed him?' Thora echoed, and her voice shook. 'Svart, who was he?'

Svart looked directly at his mother at last.

'It was Thorgrim.'

VIII

THE KINDLY ARMS of Gulbervig bay lay misty around the early morning water, and an autumnal sun turned the hillsides a bright, soft green. A skein of geese flew across the bay, their strange chants echoing. Ketil looked down at the body at his feet, and swallowed hard.

'He must have slipped on the rocks,' said Skorri, pointing to Thorgrim's head. It was bloody, and his clothes were soaked dark red. The expression on his pale, dead face was hard to read – shock, certainly, but anger?

'What was he doing on the rocks, though?' asked Ketil. 'The hall is over there, the privy to its side.'

'Lost his way?' Skorri thought for a moment. 'He didn't strike me as being very drunk. A careful kind of a drinker, I remember thinking.'

Ketil stooped to feel Thorgrim's sleeve, on the less bloody side of his body. His head swam.

'He's dry, or no wetter than the dew would make him,' he observed. 'When did the rain stop?'

Skorri shrugged. Ketil thought back. He remembered, at one point, seeing a slice of moonlight through the smoke hole in the hall's roof: maybe halfway to dawn? But if Thorgrim had ventured out in the moonlight, how had he lost his way to the privy? What might have inspired him to take a walk, not on the easy beach, amongst the boats, but here on the roughest part of the shoreline?

'Something here does not make sense,' he murmured. He caught Skorri's eye. 'What?'

'You need to be careful,' said Skorri. 'If you're thinking someone helped him on his way – and I'm not saying they didn't – then who was one of the last people to dispute with him?'

Ketil thought of the man Svart, his angry accusation and his sudden subsidence. But then Skorri's meaning came to him.

'Gunnar.'

'Aye.'

They stood in silence for a moment, neither face showing emotion. The others from the hall watched from the beach: Alf and Geirod had persuaded them to stay clear. Vigdis was not amongst them: she had collapsed where she screamed, not far from the hall door. Eyvind's wife had taken her inside, almost carrying her through the tall double doorway, and the graceful Borgny had stayed with them. Ketil surveyed the small crowd: Kolbein, the skipper of the Sea Stag, had one hand on the gunwale of his ship as if he needed comforting after the shock. Gunnar stayed close to Ketil's men, as if they were kin by association. Alfarin stood a little apart, watchful but detached. Svart had returned, and was looking with some puzzlement at the corpse. Sibbi and Kjartan, along with Svart, were with Eyvind and his men, perhaps already hoping to find a place here to settle. Kjartan looked sorrowful, but Sibbi was frowning. He struck Ketil as a sharp man: maybe he was wondering, as Ketil and Skorri were, what had really happened here. Ketil thought Sibbi could be of use to Eyvind, if he were not too ambitious: Eyvind did not seem a very clever leader. Just now he was staring over at Thorgrim's body, what could be seen of it from where they were, looking completely baffled.

'How much longer are you going to be?' he called over. 'He's dead, isn't he?'

'Yes, he's dead,' said Ketil. 'Has been for a few hours.'

'Then I suppose you'll have to bring him into the hall, and we'll organise a burial. What's taking you so long?'

'When a death is unexpected, sometimes it's a good idea to move slowly, my lord,' said Skorri. 'Just in case anything is missed.'

'Like what?' Eyvind sounded petulant. The morning was chilly: he probably wanted to get back to the fire, or get on with some work.

'Like a missing purse, or an unexpected injury,' said Alf helpfully.

'And is his purse missing? Is there an unexpected injury?' Eyvind demanded.

'No to both, so far as I can see,' said Ketil. He had pushed up Thorgrim's sleeves, so far as he could: the bloody one was very stiff. 'We can take him back to the hall, if that's what you want.'

Eyvind shrugged, as though he could see no alternative. He nodded to a few of his own men who departed and returned with a couple of boards bound together: they skidded and tripped over the rocks to where Thorgrim lay. As they lifted him, with some difficulty, on to the boards, Ketil pulled a fold of Thorgrim's cloak over his face, and shifted the purse hanging from his belt so that it lay on his body, rather than dangling awkwardly off the side of the boards. The purse was soft leather, and heavy. That was somewhere they had not looked the previous day, when Gunnar had accused Thorgrim of theft – in fact, Ketil had not even seen it. It must have been tucked under Thorgrim's cloak, and in his willingness to let them examine his pack and the silver on his arms, he had managed to distract them from any further search. So what was in the purse, then?

But the two men carrying the boards were in a hurry to get back to the level, easier surface of the beach, and Ketil left the matter for the moment. There would be time later: he would make sure of it.

The men of the hall and their guests fell into a loose procession behind Thorgrim's bier, Eyvind leading them. Ketil and his hird fell in at the back. Ketil watched the men in front of them as they walked the short distance back to the hall. No one seemed particularly upset, but then few of them had known Thorgrim well, presumably. Vigdis would be the only one here who would truly mourn him. Ketil wondered where the burial would take place, and when. He scanned around the settlement for a chapel, but could not see one, and he could not remember there being a priest at the hall last night. Perhaps they would have to walk over to Skalavagr to see the man interred – that would please Kolbein, no doubt. He would be eager to take his path, now that the rain had stopped. Or should Ketil ask him not to disappear just yet? He shrugged to himself. He might be Thorfinn's man, but he had little power here to tell anyone what to do. It might be a question of talking to Eyvind. But what would he say? And would Eyvind pay him any attention? It seemed unlikely: after all, it had been Eyvind who had fined Gunnar for attacking Thorgrim, and Eyvind who had taken the man Svart aside and somehow silenced his accusations against Thorgrim.

And what had those accusations been? Because if Thorgrim had been watching Svart, a local man, bury his silver, then what exactly was Thorgrim's connexion to Gulbervig? And if he was from around here, how did Eyvind not know him?

Ketil barely noticed the walk back to the hall, with his thoughts churning. He wished he could think more clearly. But he roused himself to watch again as they entered the hall and spread around, waiting to see what would happen next. Eyvind's wife had been busy: a table had been cleared for the corpse and draped with a cloth, with another lying by ready to cover the body. She and Vigdis had been seated by the fire, Vigdis' hand absently clutching a cup, but as the bier entered the hall they had risen and turned to face it. Vigdis' red face was soaked with tears, the front of her dress wet behind her strings of beads. Her headcloth had come undone, her black hair spiky and wild. She raised her hands, holding them out towards the body as the bearers approached, as if she could greet her husband. Eyvind's wife had an arm around her, holding her steady as she shook.

'What has happened?' she sobbed. 'What happened to him?'

'He fell on the rocks, banged his head,' said Eyvind, not without sympathy. 'He must have gone for a walk.'

'Then he's truly dead?' Her voice shook, as if she were forcing out the question against her will.

'He's dead, yes,' said Eyvind, a little more impatiently. He waved at the table where the bier was laid. 'Go and look for yourself.'

But Vigdis had taken him at his word. She sagged against Eyvind's wife.

'What am I going to do? What can I do? He's dead, he's dead!' The sobs shook her, as Eyvind's wife gently drew her back down to sit by the fire.

'We'll prepare him for burial,' she murmured. 'That will help you.'

'Have you no other kin?' Eyvind asked. 'No one you can go

to?'

Vigdis raised her head enough to shake it.

'No one here. No one at all … I'm from Orkney …'

'Then maybe you'd best go back there,' said Eyvind, with an air of finding a happy solution to a problem. 'I mean, once everything's – organised.'

'Was Thorgrim from Orkney, too?' Ketil asked, and Vigdis looked sharply at him.

'No …' she replied after a moment. 'No, he was from Hjaltland.'

'Really?' Eyvind was surprised, but Vigdis nodded, more sure of herself somehow.

'Yes, that's right. He was a Hjaltlander. And I want him buried at his home.'

'At his home? Where's that, then?' Eyvind could still see hope of being able to pass any responsibility over to someone else.

'Over in the west,' Vigdis explained. 'West mainland. St. Ninian's Isle.'

'The monastery?' Eyvind asked, taken aback. But now Vigdis was enthusiastic.

'The monastery, yes. That's where I want to bury him. The monks will allow it, I'm sure. He was a good man, my Thorgrim. A good man.'

'Well …' Eyvind seemed doubtful. 'It's a bit of a walk, with a corpse.'

'We should all go,' said Alfarin suddenly.

Everyone turned to look at him. Vigdis's jaw dropped.

'Should we?' asked his sister.

'I mean the people from the Sea Stag,' said Alfarin. 'We should all go with Vigdis on this solemn journey. Besides, I have heard of the monks of St. Ninian's Isle. I should like to see it.'

Ketil watched him, then turned his gaze to Kolbein the skipper. He would not want to lose his passengers to Orkney on a sideways expedition to the west coast. How far was St. Ninian's Isle, anyway?

Kolbein was giving the idea some thought.

'Aye, we could do that,' he said. 'I could go to Skalavagr on the way back, too.'

'And you two?' Alfarin spoke to Sibbi and Kjartan. Kjartan

48

was open-mouthed with surprise, but Sibbi, nudging him, nodded.

'Show our respects, you mean. Aye, we could do that. We're in no rush.'

'And anyone else who wants to, of course,' said Alfarin generously. He did not look at Vigdis, quite confident in his own decision. 'Ketil?'

Ketil had already decided.

'Yes, we'll accompany you. If we may,' he added to Vigdis. Vigdis looked overwhelmed.

'We'll need to get everything ready,' said Eyvind's wife. 'And food for your journey. And the corpse …' She rose, patted Vigdis on the shoulder encouragingly, and scurried off to whatever kitchen quarters the hall had. Borgny took her place beside Vigdis dutifully, and poured the new widow another cup of wine. She looked up at her brother, resigned.

Ketil sent his men off to make sure his boat was secure against whatever might strike the bay in their absence, and sat quietly at the back of the hall, head aching, watching the women in their preparations. From here he would be able to see the stripped body as they washed it, mark where the belongings were laid neatly, including that purse.

But before the women had even made a start, Svart came up beside Ketil, pointing at the corpse.

'Look at that,' he said. 'Is that not a bit odd?'

He spoke loudly enough to attract more than Ketil's attention. The women were off fetching cloths, but the men in the hall turned to look, as Svart stepped closer to the corpse and poked the back of one of Thorgrim's leather boots.

'Turn him over,' said Ketil. 'Let's take a closer look.'

Once Thorgrim was on his face, the boot was much clearer. The back of the soft leather had been torn down in a rough gash, the lace that had held it broken, and the gap glistening with sand. Ketil looked at the back of the other boot: it, too, was sandy.

'As if he had been on his back on the sand,' said Svart. 'And that boot caught on something sharp – maybe a rock.'

'But caught how?' asked Eyvind, reluctantly coming closer to inspect the boots.

'He'd have to be moving backwards,' said Skorri.

'Or be being moved backwards,' added Alf, and they nodded

at each other.

'That's what I thought,' said Svart, a hint of excitement in his voice. 'And so I went to see if there was any sign on the beach, of anything being dragged. And, well, it was hard to say,' he admitted. 'But look what I found!'

He opened his hand to show them. On it lay a penannular brooch, hammered with a cross pattern, and bent crooked.

'Was he wearing that?' asked Eyvind, confused.

'No,' said Svart. 'He was not. It's mine!'

IX

'I DIDN'T THINK that would make them think I killed him!'

'Are you sure it was our brooch?' asked Thora.

'Definite. Remember the one I trod on that time, and bent it? And I meant to fix it but I hadn't time before I was going away and we wanted to bury the silver.'

'I'm not sure I understand,' said Sigrid, hoping they would not tell her it was none of their business. 'If you buried a broken brooch, how did you find it on the beach this morning?'

'Because that Thorgrim stole our silver!' Svart snapped.

'He saw Svart bury it up on the hill, and came back and dug it up,' Thora explained, looking nowhere near as kindly as she had done till now. 'And he'd gone off to Nordvegr before Svart could accuse him. That was – that must be a year ago, wasn't it?'

'He's been back and forth since, I think,' said Svart, 'but I was never quick enough to catch him. But yesterday I accused him, in front of Eyvind. In the hall. I would do it in front of the Thing, but I've never had the chance.'

'So what happened yesterday?' Sigrid tried her sympathetic voice. She thought the neighbour looked at her suspiciously.

'I heard the Sea Stag had come in and that he was on it – someone else had accused him of theft, would you believe? So he was having to defend himself in front of Eyvind. I thought, right, now's my chance! I was too late to see what happened but I gather Eyvind decided he wasn't a thief, and made the other man pay him a fine because he had hit him – I mean, the other man had hit Thorgrim. I wish it had been me,' he added, with venom. 'There wasn't a mark on him from the other fellow. I'd have left my mark.'

Sigrid cleared her throat, wondering if she should point out to Svart that that kind of language was not likely to help him away from a charge of murder. But perhaps he was guilty – after all, she barely knew him. Barely knew any of these people. It would be nice to see Skorri and Alf and Geirod, familiar faces. And Ketil.

'So what did Eyvind say about your case?' Thora asked, though she did not look hopeful.

'He – he said to drop it. For now, he said.'

Thora was surprised.

'Drop it for now? Till when?'

Svart shrugged.

'He didn't say. He just said drop it for now. I mean, what could I do?'

You could take your revenge yourself, thought Sigrid. But then you wouldn't get your silver back.

'Eyvind and his plots again. See?' Thora waved a long spoon at Sigrid and the others. 'I said he was always up to something. And it'll just be something stupid – he'll be trying to get something out of Thorgrim, or he'll be doing some deal with Kolbein … could be anything, but it won't amount to much in the end. Stupid man,' she muttered, and attacked the pot of stew with her spoon, scraping the bits off the bottom of the pot. 'More?' she asked Sigrid.

Sigrid held out her bowl.

'So perhaps you had a reason for attacking Thorgrim,' she said to Svart, 'but what – you said you did something stupid and that made them accuse you? You told them you'd found the brooch. Was that stupid?'

'Stupid, or too clever for my own good,' Svart grunted. 'I pointed out that it looked as if the body had been moved.'

'Ketil would have noticed that anyway, sooner or later,' said Sigrid. Or he would have with her help. 'You say 'they' accused you – who?'

'It wasn't Ketil,' said Svart. 'It was Eyvind. And Vigdis backed him up. That's Thorgrim's wife.'

'What's she like?'

Svart shrugged again.

'She's a wife.' He caught Sigrid's eye. 'I mean, she travels with him, she seems upset … I think she's from Orkney. He was from over the west side of the mainland here.'

'How did you know him?'

'I have friends over there,' said Svart. 'I'd met him a few times. That's how I recognised him when he came past when I was burying the silver. I knew I had to go back and move it: I was busy. And then I went back, and it was gone. It had to be him. No one else knew where it was.'

'And if it wasn't him, how did the brooch end up on the beach today?' Thora asked reasonably. She gave her son a little nod, as if to reassure him of her support. 'You said at the time you thought it was him. The wonder is that he hadn't melted it all down months ago.'

'That's true,' said the neighbour, finding the confidence to step into the conversation. 'A broken piece, and all. Why would he not have got rid of it long ago?'

'Well, he didn't,' said Svart. 'It was on the beach this morning.'

'Where is it now?' asked Thora.

'Ketil's got it. As I said, he's trying to work out what happened.'

Thora considered for a moment, then turned to Sigrid.

'This Ketil – is he a fair man?'

'He is.' There Sigrid did not need to hesitate. 'Very fair.'

'Hm,' said Thora. 'Good. I should like to meet him.'

'I have to go back in the morning, anyway,' said Svart miserably.

'That's good,' said Sigrid, 'because in the morning, I have every intention of going to find him.'

In the morning, however, she found herself hard to chivvy along. She spent an age folding her headcloth in place, still clumsy with her injured fingers, and arranging her few beads across the top of her dress, as if they could sit in any way except their accustomed one. She had done her best to brush the salt from her skirts and her shawl, but still she lingered on the doorstep, pretending to eye the weather as if she were not sure that the rain would hold off until she and Thora – and Svart – reached the hall. The neighbour and Unnr were leaving, reckoning their job was done: they had headed for his boat, and he explained that his wife would be after him if he wasn't home soon. Sigrid shook his hand, and Unnr's, and then, surprising herself, gave Unnr a hug. She had found the silent girl strangely reassuring.

Thora appeared in the doorway, flicking her shawl around her strong shoulders with a business-like air. She, too, glanced at the sky, but it was force of habit, no particular anxiety.

'Right,' she said. 'Svart, come along. It's time to go and sort this out.'

The hall was smaller than Einar's, and much less grand than Thorfinn's: in fact, it was not much larger than the longhouse beside it, which was presumably the home of the lord Eyvind's household. Sigrid trailed in the wake of Thora and Svart, trotting along invisibly behind them, and so was able to take a good look around her before she herself was looked at much. The most striking feature of the hall was a corpse lying on a table near the back, covered up neatly, presumably already washed and prepared for its final journey. Beside it sat the women of the household, unobtrusive in the shadowy corner. Lamplight caught the uncovered, dark-gold head of one woman, taller than the others, her profile smooth as an ivory carving – not the widow, Sigrid realised, nor the wife of Eyvind. An unmarried girl, of some substance. Sigrid wondered what she was doing here: the place seemed a bit beneath her.

'Ah, Svart: I knew you would keep your word.'

The words came from the figure on the high seat. If the girl with the braided hair had seemed above the hall, this man had definitely found his station. Thorfinn could wear clothes of the same wool as the rest of his hird, cut his hair the same way, stand among them, and he would still be picked out as the leader. This man could be forgotten as soon as he was out of sight. There was neither the hint of authority in a powerful stature, nor the glint of intelligence in his eyes. How, Sigrid wondered, had he ever come to be the lord of even as modest a hall as this?

'Aye, my lord,' Svart was saying, and by the way he moved forward Sigrid thought Thora had probably pushed him. 'I would not run away.'

'Of course not. I have a very loyal hird, Ketil,' he added, and

Sigrid's pulse thumped. She shifted slightly to peer out from behind Thora, then ducked back. He was there, standing – not quite beside Eyvind, but certainly at a point of some authority at the top of the hall. She thought he did not look himself, somehow. Arms folded, he regarded Svart without expression. Did he think Svart guilty or not?

She glanced to one side and saw Skorri give her a wink, and Alf smile at her. Geirod nodded. She almost felt at home. There was a youngish lad standing with them, too, whom she did not recognise, though there was something a little familiar about him. Perhaps Ketil's men suspected him, whoever he was, and were keeping him close.

'We are here this morning,' Eyvind went on, 'to take a look at the purse found on Thorgrim's body. When you accused him of theft, Gunnar,' Eyvind pointed to the lad near Skorri, 'we searched his pack and his arms for your arm ring, but we were not aware of this purse, I think.'

A short, densely muscled man appeared to one side, his weathered face scowling.

'We were not!' he said. 'I never saw it.'

'Thank you, Kolbein,' said Eyvind. 'Maybe, as you and Ketil's man searched the pack and … the other pack, you could also search this.' He hefted a soft leather purse that chinked in a promising fashion. Alf came forward, and he and Kolbein took the purse and laid it on a table before the high seat. Alf undid the drawstrings as though expecting something nasty to be released. Kolbein flattened the loosened purse out as best he could, and they spread the contents carefully. Everything gleamed.

'That's my arm ring!' The boy Gunnar shot forward, pointing with a trembling hand. 'That's it!'

'Leave it just now, Gunnar,' said Ketil. Sigrid was surprised at his tone: it was almost kindly. The boy dropped his arm, but only stepped back a fraction, ready to grab if the opportunity arose.

'I can see some of our things there, too, my lord,' said Svart, staring down at the table. 'A couple of rings, some bangles, a pair of brooches … it's not all ours, though. And the hacksilver – well, that could be anybody's.'

'But there was hacksilver in your store?' Ketil asked.

'Oh, aye, yes – I could tell you a rough weight, but I mean,

I couldn't say to the piece. For all I know, none of that is ours apart from the bits I mentioned. That pair of brooches, that was my grandmother's. Isn't that right?' He turned to Thora, and she nodded abruptly.

'I never thought I'd see them again,' she murmured.

'So I was right,' Svart went on. 'He was a thief – he did steal what I buried.'

'And he stole my arm ring,' put in the lad Gunnar. 'I was right, too.'

'Aye, well, never mind that – and you did hit him, Gunnar, so I was right to fine you,' said Eyvind. 'The point now is, which of you killed him?'

But Svart was shaking his head.

'No, my lord. I mean, it doesn't make sense, does it? If I thought he had robbed me, and I killed him, I'd have taken my things, wouldn't I? Then there'd have been no more connexion between him and me to make me look guilty, would there?'

'Ah, now you're just trying to be clever,' said Eyvind. 'You're trying to make yourself look innocent. Or he is,' he added, jerking his head towards Gunnar.

'If I'd found the stuff in his purse I'd have brought it to you, my lord,' Svart insisted.

'Of course he would,' added Thora. 'He knows, as we all know, that he could rely on you to judge fairly, couldn't he, my lord?' Sigrid caught an undertone in her voice, and almost smiled. Thora had a low opinion of Eyvind.

'That makes sense,' said Gunnar suddenly. 'They're right, my lord. I was too rushed, I admit, and you were right to fine me for striking him. But it's true that I would have brought the proof to you. It'd be only right.'

'What are you all talking about? A voice from behind Sigrid interrupted Eyvind as he was about to speak. 'Is someone saying again that my husband was a thief? Before his very corpse?'

A woman in her middle years, face blotched with tears, slid between the witnesses and came to the front of the hall, head modestly covered – one of the women Sigrid had noticed attending the corpse.

'What do you say he has stolen now?'

'All that we said he stole is here, in his purse,' said Svart.

'See?'

The woman walked forward to the table, stared down at the heap of silver, and raised her worried eyes to Eyvind.

'But that's not Thorgrim's purse!'

X

HE SAW HER as soon as she came into the hall, behind the local man Svart and some older woman. He gave each of them a swift glance, as a good warrior should, then could not help looking back at Sigrid.

She must not have seen him. Was she expecting to find him here? Had she, in fact, followed him here?

But no: he had asked her, rashly, to come with him on this voyage to Heithabyr, on this hunt for whatever was left of his family, and she had said no. Reasonable enough: she had a business to run – injuries to recover from. Why would she want to come with him? How were her hands? His gaze slid down to them, each side of her neat skirts. Bandaged still. How would she be able to work? And what was she doing here?

Typical, though, he thought. As soon as something like a murder turns up, there is Sigrid, no doubt already with her nose well into the matter. Did she know Svart? How?

He watched with care as Kolbein and Alf examined the contents of Thorgrim's heavy purse, winced as Gunnar sprang forward to identify his arm ring, then watched with a little more pride as Gunnar argued his way – or at least followed Svart's arguments. And then heard Vigdis's denial.

'Well, if it was not Thorgrim's, whose is it?' demanded Eyvind. Ketil contained a sigh.

'We cannot prove, at this stage, that the purse was not

Thorgrim's,' he said, stepping forward.

'But it was not his!' cried Vigdis again. Eyvind raised a pacifying hand, then hesitated.

'Better ask if this one's been seen before anywhere,' Ketil murmured. 'You can't know, but you can be more certain, at least for now.'

Eyvind did not look round at him, but took a deep breath.

'But let us be as certain as we can be for now: did anyone here ever see him wear it? It was definitely on his body when we examined it this morning. Had anyone seen it there before?' He looked around the hall, first at Gunnar, then at Kolbein, who both shook their heads, then at Sibbi and Kjartan, Sibbi shrugging, then at Alfarin, just in case. Even Svart, so keen to prove Thorgrim guilty, had to admit he had never seen it on the man.

'Not that I can remember, anyway,' he said. 'I hadn't met him often.'

'So how did it come to be there?' asked Ketil quietly.

'I saw it removed,' Eyvind confirmed. 'It was laced on to his belt, just as you would expect.'

'Well, whoever put it there is obviously your thief,' said Vigdis firmly. 'If that was all your things,' she added to Svart.

'And his arm ring,' said Svart, pointing to Gunnar. 'You're sure too, aren't you?'

'Definitely,' said Gunnar, his face flushed.

'Did Thorgrim ever wear a purse that was like that?' Ketil asked.

'That's a strange question.' Eyvind picked a moment to dip back into the conversation. 'Most men wear a purse like that, particularly if they're travelling.'

'Did he?' Ketil asked Vigdis. She hesitated, frowning, then shook her head.

'No, he didn't. He either hooked things in his belt, or kept them in his pack. And of course I have a purse,' she added, 'for the journey, so odd things ended up with me.' She gave a little half-smile, a new widow remembering the habits of her husband. Ketil wondered for a moment why they travelled together – was this unusual for them? Did she normally stay behind and look after the household? Where was their household – St. Ninian's direction? If Thorgrim really had been murdered, and moved, and this purse attached to him, then there was a good deal more to find out – about everyone here.

'Has anyone seen this purse on someone else, then?' he asked. He wondered if Thorgrim could have acquired the purse accidentally, or even on purpose – more likely if he never wore such a purse himself – before he died. There was a general shaking of heads.

'This is mine,' said Alfarin, showing a finer leather one, still practical but with some wool stitches across the top. 'We all have something like it, you're right.'

Eyvind looked pleased.

'Aye, this is mine,' said Sibbi, showing a dark leather pouch, unadorned. It looked old, shaped and polished by wear and soaking and drying. 'And Kjartan, show them yours.'

Kjartan lifted a large pouch, more on his scale, with unexpected yellow tassels on the drawstring.

'My mother made it,' he mumbled, clearly feeling he owed an explanation.

'Here's mine, then,' added Vigdis, pulling out a sturdy travel purse, bulky against her skirts. 'Look, you can see.' She opened it and pulled out a couple of clean rags, a woollen cap, and a flint. 'All Thorgrim's.'

'Yet someone managed to gather Svart's stolen silver and Gunnar's arm ring, and put them into this purse, and give it to Thorgrim,' said Eyvind. 'The very items he was accused of stealing.'

'Maybe someone killed him to lay the blame on him,' suggested Sibbi, looking interested. 'You know, put the stuff there to make him look guilty.' He and Kjartan had retreated halfway into the shadows again, as they always seemed to.

'But if they had stolen the things, why hand them back so easily?' said Alf. 'What was the point in stealing them in the first place?'

'Anyway, he wasn't robbed when he was killed,' added Skorri, less inclined to ask awkward questions. 'Of this or of his own silver.'

Ketil turned to Eyvind, and lowered his voice.

'You'll need to make a decision on this before we can set out for St. Ninian's Isle,' he said.

'Me?'

'Yes. It's your responsibility. You can see there are plenty of questions to be answered, and no proof that I can see that Svart did it – he would have been a fool to point out the removal of the body and the torn boot, and even more of a fool to hide his own silver in that purse, and he does not strike me as a fool.'

'But if it was not Svart, then it could have been anybody, couldn't it? How would we ever be able to tell?' Eyvind was half dejected, half resigned. 'There's no hope. I might as well let it go.'

'It's most likely to have been someone in this hall last night,' said Ketil, trying to sound encouraging.

'Is it?' Eyvind almost yelped.

'Yes. Unless he had made arrangements with someone he knows locally – which is possible, but less likely, for I cannot see when he might have done that – then it would be extraordinary for some stranger to attack him when he happened to go outside.'

'It could easily happen,' said Eyvind, and Ketil wondered what kind of settlement Eyvind thought he was running here.

'But where did he get the purse? And if it came from his attacker, why would a stranger then fasten on him a purse containing the items he was supposed to have stolen?'

Eyvind thought for a moment, and Ketil almost felt he could see the thoughts ponderously crossing behind Eyvind's eyes.

'I suppose,' he said, 'you might be right. Does this kind of thing happen much at Thorfinn's hall?'

Ketil opened his mouth to reassure him that all at Thorfinn's hall was peace and calm, but then he reflected on the last year or so.

'Sometimes,' he said. Then, just in case, he added, 'But we always find the culprit in the end.'

Eyvind shot him a sideways glance.

'Good, good,' he muttered. 'That's the way it should be. A great man, Thorfinn. It's good to have him in charge.'

'Well, then,' said Ketil. 'What do you want to do?'

Eyvind considered again, then took a deep breath. His gaze had slid past Ketil into the hall beyond.

'I want to hand it all over to you. You're Thorfinn's man: you seem to know how these things work. I have to say we're not used to this kind of thing at Gulbervig, not at all.' Then in a louder voice, so that the whole hall could hear, he went on, 'So I'm delegating to you. You're in charge of finding out who did – whatever it was that's been done.'

'Why him?' asked Kolbein at once.

'Because he's Thorfinn's man, he has experience of this kind of thing, and I'm far too busy to deal with something like this,' said Eyvind. 'I have my hall and my hird to look after.'

For a moment, everyone in the hall seemed to be looking at Ketil. He did not enjoy the feeling.

'Well, then,' said Alfarin, and Ketil wondered if he were offended that he had not been chosen to take charge. 'What are you going to do?'

Ketil looked around at the ship's skipper, his passengers, and the few locals. And his own men, waiting with interest to see what he might decide. The body of Thorgrim, probable thief, lay covered still at the back of the hall. The weather was mild. He made a decision.

'We will go to St. Ninian's Isle and see Thorgrim buried, as Vigdis wishes,' he said. 'But each of you will give your word that if the matter is not resolved by then, you will return here for further investigation.'

'Well, Kolbein will come back anyway – he'll not abandon the Sea Stag,' said Eyvind after a moment.

'I give you my word,' said Alfarin, with the authority of a man to whom it meant a good deal. Sibbi and Kjartan looked at one another.

'Aye, we'll come back,' said Sibbi, carelessly. 'No other plans, at present.'

'I'll come back!' said Gunnar, his voice firm.

'What about you, Svart?' asked Eyvind. Svart started.

'You mean you want me to go, too?'

'We'll need help carrying the bier. How far is it? More than a day's walk?' asked Ketil.

'Aye, a day and half the next one,' said Svart.

'Then yes – come with us,' said Ketil. 'You can make sure we don't miss our way. And recommend somewhere we can stop with a dead man with us.'

He had set all the preparations in motion, including instructing Geirod to stay behind and keep an eye on their boat, before he finally approached the table where Thorgrim was laid, surrounded by the women of the party. Vigdis had returned there and was crying again, comforted by Eyvind's wife. Ketil glanced at Borgny, her lovely head bent as she sat a little distance from the others. He assumed she would also come with them on the funeral journey – should he have a word with her now? But it was Sigrid whose shoulder he tapped, Sigrid to whom he jerked his head, indicating that he would like a word outside. She excused herself to the local woman beside her – Svart's wife? Mother? – and followed him to the door.

'Well, I suppose you're going to tell me who the murderer is?' he asked, before she could say anything.

'I suppose you could not resist stopping to sort it out,' she responded. 'What about Heithabyr? What about your brother?'

Ketil turned away.

'My brother Njal is dead,' he said. 'And his wife, and one of his sons.'

'Oh.' Sigrid touched his arm. 'I'm sorry.'

'On the other hand, though,' said Ketil, 'the lad Gunnar in there is the other son. He accused Thorgrim of stealing an arm ring, and tried to hit him, and was fined by Eyvind. They came on the same boat from Nordvegr.'

'The ... is it the Sea Stag?'

'That's right. Kolbein is the skipper.'

'The dark little man?'

'That's the one.'

'Did Thorgrim steal the arm ring?' Sigrid pressed on with more questions.

'It was in that purse on his body.'

'And Svart also thinks he's a thief.'

'How do you know Svart?'

'I'm staying with the family.'

Ketil tutted.

'You have a broader acquaintance in Hjaltland than I had realised.'

'Broad enough to believe that Svart probably did not kill that man – Thorgrim, was it?'

Of course: she was already involved.

XI

SIGRID WAS NOT sure how Ketil had managed to persuade everyone to walk with Thorgrim's body to St. Ninian's Isle, in these islands where it seemed you could not go anywhere except in a boat, nor indeed was she sure why. In fact, she was not even very clear how he had involved her in the funeral procession, but here she was, plodding along with Vigdis and – what was the name of the graceful girl on her other side? Borgny, she thought.

It had not taken long to gather everyone together, ready for the journey. After all, most of them were travellers, and had their baggage to hand. Eyvind's wife had provided a hot meal for them in the late morning, and bread and cold meat and cheese to carry with them: Sigrid had not spoken much with the woman, but thought she looked relieved to see them go. Eyvind, too, waved them off with some satisfaction. Only Kolbein's crew, five men who had kept their distance from everyone else, and Geirod with his dog, stayed behind. Geirod had elected to stay in their tent, near the boat, and Kolbein's crew lived on the Sea Stag and had no need to take up space in the hall. Eyvind's work was done.

'You're sure you're going to go with them?' Thora had asked her, concerned. 'You'd be very welcome to stay at our place until they get back.'

'That's kind of you,' said Sigrid with a smile. She liked Thora. 'But Ketil wants me to see that Vigdis is all right.' And she could keep an eye on Svart, too, though she did not say that to Thora.

If Ketil were going to blame Svart for the murder, she wanted to make sure he had good grounds for it.

'Well, yes, I suppose,' said Thora. 'Poor Vigdis: she'll need a friend. And that pretty young thing doesn't look the kind who would understand. How long must she take to do all that hair-knotting? And I wonder when the last time was she walked for a day and a half? She might have to be carried.'

'We'd have to leave her by the side of the path,' said Sigrid. 'One body is enough to carry.' Even as she said it she thought the words sounded ominous, but Thora grinned.

'Well, if you're set on it,' she said with a sigh. 'But come and see me when you get back. And look after those fingers of yours!'

At least no one would expect the women to help carry the bier, she thought as she tramped along out of the settlement. They had their own share of the food and their belongings, though Borgny had left most of her things, along with Alfarin's, at Gulbervig. Thorgrim's body, carried first by Skorri, Kolbein, Svart and Kjartan, led the way as they skirted the broad, hospitable bay and took a well-worn path along the side of the hill. Heather brushed the sides of their boots, the woody stems criss-crossing the path edges, making Sigrid think of new braid patterns. The women were a few paces behind, and Sibbi, Gunnar and Alfarin, walking separately, followed. Alf took up the rear. Glancing round, Sigrid saw Ketil have a quiet word with him, then shift forward to catch up with Alfarin. He caught Sigrid's eye and nodded to her. She turned back to face the path ahead, thinking that despite Alfarin's well-made travelling clothes, Ketil looked much more – well, she had been about to use the word 'handsome', but this was Ketil she was thinking about. She gave herself a little shake, and concentrated on not tripping on heather roots.

'So where are you from?' asked Borgny eventually. Her voice was light and pleasant, as one would expect – as delicate as the rest of her. She turned her head to watch Sigrid answer.

'I live in Orkney. Near Birsay,' said Sigrid.

'But where are you from?'

Sigrid sighed.

'I was born in Heithabyr, but my family are – were – from

Nordvegr.'

'That boy Gunnar is from Heithabyr. I heard him say so.'

'I believe you're right, yes.'

Borgny gave this some thought, or perhaps not, for her next question took her back to Orkney again.

'Do you know Earl Thorfinn's court?'

'Yes, I do. I help his wife Ingibjorg with wool work.'

'Oh, really? Spinning and such?'

'No, braiding and tapestries.'

'Oh!' That was of more interest to Borgny. 'You're skilled, then?'

'Usually, yes,' said Sigrid, holding up her bandaged hands. 'Not just at the moment, though.'

'Oh. That's a shame,' said Borgny. 'I'll be married soon, and living near Birsay, I believe. Perhaps I may require your services.'

'Married and living near Birsay?' asked Sigrid in surprise. She scanned the neighbourhood of her home in her mind. Who was there who might have summoned this fine bride from Nordvegr? 'Who – um, who is your intended husband?'

'Bjorn Einarson,' said Borgny, with a hint of pride. 'He has gone to claim the hall of his father, Einar Einarson, and I am to join him.'

'Oh …' Sigrid was lost for words. How could the news not have reached her? 'Um, did you come here straight from King Harald's court?'

'No,' said Borgny innocently. 'I had been staying there for some months – that's how I met Bjorn and the betrothal came about. My brother came to collect me, but we travelled south to our home for a few weeks before taking ship at Bergvin. Why?'

'It's just …'

But at that moment, Svart stumbled with his corner of the bier, and Vigdis darted forward to seize Thorgrim's foot, as if he might escape. The procession had to stop and make sure the body was secure, and the bearers took a moment to stretch, flex their fingers, and exchange places. Svart was apologetic.

'It's all right, it's all right,' Vigdis assured him, adjusting Thorgrim's wrappings with quick, urgent fingers. 'It's not as if you can cause him any injury.' But her tears had started again, and though the path was narrow Sigrid and Borgny took Vigdis's arms and led her gently along as the procession started off again. It did not seem appropriate to break the news to Borgny of her betrothed husband's death over the head of another recently widowed woman, so Sigrid kept quiet. But she began to put words together in her head for breaking the news later. Borgny was clearly proud of her engagement to Bjorn, but how close had they been? Had she loved him at all? Or had it simply been an arrangement made by others, reasonably acceptable to both parties but not actually sought by them? For the moment, though, she should really be thinking about Vigdis and her problems.

'What do you think you will do, now?' she asked.

Vigdis sighed.

'Are you married? Yes, I suppose you must be.'

'I'm widowed,' said Sigrid, trying to make it sound like a bad thing. And in some ways, it was.

Vigdis sniffed loudly, and wiped her eyes.

'Then you'll understand. Have you family?'

'No. None in these islands, and no one close.'

Vigdis glanced sideways at her.

'Then you really will understand. How do you manage?'

'Well,' said Sigrid, 'Thorfinn has let me keep my land so far, though it's hard work. I make braids, and things like that. That helps.'

'I meant how do you manage, missing your husband? I just can't – I can't imagine life without him.'

Sigrid decided that her own example would probably not be helpful to Vigdis.

'How did you come to be on the ship from Bergvin?' she asked. 'Did you travel together a lot?'

Vigdis smiled at the thought.

'Yes, we did! Back and forth to Nordvegr, up and down to Orkney – we even went east once.'

'Thorgrim was a merchant?'

'That's right. In a small way,' she added modestly. 'It was more for the travel than anything.'

'You must have met interesting people,' Sigrid tried, wondering if she would find out anything useful for Ketil. Maybe Vigdis had some idea who might have killed her husband.

'Oh, yes! We made friends everywhere. Thorgrim was very

charming.'

'Oh!' said Borgny suddenly, and the other two turned to look at her. 'Sorry,' she said, 'I went over on my ankle. It's fine.'

'You're sure?' asked Vigdis.

'Yes, yes. Thank you, but it's probably better to walk on it.'

Certainly it did not seem to trouble her very much as they carried on.

'Where are you from in Orkney?' Sigrid asked after a little while.

'Jorfjara – do you know it? There's not much to it.'

'I've heard of it,' said Sigrid cautiously. Even those who dismissed their birthplace themselves did not like others insulting it. 'Good harbour, isn't it?'

'Small,' said Vigdis. 'Nothing like Birsay.'

'Earls have a habit of building up places around them,' said Sigrid. 'How did you come to leave? Did you meet Thorgrim there, or later?'

'There,' said Vigdis happily. 'He landed there by accident – he'd been down in Caithness, would you believe?'

Sigrid had been to Caithness herself, when her husband had been in Thorfinn's service. It had not seemed that exotic, so she made an impressed noise.

'He came to Jorfjara in a storm, blown ashore. I was serving in the hall when he came in, and – well, we were married soon after.'

Sigrid thought she detected a look of wistfulness on Borgny's lovely face, and felt a wave of guilt break over her. She would have to find a good time to break the news.

'And he whisked you back to Hjaltland!' Borgny said. The girl was a romantic, clearly. Though looking at her, Sigrid wondered just how cynical she might be.

'He did – and then to all kinds of places!' Vigdis seemed quite as easily impressed. 'As I say, we even went east. But not very far … we had plans … Places we wanted to see. Rome, perhaps. Colonia. Mikligard, maybe.'

Sigrid had met someone who had been to Mikligard, and it had not made him a more interesting person.

'Perhaps you will travel, anyway,' she suggested. 'What's to stop you?'

'But I won't travel with Thorgrim,' said Vigdis in a small

voice, and that put an end to the conversation for another while.

The sun was beginning to lower itself behind the hill to their right, darkening the ridge above them, when they reached a small settlement that Sigrid thought she remembered seeing from the boat as she had travelled from Dunrostar hofdi. The people here recognised Svart: he helped to negotiate a space in a hall so tiny Sigrid thought it only qualified as a shed. Thorgrim's body was laid on a table at the back, and the travellers were welcomed, despite the limited space. There was food and music, though the host kept the evening sombre out of respect for the purpose of their journey, and despite the attraction of visitors the entertainment ended early. Vigdis, Borgny and Sigrid were ushered to the longhouse, while the men found spaces in the hall itself. The longhouse was chilly by comparison, and the women were pleased to be sharing a bedspace together. Vigdis was first to go and use the privy outside, leaving Borgny and Sigrid alone for the first time that day.

'Can I make sure,' said Sigrid quickly, 'that you were talking about Bjorn Einarson? The Bear? Big man, dark hair?'

'That's right,' said Borgny, frowning. 'You must have met him, if you live near Birsay. He went to claim his father's hall. A splendid man, is he not?'

'Then, my dear, I have some bad news for you,' said Sigrid carefully. 'It must have missed you when you travelled by Bergvin. I'm afraid Bjorn is dead.'

And she told Borgny the whole story, as gently as she could, and whatever Borgny's feelings about Bjorn, she curled up and sobbed against Sigrid's chest like a little girl who had lost a puppy.

XII

KETIL TOOK HIS share of bier carrying after a little while, and made sure that Skorri and Alf were keeping their eyes and ears open in his place. He had changed his mind about this funeral journey because he thought they might stand more chance of finding the murderer if they all spent time together and he grew to know the others better – and it would allow him more time to clear his head, and his stomach. All the same, he was not happy about it. Vigdis had seemed so determined, which was one thing – a widow was allowed to arrange her husband's funeral, after all – but why was Alfarin so keen to pay his respects? And so persuasive when it came to making sure everyone else went, too? He had made it sound almost like a pilgrimage: Ketil wondered how religiously-minded Alfarin was. Or was he one of those travellers who wanted to see anything notable along the way, whatever it might be?

There were lots of questions to which he had no answers. He hoped he might find some of the answers before they returned to Gulbervig – assuming they all returned.

And then there was Sigrid. This time he had asked her to come along, and she had said yes. He hoped he was not bringing her into danger – or was she only here because of the mysterious Svart? How did she know him? She seemed very friendly with Svart's mother: he had seen them embrace as the funeral party had set off. But Sigrid could have nothing to do with Thorgrim's death, and that was what he was here to think about. He turned his thoughts firmly back to more useful paths, to reconsider all that had happened since they had arrived at Gulbervig.

What had Thorgrim been doing on the rocks? And was it just chance – just another unhappy coincidence – that a man accused twice of theft the previous day, accused and apparently exonerated, should now be dead? He wished he could remember more of that night – it was a blurry swirl in his head, a patchwork of vomit and shifting walls and unknown voices, faces surging up before him, arms steadying him, no sense at all.

Who had killed Thorgrim? Gunnar? Svart? He prayed it was not his nephew, but either man could have taken offence at Thorgrim's theft and exoneration. The mysterious man who had appeared and disappeared again so silently at the back of the hall? Or had it really been an ordinary accident – a man wandering in the moonlight, admiring the bay, thinking his own thoughts, straying on to the rocks and losing his footing? Ketil kept trying to see it in his mind's eye, but it was not making sense to him. There was more to this than an accident. Svart had been right about the sand and the torn boot – and really, would he have pointed that out if he had been guilty?

They were relying on Svart, too, to find them somewhere to stop for the night, and as dusk fell Ketil grew more uneasy, unable to shake off the feeling that they were somehow being watched. Yet who would bother? And there were enough of them to defend themselves in the unlikely event of an attack.

Nevertheless, he was relieved when, as all his anxieties about their journey multiplied with the failing light, Svart came up beside the bier and pointed ahead to a few scattered lights in yet another bay. The hall was small, its lord elderly, but his enthusiasm for Thorfinn was almost touching – he had fought for him years ago in Ireland, and wanted every fragment of news about the Earl that Ketil could give him. The households in the little settlement gathered enough food between them to supply this unexpected party, and stayed to exchange gossip with the visitors. The visitors in turn shared what food they had left from Gulbervig and did their best to be entertaining, in the circumstances.

'And how did you come to be the guide for this funeral?' the old lord asked Svart. Svart looked about at Ketil, then at Vigdis. The women were tucked over to the side of the hall, not expected to serve but at the same time not included in the general conversation, out of respect to Vigdis.

'I was at the hall when – well, when he died, I suppose,' Svart said.

'He died at the hall? That's awkward for poor Eyvind,' said the lord. 'Actually in the hall? I hope he wasn't ill!'

'No, no. There is no suggestion of bad food, or even some sickness anyone else could catch ...' Svart looked again at Ketil, a little pleading this time. How much could, or should, he say? Ketil, placed near the lord as Thorfinn's representative, leaned in.

'The man died outside, during the night. He was found on the rocks.'

'Ah, dear me,' said the old man. 'It happens, doesn't it? Men drink too much, then go outside and the cold air hits them and knocks them senseless, and they do things they would never do in daylight. On the rocks, eh? Poor fellow, poor fellow.'

Ketil met Svart's eye. Svart relaxed a little.

'And you're taking him down to St. Ninian's Isle? Aye, well, he'll rest peaceful there. The brothers will look after him. Where was he from?'

'From somewhere near there, apparently. I'm not sure how long ago, and the widow has not mentioned any family.'

'What will she do?'

'She says she'll go back to Orkney. She's from there.'

The old man nodded.

'I see, I see. Poor woman. It's not easy, no, not at all. Has she children?'

'Apparently not.'

'No, not easy at all. No one to look after her.'

Ketil was struck by the idea that Vigdis was more than capable of looking after herself. Was that true? Not that it mattered – she was not his responsibility, once this journey was over. Perhaps he was imagining that she was as independent as Sigrid. He glanced over at the women, seated on their bench. Sigrid and Vigdis seemed to be talking, heads bowed close together. Borgny, though, was turned a little away from them. Straight-backed and solemn-faced, she was staring at Thorgrim's shrouded corpse. It was not a friendly look.

The women retired fairly early to the neighbouring longhouse, and the men stayed to drink and sing for a while. Alf pulled out his bone whistle, and played a tune sorrowful enough for the occasion, drawing tears from more than one eye around the hall. Then someone recited a poem, and a man sang, and there was appreciative applause. Then a movement at the side of the hall drew Ketil's eye. He was surprised to see Sigrid slipping in by the side door, and making her way over to where he sat, her face grim.

'What's wrong?' he asked, as soon as he could ask it quietly.

'Did you know Borgny was betrothed to Bjorn Einarson?' she asked. 'I've just had to break the news to her of his death. I've left her with Vigdis, sobbing on each other's shoulders. Just thought I should tell you,' she added.

'I had heard that they were betrothed, but I had not had the chance to say anything,' said Ketil, though he could not remember where he had heard it. 'How had the news not reached her?'

'She left Harald's court before it happened, by my reckoning, and came here by Bergvin. That's where she and Alfarin are from, a place near there. No doubt Bjorn's hird went straight to tell Harald.'

'Most likely, yes.' He thought for a moment, but parts of his mind were still blank.

'Who was Thorgrim friendly with?' she asked. 'I'm judging by Vigdis here, but I can't see how he might have fitted in with the other passengers. Was he friendly with Alfarin and Borgny? was Thorgrim very grand?'

'No, I don't think so,' said Ketil. 'He dressed well for a merchant. But Alfarin, at least, did not think him his equal. Thorgrim might have wanted to be, but no.'

'Is this your wife, Ketil?' The old lord seemed only just to have noticed Sigrid's arrival. 'You should have said!'

'No,' said Sigrid quickly, 'just a friend. I've come along to help look after the widow. I'd better get back to her.'

'Do you have all you need?' asked the old lord graciously. 'Blankets, and so on?'

'Yes, thank you, my lord: we are very comfortable. I'll bid you good night.' She hesitated, and met Ketil's eye. 'Is everything all right?'

He held her gaze. There was no reason to worry her with

thoughts of ambush or all the other things that might happen to a party of travellers with a corpse. She would imagine them well enough herself.

'No, everything's as good as it could be,' he answered drily. She watched him for a moment longer, eyebrows raised, then turned and left. She disappeared back through the hall's side door without a backward glance.

'A pretty friend,' commented the old lord. 'I suppose her husband is here, too?'

'She's a widow,' said Ketil shortly.

'Is she indeed?' The old lord paused. 'Children?'

'None living, no.'

'Land?'

'A small farm.'

The old lord nodded thoughtfully. He murmured something to himself, which Ketil thought was,

'Could do worse, yes. Could do worse.'

He smiled inwardly, and made a note to himself not to stay at this hall on the way back.

Ketil was up early the next morning, keen to be on their way. He had had to spend the evening sitting with the old lord, pretending to enjoy the food and drink, but Alf and Skorri had been free to choose their own company around the hall, and he met them outside on the shore for a swim and a talk. The water helped his head a little.

'Nothing odd,' said Skorri with a shrug. 'Sibbi's looking for work, along with his cousin, but I don't think you'd want them. Kjartan's not bright, and Sibbi's a bit too bright, if you take my meaning.'

'Kolbein wants to get back to his ship,' said Alf. 'He'd planned to be away by now, off down to Orkney.'

'I gather he doesn't usually include Orkney in his voyages,' said Ketil. 'Why this time?'

'Extra money from Alfarin to go on south,' said Alf, and ducked under the water. He emerged, shaking his head vigorously. 'And then Gunnar wanted to go on, too, and I think that put the idea into the heads of Thorgrim and Vigdis. So it was paying him well, and I don't think he was averse to it. Anywhere he can trade.'

'Does Alfarin know that his sister's intended husband is

dead?' Ketil asked.

'He does now, I think,' said Skorri, nodding back towards the hall. Alfarin and Borgny stood outside, and Alfarin had just taken his sister in his arms, comforting her. He was facing their way, and they could see clearly the expression on his face. Alfarin was a very worried man.

XIII

SIGRID WATCHED THE men swim back and forth a few times, when they were joined by Kjartan, Svart and, reluctantly, Gunnar. Ketil liked to keep his men fit for fighting. Gunnar was a spindly, pale creature, and Kjartan was just large and strong, but Svart looked as if he could have given a good account of himself any day. Sibbi watched from the shore, making comments which were amusing, if a little cutting. Sigrid turned away, wondering. Could one of them have struck down a merchant who had stolen from them? How would they find out? Was Ketil hoping that somewhere along the way, or perhaps in front of the monks on St. Ninian's Isle, someone would break down and confess?

St. Ninian's Isle – presumably that meant another boat. Well, she did not think there would be a shortage of willing people, around the Hjaltland coast, to take them out to the island.

Their night in the longhouse had not been particularly comfortable: the old lord's wife was long dead and whoever looked after the place had even less idea of housework than Sigrid did. They had huddled together in one bedspace under stiff, ancient furs, and Borgny and Vigdis had taken it in turns to sob throughout the night. Sigrid had tried to feel sympathy, for a while at least, and had then contrived to wind a bit of blanket over her head, turn her back, and do her best to sleep. It was a relief to be outside in the cool sunlight, breathing in fresh air and listening only to the wind and the gulls, and a skein of geese flying over high in the shining sky.

She had no very clear idea of where they were – a bay on the east side of the mainland, but there were so many bays – but she assumed that today they would start to climb over the low backbone of the island to reach the western coast. The climb did not look too bad. She had not brought much with her from home, and it was all ready in a pack to be slung across her back: she never liked to travel with more than she could manage herself, without help, just in case there was no help. But she had brought her wools and her weaving tablets, just in case.

She looked at her fingers, and wondered whether or not she should try to change the bandages, or wait till she was back in Gulbervig where Thora could help her. She liked Thora. She hoped that Svart was innocent, for Thora's sake.

'I hope we'll be on our way soon.' Vigdis came up beside her, hugging a shawl around her shoulders against the morning air. 'I want to get to the island today. I want to see him safe there.'

Sigrid patted Vigdis's shoulder, feeling it was expected of her.

'I don't think it's much further, is it? We should get there today.'

'The men are so slow. Why are they wasting time swimming, of all things?' Vigdis was shivering just watching them.

'It's Ketil. He likes his men to keep fit, so I suppose the others joined in.' She was going to say something about over-competitive men, but hesitated. She did not know what Thorgrim had been like. 'It will refresh them before the day's walk.'

'I don't see Alfarin leaping into the waves,' Vigdis remarked. 'He has more dignity.'

Sigrid opened her mouth to defend Ketil, then shrugged. She thought Ketil looked quite dignified, swiping through the water. Alf, too, had a certain grace, and Skorri swam as if he just had to get the job done. But Gunnar and Kjartan could not be described as dignified.

Ketil seemed to catch sight of Vigdis and Sigrid talking, and waved the men out of the water to prepare for the onward journey. It did not take long for them to dry and dress, and for decisions to be made about who was to take the first turn at carrying the bier. Borgny emerged from the longhouse again with her hair arranged as neatly as if a dozen slaves attended her, head held high and eyes dry.

The old lord's women came out and handed over a few morsels for their day – mostly shellfish, freshly cooked and wrapped in bread – and filled their containers with fresh water.

'I'm not sure I can face another shellfish,' Vigdis murmured to Sigrid, and Sigrid grinned.

'I know how you feel. I like them in small quantities, but it's as if they spend so much time on the sea they need to eat like otters.'

'Thorgrim was partial to shellfish. But then he was a Hjaltlander.'

'From near St. Ninian's Isle?' Sigrid asked. Vigdis nodded.

'Has he family left near there? Will there be others joining us for the burial?'

Vigdis shook her head.

'I shouldn't think so. His parents died years ago. There's no one else who would come.'

Though Vigdis seemed less than eager to talk, Sigrid felt she should press on.

'What about friends? If he spent his boyhood here surely there are some who would care.'

'I don't believe he had much acquaintance here at all. He knew more people in Bergvin, I think, than here. He had traded there for years – and down to Orkney and Caithness, of course.'

'Which is how you met, yes,' said Sigrid, with a smile. But she was thinking: Svart had known him, had recognised him when he had passed the field where Svart was burying his silver. Who else might have known him, from the past or from more recent times? After all, Kolbein came here regularly and said that Thorgrim came too. 'Did you always travel with Thorgrim?' she asked. 'Or do you have a home somewhere here?'

'No … we travelled. You might think that strange, but we both loved it,' said Vigdis, her weathered face softening. 'Always on the move, meeting new people, trading, staying in new places. It was exciting, sometimes, and interesting. We probably spent more time in Bergvin than anywhere, but not even very much there. Which is why I should go back to Orkney, I suppose: a woman can't spend her life travelling on her own, and anyway, it was better with both of us.' She sighed. 'Anyway, speaking of travelling, it looks as if we're almost ready to go. I'd better see that they …' She tailed off, hurrying back into the hall to oversee the lifting of her husband's bier. This was the last journey that they would take together, after all.

As Sigrid had expected, the climb over the ridge was not particularly onerous – but then, she was not helping to carry the bier.

On the other hand, she was almost as weary, she told herself, trying to support Vigdis and Borgny. Vigdis was still susceptible to the occasional burst of weeping, but while Borgny's eyes were dry she spent most of the walk in stern silence, punctuated with the occasional sharp question concerning her betrothed Bjorn's last days. The wind had drawn hair out of her elaborate braids, and it fell in silky curtains on either side of her face, as private as bed screens. At last, after a long pause, she turned and asked:

'Did you meet him yourself? Wasn't he splendid?'

Sigrid would have been much more interested in discussing Thorgrim further, finding out more about him and about anyone who might have wished him harm in the area of Gulbervig. She could not see that Ketil was making much progress in the matter. He was lingering at the back of the procession today, and spent more time looking about him, any time she saw him, than in conversation. She dropped back a little from Vigdis but managed to angle Borgny away too, to walk alongside her, negotiating a small flock of sheep in the process.

'We know who killed Bjorn,' she said, sure that Borgny would not collapse in grief again, 'but have you any idea who might have killed – him?' She nodded at the bier, not wanting to name Thorgrim in case Vigdis heard. 'You travelled with them from Bergvin, didn't you?'

'Well, yes, but we didn't speak much to the others, Alfarin and I. And my mind was on other things,' Borgny added, as though she could hear how she had sounded.

'On your forthcoming marriage,' said Sigrid, sympathetically.

'That too,' said Borgny. 'But to begin with – well, something had happened that was – quite upsetting.'

'At the court? At Bergvin?' If it were amongst the prospective passengers, it might mean something.

'No, no, at home. At Arinbjorn's hall. Alfarin is his man. Arinbjorn's daughter Ali is my closest friend. It was Ali ...' She tailed off as they veered off the path to allow a man on a donkey go by. It was a busy route.

'Something happened to Ali?' This was unlikely to be useful, but Sigrid was happy to keep Borgny talking. It passed the time, that and admiring the girl's braided belt and trying to work the pattern out. She might indeed have been a good customer, had she stayed at Buckquoy with Bjorn as the lord of Einar's old hall.

'While I was at the court, at King Harald's court. I was away for a year, you see, and while I was away …' She swallowed hard, but did not seem likely to cry again. She was trying to find words. 'Ali was seduced. By a man not worthy of her. He broke her heart. And then, then payments were demanded to keep the story quiet.' Her pale face was flushed with anger for her friend.

'Why did Arinbjorn not punish him?'

'If he had, the story would have come out. And Arinbjorn's an ambitious man. He thought it would harm his chances with the King if he had let his daughter – if his daughter's child had a less than worthy father.'

'There's a child?'

Borgny nodded sadly.

'Poor Ali,' said Sigrid. All Sigrid's children had died – and there was Ali with one she did not want. Life was never fair.

'I should never have left her alone,' said Borgny. 'She was such a trusting girl. Her father protected her always.'

'Not quite enough, evidently.' Sigrid made a face. Girls had to be tough, too: it was no use treating them like a delicate tapestry. But she had a growing feeling that there was some toughness to Borgny, and not far under the surface. She was not as delicate as she appeared.

'Arinbjorn's a fool,' Borgny muttered, then glanced around to see if Alfarin could hear her. He was too far off. 'Don't tell Alfarin I said that! He might say it himself, but he doesn't like me repeating it.'

Sigrid thought it unlikely that Alfarin would listen to anything Sigrid had to say.

'So what happened to the man? Did Arinbjorn pay him?'

'I think he must have. Ali wasn't sure, but he had gone by the time Alfarin and I reached home. Ali could barely speak of him. I didn't really want to leave her. If it hadn't been for my brother, and

Bjorn …'

'You had other duties, of course.'

'Yes. But that's what was in my mind all the way to Bergvin, and on the ship, that and wondering what Bjorn's hall would be like, and what marriage would be like, and – you know.'

'Oh, yes,' said Sigrid. 'Of course.'

Borgny glanced at her sideways.

'What is it like?'

Sigrid had been waiting for the question. She gave a little nod.

'As much as no two people are alike, I'm quite sure no two marriages are alike. However you and Bjorn might have been is probably not what will be when you marry another man – maybe no better nor no worse, but different. If Vigdis remarries, he won't be like Thorgrim, though it might be just as happy. You can't tell, and certainly no one outside that marriage can tell. Best just to pray for the best, work hard, and be kind. That's all I can say.'

Borgny absorbed the words in silence, and then in gesture that took Sigrid completely aback, felt for Sigrid's hand, avoiding the bandages, and gave it a quick squeeze.

XIV

IT HAD BEEN a while since Ketil had had a good walk, and aside from the circumstances, and his stomach and head, he was enjoying this one. As they crossed the low ridge that formed the mainland's back, he could see before them the western coast and its attendant islands, dark brown and green in a blue sea. The land was not what anyone would call mountainous, not anyone used to Nordvegr, but it was comfortably hilly. And there was little cover to hide anyone who might wish them harm, he observed – that niggling feeling was still there, that small anxiety. Of course, the path was busy enough that anyone wanting to follow them had only, in fact, to follow: everyone they passed was a stranger to him, though Svart knew a few of them. But it looked as if they would reach their destination by daylight, anyway. Even from here he could see the distinctive shape of St. Ninian's Isle and the pale white spit of land leading out to it.

'Don't we need boats, then?' Sigrid had come up beside him, and was gazing down. 'Is that where we're going?'

'No boats necessary,' Ketil confirmed. 'I believe it's covered once or twice a year: I have never seen it. We've always had to carry boats over it, but that's easy enough.'

'Amazing to see so many Hjaltlanders with legs,' she went on. 'I had thought none of them could walk more than the length of their longhouse, and their oars were permanently attached, but it turns out they can climb across here easily enough.'

'A bit shorter than going round in a boat,' said Ketil.

'That wouldn't stop them,' said Sigrid. He had the feeling that the conversation was a blanket, covering something underneath that she really wanted to say, but he had no idea how to lift that blanket.

The party had drawn off the path to lay the bier on some level rocks, to rest and eat their remaining food. Vigdis and Borgny stayed close to the bier, Vigdis with one hand on her husband's shoulder. Borgny sat on a rock as if it were the most comfortable and beautifully carved high seat, her back straight against the wind. She stared down the path they had just climbed.

'She's upset about Bjorn,' said Sigrid, nodding to her.

'Well, that can't be a motive for killing our merchant,' said Ketil. 'No revenge there: Thorgrim had nothing to do with it, and Alfarin and Borgny didn't know he was dead until you told her.'

'Are you desperate for motives, then?' asked Sigrid, irritatingly.

'I want to find out more about Thorgrim and these people who spent his last days with him. Did you know they were delayed by bad weather in Bergvin? They had a couple of days there together before sailing.'

'Are you sure it's one of them?' asked Sigrid. 'Couldn't it have been someone in Gulbervig? I know you've considered Svart, but someone else? He was a Hjaltlander, after all.'

'There was a man who came into the hall when Gunnar was accusing Thorgrim of theft,' said Ketil, setting aside his doubts about Svart for now. 'He came in, watched for a while, then left again, all very quietly. No reason to think he might be involved beyond that. No one else seems to have seen him.'

'No one at all?' She had a mischievous look – she was going to accuse him of dreaming.

'No one but Skorri – and he is not fanciful, you'll admit. I meant none of the locals, no one who could identify him, or would, to me. He was not at supper that evening.'

'You're right, it's not much,' said Sigrid. She sighed, and looked around her. 'So that boy is really your nephew? Njal's son?'

'It seems so. I have no reason to disbelieve him,' he said carefully. 'He recognised my name, and his accounts seem convincing.'

She elbowed him hard, and he grunted.

'You're all excitement. Weren't you pleased to find him, despite his news? He looks like Njal. I mean, Njal as I remember him. When I left, Njal must have been close to the age Gunnar is now.'

'I know.'

'You don't suspect him, do you?'

Ketil shifted a little.

'He accused Thorgrim of theft, and tried to hit him when Thorgrim denied it. But it was a feeble attack. Is he capable of more? Or capable of more when darkness hides him? I'm not sure.'

'But you hope not.'

'But it's important to be careful, in something like this. When I'm seen to be Thorfinn's man.'

'Of course.' She looked away again, down at the islands and the busy sea. The wind pushed back her headcloth, showing a tangle of curling hair trying hard to escape. 'So what does that mean, anyway, meeting him here? Are you going to go on to Heithabyr, when all this is sorted out?'

'Skorri and Alf were keen on the idea – and then they wanted to go on, further east. Maybe to Mikligard, maybe further.'

Her head to one side, Sigrid seemed to be considering the idea. Would she have minded if he had disappeared east, perhaps never to return?

'I take it Geirod was not so keen,' she said. He smiled.

'Geirod was not so keen, no. And I have obligations to Thorfinn, of course. If Skorri and Alf had been interested enough, they could have gone on alone.'

'But they have obligations to you.'

'Well, yes,' he said. 'Not many people have no connexions at all.'

'No … Have you wondered at all about Sibbi and his cousin? They seem remarkably unconnected.'

He nodded, happy enough to leave the subject of his family and hird, and return to the mystery at hand.

'Yes. But then, so were Thorgrim and Vigdis, so far as one could tell.'

'She told me how they met,' said Sigrid, and gave the story to Ketil, the landing at Jorfjara, the whisking away to exciting travel. 'And she said he was from near there,' she nodded down the hill towards the island, 'but that he had no family left around here. Or no one close, anyway.'

'And nowhere to live? No duties to anyone?'

'No one's hird, it seems. How could that be? And the same with Sibbi and Kjartan. Free to move about. Owing nothing.'

'Unless they were exiled,' said Ketil, and she met his eye. She had clearly been thinking the same thing.

'Thrown out of somewhere, by someone, for something? I had wondered.'

'But how would one find out?' asked Ketil. 'I doubt they are going to tell anyone.'

'Perhaps Thorgrim knew,' said Sigrid suddenly. He looked at her.

'And that's why he's dead?' He ran the thought through his mind. 'It might be so.'

'Did either of them have the opportunity?'

He sighed.

'They all had the opportunity. There was coming and going in the hall all night, as usual: no one remembers seeing anyone specific leave or come back. It could be Sibbi, Kjartan, Kolbein, Gunnar, Vigdis, Alfarin, Eyvind if he could work up the energy, even Borgny.' A fleeting memory came to him about Borgny as he said her name, but at once it was gone, whipped away by the wind pressing up the hill where they stood.

'Or Svart?' She eyed him sideways.

'Or Svart, or any local who happened to know him, know he was there, and wanted to injure him, at least.' He thought for a moment, glancing round.

'What do you know about Svart? Was he – wherever you were – that night?'

She frowned, annoyed.

'Yes, he was. I was at Thora's house. Svart's mother.'

'Who else was there?'

'Only Thora and Svart live in the house, but the man who brought me to Gulbervig was there, too. Oh, and Unnr.' She seemed inclined to stop there, so he waited in silence. She gave a little wriggle of irritation, and continued. 'I landed at Dunrostar hofdi and said I wanted to go on up the east coast, but the ship I had taken was going up the west coast – we might even see them along here, I suppose,' she said, glancing casually down again towards the island and the sea. There were plenty of boats about. 'The woman there said her neighbour would take me as far as Gulbervig. She and her husband were having a row, and I'd say that Unnr, their daughter, is in the habit of slipping away when that happens. So she came along with us, the neighbour quite happy to take her. So we stayed at Thora's because she's the sister of the neighbour, or a friend of the sister of the neighbour, and Unnr stayed too. The neighbour, the man who brought me, went home again with Unnr.'

It seemed complicated: his head hurt. How many friends did Sigrid have in Hjaltland? But it was time to move on if they wanted to arrive in good time with the monks, though no doubt someone they had met on the path would have passed on news of their advent. 'Come on – let's gather up and get started again. It might be harder going down the hill with the bier than it was climbing up.'

To start with, it was not much harder. For the steeper parts, Alf and Kjartan took the head of the bier and Kolbein and Sibbi took the foot, using their comparative heights to keep Thorgrim's body level. The trouble there was that Kolbein and Sibbi did not seem happy working together – there was unseemly bickering about taking a fair share of the weight. Further along, the path took a turn and ran along the side of the hill, the inlet of the sea down to their right, and they were able to relax a little and walk on level ground again. But the final turn down towards the sandy beach that led to St. Ninian's Isle was tricky, and suddenly Vigdis shouted out as the bier took a dive towards the sand, Alf and Kjartan struggled to stop it, Kolbein lost his grip and one corner came down heavily on Sibbi, who stumbled and fell to the rough ground. Vigdis, with another cry of distress, was beside the bier at once, and Alf and Kjartan scrambled round to level it.

'Please accept our humblest apologies, Vigdis,' said Alf, and Kjartan looked upset. They did their best, with Vigdis flapping around them, to rearrange Thorgrim's wrapped body neatly on the bier. Kolbein crawled away, swearing, rubbing his arm where it had been wrenched by the fall. But the bier had to be shifted aside before Sibbi could wriggle his way out, clutching his leg as best he could. Ketil and Skorri held the wooden beam clear and Svart leaned over to help Sibbi, whose foot had somehow been trapped underneath him, leg bent hard back. He gasped as he tried to straighten it.

'Here, can I help?' came a stranger's voice, and a man of middle years came skipping down the steep path as though well used to it. 'Are you hurt?'

'Leg,' said Sibbi. 'Give me a moment. Bloody Kolbein – it's all his fault.'

'I heard that!' came a yell from Kolbein. 'Serve you right for not paying attention!'

'The brothers will be able to help you,' said the stranger, pushing back a hood to reveal greying brown hair. 'Are you going over there?'

'We are,' said Ketil. 'Do you live around here?'

'Yes,' said the man. 'The brothers on the Isle are my neighbours. I'd heard there was a funeral party heading this way. Whose – I mean – no one could tell me the name of the dead person.'

'Thorgrim,' said Ketil. 'That's his widow, Vigdis. None of us is related to him, I believe: we happened to be nearby when he died.'

'So you're helping the poor widow? That's good of you. But it looks to me as if this fellow's not going to be able to carry the bier any further – in fact, he may need to be carried himself.'

And Sibbi, still crumpled on the ground, looked up and groaned.

XV

TO THE RIGHT, the island ahead of them seemed to have been drawn in sweeping curves: the land rose softly in a green arc, and below that the sea nibbled gently at each side of the spit to form a narrow neck between two broad beaches of pale sand. Over to the left, though, the island was broken into chunks of rock, green on top and black underneath, dark against misty headlands beyond them. From here, standing between dunes hairy with sharp grasses, it looked like a long and chancy walk between two seas to where at last a sandy path cut up to the left through matching dunes on the other side. Low, grey buildings to the right showed where the monks must live: the rest of the place was dotted with sheep. Here, where they stood as if waiting for some kind of sign, the beach was busy with stone putters and sanderlings, and low dartings of kitticks skimmed the greedy waters without fear.

Sigrid wrapped her cloak more tightly around her, trying not to crush her fingertips in the process. Borgny was not far away, trying to keep out of the worst of the wind. Ketil and the stranger seemed to be debating the best way to transport Sibbi across the spit to the monastery – the stranger already had a pack of his own, hooked over his back, though it seemed light enough – while Vigdis and Alf and Kolbein guarded the bier, and the others hovered about, waiting. Alfarin stood halfway between the women and the men, as if he felt the need to be part of the decisions but wanted to protect his sister, though from what it was not clear.

'I can carry him,' Kjartan was saying. Sigrid could well believe it, but she was not sure if Sibbi looked reassured by this or not. She stared out at the island. There was nothing to stop a wave surging over that narrow walkway, was there? Ketil was always complaining that Orkney was too close to the level of the sea for safety, and she laughed at him. Now she could feel his anxiety, though he seemed to have put it aside.

And now he was organising the procession again, with Alf sent ahead to announce their coming, Skorri, Svart, Kolbein and the stranger at the corners of the bier, Sibbi helped by Kjartan in a half-limping, half-carried muddle that seemed to cause more pain than carrying would have done, the women walking in a line behind it as if they had been arranged that way, then Alfarin in a position of importance behind them as if he had never once stooped to help with the bier, and Ketil himself at the back, making sure no one was left behind. Or that no one would run up and attack them from behind. Sigrid was not sure, but when she glanced back she could see that his hand was never far from his swordhilt, and he was not always looking ahead to the island.

The sand was soft and vulnerable beneath her boots. At first she thought that the waves on either side were taking it in turns to strike and suck at the shore, then they seemed to attack simultaneously. But the sand in the centre of the spit was reassuringly dry, strung with crunchy seaweed that was almost sharp beneath the soles of her boots. She tramped in silence, head down, as wordless as Vigdis in front of her. She wondered if Vigdis had been here before.

But before she had had time to guess how much longer they would have to walk, she saw that the bier was rising before them, lifted up the sandy path on to the side of the island's slopes, and Kjartan and Sibbi and the women were following. She looked back again, then waited, letting Alfarin go on. Ketil caught up, raising his eyebrows.

'What?' he asked, when Alfarin was far enough ahead not to overhear.

'Nothing, really.' She was not going to say that the sand spit walk had made her nervous. 'Who is the stranger?'

'He says his name is Thorir,' said Ketil. 'He's local, knows the brothers. He seemed keen to help.'

'Nice of him,' said Sigrid, trying not to sound cynical. Really, she had no reason to. People were often kind to her – she could not survive, otherwise. 'And now we're safely here, and we haven't needed a boat.'

'I'd better go and speak to the brothers,' said Ketil, though his hand was still on his swordhilt. He clearly did not feel safe yet, and still considered himself responsible for them all. Sigrid smiled to herself. If Alfarin had not been so polite and Ketil so quiet, no doubt there would have been some debate between them over the leadership of this party. Alfarin had very much the air of someone believing himself to be in charge, while Ketil just got on with it. On the whole, she thought she would rather follow Ketil. Though Alfarin was certainly more decorative, with his fine woollen cloak and beautiful dyed leather kirtle that matched the embroidered purse he had shown everyone in the hall at Gulbervig. The braid on his shirt, too, was particularly fine. Some time she would work up the nerve to ask Borgny about it and about her own braids. Soon, surely, she would be in the market for new customers again. Her fingers were almost healed.

The monastic buildings were low-lying, snuggled into the gentle slope of the hill. Sigrid had expected them to be new, sharp and distinctive, like the work Thorfinn was having carried out on the Brough of Birsay, but these looked older. Even the chapel seemed to be keeping its head down, hiding from westerly winds with a small wooden cross valiantly topping the pitched roof. Since wood was as scarce here as in Orkney, Sigrid wondered if it had been a gift from abroad.

A man with the shaven head of the religious kind waved the bier-carriers towards the chapel, while another came forward, with Alf, to be introduced to Vigdis and to lead her towards what was presumably the brothers' shared longhouse. The land that had been cleared around the two buildings was laid out in part to crops, mostly now harvested, and to a small burying ground with several grassy mounds and a couple of small driftwood crosses marking its occupation. Vigdis went ahead with the brother and Alf, and Borgny and Sigrid followed, along with the men. Once within the roughly constructed walls around the site, Sigrid felt an unexpected sense of peace. This, too, was unlike her experience at the Birsay chapel, but after the last few days she was very pleased to accept it as a gift. A deep, contented sigh escaped her almost without her noticing, and Borgny, glancing round at her, gave a smile as if she agreed.

Ahead, two brothers were helping Kjartan manoeuvre Sibbi into the longhouse without disturbing his injured leg. Once they were through the door, everyone else squeezed in, too, and the warmth of the house settled them quickly, easing into their cold and fatigue, loosening tired limbs to drop on to the benches by the fire, silencing everything except small sounds of pleasure and gratitude as the brothers brought them warmed wine and gentle smiles.

'Sister, sit here and rest a little: Brother Aidan will pray in the chapel by your husband's body while you recruit your strength.'

For a moment Vigdis looked as if she would resist, but it would have taken a stronger woman than most. She sagged on to the bench, clutching the cup of wine in both hands, her head bowed. Sigrid shifted over beside her and put an arm around her, and Borgny joined them, staying close. Yet it was not the stiff huddle of fear or anxiety: it felt very safe here. Perhaps it was simply that they all knew the threat of being alone in the world, for a woman and even, often, for a man. One had to belong.

The monks must indeed have had warning of their arrival, for in a short time, as well as the warm wine, there was thick vegetable stew, and flatbread, and cheese made from sheep's milk. To some it gave new energy: Kjartan and Svart and Skorri, along with the local man, Thorir, volunteered to help one of the monks dig a grave for Thorgrim. Sibbi could not take part, of course. He sat sideways on the bench, while one of the other monks slopped a poultice of leaves around his knee and ankle, wrapping it in bandages soaked in hot water. His look of clenched teeth gradually dissipated. Alfarin was deep in conversation with another brother.

'Is he an abbot?' Borgny asked in a whisper. Their arrival had been confusing, and they had no idea yet which brother was which.

'I'm not sure.' Sigrid had met an abbot before, but this one was much less grand. 'I suppose he is sitting in – well, something like a high seat at the head of the hall. But then it would look odd if no one did, wouldn't it?'

Borgny shrugged, not sure.

'My brother likes to talk about religion, the old beliefs and the new,' she said, to Sigrid's surprise. 'But he would prefer to talk to an abbot than an ordinary brother.' Sigrid caught the glint of a grin in her eye.

'Sister, come now and sleep a little, and we will wake you when your watch begins,' said a monk, and led Vigdis over to a sleeping space with serviceable rugs and furs. Vigdis folded herself into them obediently, and the monk drew a curtain around her.

Now Ketil was talking with the abbot and Alfarin, politely, as befitted a respectful guest. The men of the funeral party were quiet over their wine, drinking with less energy than they would in an ordinary hall. No women served the food or drink, and there was no talk of fighting: it all seemed, to Sigrid, a little eerie. At last Vigdis was roused, and everyone, lantern-lit, left the longhouse for the chapel where Thorgrim's body lay attended by Brother Aidan. Scrubbed after their work, Kjartan, Svart and Skorri joined them, heads bowed.

'The burial will be at dawn,' the abbot announced, before leading the monks in prayer. Some of the men joined in, notably Ketil and Alfarin and, to Sigrid's mild surprise, Svart and Kjartan. Alf and Skorri followed their master, but Kolbein stayed quiet, and Sibbi, who had limped over, nevertheless did not participate but stood awkwardly on one leg, watching. The women stood at the back.

After the service they filed out back along the path to the longhouse, leaving Vigdis and a different brother by Thorgrim's bier. Sigrid turned to Borgny.

'We should take it in turns to sit with her, Borgny,' she murmured, struck by uncharacteristic charity for someone she barely knew.

'Good idea,' Borgny agreed. 'But perhaps we should leave it just for a little, let her get settled, then join her. I think the abbot is with her just now.'

'That makes sense,' said Sigrid. 'I'll slip out when the abbot comes back.'

So she waited, pinching her ears to keep herself awake, until the little thin figure of the monk returned. She gave him a moment to settle, then quietly crossed the earth floor and slipped out, pushing back the old leather curtain and easing the door shut behind her.

But when she reached the chapel, Vigdis was not there. Instead, Sigrid saw a cloaked figure with a wrapped head, slipping through the burial ground.

XVI

KETIL WAS DREAMING that Odin's ravens had come to perch on each of his shoulders. He tried to explain to them that this was not appropriate in a Christian monastery, however humble, and that they should take themselves off somewhere else, when one of them pecked him hard on the shoulder. He jumped, and woke up.

A head, half-covered in a headcloth, was poking under the curtain that marked off his bedspace, and a sharp finger was prodding him on the shoulder, then touching his lips to hush him. He could barely see, but he knew it was Sigrid.

He slipped out from under the covers, leaving Alfarin and Kolbein still snoring in the darkness, and seized his boots and his axe before following Sigrid noiselessly across the room to the door. No one else seemed to be stirring, and the night, when he saw the sky through the doorway, was bright with stars and no hint of dawn. Had he slept through some of the monks' night offices? He was not sure. He had not slept so soundly for a long time, not woken so unsure of the time. But his head felt better.

He paused by the door to pull on his boots. Sigrid shuffled impatiently.

'What's going on?' he asked.

'Vigdis's in the burial ground,' she whispered back.

'In the middle of the night?'

'She left the chapel and went out.'

'Maybe she wants to inspect the grave,' said Ketil, though it sounded unconvincing even as he said it.

'She's nowhere near the grave,' said Sigrid. 'I checked.'

'Fresh air?'

'Or exercise. Ketil, she's digging!'

'Digging? Digging what?'

'I don't know. But she has a little spade and everything. She must have come prepared.'

'She probably borrowed one. The monks are good growers.'

Sigrid made an irritated sound.

'Come and watch her. See if you can work out what she's doing.'

Ketil sighed, but he had to admit he was curious. He felt sorry for Vigdis, widowed so unexpectedly, but at the same time he was not convinced that her husband had been as innocent of the thefts as she claimed. And anything more that they could find out about Thorgrim, including the activities of Thorgrim's widow, might help them to catch his killer. Once again, he hoped and prayed that it was not Gunnar.

He fastened his sword belt around his waist and followed Sigrid along the path towards the chapel, their boots making little sound on the sandy surface, pale in the starlight. He walked with his toes flexed, trying to avoid tripping on roots and rocks, hoping their movement would not attract any attention. As they approached the low wall between burial ground and infield, they both crouched lower, coming down to its level. Over at the outer wall, the one nearest the path they had arrived along, Ketil could clearly see a figure, cloaked and bent, and moving in short, rhythmic swoops. When the wind dropped every now and again he thought that he could, indeed, hear the scrape of metal on earth.

'You could be right,' he conceded. 'And the grave they dug for Thorgrim is over this side.'

Even in the wind he could hear a little smug sound of satisfaction from Sigrid. He smiled to himself. But it did not answer Sigrid's original question – what was Vigdis digging, and why?

'Do you think she's burying something? Some possession of Thorgrim's, perhaps?' Sigrid's voice was so low he wondered if she were talking to herself and not him. 'Or is she digging something up?'

'What could she be digging up?'

'Thorgrim was from near here. Perhaps he left something here, maybe for safety. The abbot might know.'

'Or we could ask Vigdis,' Ketil suggested. Sigrid gave a reluctant shrug, clearly not keen on the idea.

'Or we could look tomorrow, when she isn't around.'

'Why don't you want her to know you've seen her?' he asked.

Sigrid turned to glare at him.

'Because she's out here in the middle of the night,' she said. 'It's obviously not something she wants everyone to know about.'

'Nevertheless,' said Ketil, 'at least three people seem to know about it now.' He looked over her head, and nodded. Sigrid turned to see where he was indicating. In the shadows of the chapel, a slight movement had caught his eye. A figure was standing there, watching Vigdis.

'I can't see who it is,' Sigrid complained, even more quietly. He bent his head to hear her, feeling the tickle of her escaping hair across his cheek. He kept his voice as low as hers.

'It's not one of the monks, I think – they're all small,' he murmured. 'And I don't think he came from the longhouse.'

'Is it a man?'

'Again, tall for a woman …' He hesitated. Borgny was tall. But this figure looked more solid than the graceful woman – so far as he could tell.

'Vigdis's finishing, I think,' said Sigrid. She was keeping very still, aware that movement could attract attention. 'She's carrying something – oh, maybe it's just the spade.'

They watched as Vigdis stepped carefully across the burial ground and made for the door of the chapel. But Ketil kept half an eye on the figure in the shadows. The moment Vigdis was inside, the figure turned to head back along the side of the little building.

'Wait! Ketil!' He felt Sigrid's hand briefly on his arm as he took a long stride in pursuit. She was already too far behind to stop him.

But the man, if man it was, must have sensed someone else there in the darkness with him. Ketil heard a quick intake of breath, then a quicker step, and suddenly the figure was off, hurrying to the end of the chapel and disappearing round the corner. Ketil sped up, too. In a moment he was at the corner, and the figure was ahead of him, a dim movement at the back wall of the enclosure. And then he was over it, a leap in the darkness, a half-laugh, and the figure vanished into the low undergrowth of the hillside. Only the distant sound of sheep, reassuring each other in the night, gave any hint as to where he had gone, and Ketil, unfamiliar with the island, had no hope of finding him.

But perhaps he could work out who it was not.

Sigrid met him by the side of the chapel. She was already thinking his thoughts.

'Did he run off? I'm going in – I was going in anyway – to keep Vigdis company for a while,' she said. 'At least I could see who is in there.'

'And I can try to see who is still in the longhouse,' Ketil agreed. 'Though I have no wish to disturb anyone – after all, what was the man doing?'

'Nothing, but he did run away,' said Sigrid. 'If it was a man.'

'Maybe Vigdis will tell you everything,' he said. 'If you ask her nicely.'

'I suppose she might.' Sigrid sounded unconvinced, and a little tired. He looked down at her with her crooked headcloth.

'How are your fingers?' he asked.

'What?' Oh … getting better.' She wiggled the bandaged ends woefully. 'They're getting better.'

'Good. I'm pleased,' he said, then thought it sounded odd, as if she would have expected him to want her injuries to last longer. 'Maybe you'll find some good wool in Gulbervig when we go back.'

'Maybe.' He felt a sudden urge to hug her, but she pulled herself together.

'Yes, that's a good idea. I have some silver left to buy some. After all, if I'm not going to Heithabyr …' She tailed off. 'Right, yes. Vigdis. Good night.' And she spun on her heel, and marched off to the chapel door.

Not going to Heithabyr. The words echoed in Ketil's head. Then she had planned to follow him – bringing her few savings with her for the journey. She had planned to follow him.

Why on earth would she do that? She must have had some ulterior motive, he told himself. She was always up to something.

And he too turned abruptly, and went back to the longhouse.

Inside, he decided it would not do to spoil the peace of the place by going about the different bedspaces, trying to work out who was there and who was not. Instead he wrapped his cloak about himself, found a stool and sat by the door, inside, ready to stay awake for the rest of the night and work out in the morning who might have been missing long enough to survey Vigdis dig in the burial ground and then run away up the hillside. He was well used to watchful nights, and he had slept soundly earlier: he felt rested, and not quite comfortable enough to do more than doze at his post.

And there was enough activity to keep him awake. The monks observed the night services, and he counted the figures as they slipped out, and as they returned. Sigrid herself reappeared, jumped at the sight of him, and scuttled off to her sleeping place, and a moment later Borgny floated by, wrapping a shawl around her as she went to take Sigrid's place with Vigdis in the chapel. Much later again, Borgny came back, solemn-faced in the grey light before dawn. As the youngest monk lit the fire and chivvied the pots into life for hot water, the longhouse roused itself: figures slid out urgently to the privy and returned, refreshed; curtains were pushed back; bedding was taken out and shaken then rolled and folded; clothes were tidied and hair and beards were combed vigorously. Ketil stood and stretched, and counted over in his head who had been in the longhouse and who had not. Kolbein, Sibbi with his injured leg, Kjartan looking after him. Alfarin and his sister, most of the time. Gunnar. Alf and Skorri. Svart and the monks, and the abbot, shaking out his dark robes. All the party who had walked from Gulbervig were there, or in the chapel. The only person missing was the local man, Thorir.

Yet Thorir was there when the bier was carried solemnly out from the chapel, his head bowed and respectful, just as if he had known Thorgrim as a friend. The monks led the procession as Thorgrim was laid in his resting place, the sandy soil held back by sacking so that the wrapped body could be lowered easily into place. Borgny held Vigdis, weeping steadily, and Sigrid stood close by, their skirts and back cloaks whipped sideways by the wind, gulls keening overhead, a chorus to the abbot's prayers. As a weak sun rose over the low mainland ridge they had climbed yesterday, the earth was scattered over Thorgrim, and thief or not Ketil prayed that he would rest in peace.

'You are welcome to stay with us longer, my daughter,' the abbot was saying to Vigdis as they ate bread and soup in the longhouse. Vigdis looked as if she had not slept for a month, and Ketil was sure that there were sparkles of sandy earth on her skirts. But then she had stood close to the grave. She was shaking her head, anyway.

'Thank you,' she said, 'but I must return to my own home now, and find a place there.'

'Of course.'

As for the rest of the company, he could already sense that they felt they had done their duty, and could now return to normal life and Gulbervig. He was sure he had already caught Kolbein suggesting they go back via Skalavagr so he could do his bit of trading. Had they forgotten that one of them was likely to be a murderer?

Skorri came into the longhouse and caught his eye, giving the least shake of his head. Ketil acknowledged it. Where Vigdis had been digging last night, then, there was nothing to be found. He glanced across at Sigrid and saw that she had caught the exchange, of course. He sighed, and slipped outside.

Thorir was standing chatting with a couple of the monks, his neighbours, and Ketil waited until the monks headed off to some work in the infield.

'Good of you to come to the burial, Thorir,' said Ketil, approaching him slowly.

'The least I could do.' Thorir seemed affable. 'A sad case, by the sound of it. He was killed, they tell me?'

'It seems that way.' He let the silence between them lie for a moment, then said, 'What's your interest in the widow? Or was it in what she was doing?'

Thorir blinked at him.

'What do you mean? I don't believe I have ever met her before.'

'Last night she was digging in the burial ground. Just over at the wall there. You were watching.'

Thorir laughed, a surprised, unbothered laugh.

'I have no idea what you're talking about, I'm afraid! I don't know what she was doing – if you're sure – and I wasn't watching. I have better things to do at night – like sleeping!'

He gave Ketil a friendly grin, waved his hands helplessly, and gestured that they should return to the longhouse. Ketil, giving up for the moment, followed him.

XVII

SIGRID WATCHED KETIL return to the longhouse with the local man, Thorir, and knew at once that Ketil had learned nothing from their conversation. Maybe there had been little to learn: maybe Thorir had chanced upon Vigdis's nocturnal activities, and was just curious. Maybe Ketil was wrong and it had not been Thorir. Or maybe Ketil had just not been very good at questioning him. She followed him with her eyes now as he went to speak to the abbot, quietly, at the head of the company. She had no hope of working out what they were saying to each other, so she let her gaze wander on around the room.

There was that respectful but relaxed feeling to the place that often happened after a funeral: the body was buried, and real life started again. For the dead person's closest relatives and friends, of course, that real life would be different, but for those who had just come to pay their respects – and after all, that applied to most of their party – the burial was the end of the matter. They had eaten, and some of the monks were already off about their daily business. How soon, she wondered, would they also leave? Kolbein at least was anxious to be on his way. If Ketil had hoped to have solved the mystery of Thorgrim's death by now, though, he would be disappointed. What would he do? He could not keep them all here, or at Gulbervig.

Her gaze strayed to Vigdis, sitting quietly by the fire. She seemed quite composed now, too, and she had her little pack made up ready to leave. Sigrid was itching to know what on earth she had been doing in the burial ground last night, but she felt she should wait and see if there was a way of finding out without asking her directly. She was not sure why, but she had a feeling that a direct question would not bring her a direct answer. After all, if you are going to sneak out at night to do something, you are unlikely to tell a stranger readily next day what it is you were doing, she reasoned.

Moving on, wishing she could be spinning or weaving to make better use of the time, she noticed that the lad Gunnar was watching her – not intently, possibly just accidentally. But when he caught her eye, he came over and hesitantly took the place beside her. His hand gripped the edge of the bench, knuckles white as he pressed his weight forwards.

'Hello,' she said. 'Ready to go back to Gulbervig?'

He nodded. He looked anxious.

'And on to Orkney, perhaps?' she added.

At that, he let go of the bench and wound his hands on his lap.

'My uncle Ketil says you're from Heithabyr too?'

'I am, yes. We knew each other as children.'

'That must have been a very long time ago.' His eyes widened. Sigrid opened her mouth to retort, then changed her mind.

'It certainly feels like it,' she agreed. 'We lived next door to your family. I remember your father, and your other uncle, Thialfi.'

'I haven't seen him since I was very small,' said Gunnar. 'But now you live in Orkney, and my uncle says you live near Thorfinn's court? That you and he are friends again?'

'You make it sound as if we were enemies!' Were they friends? 'We met again after a long time, that's right,' she said. He seemed in need of some kind of reassurance, and she tried to think what might help. 'Ketil is of good standing in Thorfinn's hird, if you're worried about that. He could make a place for you there, if that was what you wanted. You make cups, don't you? You're like your father and your grandfather?'

'That's right.' It was not clear that she had helped, so she ploughed on.

'Cup makers are useful anywhere, as you'll know. Assuming you're better at making them than your uncle Ketil, anyway.' She paused, looking at his face as he stared into the fire. 'Do you want to come to Orkney?'

'Oh, yes, yes, of course. Where else would I go?' he asked. 'Orkney is the best idea.' But he sounded more as if he were trying to convince himself than anything else. She sighed quietly. There was more here than she was going to be able to dig out, she thought. Then he asked, 'What's it like?'

'Oh … greener than here, a little. Flatter, too. Your uncle doesn't like that.' She smiled.

'Doesn't he? Why not?'

'I think he thinks it isn't safe – that a great wave will come over and swamp us. But I don't think that will happen, don't worry!'

Gunnar had looked a little tense at the thought.

'Thorfinn would not be so silly as to build his hall somewhere like that,' she carried on, though remembering what had happened to part of Thorfinn's Brough recently made her hesitate. 'Thorfinn is in charge, and the place is well run. There are two settlements that are growing as – well, market towns, though nowhere near the size of Heithabyr, of course. But you might find ready custom at Kirkuvagr or Hamnavoe if you didn't want to stay close to where your uncle works. Of course the main problem for a man who carves cups out of wood is that there are very few trees.'

'Few trees? What, like here?' Gunnar looked shocked.

'There is a striking similarity there, yes,' said Sigrid. 'Very few trees.'

'I had thought here … maybe there had been a fire, or a disease … but Orkney too?'

'But if you're clever,' said Sigrid, 'it will make your cups have more value, of course. I can't think of a single cupmaker, not from wood, in all the islands.'

'Now that's a thought,' said Gunnar, and she could already see the thoughts running behind his eyes, a hint of excitement. Good – at least he did not suffer the same miserable commercial sense as Ketil, or the poor boy would starve.

'But first, of course, we have to go back to Gulbervig,' she said. 'And who knows what will happen there, if we haven't found out all there is to know about Thorgrim's death?'

'I didn't kill him, you know,' said Gunnar at once, spinning to face her.

'No, no, I'm sure you didn't. And Ketil's fairly sure, too. He just has to be careful in these things – particularly since you're his nephew.'

Gunnar relaxed slightly.

'Has he really done things like this before? Worked out who did things they haven't admitted to?'

'Well …' With help, Sigrid was thinking. 'Well, yes, he's had some practice at it. He has some good ideas. And …' she struggled, not used to paying Ketil compliments, 'he has a kind of air of authority that is useful in matters like this. And – and he's strong.'

'He does seem to be, yes,' Gunnar agreed, frowning as he took this in. 'Alf and Skorri seem nice. Are they all his hird?'

'There's a third man, Geirod, but he's back in Gulbervig. With his dog. It's a small hird,' she acknowledged, 'but I think he likes to be able to move fast. There may have been others in Nordvegr, before he came to Orkney.' She knew of one, but he was dead.

Gunnar considered again, before asking, with some care, 'And is he a good fighter?'

'A good fighter?' She thought back to the times she had seen Ketil fight. She had been surprised at his abilities, when she had been prepared to pick faults with her childhood friend. 'Um. I think he probably is, yes. Yes, he's not bad.'

'For the son of a cup maker?' asked Gunnar, and she was not sure whether he was mocking or serious.

'He has acquitted himself well any time I've seen him.' Then she thought that sounded almost disloyal. 'He could take on any of your fellow passengers here. Even Kjartan.'

He gave a short laugh, and somehow looked older, more world-weary.

'Kjartan wouldn't fight anybody,' he said. 'Sibbi would be the more dangerous of that pair, I think, never mind their sizes. But it's Kolbein I would watch,' he added, suddenly dropping his voice. Sigrid glanced about. Kolbein was in fact sitting beside Sibbi, and if Sigrid had been asked to guess, she would have said they were talking business, and not in a friendly way. Perhaps Sibbi wanted to stay on until his leg was better, and was asking Kolbein for his money back for the passage on to Orkney. That would have fitted – nothing aggressive, nothing out of the ordinary. Sigrid took in

Kolbein's weathered face, his prickly black hair, his ready grin.

'Him? He looks strong – sailors do, don't they? But is he violent?'

'Not usually, no. But he lost his temper with a couple of the sailors one day – one was a slave, but the other was a free man – and beat them. It wasn't … it wasn't so much that it was a violent beating,' he said, scowling as he tried to explain. 'It was more what it did to the men – and what it did to him. They were completely cowed, and he … he was so pleased with himself. It's hard to describe. It made me feel cold.' And he shivered, as if he could not help himself. 'He's always like that – like a cat ready to spring.'

'But would he have had any reason to kill Thorgrim?' asked Sigrid, after a moment trying to picture this. Gunnar shrugged.

'They seemed to know each other, I mean, better than anyone else knew anyone on the boat. I mean, well, of course, Sibbi knows Kjartan and Alfarin knows Borgny and Vigdis knew Thorgrim ...'

'I understand what you mean,' she said quickly, before he started to explain that Kolbein knew his sailors and they knew each other. 'How did they know each other?'

'Thorgrim and Vigdis had travelled with Kolbein before. More than once, I think.'

'She did say they had travelled a good deal.'

'He's a merchant, so I suppose he would. But if you ask me, they were friends.'

'Kolbein and Thorgrim?'

'Yes. Not close, but friendly.'

'And Vigdis?'

'I didn't notice particularly. I mean, she's not pretty or anything. I didn't pay much attention to her.'

He's young, thought Sigrid to herself. He'll learn. And if he doesn't, and he's still in Orkney, I'll make sure someone teaches him.

'Oh! It looks as if we're getting ready to go,' she said suddenly. Vigdis had risen, and shouldered her small pack with a struggle, and Borgny was standing beside her.

'Father Abbot,' Vigdis was saying through the voices in the hall, 'I thank you for your hospitality, and for what you have done for me and for my husband Thorgrim.' She bowed low, and the abbot inclined his head.

'Daughter, you know you are welcome to stay longer. And your friend here with the injured leg –'

'Oh, I must go, too,' said Sibbi at once, and began to struggle to his feet. Kjartan was at once at his side to help him.

'But son, your leg!'

'It is well on the way, thank you, father,' said Sibbi with a grin – Sigrid thought his teeth were clenched as his bad leg took some of his weight. 'And Kjartan can help me. We have a passage to Orkney, and we should take it!'

The abbot did not look happy, and bit his lips together.

'I cannot stop you, but I can strongly advise you – both of you, perhaps, for daughter, you are very weary looking. Please stay at least one more day.'

Vigdis smiled, the smile that transformed her face.

'You're more than kind, father, but I must turn back to the world again, and go home. These people have come here with me, with my husband, and I cannot detain them further.'

It was nicely done, and despite the abbot's misgivings he was visibly struggling to find another argument to detain them. And the party themselves were ready to go: no one had much in the way of baggage for their intended three nights away from Gulbervig, and packs were quickly shouldered. The bier, which belonged to Eyvind, could now be carried by two men rather than four, and Alf and Svart took first turn at that, letting it hang down sideways. They led the way back down the sandy path to the spit that would take them to the mainland. Vigdis and Borgny followed after, and Sigrid came next, then the rest of the men in a huddle with Sibbi and Kjartan struggling along in the midst of them. Ketil took the rear, and bade a final farewell to the abbot for all of them. The monks stood at a bend in the path and watched them go. Sigrid hoped their prayers would hold back those waves that struck on either side, and kept as close as she could to the middle of the narrow path. For once, she thought, perhaps a boat would be a good idea.

XVIII

'SO WHEN YOU say there was nothing there – you're sure you had the right spot?'

Skorri thought about it for a moment, then nodded.

'It was exactly where you'd described, sir. And though she had sort of peeled back the grass, you could see the ground had been disturbed. The sand had been thrown back a bit wildly, and when I dug a bit – just with my hands – I found one of those boxes, you know, made from the local soapstone? With a loose lid. And it was empty.'

Ketil nodded, watching a flock of sanderlings peck across the sand. The abbot had explained to him, as he had wondered. Locals came to hide their treasures in the burial ground, in case of raids – or these days just in case of light-fingered neighbours. But they told the abbot before they buried anything, and they were supposed to tell him when they were taking something away, too. And Vigdis had said nothing to the abbot.

'How big was the box?' he asked. Skorri arranged his hands to show him.

'Not that big,' he said, 'but big enough to hold the contents of a biggish purse, maybe. A few arm rings and some other treasures. There were scraps of cloth, but they were only rags.'

What had Vigdis been up to? If Thorgrim had stolen the silver from Svart and the arm ring from Gunnar, and Vigdis had known and kept them – or any other treasure Thorgrim might have stolen – then this would have been a perfect opportunity for her to hide everything, somewhere safe where she could come back to it. But the things that had been found in Thorgrim's purse on his body were still lying in Gulbervig, and apparently Vigdis had not taken the chance to hide anything else. So presumably she was retrieving something, perhaps something she wanted now to take back with her to Orkney. But why had the abbot not known that it was there, whatever it was? Who had buried it? Thorgrim?

He watched the birds again, pecking, pecking and running and pecking again. He felt he was doing the same. And why? Thorgrim was dead, the things thought stolen had been recovered, and everyone here had places to go and get on with their lives. Who was he to stop them? Yet he had a bad feeling about all of this. For one thing, someone who has murdered once will hesitate less to murder again. Thorgrim might, by some lights, have deserved his fate – though who were mere humans to say that? But the next time it might be someone more innocent. And why kill a man for theft then leave with him the things he was said to have stolen? And besides, that bad feeling of his. Ketil could not shake the idea that something was happening here on a larger scale. Was it possible that Thorgrim's death was only the start?

They had crossed the land spit and scrambled back up the sandy path on the mainland side, passing the point where Sibbi had fallen. Ketil looked to see how the man was progressing. Leaning heavily on Kjartan, Sibbi was just about keeping up with everyone else.

'I wonder why he bothered coming back so soon?' Skorri murmured, seeing where Ketil was looking. 'The monks would have cared for him well. You could see that poultice was doing him good.'

'He seems keen to sail with Kolbein again,' Ketil remarked. 'Presumably he's already paid right the way to Orkney.'

'And he thinks Kolbein won't honour it if he wants to postpone it? Aye, that's possible. Kolbein looks like a sharp fellow.'

As if he had heard his name mentioned, Kolbein turned round and waved at Ketil.

'I've had an idea!' he said, hanging back to let Ketil and Skorri catch up. 'Why don't we take a boat up the coast to Skalavagr, and cross over to Gulbervig from there? It would be quicker, now we don't have a body on a bier to worry about, and I'd get my bit of business done. I'm sure we could find a couple of boats to take us, round here.'

'I know people who could take us,' said Thorir, who appeared alongside Kolbein. 'And the bier. And it would be much easier on that man – Sibbi, is it? He looks exhausted already.'

Thorir, always nearby to help. Ketil pushed the thought to the back of his mind, and glanced round at the others. Vigdis looked tired, too, and yes, Sibbi was struggling. And it would be quicker: he knew the walk from Skalavagr to Gulbervig was a short one, over the hill. And would Kolbein give them any peace until he had been and done whatever it was he wanted to do in Skalavagr?

'How close are these boats?' he asked Thorir.

'Just down there. I can run and ask if they have time to take us – two boats, I suppose? Maybe three, with the bier?' And without waiting for an answer, Thorir skipped down the hillside and back to the water's edge. Sigrid caught sight of him, and paused. She turned back to see what Ketil was doing, and saw that several of the men had stopped. Ketil heard her call out to Alf and Svart, up at the front, and gradually everyone gathered back around Ketil.

'If we can, we'll take boats from here,' he said. 'Thorir has gone to ask.' He smiled inwardly at the look on Sigrid's face.

'I thought you said it would be quicker to walk?' she said.

'We'll sail to Skalavagr, then cross the hill there to Gulbervig. Not far. And easier on Sibbi,' he added, knowing she would not argue with that.

'Assuming Thorir can find enough boats for us all,' she muttered.

'Assuming that, yes.'

'You don't have to, just for me,' said Sibbi, though it would have been hard to say he meant it. He leaned against Kjartan, trying to hide how hard he was breathing.

'We should have stayed at the monastery, Sibbi,' Kjartan murmured.

'I'll be pleased to take a boat, if we can,' said Alfarin. 'Like a true Hjaltlander!' He grinned at his sister, who gave a little smile in return.

'If it's quicker,' she said. 'Then we'll get to Orkney all the faster, I hope.' Though what she was to do now, there, Ketil could not imagine. Did she have some claim on Bjorn's goods? She would be as well to turn round and go home then, he knew, for all Bjorn's goods had been returned to the Norwegian court along with his hird and his ship. Maybe she wanted to see what might have been.

Thorir came back up the slope, his tousled head appearing first as he clutched at hanks of grass to pull himself up.

'All set,' he said. 'They can leave as soon as we get down there. Two small boats and a larger one – the bier had better go in that, I suppose.'

It was a struggle for Sibbi to try the slope – in the end Kjartan took him up on his shoulders like a sheep and staggered down backwards, while the other men did their best to steady them both. The women fended for themselves. Ketil came last as usual, allowing Thorir to complete his negotiations with the local boatmen, but discreetly making sure he had one of his own men in each of the three boats. Skorri went with the bier, and Alf with Alfarin, Borgny and Vigdis. Sigrid was in the big boat. Ketil himself ended up with Gunnar and Thorir in a little round boat at the back.

'Good of you to take the trouble,' said Ketil to Thorir when they were underway. The local boatman seemed disinclined to conversation. 'I hadn't realised you were intending to go to Skalavagr too.'

'Always ready for a journey, if I can be of assistance at all!' said Thorir cheerily.

Why? Ketil wondered. Why was he so eager to help? He had pounced on them as soon as they had arrived by St. Ninian's Isle, just when Sibbi fell. He seemed to have nothing better to do than to follow them around, helping them. And watching Vigdis's activities in the burial ground by night, of course. That, too.

'So you have no business in Skalavagr?'

'I think I'll leave that to your friend Kolbein!' said Thorir. 'He seems to have enough business to do all of us! A busy man, that.'

'Yes, indeed,' said Ketil. 'Though I barely know him. Have you met him before?'

'No, I don't think so. I know the name – his ship calls at Gulbervig regularly, I believe. I hope that boat he's in is to his satisfaction. I hear he's very proud of – what's it called? The Sea

Stag? It must be a fine ship.'

'I've only glimpsed it,' said Ketil politely. He had not been much impressed by the Sea Stag's broad beams. But presumably it served its purpose, and it must be sturdy enough if Kolbein regularly crossed from Bergvin to Gulbervig and who knew where else. 'Do you spend much time in Gulbervig?' he asked.

'No, not at all,' said Thorir. 'Busy enough on this side of the island. Lots going on here, isn't there, Erik?'

'Aye,' said their boatman shortly.

'Do you live this direction, or to the south?' Ketil asked.

'To the south,' said Thorir.

'Your own longhouse?'

'Aye, that's right. My wife keeps an eye on it, if I'm away. You know, the way they used to do when we went off in the summer.'

'Did you travel much?'

Thorir shrugged.

'Over to Irland, a bit in Danmark, you know the kind of thing. But then things got more peaceful, and there was no reason to go so far. Now I just go up and down the islands here: it makes me happy, and the wife's glad enough to get me out from under her feet.'

'Of course.' Ketil had never married, but he had often heard men justify their travels this way. If the wives were like Sigrid, he thought, no doubt they were indeed happy enough with the longhouse to themselves and the household. 'Big family?'

'A couple of children, yes. Boy and a girl.' A smile flickered over his face at the thought. 'My parents are long gone, and I have no siblings now. But the wife has sisters … Oh, they're not bad women, really.'

Ketil made the obligatory face.

'What about you, lad?' Thorir asked Gunnar, who had been listening silently to the conversation.

'My parents are dead, too. I don't have any sisters,' said Gunnar. 'And my brother's dead. But Ketil is my uncle.'

'Is he indeed?' Thorir looked at Ketil in surprise.

'Does your lord not raid any more, then?' Ketil asked, changing the subject brutally.

Thorir's expression changed at once.

'Not so much, no.' He looked at the boatman, but the boatman was concentrating on his work. The coastline was just as complicated as that on the east side of the mainland, and Ketil was happy to let him get on with negotiating it safely. He preferred, on the whole, to travel in his own boat, under his own directions, but it did make sense to take this route, particularly with Sibbi's injury. Why was everyone so eager to return to Gulbervig? Alfarin and Borgny, Sibbi and Kjartan, Vigdis, Kolbein, as long as he could go via Skalavagr ...

'Can you recommend somewhere to stay the night at Skalavagr?' he asked Thorir, since the man was so keen to be helpful. 'Or perhaps Kolbein will know someone.'

'The lord at the hall is very welcoming,' said Thorir. 'I don't know him personally, but his reputation is that of a generous host.'

That was fairly straightforward, Ketil thought. Though no doubt he would be taken up to sit beside the lord again, and not have much chance to talk with the others in the party. He would have to rely on Skorri and Alf, as before. And then tomorrow it would be back to Gulbervig, and he still had no idea who had killed Thorgrim or why.

XIX

ANOTHER BOAT.

SHE really did not mind walking: you just wrapped yourself up, put one foot in front of the other and lost yourself in your thoughts until you reached your destination. But on the boat, for one thing, she was stuck with other people. For another, she was sitting, and when she was sitting she wanted to be weaving, and her fingers still would not let her. Then she looked sideways at Sibbi, his colour much better now that he, too, was sitting and not struggling along in Kjartan's tight grasp, and thought it would be better not to feel sorry for herself.

'How are you, Sibbi?' she asked. The boat was not wide, and the bier had been jammed along the length of it, tied to the mast in the middle to stop it tipping, so it felt as if they were in a kind of half-boat on this side. There was little room for Sibbi to stretch out his injured leg, so he was stuck sideways, his back against Kjartan, half-facing Sigrid. He grinned.

'Much better like this!'

'You could have stayed on the island, if you'd known it was going to be bad,' she suggested mildly. Sibbi made a face.

'With those old monks? That's not much fun. Anyway, I wanted to get on. Kjartan and I need to find a place, and I'd be surprised if the monastery could offer us anything much.'

'Just until you were better, though? You can't go round doing much with your leg like that.'

'It's not my leg a lord would want me for,' said Sibbi, confusing her for a moment. 'I'm the clever one, see, and Kjartan's the strong one. That's what we do: we're like one perfect man in two bodies. Any lord would be glad to have us.'

She blinked at him, and he laughed.

'Not convinced, eh? Well, maybe you're right. But that's what we like to tell people – sometimes it works!'

'Where else have you served?' she asked, interested. It did not sound as if they were fleeing or exiled: it sounded as if they had a plan. More travellers, belonging nowhere.

'Oh, here and there. We like variety, don't we, Kjartan?' he called over his shoulder. The bigger man grunted. 'Mostly around Bergvin, different places. Further north, once or twice. This is our first time in the islands. Hjaltland or Orkney, I mean. But it makes sense to head for Orkney, doesn't it? That's where the power is – that's where Thorfinn Sigurdarson is.'

'That's right,' said Sigrid. 'He's very much established at Birsay. Everyone comes there.'

Sibbi grinned again, and wriggled to make his leg more comfortable. He was a wiry man, not much taller than Sigrid herself, but his hair was a lank red and lay across his head almost unmoving, even in the wind. His eyes were pale and clever: she had no doubt that he was the bright one and Kjartan the strong. But she wondered if Sibbi were really as clever as he thought he was – or, indeed, if Kjartan was strong and not clever? Sibbi seemed very sure of himself.

'Maybe we can be of service to Thorfinn, then,' Sibbi was saying. 'No point in starting too low down the hill. I'm sure he'd value people like us.'

'He certainly appreciates people with abilities,' said Sigrid carefully. 'He'll probably want some idea of things you've done for other people. If you have a few convincing stories of your achievements, it should stand you in good stead.'

Sibbi looked thoughtful. Sigrid wondered if he were planning to make something up, and then asked herself why she was so sure that Sibbi would have to make something up. She did not dislike him, but she could not quite bring herself to trust him. Why?

'What about when you told Arinbjorn about the thing? At the court?'

Sigrid could hear Kjartan's suggestion indistinctly behind Sibbi. Sibbi frowned.

'Arinbjorn?'

'You know. When we were working for him,' said Kjartan.

Sibbi turned to Sigrid and rolled his eyes, then tipped his head back towards Kjartan.

'You mean Atli! We never worked for anyone called Arinbjorn, you fool!'

'Atli, oh, yes. Atli, Atli,' muttered Kjartan, struggling to remember.

'Yes, Atli was a good master,' Sibbi settled back again, easing his leg. 'He'd found a very clever skald – just a boy who had grown up in his hall – and I suggested we should send him to King Harald's court. Atli was ambitious, wanted to impress the king, so he gave the boy a red cloak and sent him off. Worked very well.'

'A red cloak?' said Sigrid, impressed. 'The boy was that good?'

'Well … I don't know that King Harald has that good an ear for a rhyme,' said Sibbi with a sideways glance. 'But if the boy arrived at his court already acknowledged as a high-ranking skald, complete with his own red cloak – well, let's just say that Atli did very well out of it. King Harald was delighted.'

Well, that was clever enough, she thought, and if Sibbi had made it up on the spot it was fairly convincing. Would Thorfinn, a straightforward man, appreciate that kind of manoeuvre, even on his own behalf? She was not so sure. But Sibbi was moving on to other matters.

'So how do you know so much about Orkney and Thorfinn Sigurdarson? Aren't you Svart's wife?'

'Svart's wife?' She paused. Maybe it would be to her advantage if he did not know her connexion with Ketil – if that were possible. Surely she had spoken more to Ketil than to Svart in the last couple of days? But perhaps that was what Sibbi expected from a wife – and many wives would sooner speak to anyone else than to their own husband, that was true. 'Sorry, thought I'd misheard you. And a friend of Thora's,' she added for distraction. 'His mother.'

'Are you from Orkney, though?' Sibbi was persistent.

'I was brought up in Nordvegr,' she said smoothly, not wanting to reveal her connexion with Heithabyr. As to the Orkney side of things, let him find out in his own time.

'But you live in Gulbervig.'

'I'll be glad to see it again, I can tell you that.'

He nodded slightly to himself, satisfied that he had made the right connexions. The rain started, softly but insistently, and people shifted to pull up hoods and adjust cowls, squinting up at the grey sky and round at the grey water. But the wind seemed unaffected, and they sailed on, the three boats shifting around each other, the passengers huddled against the weather.

The long channel they had been following between tall hillsides, probably their best shelter, dipped and narrowed at last. They slipped through the neck, between two low headlands, and into a broad bay that split in two somehow – she was not sure, from here on the water, whether the bays were separate or whether there were more islands that could be sailed around. Maybe the Hjaltlanders were right to sail so much – their routes were probably less complex from place to place.

The bay to the left was more curved, shallower in shape, so that they could see the far end of it. There had been longhouses in evidence all along their route, but here there was a settlement of a dozen or so all nested together in the bay's high-backed shelter. It must be the famous Skalavagr.

She pulled herself up and looked around the boat, as they edged through the rain into the bay. The sailors were paying great attention to Borgny, making sure she was comfortable, eyeing her from under their woollen caps. Sigrid could see she was used to it but did not enjoy the constant interruptions, the constant watching. She was far from envious of Borgny's looks. A woman could attract the wrong kind of attention very easily, looking like that. And how much say would she have in her marriage, now that Bjorn was gone? Was it Alfarin who had the choice? They had not mentioned any other family, any parents. Alfarin seemed to be in charge. She gave him a look, across there near the stern, while he was talking to his sister. A handsome man, a self-assured man. She had not spoken much to him: she thought he was probably not interested in speaking with widows of no great standing, unless he needed something. He worked for a minor lord, if she had taken Borgny's account correctly, but important enough – or the lord was important enough – that Borgny should have spent time at the king's court, that she should be betrothed to a prominent hostage – for Bjorn had been at the royal court as hostage for Thorfinn's good behaviour. What would Alfarin and Borgny do in Orkney when they confirmed that Bjorn was dead? Sigrid could think of no other good candidates for marriage with Borgny. Ketil was hardly in her class. Though if she did marry him, Sigrid might have a chance of doing woolwork for her, and that, she thought, would be fortunate. If Borgny married Ketil …

She shook herself hard, causing Sibbi to glance at her in surprise.

'Daydreaming again,' she explained, with an apologetic smile. 'When I have nothing to do with my hands – and particularly when I'm in a boat – my mind wanders, back over the past, off into the future. It does me no good at all! I should be much more … well, you know. Sensible, I suppose.'

Sibbi nodded, and returned to his contemplation of the approaching buildings of Skalavagr. Perhaps he was planning to seek out a new place to settle, for himself and his cousin: Sigrid found herself baffled at such a process, starting again somewhere where one knew no one at all. Tolerated in a stranger's hall until one could establish one's value, or find a longhouse of one's own – which came to something similar. When she had moved, she had been with relatives, or with her husband. The idea of starting again alone was frightening.

She looked again across at Alfarin. Yes, very self-confident, she thought. A man used to being in charge. She had seen a couple of times how he expected to give an order, and was taken aback when Ketil stepped in first. Yet he had not protested, and seemed to follow willingly when Ketil gave direction. He was a courteous man, she thought. Or was he waiting for Ketil to make a mistake?

Was Ketil making a mistake? Was he any nearer to finding out what had happened to Thorgrim, and why? Or had he trailed them all across to St. Ninian's Isle and almost back, without any result? How sure was he that the killer was in their innocent little group? How sure was he that there was a killer?

Vigdis was here to bury her husband. Svart was here to show the way, and because he was suspect, even though it had been Svart who had pointed out the evidence of murder when all thought it was an accident. Gunnar was here following Ketil, and because he too had accused Thorgrim of theft. Alfarin had volunteered to be here, and Borgny had to follow him – and she and Sigrid were there to look after Vigdis. And the rest? Kolbein, so eager to get to Skalavagr; Sibbi and Kjartan, keen to find work. And then Thorir – Thorir who had appeared from nowhere, and had watched Vigdis dig up something from the burial ground, and had run away. Who was Thorir, and what could he possibly have to do with Thorgrim's death?

XX

THE SHELTERING HILLS around Skalavagr felt welcoming as they beached the boats and paid off the boatmen. The rain had darkened the day, they were all wet at least into their outer couple of layers, and it was clear that for most of them the first thought was not trade, but a warm fire and a hot drink.

'The hall is over there,' said Thorir, helpfully, though Ketil had already spotted the distinctive gable end with its great door.

'That's a good place to start,' said Kolbein with relish, and set off at once with his pack on his back, keen to do his business. Ketil watched him go to make sure he was really heading in the right direction, then gathered the rest of the party together on the beach.

'All well?' he asked generally, though he looked first to Vigdis.

'Aye, well enough,' she said, and she did look stronger.

'Sibbi?' Ketil asked next.

'Better for the rest,' Sibbi agreed, letting Kjartan lift him out of the boat. 'I'll be fine tomorrow for the last bit to Gulbervig. It's not so far from here, is it?'

'Just over the hill,' Thorir agreed. 'No time at all.'

Skorri and Svart unloaded the bier awkwardly, and carried it between them up the beach.

'I could always ride on that,' said Sibbi, 'if it gets too hard to walk.'

'Don't rush to ride on a bier,' Thorir warned him with a half-smile. 'Your day may come sooner than you think.'

Kjartan laughed, but Sibbi, though he gave a quick cackle, did not mention the idea again. Kjartan wrapped an arm around Sibbi's waist, and half-carried him up to the hall, Thorir following ready to help. Alfarin had helped his sister off the boat and lent her his arm, and Vigdis was joined by Sigrid, though she seemed in need of no support now. Ketil and Alf made sure they had left nothing in the local boats, bade the boatmen farewell, and followed everyone else to the hall. No doubt, Ketil thought, Alfarin would introduce them all and explain their coming. If he wanted, Alfarin could sit by the local lord at supper, and engage in elegant conversation. Then Ketil could sit somewhere less public, and watch what was going on. It had been easier to carry on Thorfinn's work in matters of this kind when Thorfinn had given him less responsibility: now in local halls men wanted to ask him about Thorfinn and tell him what they thought Thorfinn would want to hear, and no one would talk idly to him or drink too much next to him. It was annoying.

That was one reason he had asked Sigrid to come along on this expedition – this apparently useless expedition. People talked to her, and if she watched them talking to others, or doing things, then they paid her little attention. Just as long as she told him afterwards what she had learned, so that he could make use of the information. She probably would tell him, because she would be pleased she had found out something he did not know. But sometimes he thought she did not tell him everything, because … why? Because she thought she could make better use of it than he could? But that was dangerous: that had nearly killed her before now. He would do all he could to stop something like that happening again. But she did not make it easy: she was a very difficult person to protect. One day he would just let her manage on her own, and see how she did it. That would teach her to be more careful.

The hall was a larger one than that at Gulbervig, and looked better kept, though there were ladders leaning up against one side wall. Inside they were at once greeted by a man of around Ketil's age, an axe at his belt and a look of business about him. He had broken off from talking with several men about him to take a good look at the visitors. Ketil saw intelligence in his eyes.

'Of course you may stay. Welcome,' he said at once when Alfarin waved Ketil forward to explain who they were. 'I'm Ivar.

You look wet – let's get you over to the fire. We're taking a break ourselves till the rain eases.'

'Fixing the roof?' asked Ketil.

'Making sure it's ready for the winter,' Ivar acknowledged. 'Now, my wife will bring you something to drink. And some rugs until your clothes dry a bit.'

A cheerful-looking woman hurried forward and organised a small busy flock of her attendants to see to their needs. Soon they were indeed seated by a good fire, with warm wine and rugs, as well treated as if they had come back from a month of raiding, instead of a day's sail between the islands. Everything was done with an easy, friendly efficiency that Ketil found hard to resist. He could see that everyone else, too, relaxed almost at once, even in a stranger's hall. The thought put Ketil slightly on edge: one should not trust strangers too readily, even when they were welcoming.

But when the rain eased, Alf, Skorri and Svart headed willingly outside with Ivar's men to help secure the roof, and Ivar and Ketil joined them. Ivar was lopsided – he seemed to have had an axe blow on his left shoulder at some point. It must have made shield-bearing hard work. To compensate he had built up the arm which now looked stronger than the other, though the shoulder was still misshapen.

'You're an odd party, if you don't mind me saying it,' Ivar remarked to Ketil as they stood at the feet of two ladders, handing good bits of driftwood up to those on the roof. 'Did you say you'd been at a burial?'

'That's right,' said Ketil. 'The woman with the black hair is the widow. The rest are – well, we happened to be around when her husband died.'

'Where are you from? Gulbervig?'

'No – except for Svart.' Ketil indicated Svart at the top of the ladder. 'The man was travelling. Several people here were travelling with him.' There was no sense in telling the whole story. Ivar would know nothing of Thorgrim's death.

'Ah, in Kolbein's ship?' Ivar asked.

'That's right – some of us were in that.'

'But you're Thorfinn's man?'

'Yes.'

'Not in Hjaltland? I'm sure I would have come across you

before!'

Ivar had every right to make sure his temporary guests were not going to cause trouble – and anyone could walk in and say they were Thorfinn's man, or anyone's man, or no one's at all. He wondered again briefly if Sibbi and Kjartan were exiles.

'No, in Birsay,' he replied. 'At least for now.' It seemed a long time since he had settled anywhere, and he would not, he thought, have chosen Orkney, not when he had first seen it, anyway. But now, it seemed, Birsay was the closest thing he had to home. Unless Alf and Skorri dragged him and Geirod off east, of course. How would Thorfinn feel about that?'

'Ah, actually at his hall!' said Ivar, more reassured, Ketil thought, than impressed. Then a veil of caution passed over Ivar's face again. 'Tell me, is Thorfinn well?'

'Well?' Ketil was surprised.

'I mean,' said Ivar, with an awkward gesture, 'is everything well there? At Birsay?'

'I believe so,' said Ketil. 'And I was there only a few days ago.'

'Oh! That's good.' He seemed to think more was required. 'We haven't seen him this direction for a while, you know? I just wondered if all was well. I mean, I know he has a good deal to look after these days, and if he's happy that things in the north are settled then of course he would give more of his time to more southerly matters, wouldn't he?'

'He would,' said Ketil.

'Look out down there!' came a cry from above, and a jagged piece of old driftwood – barely hard enough to cause them any damage, it was so rotten – flopped down past them and hit the ground with a dull thud.

'Shouting before throwing is a good idea!' Ivar yelled back. 'Not after the thing's on its way!' and someone apologised distantly. Ivar laughed, and kicked at the ladder he was holding, happy enough to change the subject as far as Ketil could see.

'Can I help, at all?' Alfarin had appeared behind Ketil, smiling at Ivar.

'Nearly done now, I think,' said Ivar. 'Were you on Kolbein's ship, then?'

'Yes,' said Alfarin, who seemed to think Ivar a suitable

person to talk to. 'Travelling to Orkney, when we return to Gulbervig.'

'I heard that tragedy interrupted your stay.'

'The death of Thorgrim, yes,' said Alfarin. 'His poor widow – though she seems more … what would the word be? Content with her lot, perhaps, now that the funeral is done.'

'He died in Gulbervig, but you buried him at St. Ninian's Isle?' asked Ivar, as if the oddity of it had suddenly struck him. 'Why was that?'

'Vigdis – his widow – wanted it that way. We chose to go with her,' said Alfarin smoothly, not looking at Ketil. 'Apart from paying our respects, I was interested to see the island, and to meet the brothers. The abbot appears to be a man of deep faith.'

'Of course,' said Ivar, not looking wholly convinced. 'You're new to the islands, then?'

'Yes, I'm from near Bergvin,' Alfarin explained easily. 'But I'm taking my sister to Orkney. She was to marry Bjorn Einarson, but we've discovered that he died not long ago.'

'He did, yes,' said Ivar. 'His hird called in here on their way back to King Harald's court. A storm blew them to this side of the islands, so they were delayed a few days and then had to go back round to Gulbervig. It did not improve their general mood – he will be much missed.'

'Are you still intending to travel on to Orkney?' Ketil asked Alfarin.

'I think so,' said Alfarin. 'To make sure that we know as much as we can about the situation, before I take Borgny back to the court. Unless, of course, she finds someone new there.'

'Another betrothal?'

'Why not? I'm sure there are other men of good standing around Birsay. Perhaps whoever now has the hall that Bjorn was to inherit. Who is that, anyway? Do you know?'

'It had not been decided before I left,' said Ketil.

'Thorfinn will want to take his time over that,' said Ivar. 'It's something he'll want to get right, I should think.'

And something about his tone made Ketil look at him, but Ivar's attention was once more on the ladders and the men on the roof.

'That was a good day's work,' Ivar said as the dishes were cleared at supper that evening. He raised a cup to Ketil, sitting on one side of him – to Ketil's annoyance. Alfarin was on the other side, a gracious guest even if his travelling clothes were beginning to look a little grubby. 'Thanks to you and your men for all your help.'

'We like to make ourselves useful as we go about,' said Ketil.

'And do you go about a lot?' asked Ivar, giving Ketil a sideways glance.

'A fair bit.'

'Then … maybe you have heard things, too?' Ivar asked, his voice lower. He smiled and raised a glass to someone down the hall – keeping up the appearance of talking about nothing much, Ketil thought.

'Heard things?'

'Heard … rumours,' said Ivar quietly.

Ketil waited.

'Rumours of unrest,' Ivar went on unhappily.

'Against Thorfinn?' There were often rumours – no man ruled so great a swathe of lands without the occasional difficulty – but something about the way Ivar spoke made Ketil's neck prickle.

'Well, yes.'

'What have you heard?'

Ivar let out a long breath through his nose.

'I've heard two versions,' he said. 'The first is that King Harald wants to pay our Earl a visit, remind him where his loyalties lie. Find another hostage of standing to replace Bjorn Einarson, that's the latest I heard.'

Ketil nodded briefly. It made sense, particularly now there was no hostage for Thorfinn's good behaviour. King Harald was never very sure of Thorfinn's allegiance, and with good reason. Thorfinn was very happy to be left to his own devices.

'And the other version?'

'You remember Kalf? Kalf Arnason?'

'Oh, yes. I remember Kalf.'

Kalf Arnason, kin to Thorfinn's beloved wife Ingibjorg – beloved of Thorfinn, anyway, though perhaps less well liked by others, notably Sigrid. Kalf, one time ally of Thorfinn's, then his worst enemy. Kalf, who had thought to attack Orkney in the wake of his usual tricks and deceits, only a couple of years ago, but finding his tricks had not worked he had fled. Had he come to try again?

'They're saying he's around, that he has men loyal to him in Norway.'

'He always had.' Surprisingly, he added to himself. No one could trust Kalf.

'And in Hjaltland. And maybe, again, in Orkney.'

XXI

ANOTHER HALL. ANOTHER unfamiliar lord, with his unknown hird.

And more shellfish.

The rain drummed on the roof, but fortunately did not come through. When the men had come in from their mending work, they had claimed the places by the fire, and Sigrid and the other women had backed off into the shadows, still not quite dried out from their sea trip. By chance, Vigdis and Borgny were somewhere on the other side of the hall, while she was among the local lord's family and wives of the hird, a busy, chatty bunch, quite tiring after a day – three days, more – travelling. Once again she had had to explain about her injured fingers, and once again was excused any duty serving food and drink, though she would have relished the excuse to move about a bit. She was feeling cold and a little miserable, and wondered, yet again, why she had come. She was not normally so impulsive. But while Ketil clearly needed help here, Sigrid did not, for once, feel she was being very useful. She had walked and sailed and talked and listened and watched, and what good had it done either of them? She felt no nearer to discovering what had happened to Thorgrim, whom she had never even met. She felt lost, and a bit lonely, and very much in need of her own hearth. And she really wanted to weave, but her fingers had been throbbing all day and seemed worse than they had been before. Would they ever heal? What would she do if they did not? She felt her shoulders slump, her back sag, and let the conversation on the women's benches flow back and forth about her, as she gradually became invisible in her gloom.

'So they're all Kolbein's passengers, are they?' asked a woman's voice in a local accent. 'I didn't see the Sea Stag in the bay.'

'No, it's over at Gulbervig,' said someone else. 'You know the way he beaches there and comes over here with – not sure what he has this time. Spices of some kind, I think I heard.'

'He's always expensive,' the first woman grumbled. 'And I'm not sure half of it is what he says it is.'

There were grunts of agreement around the table behind her.

'So why did they all come over here?' the second woman asked. 'I haven't heard any of the others trading. Not that they've been here long.'

'One of the other passengers died at Gulbervig,' said the first woman, an authority, apparently. Sigrid thought she was the lord's, Ivar's, wife. 'A man. His widow wanted him buried along at St. Ninian's Isle, with the brothers.'

'There's a bier over yonder, by the wall,' said another woman.

'The body's in here?' There was a squeak from one of the younger girls, and a bit of teasing laughter.

'No! They've him away and buried. But you wouldn't leave a bier outside, not with the scarcity of wood.'

'Oh, aye, true,' said the girl, with a sheepish giggle. 'You'd be safer leaving the body on it. But he must have been well-liked, if they all came over with him.'

'They're not all from the Sea Stag,' the first woman put in again. 'That one, the tall one with the short hair – he's Thorfinn Sigurdarson's man.'

'Is he, indeed?' said the girl. 'Is he married, do you know?'

'Don't let your father hear you talking like that!' said one of the others, and everyone laughed.

'Oh, I don't know, though,' said the first woman. 'He's the kind of match I'd fancy for my own daughters. Good standing, and very bonny to look at. In fact, I'd maybe keep him for myself.'

'If he just smiled a peerie bit more,' added someone else, and Sigrid grinned to herself at last. Ketil was not known for his ready smiles.

'So that's him, and a couple of his men,' said the first woman, still in charge of the conversation. 'They weren't on the Sea Stag, I'm sure. And then there's one fellow among them … I know one of them from along the way, and I doubt he was on the ship. See him over there?'

There was a pause as they apparently surveyed and pointed towards the men, who were all well settled into eating and drinking. Sigrid, despite her mood, was almost tempted to look up and see who they were talking about, but she did not want to draw attention to herself. She could be patient.

'Oh, aye, right enough, he looks familiar. Where do I know him from?'

'His name's Thorir,' said the first woman, and Sigrid gave a little nod. 'He's from down by St. Ninian's Isle – that's maybe where they found him, for I think the boatmen who brought them all knew him.'

'Thorir? Who was his father?'

'Another Thorir,' said the first woman. 'It's an odd family. Did you not know them? There was another brother but he wouldna stay about the place, took off travelling. Not raiding, you understand. Their lord was affa young for leading men anywhere. No, this fellow set himself up as some kind of a merchant. And Thorir was left to manage the land himself, but I think he's a bit like his brother. The wife does most of the managing, and Thorir wanders about the place. From all I hear, the wife's happy enough with the arrangement.'

'So what does he do, when he's wandering about the place?' asked the girl.

'This and that,' said the first woman. 'He makes some good salves and such. For those who have no woman to do it for them, I suppose.'

'I heard something about him and his wandering,' said the second woman, warily, as if it would be a mistake to claim knowledge that the first woman did not have.

'What's that, then?'

'I heard tell that he was wandering about, looking for his family's silver. The fellow you mentioned, the brother – the story is that he took it, and hid it, before he left. And he never told Thorir where it was. And of course Thorir wants it back.'

'He would, right enough,' said the first woman generously. 'But it's a few years since the brother left. You'd think Thorir might have found it by now, if it was anywhere to be found.'

'Aye, well, the longer you leave it,' said the second woman, more relaxed now that her story had been accepted as a possibility, at least.

'Oh, aye, the longer you leave it,' the others agreed. And it was true: mark the hiding place for your silver, and anyone might dig it up. Fail to mark it, and as the time went by the place became less and less distinct – safer from robbers, certainly, but also safer from you. Sigrid's silver, such as it was, had been buried in a corner of her own longhouse, under one of her looms. Now it was mostly on her arms, what was left of it. Still, it probably was not worth stealing – there was that advantage to being poor.

'And I think I heard tell that the brother, the merchant kind of a one, was married now. What's this his name was?' The first woman pondered for a moment, and it was enough time for Sigrid suddenly to think she might know the name. Could it be ...?

'Oh, aye, that was it,' said the woman, slapping the table lightly. 'I remember now. Thorgrim, that was the fellow.'

'Oh, I remember him!' said the second woman in surprise. 'A charmer, isn't he? Didn't he –'

'Aye,' said the first woman sharply. 'He did. He'll not try that again.'

'I hadn't realised he was Thorir's brother.'

'What? What did he do?' asked the youngest woman.

'Never you mind. Time to go round with the ale again – the men are looking dry.'

'But –'

'Come on! That's enough claik for now!'

And the three women pushed up from their benches, picked up their skirts, and went to refill their ale jugs.

And Sigrid, eyes wide in the shadows, slowly stretched her back, straightened her shoulders, and felt much better.

The trouble was, Ketil's new custom of going and sitting up beside the local lord made it much harder to slip off and speak to him privately. She was not sure where he was getting these grand ideas from, but she wished he would stop. Even the thought of telling, say, Alf or Skorri first, or even having them tell Ketil she wanted a word, was not as good as going up behind him, tapping him on the shoulder and saying,

'Here's something you might not know.'

So instead, since no one seemed to be paying much attention to her anyway, she went to linger in the darkness by the door, waiting for Ketil to pay one of his rare visits to the privy. The man never drank anything like as much as the others – Sigrid wondered if he did not have the head for it – and so he was not up and out as frequently as everyone else. But at last he did slip out, and she waited just outside the hall now, in the damp night air, for his return.

'Ketil!' she muttered, as he approached. There was a sudden silence, and no movement at all for a breath. Then:

'Oh, it's you.'

'Did you think I was going to attack you?'

'Normally people do not spring out of the darkness for casual conversation.'

'Who said I brought casual conversation? I have some mildly interesting information for you, but if you can manage without it then I shall be on my way. I have no wish to linger out here in the wet.'

'Only mildly interesting?'

'It's possible you already know it.'

She could hear his smile – perhaps it was easier for him to smile in the dark.

'If you thought I already knew it, you would not be waiting to ambush me. Come on, Sigrid, tell me what it is.'

She took a breath.

'It sounds as if Thorir is Thorgrim's brother.'

There was a gratifying pause. It was news to him.

'Where did you hear that?'

'The women were talking. I don't think they thought I was listening. One of them knows Thorir by sight, and a bit of his history, and said he had a brother called Thorgrim who is a merchant, is married, is charming, travels … it all seemed to fit. You said he was, well, personable?'

'He knew how to behave to impress people, yes,' said Ketil thoughtfully. 'I don't think Alfarin took to him – people like Alfarin would think Thorgrim beneath them.'

'And he had done something to annoy the lord's wife here. I don't know what. But you know that's never a good idea.'

'No, indeed.' She heard him breathe out, considering the new information carefully.

'Oh, and here's something interesting,' she added.

'Not just mildly interesting?'

She made a face at him, even though he would not be able to see it.

'They were saying that one reason why Thorir wanders around the place is that Thorgrim took the family silver, without telling Thorir, and buried it somewhere before he went off. Thorir wants it back.'

'No,' said Ketil.

'What?'

'I mean no, you're right, that really is interesting.'

'Do you suppose,' said Sigrid, quite pleased with the effect of her news, 'that Thorir thinks that Thorgrim told his wife where the silver was buried?'

'That's what I was wondering,' he said. 'And I suppose the question is, did he?'

'You mean that that was what Vigdis was digging up in the burial ground?'

'Exactly.'

'And if it was,' said Sigrid, 'and he didn't say anything to her, or to anyone else, at the time – well, what is he planning to do about it?'

XXII

WHATEVER ELSE THORIR might be planning, the next morning he made it clear that he had every intention of travelling on with the party he had adopted, at least as far as Gulbervig.

'Don't you think we can find our own way?' Ketil heard Sigrid asking, though she made a joke out of it. Thorir laughed.

'I haven't been over to Gulbervig for a while,' he explained genially. 'I thought I'd take the opportunity. Not that it isn't a safe road for a man on his own, for there are always plenty of people back and forth on it. But it's good to have company, isn't it?'

Ketil was not sure Sigrid would necessarily agree, self-contained as she seemed. He looked about the rest of the little group, making sure they all realised that they were obliged to return to Gulbervig for Eyvind's judgement. They were packing up their light baggage, chattier than they had been before the burial but still not noisy. Vigdis, perhaps, was still subdued, but why not? Gunnar was talking to her, asking her about Orkney – he had already asked everyone else. She answered sporadically, not looking at the lad. Ketil had not seen her talking with Thorir at all. He wondered if she suspected him of anything. Had Thorgrim ever mentioned his brother, or his name? Family near St. Ninian's Isle, yes, but she had believed them all gone, or said she had. Would she be pleased to find that she had a brother-in-law and his family around?

A brother-in-law who apparently suspected Thorgrim of what was, to all intents and purposes, yet another theft.

Gunnar, Svart, and Thorir. It seemed unlikely that they were in any way conniving, and all three believed Thorgrim to be a thief, despite his respectable appearance. And he was dead, and some of the stolen goods had been found with his body. It was hard to believe that Thorgrim had not actually been a thief, with all that. Had Vigdis known? She and Thorgrim seemed to have been closer than many husbands were with their wives. And what had she been digging up in the burial ground on St. Ninian's Isle? Was that the silver that Thorgrim had taken and hidden? If so … presumably she was carrying it now. Had Thorir challenged her? Was he going to? Or was he waiting until they were back in Gulbervig, for some reason? Ketil had no right to ask to see the contents of her baggage, again, but Eyvind might, if Thorir made an accusation. And what then? If Vigdis was found to be carrying silver that did not, or did not wholly, belong to her, what would that imply about the other stolen goods? He sank his head briefly into his hands, rubbing his temples with his thumbs almost until it hurt. It did not really help. He straightened and looked about him again, trying to think.

Ketil had led this party over to St. Ninian's Isle and was dutifully bringing them back for Eyvind's judgement, but he had never felt in control of it. But at least if anyone had been following them, or watching them, or whatever it was he thought he had felt on the walk south, sailing back instead of walking had shaken off any pursuer. In that respect, if in no other, he felt easier now. Or perhaps it was just that they were almost back to Gulbervig.

He counted the company, and realised at once that they were one short.

'Where's Kolbein?' he asked.

'Oh, he said he needed to do that bit of trading,' Skorri told him. 'He said he wouldn't be long.'

'Aye,' added Alf, 'he even said if we wanted we could go ahead and he would catch us up.' He nodded drily.

'Very generous,' said Ketil. 'But I think we'll wait.'

'It's a fine day,' said Skorri. 'We could wait outside, and let them clean up the hall.'

Outside the day was indeed fine, and they sat, casually arranged, looking out across the bay with its layers of headlands to each side. It was clear to see the path their boats had taken yesterday, between that low land and the steeper climb to the right, but beyond that point it was hard to tell from here where the path between mainland and islands lay. Ketil liked it: it was like a fjord in miniature, changing perspectives, puzzling with each new angle.

Sibbi and Kjartan guarded the bier, protecting the precious wood to return to Eyvind. Ketil strolled over to them.

'How do you feel about the walk today?' he asked Sibbi.

'Better than yesterday,' said the smaller man. 'See, I can almost straighten my leg!' He demonstrated, though it made him a bit breathless. 'With Kjartan to help me I should be all right.'

'Boats today?' asked Kjartan hopefully.

'No boats, no. We'll cut straight back across to Gulbervig, over that hill. It's much shorter by land.'

'Oh, that's a pity,' said Kjartan, looking sadly out at the bay. Ketil had to agree with him: the wind was gentle, but the waves drew softly down the shore, silver to green to darkest blue. It would be a beautiful day for a slow sail, with a bit of easy rowing.

'I'll bid you farewell.' The lord of this hall, Ivar, had appeared by Ketil's shoulder, solemn-faced. 'It's a good day for a journey. And I must go with my men to deal with some sheep.' A brief smile blinked on his face, then he dropped his voice. 'Will you remember what I told you?' He turned a little, so that Sibbi and Kjartan could not hear.

'I will,' said Ketil. He trusted the man, so far as he could on a day's acquaintance.

'I know it's not much, but if I were in Thorfinn's shoes I'd want to know … that someone up here thought there was something wrong.'

'I'll tell him,' Ketil assured him. 'You're right: he'll want to know.'

What Thorfinn might do about it, Ketil was not so sure. Keep his ears open for something further, perhaps. Send Ketil back to investigate. Maybe even take a fleet and sail round the islands in a show of strength.

'Tell him he has friends in Skalavagr, anyway,' said the lord, though he looked concerned. He laid a hand on Ketil's shoulder. 'Go safely.'

'Thank you again.'

The man looked skywards, checking the weather, then nodded and strode off. His wife appeared with some cloth-wrapped bundles.

'Food for the journey,' she said briskly. 'Go safely.' She too took her leave and headed back towards her longhouse, no doubt with a busy day ahead. Ketil's arms were full of the bundles.

'I thought you said it was a short walk?' asked Sibbi, lips curling. 'Stupid woman's given us enough for a three-day hike.'

'Generous woman,' said Ketil. 'And the food was good last night. And,' he added, turning away with his burden, 'you'll be moving slowly, anyway. You might be glad of it.'

He went to find Skorri and Alf, to split the food between their three packs.

Then they waited, wondering where Kolbein had got to.

'We might have to eat the food before we leave,' Gunnar said anxiously. 'That would save us carrying it, anyway. And I'm already hungry.'

'Are you going to give him much longer, sir?' asked Skorri. 'Kolbein, I mean. What if he's found some pals to get drunk with? Or a friendly widow to make him comfortable?'

'Till midday,' said Ketil. 'We'll leave then, whether he's back or not.' But he was reluctant to leave Kolbein behind. Could he be Thorgrim's killer? He looked tough, and he must have known Thorgrim well, if they had sailed back and forth together enough. He needed more time. He had no clues at all. Or he could just let Eyvind make a judgement, abnegate all responsibility, report back, without comment, to Thorfinn.

Thorfinn, Thorgrim … Thorir.

The stranger, Thorir, was standing near to where Vigdis, Borgny and Sigrid were sitting, their baggage next to them, ready to move as soon as the signal was given. Sigrid looked bored, sitting with her bandaged hands wrapped round each other, unproductive. He was still not used to seeing her sitting still when she could be working. Thorir's conversation seemed to be mostly with Borgny and Vigdis. Ketil strolled over.

'Did anyone happen to see which way Kolbein went?' he asked. There was no sense that he should not have interrupted the conversation: they all looked to him perfectly amicably.

'Would you like me to go and look for him?' asked Thorir, always eager to help.

'No, it's all right,' said Ketil. 'One man wandering is

enough. If another should drift off, we'll never get away.'

'Are you giving him till midday?' Sigrid asked, and he nodded. How did she know?

'There's food if anyone's hungry. Skorri and Alf have most of it,' he said.

'Shellfish?' asked Sigrid. He could not quite place her tone.

'Bread, cheese, ale,' he summed up. To his surprise, the three women at once rose and made for where Skorri and Alf were sitting, leaving Thorir and him abandoned to keep an eye on their baggage.

'They must have been hungry,' said Thorir with a grin.

'Aren't you?'

Thorir shrugged.

'I'm used to irregular meals,' he said. 'When you wander about, like me – but you probably know what it's like.'

Ketil gave a short nod.

'Do you do anything, while you travel? Have you a trade or skills you bring to the places you stay?'

Thorir smiled again.

'Yes, indeed: I make medicines.'

'Medicines? Is there much call for that? I should have thought that the women of a household, or a hall, would make all that was needed.'

'True, but sometimes I can show them a better one, you know? Or bring them something with a new ingredient.'

It seemed a chancy way of making any living.

'When did you last wander as far as Gulbervig?'

'Gulbervig? I don't often go as far as that,' said Thorir, innocently. 'This west coast here, and the islands opposite. That's where I can usually be found.'

'But you live … somewhere near St. Ninian's Isle?'

'That's right.' It sounded open, but Ketil could hear a tightness in his voice – just a little wariness.

'And you're married? You have your own household?'

There was a tiny pause before Thorir replied.

'Yes, that's right. Didn't I say?'

'Parents dead?'

'Yes. It was my father's longhouse.'

'Of course.' Ketil stood almost next to him, looking out at

the wide bay, the thin sunlight on the flickering waters, the slices of headland and the busy boats to and fro. 'Any other family?'

'Me? No, not that I know of!'

'Or not any more?'

Thorir shifted slightly.

'What do you mean?' he asked.

'Oh, I think you know what I mean,' said Ketil, praying Sigrid's information was correct. 'You had a brother, Thorgrim. Vigdis's husband. Now he's dead.'

'Oh,' said Thorir.

'You knew, didn't you?'

'No.' Thorir shook his head, and a great heaving sigh passed through him. 'But I did wonder. Then it was him.'

'When did you wonder?' Ketil was not convinced.

'When I heard the dead man's name, of course, I recognised it, but it's common enough. Then someone said he'd come from – well, near St. Ninian's Isle, like me.'

'Didn't you say anything?'

'Say anything? It ... it didn't seem to be the right time,' said Thorir awkwardly. 'I hadn't seen him for years, and Vigdis was grieving. It didn't seem to be the time to claim some of that right to grieve. So I kept quiet. But you think it was? That it was my brother?'

Ketil hesitated. It seemed more than likely, but he had no more proof than Thorir himself had.

'It seems likely,' he said. 'From all you've said.'

'Did you know him in life? Did he look like me?'

Ketil turned and studied him for a moment.

'I had only just met him, but no, I should say he did not look much like you. You're fairer, and taller.'

'That fits, then,' said Thorir. 'He took after my mother, I after my father. But he was charming, I daresay? Thorgrim could always persuade people of anything.'

'That much seems to be true. Tell me,' said Ketil, drawing breath, 'did you ever hear him suspected of theft?'

'Ha!' Thorir gave a dry smile. 'Well, I wouldn't have mentioned it if you hadn't.'

'Not a surprise to you, then?'

But a shout interrupted them. Ketil turned. Kolbein was

hurrying across the shore towards him.

'Shall we go?' he said, before he had even reached Ketil. 'I think we should go. Now.'

XXIII

KOLBEIN WAS, EVEN as far as Sigrid could hear, cagey about his urgent need to depart from Skalavagr.

'Kept you all waiting too long,' he said, gasping a little as he led the whole party at a smart pace along the path towards Gulbervig. 'More than good of you all to wait for me. We'll need to catch up with ourselves, won't we?' He tried a cheerful smile, but it was a little too toothy to be convincing.

'I'd say a husband came home unexpectedly,' said Alf, bending down to murmur in Sigrid's ear.

'Or he overcharged for something that wasn't what he said it was, from what I've heard,' Sigrid responded with a grin. 'He might not be so eager to trade in Skalavagr for a while.'

'At least we're on our way,' said Skorri. 'If we're not going east, I'd like to get back to Birsay. We'll hear what Eyvind has to say, of course. But this problem doesn't seem to have a quick solution.'

No, Sigrid thought, as Alf and Skorri both hurried off, responding to a summons from Ketil. In fact, no solution or part of one seemed to be presenting itself at all. Had Thorgrim really been killed? And she was not sure what the story was about the purse that had been found with him. Where was it, anyway?

She looked around, and found Svart plodding along not far away. She changed course slightly on the path to join him. He glanced round at her, giving her a nod. Another man who did not smile readily, though in Svart's case it seemed to be that the world lay too heavy on his shoulders for him to smile.

'Not far from home now, then, eh?' she began, determined to be cheerful.

'Aye, and what then?' Svart asked, surly.

'What do you mean? I'd have thought you'd have been glad to get back from this expedition – the funeral of a man you didn't know.'

'I knew him – well, I knew his face,' said Svart bitterly. 'I should be pleased to see him buried. But I just want my silver back, and to be away out of this business of murder. I should never have opened my mouth about the boots and the sand.'

Sigrid had forgotten Svart's contribution to the investigation.

'Tell me again,' she said. 'It sounds as if you were pretty clever.'

The corners of his mouth turned down, denying the compliment.

'I just noticed that the backs of his boots were stuffed with wet sand, and one of them was a bit torn. So I looked on the sand, because there wasn't any sand where they found him, and there were a couple of sort of rough lines across the sand to the rocks where he was. So I said that someone had moved him on to the rocks, and I think Ketil agreed. But maybe I shouldn't have said anything. Everyone thought he'd just slipped and hit his head.'

'Well … I'm sure Ketil would have noticed the boots eventually,' she said. 'Or someone else would have pointed them out to him. And then, if you hadn't said anything, it might have looked bad, mightn't it?'

'Nobody else mentioned it. Does that mean it looks bad for all of them? I mean, I was the one Ketil decided to bring all the way out here, just so that he could keep an eye on me. He's waiting for me to admit that I killed Thorgrim.'

'But you didn't, did you?'

'Of course I didn't!' He spat hard at the idea, then cast her a sideways glance. 'You don't think I did, do you?'

'No, I don't,' she said, but did not add that she had no particular reason for thinking he was innocent. Except that he had, indeed, pointed out that someone had moved the body. 'And what about the stuff you said he stole from you?' she asked. 'What do you think happened to that?'

'Oh, didn't you know?' He was surprised. 'They found a purse on him, and my silver was in it. And the arm ring that lad Gunnar lost, that was there, too. I mean, a lot of mine was just bits and pieces, but some bits I knew.'

'And where is it now?' Sigrid asked, making a note to have a stern word with Ketil later. Why had he not told her? Not that he had told her much. What was she doing here?

'Still with Eyvind, I suppose,' said Svart gloomily. 'I wonder if I'll ever get it back. Still, at least now I know what happened to it.'

'How long ago did Thorgrim steal your silver?' Sigrid asked.

'Oh, over a year ago, now.'

'And he's kept it all that time?'

'What do you mean? He wouldn't have given it away. Do you mean someone would have stolen it from him?'

'No,' said Sigrid, reassessing her previously high opinion of Svart's intelligence. 'No, I mean he would either have spent it, or buried it, or at least had it melted into arm rings he could carry more easily. A purse full of bits of silver is vulnerable, wouldn't you say? And if there were bits you could recognise, why had he not, in particular, had those melted down, or sold them? Anything to get rid of something you could identify.'

Svart, initially frowning, began to nod.

'Aye, I see what you mean,' he said. 'Right enough. Why just carry it all around with him like that?'

'Did you see him wearing the purse when he came off the ship?'

'No, no one had seen him wearing it. Ketil asked everyone when the purse was opened, if they had seen it before.'

'Was it even his purse?'

'Vigdis said not. She said he just used her purse for anything he needed to carry on the journey. And everyone else showed us their purses, all different.'

'Nothing to stop someone carrying two, of course,' Sigrid murmured, 'but it would be unusual. Do you think he would have been able to hide it under his cloak?'

'Not all the time, surely,' said Svart. 'On a windy crossing? In a smallish ship? If he wanted to hide it, it would have been a bit risky.'

'So in fact it might not have been his at all.' She had been thinking about this. 'So either he found it, and was taking it back to the hall when he was killed, or someone gave it to him while he was outside that evening, or … or someone decided to attach it to his belt after he was dead. And I would assume that whoever did that would also be his killer.'

Svart opened his mouth, and shut it again. Then he tried again.

'But why would anyone do that?'

'Leave it with his body? I don't know – maybe to make the point that he had stolen the things.'

'But … but if someone else attached it, had he actually stolen the silver?'

'You were sure he had stolen yours, anyway. Maybe someone else had taken it from him.'

'And given it back when he was dead?'

Sigrid was beginning to feel that the conversation was not as helpful as she had hoped.

'Well, I don't think he just found it, anyway. For one thing, it would be an extraordinary coincidence. And for another – well, what would you do with a purse you had just found?'

'Take it to the hall, if I didn't know whose it was.'

'Would you bother fastening it on to your own belt?'

Svart thought about it. She could almost see his hands, moving as he imagined what he might do.

'If I had a lot to carry, I might,' he said.

'But Thorgrim had only slipped out from the hall. He wasn't working, or carrying baggage. His hands were free.'

'Then no, I wouldn't. It would look too much as if I was stealing it, just treating it like my own. And anyway, if I was just going to hand it over in the hall, why would I waste my time tying it on and taking it off again?'

'Exactly.' But where did that get them? They paced on up the hill.

'Where had he been on the beach?' Sigrid asked.

'What do you mean? He was on the beach, and he was

dragged over to the rocks. As far as I could see.'

'You followed the trail back from the rocks, though, didn't you? Where did it start?'

'On the beach.'

'Yes,' said Sigrid, now sadly disappointed by Svart's intelligence, 'but he must have been near something? There were boats on the beach, weren't there? Was he near those? And which one?'

'Boats?' For a moment, Sigrid wondered if Svart were a Hjaltlander at all. He seemed never to have heard the word. But no: he was better than she had expected.

'There were eighteen boats on the beach,' he said, and from the way he looked she was sure he could see each one of them. 'Mine was the first, then Aun's, then …' and he went on to list the eighteen boats with certainty, knowing their accustomed places. 'And at the end, of course, the Sea Stag.'

'Kolbein's ship?'

'Yes, that's right. Opposite the hall, there, that's where visitors bring their boats up. So that we can keep an eye on them, eh? Though Kolbein's a regular.'

'So where did Thorgrim's trail start, then? Where were you when you found the beginning of it?'

'Well, next to the Sea Stag, of course. The end boat.'

Next to the Sea Stag. What had Thorgrim been doing on the beach, next to the Sea Stag, in the middle of the night? And whatever he had been doing there – was that connected to the fact that he was now dead?

Sigrid spent the rest of the walk trying to find an opportunity to fall into conversation with Kolbein. She did not remember talking with him at all on their journey, though she was also sure he had not had much conversation with Vigdis or Borgny either – perhaps he was one of those men who barely notice women. But her efforts were in vain, anyway: Kolbein strode out at the front of the party, urging them on, barely allowing anyone to pause for a rest or food. He was clearly not popular in Skalavagr just at the moment: all he seemed to want was to return to the Sea Stag and sail off.

The Sea Stag … She should tell Ketil what she had discovered, if he did not already know. Could there be a connexion, or was it just coincidence? Why had Thorgrim been walking on the beach? Had he set out alone, or had he intended to meet someone, or had someone followed him or come upon him by chance? Had he deliberately gone to the Sea Stag – and if so, why?

This was a most annoying matter, she thought. All questions, and no answers. How could Eyvind possibly decide who had killed Thorgrim, with, presumably, even less information than they had? He was bound to come up with the wrong answer, unless he happened to choose a name by lot and strike lucky. How long might they be stuck in Gulbervig, waiting for his decision? She wanted to get home: she had had enough of other people's halls.

Even from up on the hill the gentle curve of Gulbervig's bay looked soft and welcoming, the two long, low arms of land a protective embrace from the sea beyond. She wondered suddenly how she was going to return to Orkney: would she have to potter down the coast again to Dunrostar hofdi, then find some boat to take her back south? Would Ketil take her? That seemed unlikely: his was a businesslike boat, designed for fighting men. Or could she afford a place on the Sea Stag? That might be interesting. Maybe she would at last learn something. Though of course, by then Eyvind would have made his decision, and the matter would be closed.

XXIV

KETIL FELT HIS heart sink.

'I can't say who did it,' said Eyvind, and Ketil would have called his tone petulant. 'How am I supposed to tell? Was he even killed? Was he a thief? Who knows?'

'What do you want me to do, then?' Ketil asked. He knew it had been foolish to rely on Eyvind for an answer. The man was weak. How had he ever come to be in charge of a hall and a hird?

'Well, you can make up your own mind,' said Eyvind generously. 'Or you can take the problem back to Thorfinn. He's the one in charge. Let him deal with it.'

It was tempting, but Ketil knew that if he tried to do more than tell Thorfinn what had happened, Thorfinn was most likely to hand the investigation back to Ketil. Particularly if he took the warnings from Skalavagr seriously: he would have other problems on his mind. For a moment he considered asking Eyvind if he had heard similar rumours, but then discounted the idea: he had no great faith in Eyvind or his ability to judge a situation. It would only confuse things.

'Aren't they all going to Orkney anyway?' asked Alf politely. 'That might be helpful.'

Ketil turned a glare on Alf, then reconsidered. It might just be easier to take the whole matter home (he tried to ignore the fact that his mind had used the word) and deal with it there. And yes – apart from Svart and Thorir, everyone intended to travel on, or back, to Orkney. Svart he had almost discounted, though he would like to go with him again and walk on the beach, review what Svart thought had happened to Thorgrim's body, which Ketil thought more than likely to be the truth. Thorir, though: the dead man's brother, and another man convinced that Thorgrim had stolen from him. There was nothing to stop Thorir from having been in Gulbervig when Thorgrim died. In fact, was it possible that Thorir had been the man who had slipped into the hall in the darkness, and left again in silence? Ketil thought it might well have been. And then there was the matter of other possible killers living locally, or at least other people who might have seen something that night. Eyvind was supposed to have been collecting that kind of information while they were away – supposed to have been.

'Did you make enquiries about other people about that night?' he asked, trying not to let his low expectations show. 'Was anyone local out along the shore, or nearby?'

Eyvind straightened his shoulders, a satisfied smile on his face.

'I did,' he said, 'just as I said I would. But no one else was about. I had my men question everyone in the settlement – apart from Svart, of course, who was with you. And no one saw anyone go out, or knew of anyone going out. Apart from Svart, of course.'

'Of course. What about the rest of your hird here in the hall? There were, what, a dozen of them?'

Eyvind made a face, but it was not unsympathetic. Ketil pushed on.

'You know yourself – no one seems to have paid much attention to who was going in and out. Did anyone else accuse Thorgrim of theft? Did they know who he was?'

'Some knew his name, I believe. I don't think there were any other accusations.' From his tone, it seemed unlikely that he would have believed them, anyway. Eyvind did not seem to like trouble.

'Where is the purse that was found with him?'

'The purse? Oh, it's in my house. I thought it would be safer there.'

'Good ...' Ketil was not immediately sure what to do with it, but he was pleased to know where it was.

'Can we not go yet?'

The others were around the hall, far enough back to let Ketil and Eyvind talk, but close enough for Kolbein now to attract their attention.

'My Sea Stag's keen to get on!' he said, with that toothy excuse for a smile. 'I've trading to do!'

Ketil wondered if he was impatient to make up for whatever had gone wrong in Skalavagr, or if Skalavagr had gone so wrong that Kolbein actually wanted to leave Hjaltland.

'Yes,' said Alfarin, Kolbein's unexpected ally. 'My sister and I would like to continue to Orkney as soon as may be. Are you to come to a decision here, or not? Eyvind, I thought you had said you would have a verdict ready for us – that you would have made a judgement on who had killed Thorgrim?'

'Ah, but was he killed?' put in Kolbein quickly.

'It seems more than likely,' said Eyvind, with a quick look at Ketil.

'Even if he were not killed deliberately,' said Ketil, 'Svart has shown us that the body was moved to the rocks, so someone knew he was dead.'

'But you have not come to a decision, Eyvind.' Alfarin continued. 'It would be most useful if you could do so.'

Eyvind, who was standing by his high seat, took hold of its carved arm for support. Ketil had seen it often: someone who clutched at authority, and perhaps had every right to it, faced by someone who assumed it naturally, whether they had the right to it or not. The latter almost always won. Eyvind steadied himself with a deep breath.

'My decision is to defer to a higher power,' he said. 'Thorfinn Sigurdarson will be the judge. You can all go and give your accounts to him.'

'But he's in Orkney,' Svart objected.

'Thorfinn? What about the Thing?' asked Alfarin. He looked completely taken aback. 'If you can't make a judgement, don't you call a general meeting and put it to them? Where do they meet – here? Skalavagr?'

'In the middle, by the loch,' said Svart. 'That would make sense. Let the Thing decide. Come on, Eyvind, you should call everyone.'

'I don't want to,' said Eyvind, then seemed to realise how childish it sounded. 'I choose not to. If Earl Thorfinn wants to call a

Thing, let him do so. I – I have better things to do.' And with that, he gave his high seat a brisk tap, as if to show it who was in charge, and strode off out of the side door of the hall.

'What extraordinary behaviour!' murmured Alfarin, catching Ketil's eye. 'I have never seen such a thing. Is that the way matters are handled in the islands? In Thorfinn's lands?'

'Not habitually, no,' said Ketil, tight-lipped. 'Thorfinn will soon know about this.'

'Then let's get on south to Orkney and you can tell him,' said Kolbein.

'I think we should, yes,' said Alfarin. 'This is not how things should be.'

Nor should I have to herd a flock of murder suspects about the islands, Ketil thought crossly. This was becoming ridiculous. He looked about the hall, where his men, including Geirod and his dog, were carefully stationed to prevent any incidents. Ketil felt like starting an incident himself. Still, at least he could rely on them. He looked about again, and found Vigdis.

'Thorgrim was your husband,' he said. 'Are you content for this matter to be brought before Earl Thorfinn? At Birsay?'

'I suppose so,' said Vigdis quietly. 'I want to go home to Jorfjara.'

Ketil nodded, and turned to his nephew.

'Gunnar, you are amongst those chiefly suspected of Thorgrim's murder. Are you content to go to Birsay?'

Gunnar shrugged, though Ketil could see he was shaking a little.

'My intention was to go to Birsay to find you, so yes, I am content, Uncle.'

'Sibbi? Kjartan?'

'If it's sailing, I'm willing,' said Sibbi. 'We had it in mind to go on south if we found nothing here. I'm not sure we've tried everywhere, by any means, but I'm happy to try Orkney. That's where the power is, eh?' He nudged Kjartan, who nodded, though he looked more puzzled than anything. Ketil left it – no doubt Sibbi would explain what they had decided.

'Kolbein, you want to go anyway. Alfarin, you and your sister intend to travel south. Svart, will you come?'

Svart scowled.

'I suppose I must, if I wish to clear my name. It is a hard day when you find the man who has stolen from you, and the goods he has stolen, then are blamed for his death. But I hope Earl Thorfinn is quicker at making up his mind than some people,' he added, glaring over at the side door of the hall. Svart was clearly not a great supporter of his lord just now.

Ketil's gaze travelled on, over Sigrid, then back to her. She was not involved, of course. Sigrid could stay here in Hjaltland if she wished, whatever it was she was doing here. Vigdis and Borgny could look after each other on the Sea Stag, as no doubt they had before. Or, well, Thorgrim had looked after Vigdis, and Alfarin had looked after Borgny. But that was before their walk to St. Ninian's Isle: he had the impression that the women were closer now than they had been before. Anyway, Sigrid … could stay here if she wanted to. It was nothing to do with him.

And then Thorir.

The man grinned as Ketil turned to him.

'Do you want me to go, too? I'd be happy to come along,' he said. 'It's years since I went to Orkney. No doubt I'll find uses for medicines there. And it's not bad weather for a good sail, is it?'

He said nothing about Vigdis and Jorfhara. Ketil was fairly sure that Thorir had not even spoken to Vigdis, never mind told her that he was her late husband's brother. And that was interesting in itself: families were keen to claim their own. Just look at Gunnar: there must have been friends he had left behind around Heithabyr, people he knew much better than a long-lost uncle, but he had travelled all the way to the royal court and then south to try to find Ketil. But Thorir wandered far from home, and did not make any contact with his brother's widow, when it would be so easy … but then, if the stories were true, Thorir and Thorgrim had not exactly been friends, even if they were brothers. Had Thorir been here in Gulbervig when Thorgrim had died? How could he find out? Ketil sighed: his head hurt.

'Well, then, let us go,' he said at last. 'Kolbein, when will you be ready to sail? And are you happy to take Thorir and Svart in place of Thorgrim?'

'I can take both of them, and Sigrid too,' said Kolbein, 'if she's coming.'

'I'll take my own boat,' said Svart, huffily.

'Then Sigrid will go with him, and we'll all be as comfortable as before!' said Sibbi with a grin. Ketil deliberately did not look at either Sigrid or Svart, but said,

'Certainly, if that's what you wish. But you must give your word to sail to Orkney as close to us as you can.' He thought for a moment. It would be wise, perhaps, to take one of the suspected men on his boat, and place Skorri or Alf on the Sea Stag. 'Gunnar, you can come with me, and Alf, you take his place on the Sea Stag. Kolbein, when do you want to leave?'

'First tide tomorrow,' said Kolbein happily. 'I'll make sure my crew are ready.'

'Geirod, my boat is ready, is it not?'

'Aye, sir.'

'Svart, can you sail with us? With Sigrid?'

Svart grunted.

'Aye, I'll do that, if that's what's needed.'

'Then we'll stay here tonight, and make a start in the morning.' And maybe then they would be able to straighten out this mess. Though when it came down to it, he was far from hopeful.

XXV

'MAYBE YOU WEREN'T ready to go back.'

Ketil looked almost apologetic. Sigrid smiled to herself, amused at his unaccustomed thoughtfulness. She did want to go back to Orkney, as long as she was not going to miss anything, though she regretted that she was to sail with Svart, and not on the Sea Stag with the others. With Svart, it would be a quiet passage.

'I'm interested in your little puzzle now,' she said. 'I want to find out what happened, even though I never met the man. Is Thorir really his brother? Did you ask him?' She had a feeling that Ketil was not telling her everything he found out, and that would have to change. On the other hand, it had not been so easy for them to have private conversations recently, not with Ketil sitting up beside local lords every evening. She could have asked Alf or Skorri, but she was not sure that Ketil ever told either of them everything, either.

Ketil glanced round, making sure they were out of hearing now. She had followed him down to his boat, pulled up a little apart from the others. Doubtless someone at a distance could see his head up above the gunwale, even though they were both seated on rocks, but she herself would be invisible to anyone on the wrong side of the boat. They stared out at the comfortable bay, at the entrance to the open sea, and watched gulls swing overhead: even so, she was aware of exactly how close he was, and any movement he made. As usual, he did not move much.

'Yes, apparently Thorir and Thorgrim were brothers,' he

said. 'Though I don't think Thorir has told Vigdis of their connexion.'

'Really?' She was surprised. 'I wonder why?'

'Perhaps he's not ready to trust someone who was so close to his brother,' Ketil suggested sensibly.

'Trying to get to know her first, perhaps? That makes some sense,' Sigrid conceded. 'After all, bringing her into their household is a commitment. I daresay there are a few people who would prefer not to have to adopt their sisters or brothers-in-law, but are stuck with them. But at least in this case there are no children to complicate the matter.'

'No, it seems that way. Thorir has every claim on their family silver – if he can find it.'

'So do you think he's going on to Orkney to find out more about her?'

Ketil shrugged.

'Maybe. Maybe he wants to find out who killed his brother, too. And he couldn't say that in front of Vigdis.'

'No, not in the circumstances. Hm.' She watched a flock of kittiwakes flicker across the waves, chirruping as they went. It was a dull, steady morning, not bad for a journey, nothing challenging. And she wanted to go home.

'Are those the rocks where Thorgrim was found?' she asked, nodding to their left. Ketil glanced round, and she was able to look quickly at the line of his jaw, though why she should want to was unclear, even to her.

'Yes, that's right. Just over there.'

'How did he look?'

Ketil turned back to her, and she looked away to the sea again.

'On his back, feet towards the water. He was damp with dew, and stiff. There was no damage to his clothing, back or front, but there was a wound to the back of his head, broad and flat. It looked as if he had stepped on to a slippery rock and fallen backwards, hitting his head.'

'Until Svart pointed out the thing about his boots, and the sand.'

'Indeed.'

She cast him a look out of the corner of her eye.

'Which makes Svart look innocent, doesn't it?'

There was a pause. The kittiwakes flew back with comments.

'Does that matter to you?'

'It matters to me that the murderer might escape justice, if the wrong man is blamed.'

'Well, there, at least, we agree,' he said, with the ghost of a smile.

'Are we disagreeing about something else at the moment?'

'Bound to be,' he said. 'Don't we usually?'

She laughed, then sighed.

'We don't really know enough here to disagree on anything much,' she said. 'And I know even less than you. You didn't tell me that if you follow the tracks in the sand, it looks as if Thorgrim was attacked just beside the Sea Stag.'

'He was?'

'That's what Svart said. Right beside the Sea Stag, where she's beached.' She jerked a thumb over her shoulder, towards the other boats.

'Svart said?'

'Well, he was the one who found the tracks, wasn't he?'

'Yes …' But now Ketil was frowning, as if a whole new angle to the problem had opened up.

'So it could have been something to do with the ship – that's why Thorgrim was killed,' she said firmly.

'Or Svart could have drawn attention to the tracks because he made them – because he wanted me to think about a connexion to the Sea Stag.'

'He would be giving up hope by now, then,' said Sigrid, more sharply than she had perhaps intended. 'You've only just come upon the idea, and I had to give it to you.'

'And you only did that because Svart pointed out where the tracks started, didn't you? So again: did he make the tracks himself, to draw attention to the Sea Stag?'

'But why would he do that?' But she knew the answer.

'Because he had killed Thorgrim himself, of course. Sigrid, I don't think you should travel in his boat.'

'Well, if I move now it's going to look odd. Sibbi and Kjartan think Svart is my husband.'

'What?' Now he was staring at her. She looked away.

'It was an accident, but I didn't bother to correct them,' she said.

'No? Why not?'

'Because,' she said, 'if I was Svart's wife, then that was reason enough for me to be on the journey to St. Ninian's Isle. Otherwise I might have had to explain that I was there helping you. Isn't that why I was there? Maybe I was mistaken. But it seemed to me it would make it easier for me to talk with people if they did not connect me with you.'

That had not come across as clearly as she had meant it to. It had been supposed to sound clever, strategic, as well as demonstrating to him that it would be better for him to share all his information with her as his helper, to remember and value her. Instead she just sounded confused.

'Then you'd better go with Svart, then,' was all he said, drawing in his long legs to rise. 'Just be careful.'

He rose, and walked away. The kittiwakes wheeled round once more, putting an end to the conversation. Sigrid scrambled stiffly to her feet, and walked around Ketil's boat, cross with herself and furious with Ketil.

The Sea Stag lay nearby, the largest, roundest ship on the shore. It was a wonder Kolbein brought it up the beach rather than letting it lie out in the bay, but he clearly cared for the ship. The beach was already busy around the hull, with the slave crew loading the passengers' baggage on board, organising ropes and bundles and barrels, rattling the boards above Sigrid's head. She felt dwarfed by the size of the ship, and even more by its figurehead, a stag's head with real antlers fixed on it, a clumsy imitation of a warship. She looked down and across to the rocks, a little distance away. Would one man have been able to drag Thorgrim so far? If they had really killed him because of something to do with the Sea Stag, would they have left the tracks so clear that Svart had spotted them? The sand was damp with recent rain: she was not sure she would be able to see them now. But there was a line where the sandy surface seemed a little disturbed. Was this it? Was this the point where Thorgrim had been killed?

She looked about her. Someone walking straight from the door of the great hall to the sea would almost step on this very point.

It seemed a riskier place to kill someone than the rocks, over to the east. But if Thorgrim had been lured to this place … he might have been more likely to come to the beach here, even in the dark, than to agree to meet someone on the rocks. And likewise, if he had just been outside for some fresh air, the beach was much more welcoming in the dark than the uneven surface of the rocks. Why had he been here? Whom had he met? Why, having killed him, had they dragged him over there? So that it took longer to discover him, or so that it looked like an accident?

And what about that purse?

With much masterful shouting from Kolbein, grunts and cries from his slave crew, and relief from his passengers, the Sea Stag finally set sail on the high tide that morning, followed more discreetly by Svart, pushing out a decent-sized boat and waving a brusque farewell to his mother Thora, and lastly Ketil's boat, Geirod and Gunnar and the dog already seated in it, and Ketil and Skorri running it down the beach and into the waves. Kolbein, from what Sigrid could see, looked thrilled to be back on the water in his own vessel: there was a degree of arm-waving and grinning, and then satisfied fists on his hips as he surveyed the filling sail. Ketil had his sail up, too: it took Svart slightly longer, not helped by Sigrid, to unfurl his, but once he had they made up a little on the other two boats. They were not the only sailors in the bay, and when they reached more open water still more little boats criss-crossed their paths, the Hjaltlanders going about their business between voes and bays and islands with cheerful waves and cries of greeting. It was enough to haul Sigrid out of her low mood a little as she waved back.

'You all seem so happy travelling,' she remarked. 'Always hopping in boats, skipping over to Nordvegr. Have you been to Nordvegr, Svart?'

'I like my home,' said Svart. 'I'd rather stay there.'

'Have you been to Orkney before?'

'Yes, but I didn't stay long.'

Thank goodness, thought Sigrid. She was not to hear of another devotee of her neighbour Helga, evidently.

'I don't suppose you'll need to stay long this time, either,' she said. 'Thorfinn will sort this out.'

He gave her an odd look, then asked, as if it were not quite connected with the look,

'You like living at Birsay, then?'

'I'm just across from Birsay. Yes, I do like it, I suppose. I haven't lived anywhere else for a long time. It's quiet, but there's always something happening, if you see what I mean.'

Svart shrugged.

'I'm not sure I like things happening.'

'Doesn't Eyvind do much?' Having seen him, she would have been surprised to have heard that he raided every summer.

'Eyvind does plenty, and none of it good,' said Svart mysteriously. And that appeared to be the end of the conversation. Sigrid settled back, and wondered how long it was going to take them to reach Orkney. However long it was, it seemed bound to feel much longer.

XXVI

KETIL WAS PLEASED to see Dunrostar hofdi, and to draw his boat up on the pebbly beach at the lumpy green headland. A silvery-yellow sun was considering setting over to the west, and cooking fires were already sending steady threads of smoke up above the rooftops of the several longhouses tucked into the bay. He had spent an anxious day, watching the passengers on the Sea Stag from a short distance, ignoring Gunnar's questions about Orkney, watching even more carefully Svart's boat with Sigrid seated serenely in it, it appeared to him, barely speaking. Well, that was good. If Sigrid took it into her head to start questioning Svart about his actions on the night of Thorgrim's death, her position was vulnerable, to say the least. He tried not to look as if he were following too closely, judging the distance so that if, for some reason, Sigrid ended up in the water, he would be able to pull her out. And Svart, of course.

Svart was already making his way up the beach towards a specific longhouse, and Ketil remembered something about his mother's brother living here, the one who had brought Sigrid north to Gulbervig. Everyone else seemed to be lingering on the beach, or just above it, not sure where to go.

'Where are we staying, sir? There's no hall,' said Skorri, scanning the settlement.

'Someone must take in travellers,' said Geirod, thumping down from the boat. He and Skorri hauled it more securely up the beach, and the yellow dog jumped out to join them. He did not mind sailing, but objected to wet paws.

'Kolbein should know,' said Ketil, and strode across to find him.

'I haven't been here for a while,' Kolbein said, looking more nervous than Ketil had seen him. His experience in Skalavagr seemed to have shaken him.

'If we're stuck we could upend the Sea Stag and shelter under it,' said Sibbi cruelly. Kolbein clenched his fists, but said nothing. Kjartan, propping Sibbi up, looked confused. Ketil turned to look again for Sigrid, but she was already making her way towards the largest longhouse. Ketil followed.

A woman appeared at the door, blonde and sturdy, shaking out cloths with vigour. She peered at Sigrid, then, hesitantly, smiled.

'Oh, it's you again! Come on in – Mother will be glad to see you. How are your hands? Where have you been? Are you going back to Orkney?'

'Yes, and Thora sends her greetings,' Ketil was close enough to hear Sigrid's response. 'Her son Svart is here – well, I think he's gone to your neighbour's house.'

Before this could turn into a full account of Hjaltland families and travels, Ketil stepped in.

'We are to travel on to Orkney tomorrow. Is there any chance of shelter for the night?'

'Of course,' said the woman, 'and anyone we don't have room for can go to our neighbours. Come in, come in.'

The longhouse was spacious, and the family were well enough set up to have a separate hut for the animals, such as were indoors at night at this time of the year. The space where the animals would be, therefore, was turned to extra bed spaces. Ketil assumed that being at the southernmost tip of Hjaltland, near enough, they had plenty of travellers passing by, looking for accommodation.

But fortunately this evening they had no other visitors, except for an old woman and her daughter, relatives of their host. Sigrid seemed to know them, and immediately settled for a gossip. The old woman was weaving sprang at a terrific rate. Her son, the owner of the longhouse, seemed a quiet, cowed man, but the women were hospitable enough for everyone.

Alfarin entered the longhouse warily, then seemed satisfied and ushered Borgny in behind him. Their hostess was sensitive to status, and brought them both wine before serving anyone else. Ketil smiled to himself. At least here he would not have to sit anywhere special. Kolbein, Sibbi and Kjartan, and Ketil's men, were all welcomed equally and made comfortable. Vigdis joined Sigrid and the busy sprang-weaver. There was already a large pot on the central fire, and once they were all settled the woman started chopping more vegetables to add into it. A girl a little younger than Gunnar had greeted Sigrid silently, then disappeared. She soon came back with a bucketful of shellfish to throw in, then went again for more water, never saying a word. Ketil wondered if she were mute.

Skorri edged in to sit beside Ketil, and leaned over to murmur,

'I've pulled his boat up beyond the Sea Stag and ours, and tied it in, so if he does try to slip off he'll not be able to go unnoticed.'

'Good,' said Ketil. He had not liked the way Svart had disappeared to another house without explaining himself. At the same time he did not want Sigrid to go and stay in the same house just to keep an eye on him, and to preserve the myth that they were married. Why on earth had she bothered bringing in that complication? Svart did not even look right for her. And did she really want to live in Hjaltland? Just when he was getting used to the strange, flat mistiness of Orkney? Not that she had to take his feelings into account, not at all. And he could settle anywhere, anywhere he was of use to Thorfinn. Birsay was just another hall, and Sigrid was just a friend.

He realised he was watching her, and turned away.

'Good,' he said again. 'I think we have everyone else. And tomorrow, all being well, we'll be back in Orkney.'

'Aye,' said Skorri. 'Home again. I'll get my shirts washed.'

The day dawned yellow.

'Ah, it'll be fine,' said Kolbein, stamping his feet outside the house, and surveying the Sea Stag as if she might have changed during the night. His slave crew had once again spent the night by the ship, eschewing the chance of a sleeping place in the longhouse. Ketil was pleased to see that Svart's boat was still there, though there had been no sign of him. Even as he noted that, though, the door of the neighbouring longhouse opened and Svart emerged, yawning and stretching. He raised a hand in greeting.

'Do you really think he's the murderer, then?' asked Kolbein.

'He had a good reason to kill Thorgrim,' said Ketil, noncommittally.

'But then why would he leave the purse with all his silver still on Thorgrim's belt? Why not just take it and go?'

That was a question that applied to any of the suspected killers, though. Why leave all that silver there – or even more peculiarly, why put all that silver there? Ketil had the purse now tied to his own belt: it was heavy. Why would Thorgrim bother to carry that much in a purse when he could wear it on his arms? And why had no one seen it on him, if he had carried it? But then, again, why would anyone have tied it on to his belt when he was dead?

Kolbein shrugged, as if he did not think it worth waiting for Ketil's answer.

'Anyway, we'd better get going. Let's see if your Thorfinn can come up with the solution, or tell you to leave it be. The man's dead, the silver's back, does it really matter if someone – morning, Vigdis!'

His toothy grin flashed again as he changed course. Vigdis looked wary: Ketil wondered how much she had heard.

'Are we leaving soon?' she asked, folding her arms around her as the cold morning air struck.

'As soon as may be,' said Kolbein. 'I'm just going to make sure the Sea Stag is perfect.'

'It's always perfect, as far as he's concerned,' Vigdis remarked unexpectedly, as Kolbein hurried off.

'He does seem very proud of her, and his crew.'

'Yes ... Thorgrim always wondered why. I mean, it's never particularly fast, nor steady, and it's neither big nor small. There's nothing very remarkable about it, he always said. And this time it was worse than ever – wallowing like a pig, and it always seemed to be tilting over a bit. I mean, nothing dangerous, but just not as perfect as he seems to think.'

Ketil raised his eyebrows. Vigdis was only making conversation, he thought, but it was an interesting point, given where Svart had said Thorgrim had been attacked.

'Was Thorgrim curious about the Sea Stag, then? Curious enough to ask questions about it?'

'Questions? Who would he ask?' Her mouth formed something like a smile. 'You'd not want to go up to Kolbein and ask him why his ship's sailing crooked. Not his precious Sea Stag.'

'I suppose not. If he had had the chance, though, would he have taken a look around the ship on his own?'

Vigdis frowned at him.

'You think there's something wrong? That Kolbein ... No, Kolbein wouldn't have harmed Thorgrim. They were – well, they were sort of friends, really. Thorgrim was sailing back and forth here long before I met him.'

'Always with Kolbein?'

'No, not always. But once you've found a skipper you can trust, you tend to stick with them, don't you? Look, he seems to be ready to push out. We can go.'

She stepped carefully down the rough shore towards the boats, and Ketil was pleased to see that everyone else was as eager to set off. Sigrid, tying her shawl clumsily around her, stamped past him, muttering,

'Spare me from eating any more shellfish for a year.'

Svart joined her at his boat, frowning to see how high up the beach it was. Skorri trotted over to give him a hand shifting it, smiling innocently. Geirod was readying Ketil's boat, with Gunnar doing his best to help. Kjartan helped Sibbi up on to the Sea Stag, and Alfarin handed Borgny up with the elegance of a couple of sea birds well used to such manoeuvres. Alf scrambled up after them: Vigdis was already on board. All the inhabitants of the longhouse, husband, wife, mother and sister, and the mute girl, came out to wave them off, as they slid back south past the green headlands, and out into the open sea, heading for Fritharey.

And so the whole party carried on south.

And the whole party, when they had left Fritharey just too far behind to go back, saw the storm blow up to the west.

'Get in beside us!' Kolbein cried distantly to the two little boats, and as best they could Ketil and Svart wriggled their two vessels into the shelter of the Sea Stag, not too close. The skies darkened as if someone had thrown a thick fleece over a lamp. Ketil and his men, experienced and disciplined, did what they had to do and held tight, the wind beating at them and rain driving straight across the waves stinging their faces and hands. Ketil squinted through it, trying to see the Sea Stag, trying even harder to see Svart's little boat. He sensed the wind changing, veering, growing ever colder, the rain like shards of ice now. He remembered the yellow sky at dawn, and chastised himself for his hurry, for his readiness to listen to Kolbein. You could not trust the sea, but you could read it, with experience. He wondered if his head was still affected by his illness, and scrunched his eyes closed, praying that it was not. Then just as fast he opened his eyes again, desperate to see anything useful at all. But it was hopeless: there was nothing around but wind and waves, rain and darkness. All they could do was to hold on, and to pray.

XXVII

'NO. PLEASE. NO more shellfish. And no more cold shellfish!'

Sigrid pushed away the offered dish, and found herself pushing sand. Confused, she tried to open her eyes, but they seemed sticky and reluctant.

She felt around a little more, and the back of her hand brushed wet wool, a thick, woven fabric. Exploring further, she touched the wool with the tips of her fingers, and knew she must be dreaming – where were her bandages? She wiped her eyes thoroughly with the heels of her thumbs, and despite the stinging opened them properly, and sat up.

She was on a beach, and one she did not recognise. Certainly not the one they had left at Dunrostar hofdi, nor the one where they had beached briefly on Fritharey. This one was a narrow strip of grey sand, gently curving in a very shallow bay, and lined behind with another line of smallish rock covered in dark wrack the colour of well-used leather. Behind that again a grassy slope led upwards, not far, not much more than Sigrid's head height if she stood, and was scattered with yellow and white flowers, the most cheerful thing she felt she had seen for a while. A couple of dun sheep leaned over the brow, cropping steadily. For a moment she sat, delighted by the prospect. Then she realised how cold she was, and looked at her closer surroundings.

Beside her on the sand, and the owner of the wool she had felt, was a stocky figure with black hair, lying with his back to her.

Presumably it was Svart, and he seemed to be exuding some warmth so she thought he was probably alive. She stirred again, tasted bile, and vomited on the sand. It was mostly seawater, but she flushed and scraped more sand over it, kneeling back and away from the patch to hug herself. Then she turned her attention to Svart.

He took a bit of rousing, and when he did wake he was not happy.

'Look at my boat!' he cried, then clutched his head.

Sigrid looked where he was pointing. A few broken bits of wood were flung on the beach, as of someone had tried to build something and had given up in frustration. She was not sure how he could tell they were parts of his boat, but if they were, then that boat was not going to take them any further.

'We need a fire,' she said, making use of wood in her head like a good Orcadian.

'You're not burning my boat!' said Svart, struggling to get up. 'Ow! My arm!'

'I wasn't going to burn your boat!' snapped Sigrid. 'It looks far too wet. We need to get warm, not smoke herring. What's wrong with your arm? It's your head that's bleeding.' His head was bleeding. She had not really noticed till now. 'We need bandages. Warmth, and bandages.' And a boat, she added to herself. Where were they? If they had been blown back to Hjaltland, there would be someone with a boat within shouting distance in any direction. If they were not on Hjaltland ...

Svart sat solidly on the sand and swore, clutching his head with his good hand while a steady stream of blood ran between his fingers. She wondered what was wrong with his other arm. Bandages ... She looked down at her own fingers, and realised that her own bandages had been washed away. So much for Thora's good work. She looked at her fingertips, pink and white on the ends of cold blue fingers, and tentatively pressed a finger and thumb together. They felt peculiar, part numb, part aching. But then her hands were freezing.

Something was weighing on her back. She looked around, and found that her rolled bag was somehow still strapped over her shoulder.

'That's amazing!' she said to Svart, still a bit dazed. 'Here we are, washed up from that broken boat, and my luggage in place!'

Then the mists in her head cleared and the significance dawned on her. 'Oh, of course. Stupid of me. There'll be something in it we could use.'

She hauled the bag round, and felt clumsily inside it. Her spare shift. It had been rolled so tight that parts of it were almost dry. With difficulty, she ripped it into strips, folded part of it into a pad, and wrapped the dressing around Svart's bleeding head.

'Right,' she said briskly, partly for Svart's benefit and partly for her own – after all, that had been her only spare shift, and she had no idea how she was ever to replace it – 'let's get your tunic and shirt off. Carefully now – good arm first!'

'It's cold,' Svart grumbled.

'You're right, it is,' said Sigrid, trying to stop her own teeth chattering. 'And the sooner you're strapped up, the sooner we can try to find somewhere to shelter, or something to start a fire. Or some way of finding out where we are.'

Svart gave the beach a look of deep disgust.

'I think you're home, if that's any consolation.'

'Do you mean is this Orkney? My home?' Sigrid stared at the bank again. 'It's hard to tell from here. It's not a bit I know.'

Svart, not speaking, waved his good hand out to sea, and Sigrid turned on her knees to look. Through the smirr of rain, trying its best to replace the salty water in their clothes and hair with fresh, she could just see a long, flattish tongue of land stretching out from their left along the horizon. It did look vaguely familiar.

'What about my arm? I'm freezing here!' Svart seemed more like a sulky child than anything, but Sigrid sighed and told herself he was probably in pain. And indeed, when she looked at it, his upper arm was swollen and blackened, the skin taut.

'I'll do what I can,' she said, and she did try hard to be gentle as she wound the rags of her poor shift around the arm, and then around Svart's chest to hold the arm as still as possible. He was not going to be much use collecting firewood, that was certain.

Then Svart cried out more loudly, and she jumped. He swore.

'Well, if you wouldn't startle me,' she complained, but Svart was waving.

'Be quiet, woman, and look!'

Sigrid spun again on her knees, then jumped up in

excitement. Crossing the bay were two boats, one large and one small. It was hard to see the small one clearly, but the large one had very much the heavy, bovine roll of the Sea Stag.

She snatched up Svart's shirt before he could pull it back on, and danced along the beach, waving it above her head. Even Svart managed to get to his feet and wave his good arm in the air, and the yells he gave would probably have been audible in Dunrostar hofdi. Sigrid joined in, and after a moment of terrible suspense, she cried,

'They're turning! They're coming this way!'

It seemed to take an age, but at last Ketil ran his boat up the beach, and he and Skorri leapt out.

'We thought we'd lost you!' Skorri shouted, as if he were still out at sea. To Sigrid's extreme surprise, he took her up in a great bear-hug, then set her down, delighted. 'We all thought we'd lost you!'

Sigrid blinked: she must have got some seawater in her eyes, stupidly.

'My boat's wrecked. Look,' said Svart, nodding and wincing.

'Bad luck,' said Skorri. 'We'll get you and the wood on to the Sea Stag, but I don't think there's much hope for a repair.'

At once Svart began to gather what pieces he could find with his good arm. Gunnar went to help him, while Ketil turned to wave the Sea Stag closer to the shore.

'Stay there if you want, and we'll ferry them out to you,' he called. 'It's a short beach.'

Kolbein raised a hand in acknowledgement, while the other passengers, hanging over the gunwale to see the wreckage, called their greetings.

'Thought you were lost!' Sigrid heard, several times. 'Can't believe we've found you!'

'Where are we, anyway?' she asked, standing close to Ketil. She should help Svart, too, but for a moment she just wanted to stand and be glad they were all safe.

'Hrossey,' he said, as if it were obvious.

'Hrossey?' She looked about her, feeling stupid. The Orcadian mainland, her home.

'The east,' he explained, with a look half teasing and half kindly. She resented it at once.

'I don't often go east,' she said with dignity. Then she thought about what must have happened. 'We sailed right through the northern isles? Right past them all?'

'I assume so,' he said, his face still straight, 'though I did wonder if you might have flown over them, in that wind.'

'And all through the night … We were lucky to hit a beach, and not something harder.'

'You were,' he said, and quickly put an arm around her, and held her close. Then she was standing alone again, heart hammering, and he was organising the best way to load the injured Svart and his collection of not-quite-firewood on to his boat for transfer to the Sea Stag. She went to see if she could help.

Loaded on to the Sea Stag herself, she thought that probably what Kolbein liked about the ship was that it seemed to be capable of taking in any number of passengers, and a quantity of cargo, too. He kept the passengers mostly to the starboard stern, while some bulky, well-wrapped bundles were stacked in the prow, towards the port side. Always the trader, she thought, wondering what Kolbein had been trying to deal in at Skalavagr. The cargo looked well enough wrapped to be barrels of spices or salt, perhaps, something you would want to keep dry. If it were something really exotic, she would have to warn her friend Helga to stay clear, or examine her bargains carefully – but then Helga was a very canny trader herself. And Kolbein was unlikely to appeal to her in any other way: Helga liked her traders large and well-muscled, not small and wiry.

'Here, here's a dry cloak,' said Borgny with a smile, holding out to Sigrid cloth so soft and warm she almost wanted to apologise for taking it with less than clean hands. 'You look frozen.'

'Thank you, Borgny. I'm not warm, that's for sure.' Sigrid wrapped it around herself, and Borgny sat beside her, adding her warmth. Sigrid grinned.

'We thought you were gone,' said Borgny, 'but that man Ketil wouldn't let us go on until we had searched every inlet. He's very thorough. That's why I'm sure we'll never find out who killed Thorgrim. Someone like Ketil would have discovered it by now, if it was there to discover.'

'He is quite clever, it's true,' said Sigrid. 'But sometimes information comes together slowly. Sometimes not all the answers appear straightaway.'

'I suppose.' She settled more comfortably, keeping them both warmer. 'What is Earl Thorfinn like? My brother doesn't seem to think he will be able to do much in the matter.'

'He's a good leader,' said Sigrid, 'and he thinks, he doesn't just fight.' She was about to make a comment on his choice of wife, but then reconsidered: Alfarin and Borgny were likely to be Thorfinn's honoured guests, and could make their own minds up about Thorfinn's wife. 'He and Ketil will be able to sort it out, if anyone can.'

As long as they remembered to include her, of course. She would have to make sure of that.

XXVIII

THORFINN SIGURDARSON, FISTS on hips, was not looking happy. He might have been shorter than Ketil by half a head, but there was no doubt who was in charge here. Ketil kept his account of Hjaltland economical, and stood back in silence, waiting.

They were alone, outside the great hall on the Brough of Birsay, but in the shelter of its wall. Inside, the hall was busy with their new guests, just arrived, warming up after the sail from Deerness and the east. Ketil counted them over in his head, making sure he had lost no one. Not that that was much of an achievement to bring to Thorfinn. Thorfinn did not want problems brought to him: he wanted Ketil to sort things out before Thorfinn even heard about them. It was not that Thorfinn was lazy, or old, or stupid: he just had a great deal to do, with all the lands he oversaw. He needed to be able to delegate. Ketil understood all that. Eyvind, perhaps, did not, but it was too late now to persuade him.

'So we have a dead man who seems to have been a thief. Three men who accused him of theft – one of whom is your nephew. Two of them were nearby, and the third might have been. A widow, and four other passengers who spent time with the dead man, and the skipper of the ship he came on, who seems to have known the dead man for some time. And the man was killed near this skipper's ship, and moved away. And the silver he was accused of stealing was then found in his purse.'

'A purse, my lord. It may well not have been his own.'

'A purse.' Thorfinn stared across at the mainland, green fading to brown as the daylight blew away. Down in the harbour the

Sea Stag was the largest merchant ship drawn up on the beach, though some of Thorfinn's own warships outdid it in length and style. Ketil's own boat was hidden behind it. Svart was in the hall, carefully guarding his heap of scrap wood. Thorfinn asked, 'And why did Eyvind see fit to send his problems here?'

Ketil hesitated.

'Eyvind is an odd man, my lord. He does not seem to be much liked locally, from all I could gather. I hear – though not directly – that he spends more time playing his men off against each other than drawing them together, and is not as clever as he believes he is.'

Thorfinn looked at him.

'If you didn't hear that directly, I assume Sigrid Harald's daughter has something to do with it?'

'She mentioned it, yes, my lord.' There was no point denying it. 'I believe she heard it from the mother of the man Svart – the one with the broken arm.'

'And the broken boat, yes.' Thorfinn looked away again. 'What was Sigrid doing in Hjaltland?'

'I'm not sure, my lord. She seemed to have some acquaintance there.'

'Does she have any idea what happened? With the dead man, I mean.'

'I don't think so, sir.'

'Then it really is a mystery.' Thorfinn sighed. 'You've spent – how long? A week? Tramping about Hjaltland, with nothing to show for it?'

It was hardly a waste of Thorfinn's time, since he had given Ketil and his men permission to go to Heithabyr, which would have taken much longer. Thorfinn must have remembered.

'Still, I'm glad to see you back, sorry about your brother, and pleased you have found your nephew. He seems … well, no doubt he'll settle down. Is he any good at making cups?'

'I believe he is quite skilled, my lord. I haven't seen any yet.'

'No, I suppose not. Now, about this man at Skalavagr.'

'Ivar. That was nothing definite, my lord, but he did mention Kalf Arnason. I thought you'd want to know.'

'Kalf?' It was surprising just how quickly Thorfinn's face darkened at the name. 'Kalf is supposed to be in the Western Isles.

He can't be back?'

'I'm not sure, my lord. That was the rumour the man had. He had nothing more, except a sense that trouble was on the way. He seemed a sensible man.'

'Not like Eyvind?'

'I was going to ask Eyvind if he had heard anything similar, my lord, but then I decided not to.'

'Why was that?'

'Because I wondered if he might be involved in some way.' Ketil cleared his throat. 'If he wasn't involved, I didn't think he could have given me any useful information. And if he was involved, I would have shown him that I had heard something, and was suspicious. It seemed sensible to keep quiet.'

'Hm. Yes, all right. But I don't like the sound of this. I wonder if King Harald is behind this, though, rather than Kalf? Checking to see if we are being loyal? I thought I had made it very clear to Kalf that he would not be welcome in these islands again.'

'I couldn't say definitely, my lord. But I'll be bearing Kalf in mind, just in case.'

'Yes ... I think you're right. I don't like to say it about one of my wife's kin, but there is very little honour in Kalf. A show of force is all he seems to understand.' He pondered for a moment or two, looking down at the harbour. 'I think it's time to send a couple of warships up and around Hjaltland, before the winter comes. Just as a gentle reminder that we have them.'

'Will you go yourself, my lord?'

'I'd like to, but I think not. Better to let people know that I have long fingers: I don't have to be there all the time. Besides,' he said with a sigh, 'you have brought me an interesting selection of guests. It would be rude of me to leave while they are settling in.'

'Then do you want me to go?' It was a while since Ketil had been on a warship: he would enjoy that thrill of speed and power again.

'No, I want you to sort out your dead man and his friends. I want it done quickly, and I want a message sent back to Eyvind telling him what happened, explaining how it was discovered, and reminding him to sort out his own problems in the future, and not to involve my men.' He stopped, and looked more closely at Ketil's face for a moment. 'Are you feeling all right? I'd say you look pale, but you always do.'

'I'm fine, thank you, my lord.' He almost was.

'We don't want sickness on the Brough. Not if things are starting to happen in Hjaltland – the men need to be healthy. Right, I suppose I'd better meet these guests.'

Ketil would have liked to have stayed outside a little longer, marshalling his thoughts in peace, but Thorfinn seemed to want him to follow him back into the hall. He strode up to his high seat, and waved to Ketil to make the presentations. Ingibjorg, Thorfinn's wife, took her seat beside him. Sigrid referred to her, when in private, as Sheepface.

'My lord, Alfarin and his sister Borgny, from the hall of Arinbjorn Egilsson, near Bergvin.'

Alfarin led Borgny forward, well aware of their own status and looks. Borgny, head high, kept her gaze modestly low. Ingibjorg looked impressed.

'Good day to you, Earl Thorfinn,' said Alfarin, much less modestly. 'I am here to escort my sister who was betrothed to marry Bjorn Einarson, but we met with sorry news on our way. Can you confirm that Bjorn is indeed dead?'

'Dead, yes, and buried here with his father,' said Thorfinn. 'I am sorry for your loss, but we had no idea of your coming. Bjorn had no chance to mention his betrothal. Your loss is ours, too: he might have made a fine lord for the hall at Buckquoy across on the mainland.'

'Might have?' Alfarin caught the words at once, haughty at the apparent insult.

'Yes,' said Thorfinn, unmoved. 'There were several candidates for the hall. I had not made my decision at the time of Bjorn's death.'

'Then who holds the hall now?' Alfarin made it sound as if Thorfinn had made a great strategic error of some kind.

'No one, as yet,' said Thorfinn, still quite cool. 'Einar only died a matter of weeks ago. It is not an appointment I should wish to rush into. And the other candidates are also, sadly, dead.'

That took Alfarin by surprise. Ketil wondered if he had been planning to have his sister re-betrothed to the next in line. There was no other obvious partner for her around Birsay, not at the moment.

'But welcome to Birsay,' Thorfinn continued, as if he had said nothing untoward. 'Welcome to my hall. There are baths, of course, and a hot room, and a chapel – just ask and be free of them. My wife will have you shown to places for your baggage and your beds. I look forward to conversation with you later, and news from Nordvegr. Ketil?' He turned from Alfarin and gestured for more guests to be brought forward. Ketil, out of the corner of his eye, saw Alfarin's fine nostrils flare, but Borgny took him discreetly by the elbow and led him away towards where Ingibjorg's women were waiting to direct them. Hm, Ketil thought. Alfarin did not have high expectations of Thorfinn and his court. He wondered why.

'Kolbein,' he said out loud, and Kolbein bowed. 'Skipper of the Sea Stag which brought most of the party here.'

'And brought the dead man, Thorgrim, from Nordvegr – more than once, I gather?' said Thorfinn. Kolbein straightened, looking surprised.

'Yes, my lord: I knew him slightly. A sad loss.' Kolbein held his toothy grin in check, the corners of his mouth turned down.

'What are you trading?' asked Thorfinn.

Kolbein brightened.

'I have spices from the East, my lord – just the thing to enhance your dinner, and also good for medicine. If I might have your lordship's permission to speak with your wife …'s women,' he changed his sentence as he saw Ingibjorg facing him down grandly, 'I am sure they will be delighted.'

'Of course,' said Thorfinn, nodding him away. Ketil heard him add, in a murmur, 'You can try.'

'Sibbi and his kinsman Kjartan, my lord,' Ketil went on.

'Seeking hard work and a good place to settle, my lord,' Sibbi explained boldly. He stood as straight as he could, and set aside Kjartan's supporting arm. 'I'm a clever man, and my cousin Kjartan here is a strong one. Together we are worth more than three men.'

'In confidence, if nothing else,' Thorfinn remarked. 'Well, make yourselves useful, and we'll see.'

'Thank you, my lord,' said Sibbi smartly, bowed to Thorfinn then to Ingibjorg, then leaned on Kjartan to walk away.

'Is he a cripple?' Thorfinn asked Ketil.

'He was injured on our travels, my lord. I believe it is not permanent. But Kjartan is the stronger man, certainly.'

'Any word on where they came from, or why they are travelling?'

'Again, somewhere near Bergvin. I wondered if perhaps they had been exiled.'

'I wondered the same. Next.'

'This is Thorir, my lord.' Ketil hesitated before saying anything about his relationship to Thorgrim, but it seemed Vigdis had gone off with the women, not expecting a personal presentation to Earl Thorfinn. And Thorfinn had remembered, in any case.

'You helpfully attached yourself to the party, I gather,' he said. 'But you were not on the original voyage. You live in Hjaltland?'

'Aye, my lord.' Thorir had bowed very low, his blond fringe flopping over his eyes. 'Near St. Ninian's Isle.'

'I have been there,' said Thorfinn, thoughtfully. 'Welcome.'

Thorir bowed again, smiled, and backed away. He did not seem to crave attention.

'The dead man's brother?' asked Thorfinn.

'Yes, my lord.'

'But the widow doesn't know?'

'I don't believe he has told her.' He remembered something he had not mentioned before. 'When we were on the island, the widow dug something up from the burial ground, at night. The brother was watching, but ran off up the hill. He denies he was there, but we both – Sigrid and I both saw him.'

'What did she dig up?'

'I have not asked. It was only later that I heard that Thorir believed his brother had hidden the family silver before he went off on his travels. Presumably he had buried it at the monastery for safekeeping, as people do.'

'Did the abbot know anything about it?'

'No, my lord. But then there are those who do not even trust monks.'

'Nevertheless, to keep a record of where family treasures are … Well, and where is the widow?'

'Gone out with the women, my lord.'

'I suppose I should see she is comfortable – and that girl Borgny,' said Ingibjorg, as though it might be the greatest trouble in the world.

'Where is Sigrid?' asked Thorfinn. 'I had better hear what she has to say. Or no doubt she will manage to convey her feelings in some less convenient way.'

'Hmph,' snorted Ingibjorg, and rose from her seat, and left the hall.

XXIX

'I DON'T KNOW what I can tell you, my lord,' said Sigrid. She wanted to add that she hadn't been asked to help, and that she was sure she had not been told everything that Ketil had found out, but something stopped her in time. She did not really want to get Ketil into trouble: she had the impression that Thorfinn was not pleased, and also that he had other things to think about. She wondered if she should have been told about them, too. Really, how did people expect her to help them if they did not give her all the information? She was a woolworker, not a miracle worker.

'Don't tell me you haven't formed some opinions about the people you were travelling with?' Thorfinn was casually sarcastic, his heart not really in it. 'I know you have given Ketil a bit of assistance in the past.'

A bit of assistance? She bit her lip. Ketil was there, too, of course: he had reported to Thorfinn first, and now stood a little to one side, watching her. Maybe he thought she was reporting to him now. He would be wrong, of course.

'I think Ketil and I need to discuss everything properly, now we are back here. Just in case there is anything one of us has found out, and not yet passed on to the other.' She managed not to look at Ketil, and stared straight at Thorfinn. 'And anyway, I spent more time with the women. With Borgny, and of course with Vigdis, Thorgrim's widow.'

Thorfinn nodded.

'What like of a woman is Vigdis?'

They were speaking quietly, up at Thorfinn's high seat, and the hall was nearly empty, but Sigrid still looked about her before replying.

'Well, she's just lost her husband, so I was probably not seeing her at her best. She's from Jorfjara, and that's where she wants to go back to now. She has no family.'

'Except for her husband's brother and his household.'

'About which, I believe, she still knows nothing, my lord.'

Thorfinn nodded again, acknowledging that.

'Where was their household?'

'I don't think they had one, my lord. They travelled and he traded. Stayed a little while here and there, around Bergvin, I think, but also further east and north.' It sounded terrible to Sigrid, but Vigdis had clearly relished it. Perhaps she was as bad at cooking as Sigrid was: that would be one advantage. 'You asked what like of a woman she is, and I suppose the like of a woman who can cope with that kind of a life. She seems independent, able to manage moving about, organised, keeping track of her baggage, perhaps able to look after herself. She made her decisions about the funeral: if the rest of us had not gone along she would have hired some bearers and set off regardless, I'm sure. It's nothing to her to travel alone from Gulbervig to Jorfjara. How she might find settling down there when she arrives, I do not know.'

'Ketil says her husband was most likely a thief. Did she know?'

'She has not talked about it. It – the chance did not arise to question her, on her husband's funeral journey.'

'No, I suppose not. Does she grieve for him?'

'For him and for the way of life he shared with her, yes, I believe so. Yet once he was buried – well, you know how it is, my lord. That can help, whatever the loss or even the manner of death. But it struck me that whenever I saw her after St. Ninian's Isle, she looked – well, cheerful. But then I didn't see her so much: we were on different boats from the isle to Skalavagr, and at Skalavagr I was talking to the local women, and then on the walk back to Gulbervig I was with other people, and then on the way here I was with Svart.'

Thorfinn took in the details, then looked across the hall to where Svart was seated, feeling sorry for himself, but in deep conversation with a couple of the local boatbuilders.

'And his boat was wrecked, this Svart.'

'Yes, my lord.' She had no particular wish to dwell on that. Nor, probably, did Svart, though he did seem to be a man that enjoyed a grumble.

'Hm. It has not been a lucky journey, this one.'

'Well, we're all here safely,' she said briskly. She had been stupid even to go: a waste of silver, leaving her home, chasing Ketil like a child, when it was clear he had no need of her, or no need he would acknowledge. She had not yet had the chance to get back to her own little longhouse. She wondered if she would be able to sleep there tonight – if her young helper Gnup had the place warm and dry or whether he would have abandoned the house in her absence and gone to beg food from her neighbour Helga's well-appointed fire. The thought of having the place to herself, even if it needed to be warmed up, was remarkably tempting.

'Right,' said Thorfinn, and turned to Ketil. 'I need to organise those warships. You and Sigrid share whatever information you need to share, and sort this problem out. I don't want these people hanging around my hall any longer than necessary. And what am I supposed to do with those two? Alfarin and his sister? I don't understand why they came here, if they knew Bjorn was dead. I can't just provide a suitable husband for the girl.'

Of course not, thought Sigrid. But warships? What was that about?

But before she had a chance to ask, they were interrupted.

'I'm sorry, I don't want …' said Kjartan, the big man rubbing his fingers together nervously. 'But has anyone seen Sibbi?'

'Is that your kinsman?' Thorfinn asked, though Sigrid was sure he remembered the greasy-haired man with the confident attitude very well. Kjartan nodded.

'He's usually with you,' she said. 'Can he walk far without you?'

Kjartan looked desolate.

'He wanted to go outside and see the place – you know, there are hot baths and a chapel and all and the smithy – I like the smithy – and the bit where everything fell into the sea and the new building work – he was very interested in all of that, so he told me to take him outside. And, well, it's chilly out there, so I asked him if I could go and find the privies and he said I could, he would just stay where he was till I came back. And I came back and he wasn't there.'

'And where was that?' asked Thorfinn irritably. Presumably if he had warships to see to, he had no wish to be bothered about a man who could look after himself, mostly.

'It was over near where the buildings had fallen into the sea. He'd found himself a wee sheltered bit there, out of the wind, and he said he was quite happy to stay and wait for me.'

'I hope he hasn't fallen over the cliff,' said Thorfinn. Kjartan looked horrified.

'Not Sibbi!'

Thorfinn tutted impatiently.

'I did warn people – and it's broad daylight. Surely he would have seen the danger.'

'He would! He would,' Kjartan said at once. 'Sibbi's the clever one. He'd know.'

Thorfinn looked to Ketil.

'How far could he walk without you?' Ketil asked.

'He's getting better. He can manage a bit – maybe ten, twelve steps? Then he has to rest.'

'But then he could do another ten or twelve, presumably.'

'I suppose …'

'How long were you away at the privy?'

'Well, I had to find them first,' said the big man, reasonably. 'And that took a wee while. I got a bit confused and I found the dairy, and the brewhouse. So maybe I was away a wee while.'

'Sibbi will have started feeling the cold and headed back towards the hall, no doubt,' said Sigrid.

'But I couldn't find him anywhere!'

'All right,' said Ketil, with a look at Sigrid, 'we'll get some people organised and go and look for him. Skorri!'

Skorri hurried up from the back of the hall. Sigrid saw he had already gone and found himself a clean shirt. Alf and Geirod followed, and in a moment Ketil had told them what had happened. They split into two pairs and set off to search half the headland each, leaving Kjartan bewildered and Thorfinn nodding in satisfaction, before murmuring,

'Warships,' and moving away to talk to some of his other men. What could he need warships for? But he was unlikely to tell

Sigrid just now. She might as well make herself useful.

'Come on, Kjartan – let's go and take another look.'

Outside it was not as broad a daylight as Thorfinn had suggested. The sky had darkened, and the air was wet, slapping the ends of her shawl against her skirts before she had even stepped through the doorway. She hoped they would find Sibbi quickly, if not for his sake then for their own.

'I suppose it makes sense to start over near the cliffs,' she said, though she had no wish to go anywhere near them, not after what had happened so short a time ago. Her injured fingers tingled at the thought. But it was the place where Sibbi had last been seen. 'We'd better get started, or we're going to need torches. Come on.'

Kjartan followed her, reminding her slightly of one of her less intelligent sheep. They had to keep wiping the damp from their faces as they walked, asking anyone they met, peering around as they went. Kjartan displayed an understandable tendency to want to stay by the smithy, where the fire was hot.

'But I need to find Sibbi,' he said, half to himself. 'What would I do without him?'

Sigrid patted him on the arm, and continued towards the cliff.

'We should look over the side, in case he's fallen,' she said reluctantly. The cliff was not very high, not at this point, but the rocks below were laid out like long teeth, dark and unwelcoming. The rubble from the latest cliff falls was probably softer, muddy and with smaller, rubbly stones: if Sibbi had somehow rolled down that, he might have a chance. The tide, she noted, was going out.

'I can't see him,' Kjartan moaned. 'I can't see anything!'

'Well, that's not true, Kjartan: I mean, there are birds down there, and rocks, and waves … just cast your eye slowly over it all –'

'And a cloak!' cried Kjartan, so suddenly she almost went over the edge herself. She snatched at his arm for support.

'Where?'

But she had already seen what he was looking at. A darkish piece of cloth, flapping slightly at one edge where the wind caught it. And under it – well, that was not clear.

She turned to see who was nearby, who might be able to help. And at that Alf and Geirod came into view, out on their search.

'Alf! Over here! We think we've found him!'

Alf glided towards them, with Geirod and his dog following. From the expressions on their faces Sigrid knew they, too, were remembering the last time they had attempted a rescue on these cliffs.

'Where?' said Alf at once. Sigrid pointed. 'Geirod's brought rope,' he said, and looked at Kjartan assessingly. 'You stay here, and tie the rope around your waist. We can scramble down, and tie the other end to him. Then we'll lift him, but we'll need you to give us support if we slip or if he's too heavy. Right?'

Kjartan nodded eagerly: anything to get Sibbi back safely.

He really had fallen on an easy bit of the cliff. Alf and Geirod, as Alf had suggested, scrambled down over the newly fallen rubble, leaving the yellow dog to watch them quizzically from the cliff's edge. Indeed, the fall would not have been a steep one. It was hard to see how he could have knocked himself out, unless he had slipped and fallen further down.

Sigrid watched Alf and Geirod sort out their rope and then turn the body on its back. For a moment she thought she had heard a cry of surprise, but almost at once they were lifting it, the cloak wrapped carefully around it, and carrying it up with surprising ease towards where Sigrid and Kjartan were waiting. They had covered the face. Sigrid glanced at Kjartan, but he did not seem to have taken in the meaning. In a few steps they had reached the top, and set the figure down gently, some distance from the cliff edge.

'What's – what's the matter with him?' Kjartan began. 'What's wrong?'

'Well, firstly,' said Alf, with an odd expression, 'it's not Sibbi.'

He pulled back the cloak with one delicate finger, revealing the face.

It was Vigdis.

XXX

THE GATE GUARDS had not seen Sibbi limp past them, nor anyone of his general description walking normally. Ketil asked both questions, just in case: he had known people fake injuries before. So either Sibbi was still on the Brough, or he had fallen off it into the sea. Or at least on to the rocks. Ketil had not much liked Sibbi, but he still felt the need to look for him and make sure he was safe, if at all possible. Sibbi was still, sort of, Ketil's responsibility.

'Come on, we'll check around the new building work,' he said to Skorri.

'There's always new building work to check,' said Skorri. 'When will Thorfinn stop building?'

'He has to replace the bathhouse that fell over the cliff,' Ketil pointed out. 'And the other buildings there. After that … but you like all the new things, don't you?'

'I like a smart new longhouse, aye,' said Skorri comfortably. 'Maybe one day I'll have my own, with a fine wee wife, and I can put all my nice things in it and sit there and admire them. Is that not what you want? Eventually, I mean.'

'I think work has started on the pits for the bathhouse,' said Ketil after a moment. 'Let's take a look.'

He thought he heard a little snort of laughter from Skorri, but let it go. Skorri was a good man, if a little too interested in the pleasures of life. Now for Ketil, the main thing was his work. Sitting about the fire in a cosy longhouse with a wife and maybe a family

... the picture floated into his mind, unbidden. A quiet longhouse certainly had some appeal over the drunken noise of a lord's hall. But it depended very much, he thought, on the longhouse. And of course the wife. He shook himself, and led the way past the chapel and the little monastic site, past a pig enclosure and over to where Thorfinn was having the new bath house constructed, a sensible distance inland from where the old one had crumbled into the sea. No one was working on the site just now, for some reason: there were shovels and buckets lying in a neat row under a bit of sheltering cloth, but that was the only evidence of work. The hole was already quite deep, with a pile of slabs in one corner, so perhaps they were waiting for precious wood to form part of the structure.

But as they approached he could see that actually, there was one figure in the ditch, sitting in the light rain and looking miserable.

'Is that someone? Can someone help?' he heard, as their footsteps must have been audible to him. It was Sibbi, wet and muddy, and looking heartily relieved.

'We've been looking for you,' said Skorri cheerfully. 'What are you doing down there?'

'I slipped and fell in!' said Sibbi. 'Can you help me get out? I know it's not high, but my legs won't hold me any more. I walked too far.' He sounded cross now, let down by his own limbs. Close by where he was sitting Ketil could see a gouge in the earth, as if someone had placed a foot there and then skidded into the hole: Sibbi must have been struggling to pull himself out, for there were also fingermarks in the gouge, and his hands were filthy. Skorri jumped down into the ditch beside Sibbi, and made short work of hauling him up and passing him into the hands of Ketil above.

'Where's Kjartan?' asked Sibbi, as soon as he was steady.

'He's looking for you, too,' said Ketil. 'He came to the hall to say you were missing.'

'You're a right mess, son,' said Skorri. 'You'll need to go to where the baths are, not where they're planned to be.'

'I tried to get out,' said Sibbi again. 'Useless. I need Kjartan.'

'We'll take you back to the hall, and then Kjartan can take care of you,' said Skorri. 'Come on, arm around my shoulders. I'm not as big as him!'

They made their way awkwardly back between the buildings, passing people heading home for the night now that the rain grew heavier. Ketil asked each of them to pass on the word that the missing man had been found, alive and fairly well. At the entrance to the hall, though, he sensed disturbance: had word come back before them? At least it was good news, he thought.

Ingibjorg met him at the door, and stopped.

'What now?' she demanded, looking at Sibbi.

'He had a fall,' said Ketil. 'Into the ditch for the new bath house. He'll need a wash.'

'His friend can do that: it'll give him something to think about,' snapped Ingibjorg, turning to Skorri. 'Take him inside – that lump of a fellow is waiting.' She made way for Skorri and Sibbi to stumble past, then laid a hand on Ketil's arm. 'I didn't say earlier, Ketil, but it's good to have you back safely. Thorfinn depends so much on you in all his work. I'm glad you decided not to go on to Heithabyr – though of course, the reason is very sad,' she seemed to remind herself. He could feel the pressure of her warm fingertips through the wet linen of his shirt. 'And of course so good to have your men back safely, and – and Sigrid. Of course, Sigrid. Although I could wish that she caused less trouble, generally.'

'Trouble, my lady?' Ingibjorg and Sigrid detested each other, but he was not aware of anything Sigrid might have done recently to cause a problem. Ingibjorg sighed, as if the troubles of the world were on her shoulders.

'Always trouble. Dear Ketil, couldn't you just – maybe keep her away from here? Only Sigrid could go out to look for an injured man, and bring back a dead woman instead.'

'A dead woman? Who?' Ketil's spine tingled. At least it could not be Sigrid herself.

'That widow you brought from Hjaltland. Cheerful little thing, I thought, though she was eager to be away home to – was it Jorfjara, or Hamnavoe? Anyway, she'll not be going now.'

'Is she here?'

'Who, Sigrid or the widow?'

He took a breath.

'Both.'

'Oh, yes. They're both inside.'

She could just have said yes, Ketil thought. She was always so peculiar about Sigrid. Ketil had no means of keeping Sigrid away from the Brough, but he thought she might be happier if she never had to see Ingibjorg again. He excused himself to Ingibjorg, and pushed past her as politely as he could, into the hall.

A cry of joy met him, but it was Kjartan, seeing Sibbi safely back. At least someone was happy, he thought. A table had been laid out at the back of the hall, a covered shape on it, and Sigrid was standing next to it, her back to him. Even from the back she looked small and tired, her hair, still freed from its headcloth, wild about her head. Not for the first time, he felt an urge to go and wrap his arms around her. Heaven knew how she would react to that.

Instead he walked over to the other end of the table, caught her eye, and said,

'Vigdis?'

'Yes. It looks as if she fell down where we were expecting to find Sibbi. The ground must have slid from under her.'

They met each other's look again: they both knew what that felt like.

'Sibbi's safe, anyway,' he said.

'So I hear.' A half-smile: it would have been hard to miss Kjartan's shout. 'That's good.'

He moved closer to her, on the other side of the table. They might not have long until the women came to clean the body and prepare it for burial.

'It seems a harsh thing to ask, here,' he said quietly, 'but was anything found with her? A purse, or her baggage?'

'She'd hardly have taken her baggage out for a walk in the rain,' said Sigrid. 'There is no purse on her belt, though. Maybe the ties broke when she fell?'

'Maybe.'

'Alf and Geirod brought her up from the rocks. But if they had noticed something, they would have brought it, wouldn't they?'

'I'd like to think so.'

'They're sensible,' she said, as if he didn't know it.

'Is she much damaged? There's no doubt that it's her?'

'I don't believe so, but take a look. She won't mind.'

He raised his eyebrows, then leaned over to lift the cloth that covered the corpse's face. They were close to a lamp, and he could see easily that it was Vigdis. Her face was hardly marked. She was still in her gown and shift, her belt in place, boots on her feet, all a bit rumpled and torn.

'We tried to tidy her up a bit,' said Sigrid apologetically.

'You'll tell me if they find anything odd when they prepare her, won't you?' he asked, and was about to cover Vigdis again when something caught his eye. A bruise, just forming, on one side of her neck.

'What is it?' asked Sigrid, quick to see his frown.

'Look, there.' He reached out a hand and gently turned Vigdis's chin towards the lamplight. 'And one on the other side, too. Can we – do you think we can turn her over? Just a little? She's not stiff yet, and –' he glanced quickly about the hall, 'and no one is paying much attention.'

Sigrid at once leaned over and took Vigdis's left shoulder, pulling it towards herself. Ketil supported the head, turning the chin away from him. He brushed Vigdis's coarse black hair up and away from the back of her neck.

'Fingermarks?' asked Sigrid, craning to see for herself.

'She's been strangled,' Ketil murmured. 'Two handed. Well, at last we can be completely sure about Svart. He can barely use that broken arm.'

He thought it would please her, but she scowled.

'He'll find something else to be grumpy about,' she muttered. He managed not to look at her as they eased the body back to its original place. 'But I'm not sure it lets anyone else off. Everyone has been outside the hall since we arrived, except for Svart and you and me and your men. And even Kjartan and Sibbi were not together. Alfarin and Borgny both went out, at different times, and Kolbein was off trying to find out about local traders.'

'And Gunnar went to see the pigs,' added Ketil, scrupulously honest. 'Can you see Alfarin or Borgny doing something like this?'

She shook her head, but said,

'Unless one of them was desperate. And they are both bigger than Vigdis.'

'They are, it's true.' He let out a long breath through his nose, thinking. 'You and I need to have a talk about this,' he said. 'Why would someone kill her? And if it is someone from our party – and why would it not be – why wait till now?'

'We've been together so much,' said Sigrid at once. 'This might have been someone's first opportunity.'

'Then do you think someone set out, from the start, to kill

both of them?'

'Maybe … or maybe when they killed Thorgrim they realised they needed to kill again. I mean … well, you've got the purse, haven't you? The one with the stolen silver in it?'

'I gave it to Thorfinn.'

'But it's safe. But what if she – wittingly or unwittingly - had something else that Thorgrimm had stolen? What if she was carrying it for him? And someone, when they killed him, couldn't find it on him, so thought Vigdis must have it?'

'Then let's hope they have found it now,' said Ketil. 'I don't want more deaths. Who would they try next?'

'We need to look at her baggage,' said Sigrid suddenly.

'Well, of course, but straightaway?'

'Yes. We need to know if she dug anything up from the burial ground on St. Ninian's Isle. And then,' she added, looking about the hall, 'we need to find out where Thorir is.'

XXXI

'I SAW INSIDE her pack when Gunnar accused Thorgrim of theft in Gulbervig,' Ketil said, as they searched the side of the hall for Vigdis's belongings. 'Very neat and tidy.'

'You'll have to tell me all about it,' said Sigrid, still resentful that there was so much she did not know. 'Here – isn't this it? And that, beside it, is Thorgrim's pack that we collected when we came back to Gulbervig.'

'We searched it, too,' said Ketil. Sigrid wondered if he were being deliberately annoying.

'We'll still need to search it again, won't we? Since St. Ninian's Isle.' She looked at the smaller pack. 'I'd swear this one was bigger – just a bit – after the Isle. But now it looks smaller again. Which shall we start with?'

'Whichever you like,' said Ketil politely. She gave him a look.

'Thorgrim's, then. I hope he washed his hose regularly.'

She untied the pack carefully, realising it was the first such job she had tackled since her bandages had washed off in the sea. She tried not to wince at the tenderness of her fingertips. Thorgrim's pack fell open, showing clothes and not much else.

'This is very much as it was when we inspected it,' said Ketil. 'But then, she would hardly have had time in private to move anything into it from her own pack, would she?'

'I suppose that's true. Let's look in hers.'

This time Ketil undid the strings, and she wondered if he had noticed her pain undoing the first pack. The cloth unrolled, and they could see that everything inside, the bulk of Vigdis' clothing, had also been rolled, in regular layers. Between each layer, placed so as not to chink together, were pieces of silver – finger rings, arm rings, and fragments, amounting to a nice little family treasure.

'Thorir's, do you think?'

'He'd have to be able to prove it, after all this time,' said Ketil. 'I can ask him to describe some of it.'

'Well, who else's treasure would she have been digging up in a burial ground at night? Thorgrim must have told her where it was.' She thought for a moment. 'And presumably that was why she wanted him buried on St. Ninian's Isle, so that she could retrieve it.'

'From under Thorir's nose,' Ketil added. They looked down at the silver, trying to pick out pieces distinctive enough to be memorable. There were a couple of old-fashioned brooches intended to fasten a woman's dress, and a penannular brooch with a zig zag pattern beaten into it: they could have belonged to Thorgrim and Thorir's mother, perhaps.

'Thorgrim must have told her where to find it. No wonder she looked cheerful. But I still don't think this pack looked quite as heavy on the way here as it did between Skalavagr and Gulbervig. Where is her purse?'

'I'm sure if Alf or Geirod saw it near her on the rocks, they would have brought it in,' said Ketil. 'As you said.'

'It's too dark to look for it now,' said Sigrid. 'Unless … do you think the tide could get it?'

Ketil looked around, caught Alf's eye, and summoned him with a gesture.

'Was Vigdis' body above the tideline?' he asked.

'Oh, yes, sir. Long way above it.'

'Did you see anything that looked like a purse anywhere near her?'

'No, sir. I did glance around, just in case we had missed anything, but I didn't see a purse or anything else but rocks and mud.'

Ketil nodded.

'Take another look in the morning,' he said. Alf looked

down at Vigdis' open pack.

'That's hers, isn't it? I remember it from Gulbervig.'

Sigrid sighed. Everyone seemed to know everything except her.

'Without the silver, of course,' she said.

'Yes, the silver wasn't there. But there was a nice string of beads, I remember – amber ones, quite big. I remember thinking they would be heavy on her – she wasn't a large woman.'

Sigrid picked carefully through the clothing in the pack, setting the pieces of silver to one side.

'I don't see any amber beads,' she said. 'There's this string of glass ones – she wore these on the day of Thorgrim's burial.'

'I remember,' said Alf. 'But not the amber ones. Are they on her now?'

'No.' Sigrid answered definitely. 'She's wearing a set of carved wooden ones, and a string of mixed glass and stone – nothing valuable. It was probably what she preferred to wear for travelling.'

All three of them looked at each other.

'Stolen when she was killed?' asked Ketil. 'Perhaps they got in the way, and broke?'

'But I don't think she was wearing them earlier, either,' Sigrid objected. 'If they were heavy, they would have been uncomfortable for travelling. I don't remember seeing her wear amber at all.'

'Where did the silver come from?' asked Alf.

'We think it might be Thorir's family treasure. Have you seen him?'

Alf shook his head, turned to scan the hall to be sure, then shook it again.

'I don't think I've seen him since Thorfinn spoke to him,' he said. 'Most people went outside around then.'

'Do you know who went where?' asked Sigrid. Alf was more observant than he looked, but he shrugged now.

'Skorri and Gunnar had been talking about pigs, and Skorri took him to see the pigs round the back,' he said. 'But Skorri left him there and came back, in case he was needed.'

'Svart is still here,' said Sigrid, and caught Ketil's quick look at her.

'Yes, I don't think he's going to go far, not until he has an offer to mend his boat,' said Alf. 'He's convinced it's only a matter of putting it back together.'

'Ah, well, no doubt an Orkney boat is not as good as a Hjaltland boat,' said Sigrid. She hoped Thora was not worried about her son, though perhaps the longhouse was a happier place without him.

'What about Kolbein?' Ketil asked.

'Oh, yes, he went out as soon as he could. Trading, I suppose.' Alf smiled. 'Let's hope he doesn't offend anyone here! And let me think – Alfarin and Borgny went out about the same time, but very much not with Kolbein.' The smile lingered around his lips as he spoke of Borgny: Alf was evidently appreciative. Sigrid thought they would go well together, if Alf were perhaps a lord. It seemed unlikely that either Alfarin or Borgny would look at him otherwise.

'When did Vigdis go out?'

'I'm not sure,' Alf admitted. 'I remember having the impression she had gone over to the longhouse to sit with the women.'

'I think you're right,' said Sigrid. She felt a pang of guilt: she should really have been keeping an eye on the widow. Ketil was better at making sure of his responsibilities, she had to admit. He had herded them very well from Gulbervig to St. Ninian's to Skalavagr and back to Gulbervig, and only the storm had separated them briefly on the way here. Maybe he should keep sheep, when he grew too old for soldiering. If that was really what he could call what he did.

'We'd better wrap the silver up,' said Ketil. 'Alf, have you a bag?'

Alf produced a cloth bag from his own purse, and lifted the silver quickly into it, checking to see he had not missed anything.

'What do you want done with it, sir?'

'Take it to Ingibjorg in the longhouse,' said Ketil. 'The purse is there too – the one found on Thorgrim's body. I want it safe, and I don't want Thorir to see the contents before I have the chance to hear his descriptions of some of the pieces.'

'Sir,' said Alf, and floated off, leaving Ketil and Sigrid alone with the two packs.

The rest of the hall was growing busier, as the evening drove people back inside, and Ingibjorg's women quietly finished their work with Vigdis's corpse down near the door. Bolla, one of the maids, was starting to arrange pots at the central fire, while others brought food already chopped to pour in for the stew. Sibbi and Kjartan, Sibbi now bathed and cleaner, and Kolbein and Gunnar, were already at the long tables, anticipating the evening. Alfarin and Borgny returned, separately, but sat together now near the top of one table, ready to be ushered to seats near Thorfinn as honoured guests. Svart still sat with his bits of broken wood, though now he was at least chatting with a couple of the older men in Thorfinn's hird, men long retired from fighting but ready to do their duty in a night's drinking in the hall. But here, over at the side, away from the glow as the lamps were lit, Ketil and Sigrid found a bench, and sat, and watched for a moment or two in silence.

And Sigrid could think of no way to break the silence.

It was not as if they did not have plenty to talk about. For one thing, she had to ask him to tell her, properly, from the start, all that had gone on from the moment he met his nephew Gunnar and the rest of those sailing on the Sea Stag. Surely that was not hard to do? Then she had to make sure that he knew, and understood, anything she had heard or seen or any conclusions she had come to. Thorfinn had told them to share their information, after all. He was not going to say no, or refuse to listen to her. And why didn't he say anything? Only that he was not exactly the most talkative man in the world. So she would have to start, as usual. Or she could just go off to her longhouse, off home, and pretend that none of this was happening. After all, what had any of this to do with her? Only her new friendship with Thora and tentative connexion through her to Svart had made her remotely involved in this, and now even Ketil admitted that Svart had to be innocent, of Vigdis' murder at least.

If one of them did not speak soon, she felt they would never speak again.

At last she cleared her throat, as if she had not used it for a month. It was still sore from the seawater.

'Well, at least we know that Svart is innocent,' she said.

Ketil shifted on the bench.

'Yes, that's important, of course.' Something in his tone was less than sincere.

'Well, it is!' She spun to face him. 'It's one possible killer eliminated, isn't it? Now we can stop worrying about one of them, and try to work out which of the others we can cut out, too!'

'I thought it was only Svart you were worried about. That was why you came to St. Ninian's Isle, wasn't it?'

'To St. Ninian's Isle? I thought you wanted me to come along – I thought you wanted me to keep an eye on Vigdis. To look after her. Well, I'm sorry if I intruded where I was not wanted, but it was a genuine mistake on my part. Next time be a little clearer in your instructions.'

'You didn't have to come if you didn't want to. You and Svart can go back to Hjaltland now,' he said, and his voice was quite cool and calm, 'once he's fit to travel. I daresay you won't be troubled again.'

'To Hjaltland? I don't want to go back to Hjaltland, with Svart or with anyone else. I only went there in the first place because –' She broke off. How stupid did she want to look? 'Anyway, I only know Svart because I happened to stay with his mother Thora, because she was the sister of the man who took me from Dunrostar hofdi to Gulbervig, because he was the neighbour of the people we stayed with. And I only stayed with them because the old woman on the boat to Hjaltland was the mother of that man in the longhouse there.'

She glared at Ketil, who stared back. For another horrible moment neither of them spoke. Then Ketil looked away, and almost at once leapt to his feet.

'Thorir,' he said.

XXXII

SIGRID DID NOT want to go to Hjaltland with Svart.

Ketil put the thought to the back of his mind, delicately, as if it might break, and strode down the hall to meet Thorir. Thorir was standing just a little distanced from where Vigdis' corpse lay, covered, on the table to one side: the makeshift curtains that had been pinned up hid it quite well, but there was a gap at one point, and Thorir's eye had evidently been caught. He bowed his head respectfully, and only raised it when Ketil approached.

'Has some member of the household died?' Thorir asked, keeping his voice low.

'Not a member of the household, but one of our own party, I'm sorry to say.'

'Our own party?' Thorir's gaze flickered around the hall, his expression taut – was it guilt? Fear? Or was it just a quick scan to see who might be missing?

'Where have you been?' asked Ketil. 'I'm looking for people who saw what happened.'

'I was … I was just wandering around,' said Thorir. 'I like walking, and meeting people. I was just chatting, here and there. Who – I can see some of our group.' He shifted sideways to see better around the wooden pillars. Ketil saved him any more trouble.

'Vigdis, your brother's widow.'

'Vigdis is dead?' He did look surprised, though any killer might not have expected his victim to have been found so soon. Why had he really come with them so willingly? Ketil wondered. Was it to try to recover whatever Vigdis had dug up in the burial ground – presumably the silver they had found in her pack? If so, had Thorir felt the need to kill her to do it? Thorir swallowed heavily. 'How did she die? She seemed well, today.'

'She fell on the rocks, where the cliff had broken away,' said Ketil. 'Thorfinn did warn everyone about it, but she seems to have gone there, nonetheless.'

'Outside, of course. You did ask where I'd been. Well, I don't believe I was anywhere near the cliffs, only that I looked at them from a distance, from near the smithy. I'm not a foolish man – or not in that way, anyway.' He gave a thin smile. 'I should have spoken to her earlier.'

'Why?'

'She would have known she had some family still, in Hjaltland, if she had wanted us,' he said sadly. 'She might not have felt so alone.'

'You think she felt alone?' Ketil was surprised: the idea had not occurred to him.

'She must have done, mustn't she? A woman on her own like that.'

'This is not a case of self-harm, if that's what you mean,' said Ketil. A flicker of something darted across Thorir's face, and he frowned.

'She was found on the rocks … that's what you said about my brother, too. Found on the rocks, but you said there was reason to believe he had been murdered. So, Ketil, what about Vigdis? Was she murdered?'

He would have found out sooner or later, anyway.

'Yes, she was,' said Ketil. 'So if you can give me an idea of who you visited, what you looked at and who you gossiped with, and who else might have seen you, that would be very useful.'

'That's … that's reasonable, I suppose.' Thorir's voice was unsteady. 'So no one has claimed it, just like my brother. Let me think. I spoke to the smith, and I visited the chapel – the priest was there, he might remember me. I went to the dairy, and helped the women lift some cheeses. And I spoke to the gate guards, just asking them what the place was like, how busy they were. That kind of thing.'

'What order did you do that in?' Ketil asked. Thorir glanced at him, trying to find significance in the question.

'I spoke to the smith first. He was fixing a tripod for cooking – you know, like those ones.' He pointed towards the cooking fire. 'It was nice and warm there, but he was busy. So I walked down to the gate, wondering if I might go off for a longer walk. But it seemed to me to be getting dark, and there was lots still to see up here. And besides ...'

Ketil waited for Thorir to go on.

'Besides, I saw Kolbein heading down the path to the harbour, and I didn't much want to meet him again just then. I mean, you know what it's like – sometimes you just want to meet someone new.'

'It can happen,' Ketil agreed. He would be glad to part with most of this party.

'So I asked the guards where the chapel was, and they sent me there. I talked with the priest, as I say – a small, dark man, didn't get his name – and admired the building, which is very fine! I have never seen the like. And then I just wandered, and that was how I came across the dairy. I could smell the tang of the cheese – delicious! Then one of the women said they had to make a start on supper, so I carried a couple of cheeses over here for them and came on round to the main door – it didn't seem right going in with the women by the side door. And that's – that was how I spent my time,' he ended, his mouth turned down. 'I am sorry I didn't speak to her. Make some connexion. It might not make sense to you, but I'm sorry.'

Ketil let him dwell on that for a moment, then said,

'I have something more to ask you.'

There was that flicker of the eyes again. What was it?

'Yes? What do you need?'

'We talked about your family silver that Thorgrim took away and buried. Can you describe some of it for me?'

'You've found something?' Thorir spoke slowly, not eagerly, as if he had been disappointed before.

'We've found something,' Ketil conceded. 'It may not have anything to do with you.'

Thorir puffed out a long sigh.

'Well, most of it was just bits and pieces, you know?

Wrapped in a cloth in a wooden pot, when I last saw it, but he might have wrapped it differently.' There had been no cloth nor wooden pot, thought Ketil, but they might not have survived the burial anyway. 'And it's been a long time. I remember there was a ring with a dark brown stone in it.' He glanced at Ketil, but Ketil kept his face still. There had been no ring like that, that he could remember.

'A piece of silver with my father's name on it, just scratched on,' Thorir tried again.

That could have been there, Ketil thought. They had not examined every piece closely. It might help.

'Oh! I know what there was, though,' said Thorir suddenly. 'My mother's brooches! You know, the old style, like stretched-out shield bosses. One for each shoulder. When my mother died, my sister didn't want them, and we didn't want – not yet – we didn't want to melt them down and turn them into something else. They had blue stones, four on each brooch, polished round like beads. You know the kind of thing?'

A match for the pair of brooches in Vigdis' pack. Ketil was content, but he was not yet sure that Thorir had not murdered for those brooches and the rest.

'We may have found something, but it is in safe keeping for now,' he said. 'Like the pieces belonging to Gunnar and Svart, everything will be restored when we know who the killer is.'

'I can't believe you've found it!' Thorir looked stunned. 'I'll not believe it really until I see it myself. But I can be patient, Ketil! I can wait. And if I can help you find out who killed my brother and my sister, I shall.'

Ketil left Thorir to prepare for the evening meal, and was not entirely surprised to see that he settled quietly to the side of the hall, not close to any of his acquaintance. And as he saw the shadows cross Thorir's face, he realised that it was almost certainly Thorir he had seen at the back of the hall at Gulbervig, watching as Gunnar accused Thorgrim of theft, then silently slipping away. Why had he not come forward then? He could have added his accusation to Gunnar's. Or did he prefer to take his revenge on his brother in his own, more violent way?

He could have arranged to meet Thorgrim outside that night, on the beach. Maybe he had no intention of killing him, but if, say,

Thorgrim had denied all knowledge of the family's silver, or refused to tell his brother where it was buried … what might Thorir have done, in his long-built frustration?

He needed to talk to Sigrid, properly, tell her everything he knew. Tell her, too, that while he had been in Gulbervig the first time, he had not been as clever or observant as he might have been. Yes, she would probably mock him, but he had to explain. Then they would have all the information between them, and sit down and sort this matter out once and for all.

But when he looked around, he could not see Sigrid: she must have gone into the longhouse. Before he could take two paces after her, someone called him.

'Ketil,' he heard, and knew he was expected to obey the summons.

Alfarin and his sister Borgny were seated as he had seen them before, up near the top of the hall, at some distance from the other travellers, both looking his way. Well, he needed to talk to them anyway. He went over, deciding to sit by Alfarin on the bench, not stand like a servant, just in case Alfarin made the mistake of thinking he was in charge. He had not liked the way Alfarin had seemed to be assessing Thorfinn, and finding him wanting.

'Has something happened?' Alfarin asked. 'Thorir looks worried.'

'There has been a death,' said Ketil. 'Did you not notice the curtains at the back of the hall?'

Borgny looked round faster than her brother.

'The body is there?'

'They'll likely move it to the chapel,' he reassured her.

'But who is it? Is it someone we know?' Borgny had all the questions. Alfarin looked from the back of the hall to Ketil, apparently with nothing to say.

'Yes, it is,' said Ketil. 'One of our party.'

'Not that poor man Svart?' she asked at once. 'His head injury –'

'No, not Svart,' he cut across her, sick of the name. 'It is Vigdis.'

She gave a little gasp.

'Oh, no! But she seemed … please tell me she did not …' She broke off, her wide eyes alarmed.

'She did not take her own life, no.'

Alfarin gave a little shake, as though his mind had been elsewhere.

'An accident, then. This has been an unlucky journey. I shall be glad to be going home.'

Ketil saw Borgny glance at him quickly, surprised. At his opinion, or at his intention of leaving? Maybe she was still expecting to stay.

'Where were you both today, since you were presented to Thorfinn?'

'Why do you ask?' Alfarin was quick to block him, but perhaps he just felt that his business was his own. Ketil could not see why he might have wanted to kill Vigdis, or even Thorgrim, but he was careful, all the same.

'There are one or two questions about the accident – a couple of things that aren't quite clear. No one seems to have been near her, but I'm asking people who they saw, and where and when.'

'I doubt we can be of use to you. We thought we would walk over to Buckquoy, but the day was later than I had expected, so we stood by the cliffs over the harbour and looked from a distance.'

The gate guards would probably have seen them, or anyone in the houses that side of the Brough. It would be easy to ask.

'Did you go anywhere else?'

They exchanged glances. He could almost hear a brief debate, then saw a tiny shrug shared.

'I wanted to walk to the far cliffs, the ones we sailed around to come into the harbour. Borgny did not want such a long walk. So I went alone.'

'And you, my lady?' He was happy to give her the courtesy, since she did not seem so much to feel she deserved it.

'I came back here, and went to the longhouse where Lady Ingibjorg made me welcome. When my brother returned, he came and found me, and then we came in here.'

'And did either of you see Vigdis when you were out? Or any of the others from our journey?'

'I believe I passed the boy Gunnar talking with a pigman,' said Alfarin, with a smirk.

'We saw Kolbein going down to the harbour,' added Borgny, with a scowl at her brother.

'He does not like to be parted from his precious Sea Stag, of course. And Thorir, I think, was also going to leave the Brough, but he had a word with the gate guards, and then he changed his mind. Perhaps, like us, he though it too late in the day,' said Alfarin.

Perhaps, thought Ketil. Or perhaps he was looking for Vigdis.

XXXIII

SIGRID HAD RETREATED to the longhouse next to the great hall, and huddled over by the fire. Her fingers hurt: true, some of them were healing well, but some of the deeper cuts, where she had caught the sharpest stones, were still raw. Would she ever be able to weave again?

She wanted to go back to her longhouse and avoid seeing anyone again this evening, particularly Ketil. Words from their conversation dropped into the pool of her thoughts and splashed, making more mess in her head than they had at the time. She should go home – but she was cold and tired, and the fire here was warm. Ingibjorg and her women were busy with supper, or with Vigdis' body. It was quiet. One of the bed spaces sheltered Ingibjorg's twin boys, and their nurse, all asleep. An elderly dog lay on the other side of the fire, too frail to follow Thorfinn around as he used to. If she fell asleep here, no one would mind – well, not until Ingibjorg came back and quite possibly threw her out into the night. Yes, she should rouse herself and go home.

But just as she managed to get to her feet, and remembered once again that she had no headcloth since the storm, the longhouse door swung open, and Ketil appeared.

'Oh,' she said quickly, 'I was just going.'

'With no supper?' He raised his eyebrows, almost smiling. She hesitated.

'That's a good point,' she admitted. 'It would be a shame to miss it.' Particularly when there's probably no food at home.

'And I think we need that conversation sooner rather than later,' he went on. 'I need to tell you something. I was sick in Gulbervig, the first time we were there – well, and for a while after that. Bad stomach, bad head, not sleeping well. It might sound like an excuse, but I don't think I was thinking straight.'

She opened her mouth as a choice of ripostes came to mind, then stopped. He had at least admitted it, and it was true she had noticed he had been paler than usual while they were in Hjaltland.

'Probably some of their shellfish,' she said instead, and sat down again by the fire. Ketil joined her, so they were sitting side by side again as they had done in the hall not long before. This time she would try to make sure they had a useful conversation. 'Do you think you missed anything in particular? Anything you've realised since?'

'That I don't know yet. But maybe, after you joined us, you saw something useful I missed.'

All too likely, she thought. She resisted the urge to try to comb her hair back into some kind of order, and wrapped her hands in her shawl, as if they might give something away.

'I don't see any point in going through Hjaltland step by step,' she said. 'It seemed long enough without doing it again. Let's concentrate on who might have killed your man Thorgrim, and why. And Vigdis, of course.'

'Yes,' Ketil said. 'If we can assume that the same person killed both of them, that helps a lot, doesn't it? It cuts out any passing local in Gulbervig, for a start, or any of Eyvind's hird in the hall there.'

'It's Kolbein and his passengers,' Sigrid agreed.

'Not all of them.'

'Who would you take out?'

'Well, Borgny and Vigdis, for a start.'

Borgny, of course. How could a pretty girl be a killer? She was about to protest when he went on.

'Because while I suppose either of them could have been responsible for his death – head wounds can be accidents, or can end up worse than intended – I don't think either of them would be strong enough to haul Thorgrim's body over to the rocks.'

'They could have had help,' said Sigrid. 'Alfarin could have helped Borgny.'

'But who would have helped Vigdis? Kolbein, as an old friend?'

'Maybe. What about Thorir?'

They both stopped and thought at that. Ketil was the first to speak.

'A woman conspiring with her husband's brother to kill him – for the silver, I suppose?'

'I suppose so. Thorgrim tells Vigdis where it is – which he must have done, or how would she have known where to dig? And Thorir kills his brother so that they can retrieve the silver and split it between them.'

'We saw her dig, and we saw him watching. I don't know that it looked as if they were working together.'

Sigrid considered.

'And if they really knew each other, they were very good at pretending they didn't. But ... but Thorir could still have killed Thorgrim, then followed Vigdis to see where the silver was, then killed her to get it!'

'How would he know that she would know where to find it? And why not just steal it from her?' But Ketil did not look entirely convinced. 'I think that needs to be taken as a possibility, though. He might have killed Thorgrim, maybe in anger, and then just hoped that if he followed Vigdis she would lead him to the silver. After all, he did follow us from Gulbervig to St. Ninian's Isle.'

'He did, didn't he? I thought you looked suspicious on our walk there.'

'Stupid of me not to recognise him at once as the man in the hall.'

'Shellfish,' said Sigrid. 'They're not good for you.'

'I'm a lot better now,' he said firmly.

'Then let's keep going. You said Borgny, with Alfarin's help. But why? I don't think Alfarin would have killed him just because he was not grand enough to associate with.'

'I can't think of any reason why Alfarin or Borgny would kill him, to be honest,' said Ketil. But she saw he was frowning, rubbing his forehead hard with the heel of his hand. His head must be starting to hurt again.

'Right, well, he could still have done it. And what about Vigdis? Where was Alfarin today?'

'Oh, everyone was out wandering,' said Ketil, irritably. He must definitely be in pain. 'Alfarin and Borgny went out to stare over at Buckquoy, then went their separate ways until just before they returned to the hall. He says he walked out to the head of the Brough, and she's supposed to have come in here.'

'I think she was in here, for a bit, anyway,' said Sigrid.

'We can ask the women later. I don't know if anyone saw Alfarin.'

'That's a shame,' said Sigrid. 'He's a man who likes to be seen. So who else is there What about those two, Sibbi and Kjartan? They go in a pair, too, like Alfarin and Borgny.'

'Yes,' said Ketil, 'and like Alfarin and Borgny, I'd have said that Sibbi might not have been strong enough to move Thorgrim, but Kjartan would have done it for him.'

'That's probably true,' Sigrid agreed, 'but again, why would they? Had they even met Thorgrim before this journey? And if we don't know why they killed Thorgrim, then how could we possibly work out why they killed Vigdis?'

'They were out and about, though,' said Ketil. 'We know that much.'

'On the list, then,' Sigrid sighed. 'Who else?'

Ketil's shoulders straightened.

'Gunnar,' he said. Sigrid drew a breath.

'I like him,' she said, as if that might be consolation for considering him as a killer.

'I like him, too,' said Ketil, 'and he is my nephew. If he admitted to it, I would help him to pay the price – though I wonder who that would be for, now? Thorir? But he has a temper, and he accused Thorgrim of theft and Thorgrim persuaded that fool Eyvind that he was innocent. Unlike some of our other possibilities, Gunnar actually had a reason at least to confront Thorgrim. And then, another hasty punch, an unlucky angle, and he finds himself with a dead body. He's not a fighter, Gunnar, not a killer. It would have been some kind of accident.'

Sigrid was surprised at Ketil's apparent attachment to Gunnar, but then she thought again. All he had said made sense, whether he was Gunnar's uncle or not. Gunnar was not a killer.

'You should have seen how he punched Thorgrim when I first came across them,' Ketil went on. 'It was astonishing that the blow connected at all. I'm almost ashamed of him.'

'If he had done it, though, by accident, surely he would have admitted it?'

'To Eyvind? Who knows what he might have ended up having to do to atone. But you're right: I would have expected it. And I can't imagine why he would then have killed Vigdis.'

'No, nor can I,' said Sigrid, attempting a gentle tone. 'I can't see him killing a woman at all. And while a bang on the head might be an argument gone wrong, throttling someone is harder to do by accident.'

'But he still has to be on the list. I barely know him,' Ketil insisted.

'So that's Alfarin, Thorir, Sibbi and Kjartan, and Gunnar,' said Sigrid, wanting to count on her fingers.

'And Kolbein,' said Ketil suddenly. 'Though several people said he was down at the harbour today.'

'He can't leave his precious Sea Stag for too long!' Sigrid laughed. 'Could he have killed Vigdis at all?'

'If he did it earlier, then yes, perhaps. I'd have to talk to the guards again, and Alfarin and Borgny. They saw him. Oh, and Thorir mentioned him, too. It put Thorir off going down there.'

A lot of people.

'Maybe he wanted to be seen,' she said, not sure if that helped. 'So what reason would Kolbein have had to kill Thorgrim? I thought they were friends.'

'Old acquaintances, perhaps,' Ketil corrected. 'That was my impression.'

'Vigdis said they had travelled on the Sea Stag several times.'

'Yes, that's all. But then if Svart is right – and I think he is,' he added quickly, with a look at Sigrid, 'Thorgrim was killed right beside the Sea Stag. What if he did something to it?'

'What could he do? And why would he? He was intending to sail on in the ship, wasn't he?' Sigrid objected. 'More likely he saw something he shouldn't have. That Kolbein and his trading – I wouldn't be at all surprised if he was up to something. The women in Skalavagr didn't trust him at all. And look at the way he had to leave there fast!'

Ketil was nodding, which was good to see. Then he paused.

'But why kill Vigdis?'

'Because ...' But Sigrid tailed off, lost for an idea.

'I wish I had taken Gunnar and left Gulbervig at once. Whatever made me sick I ate that evening. Every time I think of the place, I hear Vigdis' howl that morning, and the way it went through my head.'

She gave a sympathetic smile, imagining his pain. He was rarely so descriptive: it must really have hurt. Then she pictured the scene.

'What was Vigdis doing down by the rocks that early in the morning?' she asked.

'She wasn't. She was kneeling on the ground, right outside the hall. That's why it was so loud when she howled.'

'Right outside the hall? At the door?'

'Yes. Why?'

'She couldn't have seen Thorgrim's body on the rocks from there.'

Ketil turned and stared at her.

'I think you're right. She couldn't. But –'

'But, as far as I can remember, she would have been able to see it if Thorgrim was lying where he first fell, beside the Sea Stag. The ship was pulled up right opposite the hall, wasn't it?'

'Yes, but he wasn't there.'

'But what if Vigdis was expecting him to be there?'

'Because she'd killed him?'

But Sigrid shook her head, feeling her hair shift. She scowled.

'I don't think so, no. But I think she saw him being killed, and went back into the hall, and had no idea he'd been moved.'

'But then –'

'Then she could well have seen his killer.'

XXXIV

'AND SHE DIDN'T say … for what reason?'

'Because – well, what do we know about Vigdis and Thorgrim? They both like their silver. I'd guess – and it is a guess – that Vigdis didn't say because she could get the killer to give her silver not to say.'

'That's a very dangerous thing to do,' said Ketil, rubbing his forehead again. Sigrid's idea seemed to be making sense.

'Well, obviously,' she said. 'That's why Vigdis is dead. So whoever killed Thorgrim had a reason then to kill Vigdis – we don't need to look for anything more for any of them.'

'Although some of them might have further reason. Like Thorir, perhaps.'

'Yes, that seems right.'

'And, since she kept everything to herself, this doesn't help us towards finding the killer.'

'Unless we discover that someone today could not have killed Vigdis. Or, I suppose, find out that someone saw the actual killer. That would be good,' she said, a little wistfully.

'So,' he said, making sure they had their list straight, 'Alfarin and Borgny, with no known reason. Sibbi and Kjartan, with no known reason. Thorir, for the silver. Kolbein, perhaps to do with his boat. And Gunnar, for the arm ring Thorgrim stole.'

'Wasn't it in the purse you found on his body?'

'It was. Along with Svart's missing silver.'

'Why on earth, if Gunnar killed him to get his arm ring back, would Gunnar then leave it on the thief's corpse?'

'I've wondered about that,' said Ketil, pleased she had asked. 'I think that someone who found his silver on the body of the man he had murdered might well leave it there, so that it did not look as if he had killed the man. He would be fairly sure of getting it back eventually, when the hunt for the killer had died down.'

'Or he could take it, and not risk anyone making the connexion between him and the victim,' said Sigrid.

'But if the connexion was already there, there would be no point in that.'

He could see she was unconvinced.

'Anyway,' she said, 'where had the purse come from? You said that no one had seen him wear it. Was it even his? Or was somebody trying to blame him for the thefts?'

'I've heard three different men accuse him of theft, men who did not know each other. I think I am persuaded that Thorgrim was a thief. And I have the feeling that Vigdis knew what he was up to. The way she and Thorgrim opened their packs for searching and stood back – at the time I was sure they were guilty, but they were very confident that they were not going to be caught. So what if the purse was their hiding place? In which case, where had he hidden the purse?'

'On the Sea Stag,' said Sigrid at once. 'That's where he was killed, wasn't it? He had hidden it there, and gone to retrieve it.'

'Or he had taken it out to add to it, and was putting it back in its hiding place,' Ketil countered.

'Or he had just gone to check it was safe,' Sigrid tried. They grinned at each other.

'One of those things, yes,' said Ketil. 'It's a good reason for him to have gone to the ship in the middle of the night.'

'And perhaps Kolbein followed him, and thought he was – maybe stealing something? And struck out, then tried to hide his mistake.'

'He could have declared it, and paid the fine,' said Ketil.

'He wanted to get on, to trade and to come here to Orkney,' said Sigrid. 'If Thorgrim's death was considered an accident, he could have left sooner.'

'That's … that's not a very strong reason, I'd have thought,' he said, and after a moment Sigrid shrugged.

'Yes, you're right.'

He cherished the statement for a little while: it was not one he heard often from her.

'He might have killed him deliberately, though.'

'But why?' she asked. 'Why kill one of his passengers? And why at Gulbervig?'

'Because of something to do with the Sea Stag, surely,' said Ketil. 'Kolbein seems to care about nothing but that ship.'

'Is it really such a remarkable ship?' Sigrid asked.

He made a face.

'No, not at all. It's an odd shape, and it wallows. Coming here from Hjaltland it almost seemed to be going sideways. But I suppose if he's had it for a long time, and he and his crew know how to handle it, he might feel some affection for it. I doubt he would get much for it if he tried to sell it, but it must serve his purpose.'

'Odd all his crew should be from the East,' Sigrid commented. 'At least, all the ones I saw. They only speak their own language, and keep themselves to themselves.'

'Again, they must know how to handle it. I'd have said the slaves were more valuable than the boat.'

'So why would he be so protective of it, then? And if we think he might have killed Thorgrim there on the beach at Gulbervig, what could Thorgrim have been doing?'

'Hiding his purse or retrieving his purse,' said Ketil with a hint of a smile. This was better. He could stay here all evening, and never bother going back into the hall and people and business.

'Which would not trouble Kolbein at all, surely, if it was Thorgrim's own purse. But what if there was something in the Sea Stag, not the Sea Stag itself, that Kolbein wanted to protect?'

'Like what?'

'I don't know,' she said, as if she thought he should do some of the work himself. 'He doesn't bring all his stuff off when he lands, does he? His cargo, the stuff he trades. What if he thought Thorgrim was stealing it?'

'It would be a reasonable thing to think, when he had already been accused of two thefts.'

'Only,' said Sigrid, 'if he has valuable things on his boat, he probably leaves his crew there to keep an eye on it.'

'Maybe they don't stay.' Slaves were not always obedient.

'Or maybe he gives them time off to relax, after all their hard work on the ship,' she suggested. 'So that they're fresh for the next day's sail.'

'Why don't I go and find out?' he asked, looking round at her.

'What, now? Do you mean you're going to go and ask Kolbein?'

'No,' said Ketil, 'not that. And not now. I'll wait till later, see him settled in the hall with his supper, and then go down to the harbour and have a look at the Sea Stag. If there isn't anyone guarding it, then I'll take a look inside, just in case whatever Kolbein was protecting – if we're right – is still there.'

'Thank goodness. I thought you might be thinking of going and asking him if he kept anything on his ship worth killing Thorgrim for.'

The longhouse door opened, and Skorri pushed back the inner leather curtain.

'Oh, you are in here! Alf said he thought he'd seen you, sir. And Sigrid.' He gave her a little wave of greeting, and she waved back. Ketil was glad she liked his men – at least that was something in which she seemed to find no fault in him.

'What is it, Skorri?'

'Just that it's supper time, sir. Thorfinn wondered where you were.'

'Coming?' he said to Sigrid, standing up. 'You don't want to go home now, not when there's food and warmth here.'

'And not if you're going to do something daft, I suppose,' said Sigrid, and stood, too. Her fingers were still wrapped in the tails of her shawl. Skorri let the curtain fall back with a slap, and disappeared. Sigrid looked up at Ketil, blue eyes serious.

'You'll be careful, though, won't you? No turning your back on anyone with a rock, or a rope, or anything. I know what you're like.'

'I'll try my best,' he said. At least she seemed concerned. She nodded, and turned towards the door.

'Although,' she said, suddenly cheerful, 'I'll be keeping a close watch on everyone in the hall. If anything happened to you, we'd be a good step nearer to finding the killer. We'd have to balance the loss and the gain.'

And she marched over to leave the longhouse, leaving him to wrestle with the curtain behind her.

He found it surprisingly good to be back at supper in Thorfinn's great hall. Alfarin and Borgny sat as Thorfinn's honoured guests at the head of the hall, Borgny beside Ingibjorg and Alfarin at Thorfinn's right hand. No one paid much attention to Ketil or his men, and they scattered themselves as usual, gossiping where they might hear something, watching where they might see something, keeping an eye on Svart, Thorir, Sibbi and Kjartan, and Kolbein. Vigdis' body had been removed from the hall to the chapel, where the priest would watch over it: with that gone, the others could relax, eat and drink, and perhaps give something away. You never knew.

Svart he was sure had had nothing to do with Vigdis' death and probably nothing to do with Thorgrim's, either. But he was not stupid: he had seen that Thorgrim's body had been moved, and even injured and mourning the loss of his boat, he might have heard or seen something here on the Brough that could help them find Vigdis' killer. Ketil told himself to speak with Svart soon.

Thorir also needed close attention. There was more to him than he pretended, with all his cheery helpfulness. The way he had slipped into Eyvind's hall at Gulbervig, and out again, and the way he had followed them to St. Ninian's Isle, only showing himself at the last minute – the way he had followed Vigdis to the burial ground, and watched her, and then run off into the darkness. He was far from straightforward, Thorir. And he had reason to distrust and dislike his brother, and no reason to like or trust his brother's widow.

Sibbi and Kjartan – it was hard to imagine either of them working alone, particularly since Sibbi had hurt his leg. But it was also hard to imagine why either of them might have wanted to kill Thorgrim or Vigdis. Ketil did not like Sibbi, but that was no reason to think him a murderer. Sibbi and Kjartan wanted a new place to live and work, that was all. Wait, though: had he and Sigrid not wondered if maybe the pair of them had been exiled from somewhere? And if so, might Thorgrim have recognised them, and threatened to tell any future lord what they had done?

But they did not have to travel with Thorgrim. All they

would have to do was leave him and take a different direction: there would have been no need to kill him. Sibbi was clever enough to work that out. In fact, Kjartan was probably clever enough to work that out.

Then there was Alfarin, up in his seat beside Thorfinn, bending his head graciously to listen to his host. He looked almost happy for once, and Ketil wondered what Thorfinn was saying that might please him. What would a man like him have had to gain from killing Thorgrim? And would he have killed a woman? Ketil found it difficult to imagine, but then if Alfarin had been desperate, he could have done anything.

The evening went on. Kolbein looked very content, laughing and joking with some of the locals, flirting heavily with the serving women. Ketil bided his time, trying to choose the best moment. One of the younger men lurched to his feet and staggered to the hall door, and Ketil took his chance.

'I'll make sure he's all right,' he said to the men seated near him, and headed out after the drunkard.

The man was throwing up copiously against the wall of the longhouse. Ingibjorg would not be too pleased in the morning, Ketil thought.

'Are you all right, there?' he called.

'I will be now,' said the young man, voice bitter with experience. A movement behind him caught Ketil's attention: by the light from the open hall door he saw Borgny, with one of Ingibjorg's maids, making her way back presumably from the privy. The women gave Ketil and the young man a wide berth.

Something was niggling at the back of Ketil's mind … something to do with Borgny, and darkness, and vomiting … He set it aside for now: he wanted to get down to the Sea Stag before Kolbein suspected anything.

He took three paces towards the gate, and remembered. Outside the hall at Gulbervig, while he was sick, Thorgrim had tried to seduce Borgny.

XXXV

SIGRID NOTICED KETIL drift quietly out of the hall. It was a good moment to go: the evening had reached the point where things were a little less clear-cut. Men had eaten enough to be less intent on food, and drunk enough to grow noisy, confident, friendly – in most cases, anyway. At the upper end of the hall, Thorfinn still kept a watchful eye over some well-disciplined poetry and singing, and even Alfarin pronounced with courtly skill a longish verse about a battle he was probably too young to have fought in. Sigrid admired his wordplay, but his voice was too smooth and she felt her eyes closing as she watched from the side of the hall. She had to stay awake. It seemed an age since she had woken on that beach this morning, with Svart and his smashed boat.

Alfarin bowed, and there was some admiration in the courteous applause. Ingibjorg in particular seemed to find the handsome young man unusually talented. Sigrid scowled to herself. She could never understand what Thorfinn saw in Ingibjorg, or Sheepface as she privately called her. If it were not bad enough to be married to Ingibjorg, then there was trouble with her kin, too: she cast her mind back only a year or two to when Kalf Arnarson, Ingibjorg's cousin, always jealous of Thorfinn's extensive realm and influence, had done his best to unsettle Thorfinn's mind and raise islanders against him. Kalf never bothered so much with men of his own: he preferred to instigate treachery and betrayal, insinuating himself where he saw cracks in anyone's loyalty, or where a nasty little nibble of gossip could weaken and wear at the truth, until it was full of holes and worth nothing.

But Kalf was many miles away in the Western Isles – no need to be distracted by thoughts of him, and lose sight of working out who had killed Thorgrim and Vigdis. She glanced quickly round the hall, checking to see where each of their possible killers was again. Thorir, near the door to where the women kept the food, offering help when a woman came in with something heavy, and otherwise keeping in the shadows, like her. He was an odd man, but was he a killer?

Alfarin had returned to his high seat beside Thorfinn. Borgny was missing – ah, but there she was now, coming back into the hall with Bolla, the maid. It was wise for a lady like Borgny not to go out alone in the dark to the privy – who knew what might happen? And Bolla would have made sure she did not miss her way. Borgny swept, faultless as a gull in flight, up the hall and back to her place beside Ingibjorg. Ingibjorg did not look that pleased to see her back, but then she had never been as beautiful as Borgny, and Ingibjorg was one to note and resent any possible competition. Borgny smiled sweetly at her hostess, but Sigrid could imagine there had been little delight in her evening so far.

The young man who had looked perilously drunk now also returned to the hall, walking with great care, and Sigrid was fairly sure that Ketil would now be making his way down to the harbour, to see what he could find out about the Sea Stag. As long as Kolbein stayed here, and did not decide to take a final look at his precious ship for the night, Ketil should have a fair chance - and as long as Kolbein's slaves were not guarding it against any possible attack. It was strange behaviour, too, she reflected. Down at the harbour, apart from two or three guards who watched Thorfinn's under-used warships, the boats were usually left alone. What had Kolbein to protect, more than any other trader? Perhaps his spices really were as valuable as he said, despite the opinions of the women at Skalavagr. Or given Thorgrim's love of silver, perhaps there was something more of that nature on the ship. But how much could there be, that Kolbein could not just wear it or carry it? Could a huge treasure onboard explain why the Sea Stag wallowed and ran sideways, or whatever it was Ketil had told her it did?

'Are you all right?' came a voice near her. She glanced up in surprise to see Borgny standing, holding a cup of wine. 'I saw your hands were still unbandaged, and you haven't had a chance to get home, have you?' She nodded at Sigrid's uncovered head, but her look was one of shared amusement, not criticism.

'I wanted to, and then it seemed a lot of effort,' Sigrid confessed. 'What are you doing over here? Shouldn't you be up with Ingibjorg?'

Borgny sat on the bench beside Sigrid, and took a generous sip of wine.

'I was admiring her tapestries, since I thought you might have had a hand in them,' she said innocently. 'After a little persuasion, she admitted the name of the artist, and I said I simply had to go and speak with you about them. So here I am. There's a limit to how many times I can go out to the privy, and I should like just to sit and look and not have to talk intelligently. I don't know if you're used to this kind of thing, but I'm exhausted.'

And she did look it, at last, Sigrid thought. There were dark circles under her eyes, and her complexion was not as bright as it had been.

'You have every right to be,' she said. 'We all have. Just sit and be still for a while: no one will bother us over here.'

'Thank you,' said Borgny, and leaned back against the wall, her eyes closing. She had done well, Sigrid thought, for one delicately raised – all that walking and sailing and worry, and then to find out that her betrothed had been killed. Would Kolbein take them back to Bergvin?

She looked about for Kolbein, suddenly uneasy. He had such a knowing grin always, and quick eyes – he seemed to miss nothing. He would probably have noticed Borgny coming over here. Had he seen Ketil leave the hall? She shook herself. Even if he had seen Ketil go, what reason would he have to think that Ketil intended to look at the Sea Stag?

But Kolbein did seem to have an eye on the hall's door, even as he drained another cup of wine. She had watched him eat, too: he seemed to want to make his stay on the Brough worthwhile, at least in food and drink. And he appeared to be enjoying the entertainment, too: she watched now as he turned his attention back to Alf, playing his sheepbone flute while someone else beat a small drum. Kolbein beat time, too, with one hand, still grinning. Then a fellow at the other side of the hall started up a familiar song they knew Thorfinn liked, and Kolbein joined in along with everyone else, beating time with his cup, now.

'Is Ketil anywhere nearer to finding out who killed Thorgrim?' Borgny asked, breaking into her thoughts.

'I'm not sure how I would know,' said Sigrid cautiously. Borgny smiled.

'Well, you're not Svart's wife, whatever Sibbi says,' she replied with a mischievous look. 'You're not Ketil's wife either, I should say, but there's more between you than just acquaintance, isn't there?'

Sigrid hunched.

'We've known each other a long time. On and off,' she added.

'Ingibjorg likes him,' said Borgny.

'She docs. She wanted him for her daughter, but she has married elsewhere.'

'And he's in good standing with Thorfinn, evidently.' She hesitated. 'What do you think of Thorfinn?'

'I like him,' said Sigrid simply. 'You'd expect me to say that, living here. But I do. He's a sensible man, makes good decisions for his hird and his people, listens to reason, has practical ideas. Whoever he chooses to replace – well, Bjorn, I suppose, at Buckquoy – he'll choose well.' She eyed Borgny with interest. Was she thinking of waiting to see if the new lord of Buckquoy needed a wife? She was beginning to think she would like Borgny as the lady of her hall. But who would Thorfinn choose as the lord?

But this was distracting. She needed to watch Kolbein.

He was still there, thank goodness, just where he had been sitting all evening. She was about to look around for Sibbi and Kjartan, just to account for everyone, when she saw that they had moved to where Kolbein was sitting, across the table from him. Kjartan was singing with enthusiasm, beating both large hands on the table, while Sibbi sang much more quietly, his eyebrows raised as if to ask if no one else found this as ridiculous as he did. As the song drew to a close in a thunder of cheering and thumping, Sibbi leaned across the table and said something to Kolbein. Sigrid was just near enough to see Kolbein's eyes tighten, the grin set on his face. Sibbi was smiling now, the smile of one who knows he is tremendously clever. Kolbein's brow twisted as he responded, in some way Sigrid could not hear. Sibbi's smile stretched still further as he shook his head. Sigrid tensed: she had just noticed Kolbein's hands snap into fists.

'What would you say to the idea that Earl Thorfinn has a man in mind for Buckquoy?'

Sigrid shrugged, still watching Kolbein.

'I should want to know who it is,' she said.

'I think,' said Borgny, 'that he's thinking of your friend Ketil.'

'What?' Sigrid's head snapped round so fast that her hair came loose again, springing around her face. She scrabbled to catch and contain it. 'That would be ridiculous! Ketil couldn't run a hall! I mean – you know, it's not what he's used to.' But she was sure in her mind that Ketil could, in fact, run a hall and his own hird. With the appropriate help, of course. Skorri, and Alf, and Geirod. And Borgny? 'Are you sure?' She hoped Borgny could not hear the wobble in her voice.

'No, I'm not sure,' said Borgny, her smile a little less certain now. 'I'm sorry if I upset you. It's just the impression I had, listening to my brother and Thorfinn speak, and listening to Ingibjorg. I mean, you're right – Thorfinn seems a very sensible man.' She smiled more fully again. 'I like him, too. I wish our lord was like him.'

Just an impression … she would have liked to have talked more about this with Borgny, about her impression and how she came to it. But for the moment, there were more important things to think about. She made a last effort to pull back her hair, catching her fingers and wincing, tried to look as if she were just considering Borgny's words at greater length, and turned her attention back to Kolbein and Sibbi.

Sibbi, as if he had not noticed Kolbein's fists, leaned forward to speak more softly to Kolbein. That superior smile was still on his face - Sigrid thought she would have punched it herself, if it had been directed at her. But Kolbein held still, for now. Beside Sibbi, Kjartan, oblivious, was cheering someone else who had come forward to perform. Sibbi dug him in the ribs, and he gave a yelp even Sigrid could hear. He turned his attention to Sibbi and Kolbein, his expression somehow puzzled and stern at the same time. Sibbi said something more, his smile insidious. And Kolbein smacked his cup down on the table, swung himself over the bench, and strode out of the hall.

'Oh, my,' said Sigrid, and this time when she used her hands to push herself up from the bench she felt no pain.

'What?' Borgny was confused, thinking she had done something wrong. But Sigrid shook her head, and scrambled out to follow Kolbein to the door.

'Excuse me, Borgny. I have to go.'

XXXVI

THERE WAS NO moon, and the stars were well concealed behind banks of low cloud. Ketil could not see them but he could imagine the thick grey fleece of them dragged past by the wind. Wind and cloud were normal here, but he had the sense that perhaps another storm was coming, bowled along towards them. He wondered if Thorfinn would get his two warships up to Hjaltland or whether the show of strength would have to wait for better weather. Once the autumn set in properly, and the days grew shorter, it would be harder to find a good time, yet Ketil remembered that sense of urgency at Skalavagr. The lord at the hall there had certainly felt there was no time to waste.

He took a torch from inside the hall door and lit it from one of the sconces outside, the flames licking sideways. He could see the gate lights from here, anyway, and knew the ground well.

'All quiet?' he asked, as the guards inspected and identified him.

'Aye, sir, quiet enough. Weather's coming in,' said one.

'Anyone been in or out since dusk?'

'A few came in, but we knew them all, sir.'

'What about the newcomers? From the Sea Stag down in the harbour?'

The guard made a dismissive sound.

'The skipper's been away down to the harbour – he was

218

down there a good while. The others – well, there was a man and his sister but when they saw the path I think they thought it was too rough for them to go anywhere. And a fellow came on his own, but he changed his mind and went back up round the buildings. Don't know what he thought he was doing, but he seemed nice enough.'

The other guard grunted agreement, then added,

'There was a younger lad, too, sir, but he just walked about, looking around him. He nodded but he said nothing. Just seemed to be seeing what was going on, ken?'

Gunnar, Ketil thought. He had gone a little further than the pigs, then. But as for Alfarin and Borgny, and Thorir and Kolbein, the story was much as he already had it.

'I'm going down to the harbour myself just now,' he said. 'I shouldn't be long.' It was never a bad idea to let someone at the gate know where you were going, at this time of the night. He had told Sigrid he would be careful, but it would be a cold night to lie out on the path if he tripped and broke his ankle. He lifted a hand to wave to the guards, and used the torch to help him see where the path was, the steeper one that led straight down to the harbour.

Thorfinn's warships were beached furthest away from the Brough, where the shore was more suitable for a quick launch. He could see lights around them: there were men to keep an eye on them all the time, but just now there would be others there, too, checking every board, mast, rope and sail for the voyage up to Hjaltland. It would not send out a good signal if something went wrong, and if they did encounter trouble, they would be more than ready.

Between them and the end of the path, where it reached the beach, lay all the other craft belonging to anyone living this side of the headland of Buckquoy or on the Brough itself – fishing boats, small traders, boats for the quick daily transport of sheep or feed or family south towards Hamnavoe or round the Brough and east, the way they had come today, towards Tingwall and the northern isles. He pictured briefly the search for Sigrid and Svart that morning: he could barely remember thinking or reasoning as his eyes scoured the coast for any sign of Svart's cursed little boat. He gave thanks again for their safe discovery, and tried to pay attention to what he was looking for.

His own boat was beached near the path end. He gave the gunwale an affectionate pat on the way past. The Sea Stag was further along, bulky among the other boats, with a large, greased cloth draped over it to protect it, or whatever was on board. There was no movement near it – why would there be, at this time of the night? Even the seabirds were asleep, and the activity around the warships was the only movement on the beach apart from the soft lapping waves. Ketil held his torch high, watching out for ropes on the sand, and carefully approached the Sea Stag.

A corner of the greased cloth flapped in the wind, but the rest seemed well tied down. It was the only movement about the vessel. Ketil walked slowly around it, footsteps unheard above the wind and the sea-stir. To the downwind side of it, he thought he detected an odd smell, and sniffed carefully. But the wind was strong, as were the smells of wrack and spray. Was it whatever the covering cloth had been greased with? It did not smell like the fat of any animal he had ever come across. There was a bright, fresh scent, almost like the pine forests in Nordvegr, but under it an odd sharp spiciness. Whatever Kolbein had been trying to trade in Skalavagr, presumably, though again he could not quite place it. He reached the point at which he had begun his tour of inspection, where the loose flap was, and stretched out a hand to lift it.

At once it was snatched from him, and two figures were standing up on the boat before him, breathing hard. For a moment no one said anything, then there was a cry from one of them and Ketil found his torch snatched from his hand and tossed, hard, into the sea. It sank with a hiss. His knife was in his hand before he had time to think about it.

But the men made no effort to attack. He could only see them in outline against the glow from the warships along the beach, but he could work out that they were waving empty hands, gesticulating frantically but not threateningly.

'No fie-er!' cried one after a moment. 'No fie-er!'

The other one echoed him, more emphatically.

'No fie-er, man! No fie-er!'

'All right,' said Ketil, holding his knife up to show he was not about to use it. 'All right. I'm glad to see Kolbein's ship is well-guarded. Good night.'

They showed no sign of understanding any more than his tone: when he raised his knife they jumped, but then seemed to see the gesture for what it was, and let their arms fall.

'No fie-er,' repeated the first one, almost apologetic but quite firm.

'No fire,' Ketil agreed, backing slowly away.

There was no point in trying further just now: the slaves evidently slept on the ship under that greased cover. He would come back in the daylight. Was that what they were worried about, though, the greased cover? No fire – because they thought it might burn? If it had been soaked in pine resin, somehow, he thought they might be right. He shuddered suddenly. They might all just have had a lucky escape.

He was about to make his way further along the beach to beg a light from the men working on the warships, when he glanced back at the path from the Brough. Someone was coming down it, carrying a torch. Who could that be, at this time of the night? If it was someone else going to work on the warships, it would be quicker to ask for his light – after all, once he was down on the shore he would barely need it to find his way. Or it could be Kolbein, coming to check once again on his ship and its cargo and its guardians. And Ketil thought that might give him a chance to ask some questions.

He stepped over quietly to where the path came down to the shore, wary of casting his own shadow in the light from the warships. Whoever it was, they paused for a moment, as if taking in the scene of the work in progress. And for that moment, he was just able to see the man's face. It was Kolbein.

He kept very still, keen to take the man unawares, but before he could step out, Kolbein cried out.

'Oh! What are you doing here?'

He did not sound alarmed, just taken aback. Ketil opened his mouth to reply, when another voice, close beside him, said:

'Oh! I'm … I'm just going home. I live over there.'

Sigrid. What was she doing here?

'You're late to be walking about on your own, and with no light,' said Kolbein. He seemed concerned, but there was a hint of something in his voice – laughter? He stepped on to the path.

'She's not alone,' he said firmly. 'And we both know the path very well, thank you.'

Sigrid gave a little gratifying gasp: and serve her right if she was shocked, he thought. What on earth was she doing down here, when he had left her safely in the hall?

Kolbein swung the torch's light from one to the other of them, and through it Ketil could see that sly smile spreading across his face.

'Oh, aye? What have we here, then? Your poor husband stuck up there with his arm bandaged and useless, and his boat in pieces, and you're here being walked home by Ketil?'

'You could think about that for a moment,' said Sigrid, tight-lipped. 'If Svart lives in Gulbervig, and I live just over there, how does that work?'

For a moment, Kolbein looked confused.

'Then what were you doing with Svart?' he asked. 'Aren't you his wife?'

'No, I'd barely met him. And I'm not Ketil's wife, either, before you ask. I'm a widow who would very much value a quiet night on her own in her own longhouse, and no more nonsense about husbands!'

Kolbein made a mock apologetic face.

'I'm so sorry,' he said, 'but everyone thought you and Svart –'

'It was Sibbi. Sibbi jumped to that conclusion and at the time – at the time it was complicated. There was a lot happening.'

'Sibbi got it wrong?' Of all of it, Kolbein picked out that. 'Sibbi got it wrong! Ha!'

'I suppose he does, sometimes,' said Ketil mildly.

'More often than he'll admit,' said Kolbein, and it was almost a growl. 'That wee man thinks very highly of himself. More than anyone else does – except maybe Kjartan. But oh, no, Sibbi can get it wrong, too!' The growl sank into a low and satisfied chuckle.

'It sounds as if you've known Sibbi a long time!' said Sigrid, suddenly brighter. 'Old grudges, eh?'

But Kolbein's chuckle stopped.

'No, Sibbi only appeared at the harbour a week or so ago, asking for a passage,' he said. 'I'd never seen him before in my life. Why would I?'

'I don't know,' said Sigrid. 'You were stuck there for a while, weren't you? You and Thorgrim and Borgny, and Sibbi and Kjartan, and Gunnar, and Alfarin and Borgny.'

'Not Alfarin and Borgny, not from the start,' said Kolbein, eager to change the subject from Sibbi. 'The boat they were expecting was damaged in the same storm that delayed us, so they joined us, too.'

'And apart from you and Thorgrim, no one else knew each other? Was it a happy voyage?'

'What?' Kolbein asked. 'What's that to do with anything? Thorgrim was killed because he stole things, wasn't he?'

'Things he had hidden on your boat, hadn't he? On the Sea Stag?'

There was silence for a moment, broken only by the torch in the wind, and the fluttering of waves. Then Kolbein said,

'I think so, yes.'

'You saw him, didn't you? The night he was killed.'

'He was next to the Sea Stag. That's my favourite thing, the Sea Stag. It's like a wife and a son to me, and a home and a living. And there he was, rooting round in it.'

'You had no guard posted?' Kctil asked.

'I did after that. I thought she'd be safe at Gulbervig.'

'So what did you do?' asked Ketil.

'I left him a moment. I'd only come out of the hall to go to the privy. I was puzzled, but I had to do that first, you ken?'

'Of course.' He hoped Sigrid would not laugh.

'Then I went to look, and – well, he was dead. Lying beside the Sea Stag.'

'Did you move him?'

'No! I had no intention of touching him! It was nothing to do with me!'

Something caught Ketil's attention.

'You had no intention of touching him – but you did, didn't you?'

In the torch light, Kolbein looked sulky.

'I had to look and see if he'd disturbed anything. And I found a purse – that purse that was on him. I don't know who put it on him, but I threw it out of the boat to land beside him, and then I went back into the hall. And I didn't say anything to anybody.'

XXXVII

SIGRID WAS STUNNED. Someone who had actually been there, or been close to the spot, when Thorgrim was murdered, and had moved that wretched purse full of silver, and he had never said anything about it till now.

'But did you see anyone else there?' she asked, unable to stop herself. 'You can hardly have been in the privy long – you must have seen someone else near your ship, or near the hall, or something!'

Kolbein looked at her.

'You're a nosy one, aren't you? Why, are you worried one of your menfolk might have been there?'

She heard Ketil draw a deep breath, and managed to hold her own.

'It's a good question: answer it.'

'I didn't see anyone,' said Kolbein heavily. 'Not near the Sea Stag, nor near the privy, nor on my way to the hall, nor on the rocks. I went straight back into the hall, and I stayed there. I didn't notice anything else at all. I'd had,' he added as an afterthought, 'a fair bit to drink, of course.'

'Not so much that you didn't notice there was someone at your ship,' said Ketil, just as Sigrid thought the same thing. 'Why didn't you mention all this before?'

Kolbein sighed.

'The Sea Stag is more important to me than any fool I might

have seen wandering around Gulbervig. Including Thorgrim, dead or alive. And now I've had enough of this – I'm going to go and check on her.'

He waved his torch just enough to look dangerous, and made to pass them.

'Your slaves are keeping a good eye on her,' said Ketil. Sigrid was surprised: she would not have expected him to admit he had been there. 'Though they disposed of my torch quickly enough.'

Kolbein spun on his heel. The torchlight flickered across his face, casting shadows as black as his hair and eyebrows, as if he had been drawn with charcoal.

'You took a torch near the Sea Stag?'

'I did. I was passing.' He nodded along the beach. 'We're working on Thorfinn's warships.'

Sigrid crushed a smile. Ketil was not remotely working on Thorfinn's warships. There was a pause.

'I doubt they'll be away tomorrow,' said Kolbein, and jerked his torch at the sky. 'Storm closing in.'

'Then you'll be here a bit longer, too.'

'Plenty trading to be done,' said Kolbein, and the grin came back. 'I'll keep myself busy, don't worry.' He jerked the torch again, and turned and left without another word. Ketil and Sigrid were left in darkness.

'What happened to your torch?' Sigrid asked, when she was sure Kolbein could no longer hear.

'The slaves were under a cover on the boat. They took exception to the torch, and threw it in the sea.'

'They attacked you?' The slaves had looked competent: they could have done him some serious harm, but she could not see him to check.

'Not really, no,' he said.

'Then what?'

'It was just the torch. They just kept saying "No fire".'

'No fire?'

'The boat's cover is soaked in something to keep the water off – maybe painted with pine resin. I could smell something of the kind.'

'Well, that would certainly burn well. You can see their point, if they were sheltering underneath it. And look, he's being careful himself.'

She pointed to where she had just noticed Kolbein's torch, stuck on its handle in the sand. Kolbein himself was a lurking shadow, leaning in to something at the Sea Stag's side. 'I take it you didn't have the chance to look onboard, then?'

'No, but I did smell the spices.'

'It must be the spices he's trying to protect,' she said. 'I mean, you wouldn't want spices getting wet, would you? Particularly if they're very valuable, rare ones.'

'For the sale of which you might be chased out of Skalavagr?' he asked. 'Come on, we can't stand here much longer.'

She felt him take her elbow, so they could stay together. With great caution they began to climb the path back up to the Brough, a task made slightly easier after a few minutes, when they could see the torches at the gate. At least they knew now they were heading in the right direction, even if they still had to be careful where they put their feet. Once out of the shelter of the land bridge between the Brough and the mainland, they hurried forward to greet the guards and be admitted once again.

'That fellow Kolbein's away down to see his boat again,' one of the guards remarked.

'You can let him in when he comes back up,' said Ketil, 'but tell him that's his last outing tonight. You're not here for his convenience.'

'Yes, sir!' said both guards, grinning.

They walked on a few paces, their path easier now with more torches about. Sigrid's mind was busy with what they had learned – not much, in some ways, not about the Sea Stag, anyway. But what Kolbein had to tell them was more interesting.

'Why did he wait until now to tell you what he'd seen?' she asked, without preamble.

'And if he waited this long, why tell us at all?' Ketil countered. 'Do you think he was telling the truth when he said he hadn't seen anyone?'

'No,' said Sigrid, who had already made up her mind on that. 'How could he not have seen someone? He was only away for a moment or two. And then he mentioned the rocks, didn't he?'

'Did he?'

'He said he saw no one at the privy, around his boat, at the hall, or at the rocks. Why mention the rocks? Unless that was actually where he saw someone.'

'You mean … but wait,' said Ketil. 'He told us he saw Thorgrim at his boat, went to the privy then down to the beach to confront him, and found him dead. Dead, beside the Sea Stag, on the beach. The killer had not had the chance to move the body, so the rocks would mean nothing. And it looks as if he spoke the truth about that, or how did the purse come to be with the body?'

'All right,' said Sigrid, thinking busily. 'First, he could be the murderer and just trying to invent distractions. He tried to drag the body over to the rocks to conceal the connexion with the Sea Stag and with him.'

They were outside the hall, now, and could hear singing and noisy talk still going on inside. Neither of them made any effort to cross the threshold. Close together, they could speak quietly, sheltered from the wind.

'I think he would have tried harder,' said Ketil. 'He could have rubbed away the marks on the sand.'

'Hm,' said Sigrid, though she thought he might well be right. 'Anyway, the other thing is that we know how often Kolbein goes to check on his beloved ship. What if he went out of the hall at Gulbervig twice? Once, as he told us, seeing Thorgrim and then finding the body. The second time he sees the body has been moved, and maybe even follows the trail to the rocks and sees the murderer.'

'That's possible,' he said, though he did not sound convinced. 'I suppose.'

'Anyway, I'm sure he was lying,' said Sigrid, not sure how she would prove anything yet. 'Either he's the killer, or he saw the killer on the rocks. However many times he had to go down to the beach to do it.'

'But if he did see someone else,' said Ketil, 'then why does he not tell me who it was?'

'Because he's a selfish, stupid man who has no idea where his duty lies,' said Sigrid.

'Or he's afraid of the killer.'

'Then why not just say? He would have to go on being afraid if the killer stays unknown and unpunished. Anyway, he didn't look like a frightened man, did he?'

Ketil gave a soft laugh.

'No, that's true. Nor can I think of any reason for him to protect anyone, can you?'

'He didn't know any of them well, he said. So no, why would he?'

She heard Ketil draw in a swift breath.

'Unless it was Vigdis?'

'But she couldn't have dragged Thorgrim on to the rocks on her own – oh! You mean Kolbein helped her? Like we said before?'

'It seems to be a possibility.'

'But why would Vigdis want to kill Thorgrim?'

Ketil leaned a little closer, and she could feel his breath on her loose hair.

'Jealousy.'

'What?'

'It's a possibility.'

'Pft, possibilities! Who would she be jealous about? I mean, I never met the man but no one has mentioned anything like that.'

'The night we arrived at Gulbervig, the night before Thorgrim died, I was sick. Very sick.'

'That'll be the shellfish, I told you,' she said at once. 'What has that to do with Vigdis and Thorgrim?'

'I can barely remember what happened that night, or what order it came in,' Ketil pushed on. 'And this bit – I'm sure it really happened, and it must have been that night, but it's only just come back to me.'

'Well?' she said, impatient. 'What is it?'

'I went outside to throw up. On my way back, I saw Borgny coming back on her own from the privy. And I saw Thorgrim accost her.'

'You mean he tried to rape her?' Sigrid gaped – a woman of Borgny's standing? By a man like Thorgrim?

'No – no, not that,' he said, frowning. 'It was more … persuasive than that. He was trying to seduce her – the first steps, I should think.'

'What did she do?'

'Told him she was betrothed, and not interested. And at the time, of course, she believed she was still betrothed.'

'But you think he would have tried again? You said the first steps.'

'I think so. If he had lived. I – I think I staggered over and broke them up, though I'm not sure about anything. But he didn't look unhappy, not at all.'

'That's – well, that's odd. What hope did he think he had?'

'He was, I suppose, a handsome man, and well dressed. Maybe he thought –'

'But he was married. Did he really think he could get away with the seduction of someone like her? It doesn't make sense.'

'Maybe I imagined it all.' Ketil sounded miserable. 'Maybe I can't rely on anything I remember from that time.'

'You must have been very sick,' she said, tempted to put an arm around him. 'I know it doesn't make sense, but … well, I could ask Borgny.'

'You could?' said Ketil, dubiously.

'I think I could. She seems to want to be friendly.' She took a breath, and galloped on. 'I think she has plans to stay here, you know. Maybe marry whoever Thorfinn puts in Buckquoy, after all. I think I'd like that: she would be a good woman to work for. The question is, who is Thorfinn going to put in Buckquoy?'

There was a pause. She could feel Ketil breathing. What would he say? Did he think he had a chance at the Buckquoy hall? Would he want it?

'You'd better go and talk to Borgny, if she'll tell you anything,' he said at last. 'Just in case something happens to her, too.'

Feeling as if she had backed away from the edge of a precipice, Sigrid went back into the hall, leaving Ketil outside for now. Borgny, she saw at once, had returned to sit beside Ingibjorg, and Sigrid had no intention of asking her anything while old Sheepface could hear her. But the evening was drawing to a close, and Borgny was gathering herself to go to a sleeping space in the longhouse, as Ingibjorg's guest. Sigrid would have preferred to skirt around the conversation for a while, lead gently up to questions about attempted seductions, but Ketil's last words had made her uneasy. Vigdis' killer, if not Thorgrim's, was still amongst them. She needed to move fast.

She drew Borgny aside in the gap between the buildings, away from Ingiborg's women as they tidied things away for the night.

'Can I ask you something about Thorgrim?' she said, shifting sideways so that Borgny, opposite her, caught the torchlight on her face. Borgny looked surprised, but not alarmed.

'About Thorgrim? I'm not sure what I could say about him. I barely knew him,' she said.

'It's about something that happened at Gulbervig.'

'Oh, yes?' Was it Sigrid's imagination, or was that reply more wary?

'Someone told me he tried to seduce you,' said Sigrid, before she could waste any more time, or anyone could interrupt them, or Borgny could take offence and walk away. She held her breath.

'Yes, I believe he did,' said Borgny. 'The little worm.'

XXXVIII

'YOU REMEMBERED FAIRLY well, considering,' Sigrid told Ketil kindly. 'But she says it wasn't the first time he had tried to charm her. Once or twice, maybe three times, in Bergvin, before the ship sailed, he made some approaches.'

'What did she do? She must have told Alfarin.' Alfarin would not have been pleased.

Sigrid shrugged.

'I don't believe she did, at first. I suppose someone like Borgny must attract a certain amount of attention.'

He looked down at her for a moment. They were sheltering in the lee of the longhouse again, keeping a wary eye out for anyone who might overhear them. Borgny had retired for the night, but Sigrid had wrapped her shawl around her head and come back to find him, tucked close to him again so that they could keep their voices low. She had still not been home to her own longhouse – she must be exhausted. But he had to pay attention to what she had found out.

Borgny was from a good family, and there was probably a sizeable dowry, but at the same time because of that she would not be married off to just anybody.

'Oh, you mean because men find her attractive?' he said belatedly. Sigrid gave him an odd look, but then she often did.

'She says she didn't take it seriously the first couple of times. She decided it was just flattery, much the same as the way people like Thorgrim and Kolbein talked to her brother, trying to build up their own self-importance. She said he was handsome and well turned out, but vain, and certainly not of her standing, even if she had not thought herself betrothed to Bjorn still.'

'And he was married, too.'

'Of course. I'll come back to that, though.' She took a breath, finding her place in Borgny's story again. 'Then she said there was an incident the night before they sailed – again, Thorgrim was careful. She felt he had said more than he should have, but it was hardly anything she could put her finger on, or describe to Alfarin. They were alone, so she had no witnesses. What happened at Gulbervig was the next stage, though. She was very glad that you had interrupted it – told me she had not gone out on her own to the privy since.'

He tried not to think about that night, and his interruption.

'So she only told Alfarin then? And Thorgrim died that night.'

'She says she only told Alfarin the next morning. I think I saw her do it, outside the hall. It was some serious news she was telling him, anyway.'

'They could have made it look like that, couldn't they?' He considered. 'It's the perfect reason for Alfarin to kill Thorgrim – an insult to his sister. And yet ...'

'He would have admitted to it, surely?' Sigrid put in.

'He would ... but despite the good reason, I can't see him doing it. He would have beaten Thorgrim, perhaps, and left him alive and punished. Challenged him, perhaps, if he thought him worthy of a fight. But to hit him from behind and kill him with one blow, that does not seem like Alfarin, to me.'

'I know what you mean. Nor could I see him kill Vigdis, a woman.'

'No.' He tried to imagine it, but Alfarin, he was sure, thought too highly of himself to have behaved like a coward, in either case. He had not warmed to the man himself, but he could acknowledge the good points in his character. Then a thought struck him. 'What were you going to say about Thorgrim being married?'

'About Thorgrim being married? Was I?'

'You said you'd come back to it.'

'Oh! Ah, yes, well, not quite about him being married. It was just something Borgny said about the times Thorgrim tried to charm her. Well, the first couple of times, when he flattered her. She said that one reason it didn't worry her too much was that in both cases they were out in the open, in the sight of others – including Vigdis. And, she said, Vigdis was watching them, and seemed perfectly happy. Borgny's convinced that Vigdis knew Thorgrim was making advances to her.'

'That's odd,' he said. 'Why would she be pleased?'

'The thing is, if that's true then it takes away the possibility that Vigdis killed her husband because she found he was approaching other women, doesn't it?'

'If that's true,' he repeated.

'I don't think Borgny was lying. Why would she lie about that?' She had wound her hands into the tails of her shawl again, he noticed. She must be cold.

'She might just have misunderstood a look, or something.'

'I suppose. She seemed very sure, though.' She yawned. 'I don't think I can think any more today.'

'Are you going home?' He paused. 'I'll walk with you, if you like.'

'No, Bolla's found me somewhere to sleep here, where Ingibjorg's not likely to see me. If I rise early enough, anyway.' He caught the sound of a rueful smile he could barely see in the dark. 'Are you sleeping in the hall?'

'I'd better see if Thorfinn needs me for anything, first,' he said. 'Sleep well.'

'You too, when you get the chance.' Her hand brushed his arm before she turned and headed towards the longhouse. He watched her safely through the door, then went back to the hall.

'Ah, there you are. Any progress?'

Thorfinn was waiting at the top of the hall, watchful in his high seat. He spoke quietly: already men were sleeping, rolled in their cloaks and blankets, around the sides of the building. The fire in the middle, cooking apparatus removed, burned low and warm.

'Not much, my lord,' said Ketil, just as softly. 'We still have five possible killers: Kolbein the skipper, Sibbi and Kjartan, my nephew Gunnar, and Alfarin. Though I can't see Alfarin killing either Thorgrim or Vigdis.' He explained why, and Thorfinn nodded, scowling.

'I've only spoken to him this evening, but I can see what you mean. Still, he wasn't easy company. I suppose he's wondering what to do with his sister now. There was certainly something on his mind.'

Ketil raised his eyebrows, and took that in. Thorfinn was a good manager of men, and noticed these things.

'I tried to take a look at Kolbein's ship while he was up here, but he has it well guarded by his crew – slaves from the east, I think. But we – I met him on the way back, and discovered that he almost saw Thorgrim being killed.'

Again, Thorfinn listened carefully, eyes widening at the account.

'Do you believe him?'

'I'm not sure. I've never trusted him, but I wish I could find out if he is hiding something on his ship that is important enough to him to be kept secret. To kill to keep secret.'

'I don't like that grin of his,' said Thorfinn. 'But what could he be keeping secret?'

'He trades in spices, apparently, and there was certainly a smell of something spicy about the boat.'

'Something from the east, perhaps.'

'Perhaps. The women at Skalavagr didn't seem to have much faith in him, anyway, and thought he overpriced his wares. We had to leave quickly because of something he did there. He wouldn't say what it was.'

'Did you, indeed?' Thorfinn considered. 'Maybe we'll both go down tomorrow and take a look at his ship. It looks as if the warships might not be able to sail north anyway, if the storm comes in.' He frowned, but it was more thought than annoyance. Then he brightened a little. 'But at least you likely know about that purse now. Should I hand the contents over to your nephew and that miserable man Svart?'

'Some of the silver may belong to others, too,' Ketil pointed out.

'Svart seems honest to me, and your nephew only lost one arm ring, didn't he?'

Ketil could see that Thorfinn was keen to hand the silver back and have one responsibility gone.

'Yes, my lord.'

'I can't see what else we can do tonight. You've spoken with Sigrid?'

'At length, my lord.'

'Good. Good. She's a sensible woman. How are her hands?'

'Not fully healed yet, my lord, I believe.'

'Hm. I'll need to think about that. Why did she go to Hjaltland? Have you found out?'

'I think she has friends there, my lord.'

'I had no idea. Well, that's enough for tonight. I'll see you in the morning – we'll know then whether the warships can go, and we'll take a look at that fellow's boat.'

Thorfinn stood and went to the side door that led to his longhouse and his wife's bed. Ketil remembered where his bedding roll was, and made his way to the back of the hall, careful not to tread on anyone or stumble too loudly in the fading firelight. Even in this light he could make out where his three men were, scattered about the room, as well as the huddle that was Sibbi and Kjartan – emitting heavy snores – and Alfarin's place, near the top of the hall, a little separate from everyone else, and with more in the way of baggage around him, his own little fortification against the world beneath him. Had he expected to be invited to a space in the longhouse? Or did he consider this to be more of an honour? Ketil shook his head. Thorfinn might be right, and Alfarin might have something on his mind, but Ketil was still fairly sure that it was not guilt at the deaths of Thorgrim and Vigdis.

Near the main door he found his bedding roll and undid it, knowing the fastenings even when he could not see them. He had laid it out and was about to settle down when he heard a low word from just beside him.

'Uncle!'

'Yes?'

Gunnar had been curled up against the wall, but he seemed to have been waiting for Ketil to return. Ketil hoped he was not in the mood for a long conversation. Gunnar was breathless.

'Uncle, was that you talking with Earl Thorfinn?'

'Yes.'

'Was he angry with you?'

'No. Why should he be?'

'Well, he was talking to you, on your own.'

'I work for him,' said Ketil. 'We talk a lot.'

'I know you said you worked for him, but I mean, lots of men work for him. But you actually know him!'

'Well, yes.' He hoped that would be enough excitement for Gunnar for one evening, but Gunnar clearly had more to say.

'I had no idea. He's not very popular at the King's court, you know.'

Ketil began to pay attention. Thorfinn's credit rose and fell at the King's court depending mostly on how recently Thorfinn had gone to reassure the King of his loyalty. Perhaps he was due another visit. Could this have anything to do with what Ketil had heard in Hjaltland, though?

'Isn't he?'

'No. King Harald thinks Earl Thorfinn needs to be reminded who his liege lord is.'

'Where did you hear that?'

'Oh, at the royal court. Nobody really noticed me there, and I was very interested in all that was going on, so I listened to quite a lot of conversations.'

'Did you, indeed?' Ketil took a look around. No one was close enough to overhear, and the nearest men were indulging in a late night game of dice under a low lamp, muttering to each other over the results. 'And did you happen to hear what King Harald was going to do about this?'

'Well … someone said that he wanted to give Earl Thorfinn a chance first, and that he had sent someone from the court to Orkney to see how the land lay. Or not someone from the court, exactly, but someone who was supposed to be coming here anyway.'

'Who?'

'Well, that's interesting,' said Gunnar, all eager innocence. 'It wasn't anyone I met, because he'd already left. But his name was Alfarin. Do you think it could be the same one?'

XXXIX

'YOU WONDERED IF what?'

The day was not starting well for Sigrid. First, the sleeping space that Bolla had found for her in the longhouse was where the maids kept their belongings, and it was draughty and full of things that poked into her ribs in mysterious shapes through what had been left of the night. The only advantage to it was that it was very near the door, so that when Bolla woke her before dawn, she had only to disentangle herself and roll outside. Second, there was of course no hot water to wash with at that time of the day, before the fires were lit, and she was longing desperately for a bath. Third, her hair was beyond hope, she had no spare headcloth, and she had sacrificed her only spare shift to bandage Svart's arm and head. Fourth, when she had emerged from the bath house, frozen and irritable, she had nearly taken off into the sky when Ketil spoke to her from the corner of the building, almost invisible in the thin light. She wanted to slap him, but when he told her why he had brought his miserable nephew along, and what the nephew had to say, and when the nephew had then told his story, she changed her mind. She wanted to slap both of them.

'Why didn't you tell us before?' she said crossly.

'I don't even know why I'm telling you now,' said Gunnar, looking baffled. 'I thought you were Svart's wife.'

'I'm not,' she snapped, at the same moment as Ketil muttered, 'She's not.' They scowled at each other.

'It might not be the same Alfarin,' said Gunnar, looking from one to the other of them, not sure yet how he had offended.

'How many Alfarins do you know?'

'There was a woodcarver in our street in Heithabyr: he had a boy named Alfarin –' Gunnar started helpfully, but Sigrid cut across him.

'I doubt King Harald would be sending a woodcarver's son from Heithabyr to spy on Thorfinn. It would explain a lot, wouldn't it?'

'Would it?' asked Gunnar, but she was speaking to Ketil.

'It was strange that they wanted to continue to Orkney when they knew Bjorn was dead and all his ships, men and possessions gone back to Nordvegr,' said Ketil. She was not sure if he was as cross with his nephew as she was, but then his heart probably was not still racing like a puffin's wingbeats from having been pounced upon before he was properly awake. And anyway, he had had half the night to think about it. 'Thorfinn said last night that Alfarin seemed to have his mind on other things. I suppose this could be what it was.'

'Why were they talking about it in front of you?' She rounded on Gunnar, who flinched.

'It wasn't really in front of me. I was just listening. I'm interested in things,' he said.

She bit back a reply, trying to think instead. After all, he was Ketil's nephew. And he was very young.

'What else did they say, then?'

'It was at supper. They were just talking, you know?' He cast an anxious look at Ketil. Ketil's face was blank. 'They started talking about how they might end up going down to Hjaltland and Orkney, you know, to sort Earl Thorfinn out. I didn't know my uncle knew Earl Thorfinn, or I'd have paid more attention.'

'Sort Earl Thorfinn out. There's a happy prospect,' she said. War would not be good for business. Who wants to decorate their halls and their clothes with woven bands when they're about to be killed? 'What else did they say?'

'One of them said that Alfarin had been sent to find out more about Earl Thorfinn's loyalty. And another one said that was a shame, because he liked Alfarin's sister. I didn't know who they were talking about, you see,' he added plaintively. 'Alfarin and

Borgny had gone before I arrived at the court. Just before I left a ship came in and it was – it had belonged to Bjorn Einarson, and someone said that Borgny would be free to marry someone else now, but I didn't really know who they were talking about. Not until I met them.'

'Did you tell either of them that Bjorn Einarson was dead?' Sigrid asked, trying not to be distracted. Gunnar looked at her as if she had turned into a troll.

'Speak to Alfarin? Or Borgny? Me?'

'Fair enough,' said Ketil briefly. Sigrid turned back to the main subject.

'Anyway, Alfarin and his intentions in Orkney,' she said.

'Oh. Yes. Well, they liked his sister. And then someone else said he didn't really mind if Alfarin went, because he was a miserable man and not good company. And the first fellow said that he had heard Alfarin complain that he had been in good standing in his own place, you know, near Bergvin, until some newcomer came in and got everything his own way and his lord only listened to the new man because he was ambitious and the new man was helping him. But I don't know who they were talking about. I only heard anything about the lord – Alfarin's lord near Bergvin – when they talked a bit about where they were from. Alfarin never said anything against him that I heard myself.'

'I suppose he would only talk like that to others of his standing,' said Ketil, and Sigrid nodded.

'Can I ask something?' asked Gunnar.

'I'm not sure why you need permission,' said Sigrid. 'You never have before.'

Gunnar blushed, and Sigrid felt mildly guilty.

'I'm interested in things,' he mumbled.

'I'm sorry,' she said. 'That's a good thing, to be interested in things. What thing are you interested in this time, though?'

Gunnar was not going to let the opportunity slip.

'I wanted to know why I had to tell you this, and why aren't you Svart's wife?'

Sigrid looked at Ketil, but Ketil had inexplicably turned away. Was he laughing? That was most unlike him.

'I'm not Svart's wife because I barely know him and have no particular interest in being his wife. I'm a widow and quite happy that way, thank you,' she added, and then wondered why she had. 'Your uncle Ketil works out problems for Earl Thorfinn. It's a good position, if a bit unusual. At the moment he's trying to work out the problem of Thorgrim's death, and Vigdis' death. And the theft of various bits of silver, including, I believe, your arm ring.'

'That doesn't explain ...'

'Ketil works out problems for Thorfinn, and when Ketil gets stuck, I help him,' she said, casting a glare at Ketil's back. Ketil must have felt it: he cleared his throat, and took a breath. When he turned round, his face was almost straight.

'Thorfinn wants to walk down and see what's on Kolbein's boat,' he said. 'And then see if the weather's fit for the warships to go north. Will you be here when I get back?'

'I want to go home,' said Sigrid, and tried hard to keep the whine from her voice. 'But I also live in hope of a bath, and the water will be hot sooner here than anywhere else, with Thorfinn's great fires. So yes, I might well be. Are you going to tell Thorfinn what Gunnar heard?'

'Gunnar is going to tell Earl Thorfinn, aren't you?' said Ketil, and Sigrid watched Gunnar turn white. 'And then we'll see what happens next.'

When they had gone, Sigrid pushed up her sleeve and counted the few silver arm rings she had left. She had a couple of braids still to exchange, but she did not want to use them on this occasion, and it looked as if the silver she had not spent on getting to Heithabyr would not last long. She sighed, and rolled down her sleeve, and turned her steps back towards the buildings around the great hall.

At most houses, there was some sign of stirring: the first scent of smoke from the roof hole, the door already ajar while the householders scuttled out to the privies. At the longhouse she sought, the door was wide open and the leather inner curtain tugged back over its hook. When she knocked and went in, she could see the cooking fire was well-established, and there was hot water coming to the boil over it. Two women sat over it, but one rose quickly when she saw Sigrid.

'Come in, come in! What can we do for you, Sigrid?'

'I need a new shift and a new headcloth,' she said, her hand already going to her sleeve. 'I was shipwrecked yesterday – it's all a bit of a mess,' she explained, and was annoyed to find she had to bite back tears.

The woman who had greeted her, hard-chinned but with kindly eyes, brought her over and sat her down by the fire.

'Something hot or a cup of milk?' she asked.

'Milk, please,' said Sigrid with sudden longing. She took the cup in both hands and tried not to gulp at it. 'The thing is, I can't sew them myself at the moment.' She raised the cup to let them see her bandages, replaced by Bolla last night. 'Would you ...?'

'I think we can go one better,' said the woman, looking Sigrid up and down with a professional assessment. 'There's a shift here we made for a woman who had to set sail without it, and she was small, like you. Never been worn, of course. And we always have a headcloth or two hemmed, just in case!'

It would be more expensive than buying the fine linen and sewing it herself, and more expensive still than trying to find an old one to refit, but she needed something as soon as possible. They argued amicably over the price, then the other woman went to dig out the new shift and headcloth while the first took the quarter arm ring Sigrid broke off. She tucked the other part safely into her purse, and received the fresh linen with delight. Now for a bath.

She glanced over towards the harbour as she left the longhouse with her precious parcel. The day was grey and sodden, but there was no sign of the promised storm, and from here she could just see movement around the two warships that Thorfinn intended to send north. She wondered if Ketil would have liked to have been sailing with them, and found she was glad he was detained here by the problem of the murders. Not that there was any intention of fighting, as far as she could work out: it was just a tour of inspection, a check to see that nothing untoward was happening in Hjaltland – up the west coast, call at a few settlements, sail on in dignified majesty to the northernmost point, turn and come back down the east coast. No doubt Eyvind would welcome his important visitors to Gulbervig, and the family at Dunrostar hofdi would wave as the warships surged past and back down south and home again. That mute girl Unnr might even draw them. She watched for a moment, but it seemed they had only pushed the ships out on to the water to fiddle round, no doubt, with oars and things, and probably vie with each other to prove themselves the better boat. No dragons on the prows this time as they came in peace, but the men would probably wear all their best fighting gear, axes polished, gloves oiled, helmets gleaming. Tutting at it all, she turned on her heel and set off for the bath house, hoping that the water was already nice and hot.

When she emerged, she felt so much better. Her shift was clean and crisp, her hair washed and combed and tied firmly under her headcloth, and she had managed to find clean hose. She stepped out into the fresh air, ready to face another day.

And that was when the screaming started.

XL

KETIL'S PLAN TO have his nephew Gunnar explain all he had heard at the King's court to Thorfinn failed almost straightaway.

Thorfinn, sturdy and dark, eyes quick to notice Gunnar's presence, was ready to go down to the harbour when Ketil came into the hall, and Ketil waved to Skorri and Alf to join them. But standing beside Thorfinn, a head taller and two-thirds the width, in cloak and boots and with a look that said he had slept the sleep of the just, was Alfarin.

'Then you can see the warships prepared before they go,' Thorfinn was telling his guest as Ketil approached. 'Not that they're going into battle, of course, but it's always wise to have everything to hand, just in case. Don't you think?' Thorfinn's tone was friendly, open, inviting conversation. Ketil assumed he was trying to find out more about Alfarin's intentions in Orkney. Gunnar could tell him. 'How many ships does your lord – Arinbjorn, isn't it? How many does he have?'

'He's in the middle of building more just now,' said Alfarin, without giving a number. 'The weaving houses are full of sails.' He sounded weary of it. Thorfinn nodded.

'Is he expecting some action, then? Or has he plans for raiding?'

'As to that, who knows?' Alfarin seemed to pull himself together, and favoured Thorfinn with a fine smile. 'He has plenty of ideas, some his own, some from others. I am not privy to all of them,

I'm afraid!'

He made his tone light, but Ketil remembered what Gunnar had said he had heard: Alfarin had been in good standing in his own place, until some newcomer came in and found favour with the lord, Arinbjorn. Alfarin was jealous. Was that why he had decided to come to Orkney with plans to spy on Thorfinn? Was it to regain favour, or just to get away for a bit? And if he were taking his spying seriously, a little walk down to look at Thorfinn's warships would stand him in good stead, no doubt. A spy, but a murderer? Ketil was not convinced.

'Let's go, then, if we are all ready. The weather looks better than I had expected,' said Thorfinn. He led the way down the hall to the door. 'I did not tell you, Alfarin, but I have another purpose to this walk. Tell me, what did you think of Kolbein's ship? You came on it from Bergvin, did you not? And then down here from Hjaltland?'

Alfarin's eyes widened at the question.

'The Sea Stag? It's … it's not a ship I should choose to own, my lord, if I were offered the opportunity.'

'I'm not thinking of buying it,' said Thorfinn. 'I don't believe Kolbein would sell it, from what I hear. He is very attached to it, is he not?'

'Oh, very much so,' said Alfarin with a smile. 'He could not be prouder if it were his own son. Yet – it sails very strangely, almost lopsided. His slaves must be very clever to manage it well. He told me he had taken it all the way east to Russland, which I found very surprising.'

They had reached the gate. Thorfinn nodded to the guards, and paused to point out to Alfarin the hall at Buckquoy, across the landbridge to the mainland. Ketil dropped back.

'Is the man Kolbein in or out this morning?' he asked.

'Never came back last night, sir,' said the guard. 'I think I saw him still down at the harbour this morning, though.'

'Thank you.'

'A shame about Bjorn,' Thorfinn was saying. 'I daresay he would have made a fine husband for your sister. But there: perhaps she will be happier with the next man you choose.'

'Perhaps,' said Alfarin. 'She knows her own mind: I shall have to choose carefully. I suppose you might know of some suitable husband here in these islands?'

Thorfinn had already begun to pick his way down the path to the harbour.

'I'll give it some thought,' he tossed back over his shoulder. 'There's no one obvious.'

Ketil smiled to himself as he listened, following them down: Thorfinn had not much enjoyed trying to find a match for his own daughter, now down in Caithness: he would not want to involve himself in another man's problems. And Borgny might not be that easy to match: her brother had no hall of his own, and Alfarin had been ambitious, matching her with Bjorn Einarson. Would he be prepared to make do, now, with someone lower in status? Ketil, too, was glad he had nothing to do with such matters: finding murderers, however elusive, was easier any day.

'It looks as if the Sea Stag is already setting sail,' said Alfarin. He pointed ahead, and Ketil looked up quickly, a cold finger on his spine. Perhaps he should have made sure that Kolbein was back last night, instead of sleeping. Thorfinn stopped and stared.

'I gave no permission for him to leave until this matter is settled,' he growled. 'You told me he wanted to trade, Ketil.'

'I thought he did, my lord.' Out in the little bay, the Sea Stag wallowed and turned. 'And I'm not sure he's going anywhere.'

All of them stopped and watched. The Sea Stag's crew had stopped rowing, and there seemed to be no move on board to raise the sail, though Ketil could see some activity at the prow of the boat. Maybe Kolbein was finally trying to deal with the strange tilt of the vessel. How it had come safely through the storm on the way south here it was hard to say.

'You can hail him from the beach and remind him he has to stay here a while longer,' said Thorfinn. 'Meanwhile, we shall go and inspect the warships, and let them be off.'

When they reached the point where the Sea Stag had been pulled up, Ketil nodded to Skorri, who was better at hailing than most.

'Sea Stag! Kolbein!' Skorri bellowed. 'Are you off?'

Kolbein raised a hand, greeting them from the Sea Stag's prow as the ship sat sideways on to the beach. An occasional flurry of oars kept them roughly in the same place as some of the slaves worked at something with, Ketil thought, ropes and metal.

'We'll be back in soon,' came Kolbein's faint words. 'Just testing something – make her run even better!' They could see his grin from here.

'Skorri, stay and keep an eye on him,' said Ketil, and left him there.

A little further along the beach, they came across Svart with his pile of scrap wood, and with big Afi, the boatmaker from Buckquoy.

'See, there's no enough there to make a raft for a wee pet lamb,' Afi was explaining kindly. 'And if I tried to build a boat round them, there would be an awful risk of it breaking at the joins. Would you no just build a new one?'

'It's my boat,' said Svart, stubborn beyond reason. Ketil tried to imagine for a moment a longhouse with Svart and Sigrid in it. Neither would give way over anything: the marriage wouldn't last a week.

Afi caught sight of Ketil.

'How's your wee boat?' he asked, as if it were family.

'It's doing well, thank you,' said Ketil.

'Better than yon thing,' said Afi, nodding out at the Sea Stag, now turning in slow circles. 'Did you ever see such an object unless it was sunk?'

'I think he's trying to fix it,' said Ketil.

'There was an awful strange smell off her this morning,' said Afi. 'I never smelled the like. And the crew – not a word of any language I've ever heard between them.'

'We'll come back and look at it later again,' said Ketil. 'I need to go with Thorfinn.'

'Oh, aye,' said Afi easily, but he frowned as he watched the Sea Stag. Ketil hurried to catch up with the rest of them, heading on along the beach towards the warships.

'I'm only sending two,' said Thorfinn. 'They'll go up and round Hjaltland, stopping here and there to see that all is well before the winter. I'd have offered you and your sister a passage, but these two are travelling light, and the route might be unpredictable if any problems occur. You would be better waiting for Kolbein, if you don't find another ship.'

'We're in no rush,' said Alfarin, not looking at Thorfinn. Already he had fixed on the warship ahead, and Ketil could not blame him. Even without the dragon's heads on their prows, they were beautiful: the keels sharp, the lines pure, everything just where it should be. Ketil gave a little sigh of satisfaction, and for a moment wished he were going, too. It was a while since he had sailed on a warship. And soon these two lovely creatures would be rowed out of the bay on smooth oars, and the sails would be unfurled and swell with the generous wind, and they would slip like smoke over the waves, Aegir's daughters, and along the whale path to the north, sweet as any song sung at a feast. And he would stay here, on the land, doing his heavy duty.

'New masts in place, my lord,' snapped a man smartly. 'Everything is boarded and the men are all here. Ready to go when you give the word.'

Thorfinn cast an eye at the sky.

'I was going to show this man around the ships,' he said, 'but maybe you'd better get off now, while the wind is good. You know your orders. Let us pray for a good voyage and a safe return. Now, off you go.'

The man bowed his head briefly, as in a brisk prayer, and turned to raise his arm to the crews of both ships.

If Thorfinn felt some pride at the smooth launches that followed, Ketil would not have blamed him. The ships were slid swiftly down the gritty sand with a deep swoosh that made Ketil's pulse race, and in no time they were afloat, the men pulling themselves and each other on board. The oars glided into position, the helmsmen called, and one after the other the two ships took their positions in the bay.

A shout went up from somewhere back on the beach. For a moment Ketil thought it was a cry of enthusiasm, someone giving voice to the same kind of delight that was in him. Then he realised he was wrong.

'There's smoke!' Afi was calling. 'Smoke from that Sea Stag!'

And Skorri was yelling, too, running towards them. Ketil spun to stare at the Sea Stag. Its blunt prow was facing the two warships, oars holding it steady, its weight somehow forward. The warships edged on, slow here in the harbour. Kolbein was standing just back from the prow, and raised his hand, an echo of the warship's commander. But when he gave the signal, a jet of flame sprayed from the Sea Stag's prow, and shot straight across the water to the leading warship.

Cries of horror echoed along the beach. The warship caught fire, burning incredibly quickly. Men leaped into the water, but some took the wrong side. Flames burst from the Sea Stag again, a dragon's tongue of fire to catch the second warship, and the men in the sea between vanished.

'Greek fire.' Thorfinn said the words so quietly Ketil only just caught them: the roar and crackle from the burning ships thundered across the water, the shouts of agony from the crews and despair from the shore beat back and forth. And now others were on the beach, too: women from the nearby longhouses, people running down from the fields and pastures, appalled at the scene. Only Kolbein and his crew seemed unconcerned, concentrating on whatever hideous thing in the Sea Stag had caused this destruction.

And then something went wrong on the Sea Stag. There was a flustered panic, a flash of horror on Kolbein's face. Slaves jumped for the water, and before Kolbein could follow them there was a mighty crack, as if the gate to Isengard had split in the heavens above them. And in an instant the air was full of flying wood, and metal, and rope. Ketil flung himself with Gunnar to the ground, along with Thorfinn and Alf. Alf dragged Alfarin down with him. There were cries of pain and shock all along the shore, and then the hail was over.

And when Ketil poked his head up to see, the Sea Stag was gone.

XLI

LIKE EVERY OTHER woman on the Brough and in Buckquoy, Sigrid spent the next couple of hours soothing and wiping and bandaging, though at least this time she had no need to sacrifice her shift or her headcloth. Some of the injuries were terrible: she was glad she had not had much to do with the poor burned men, the few who had escaped from the warships, now wrapped in cold, wet cloths and laid by the fire in their homes or in the hall. Burns often turned bad, and needed careful attention: Thorir had produced from his pack a paste he said would help, though he had nowhere near enough for all the men so he was now overseeing the gathering of herbs and grease and honey, mixing and pounding, warming and cooling, to make up more of it. Sigrid and Bolla, instead, with a couple of other women, walked along the shore, finding men with huge splinters in their heads, or metal in their arms, or dark bruises where something heavy had hit them at an unbelievable speed. Two were dead and one had lost an eye, another three fingers, and there was blood everywhere. Boats were damaged, too, with chunks of metal shoved into their woodwork by the blast, sails ripped by flying debris. It was as if the Sea Stag, in exploding, had decided to take revenge on anyone who had mocked it.

'Maybe we should take a quick look the length of the shore and see who needs help most urgently,' Sigrid said when they had tended to the first two or three men. Her fingers were clumsy and she feared causing more damage instead of helping. 'Otherwise we could be spending time on those who could just go home to their wives.' She knew Ketil and Thorfinn had been on their way to the warships, and she had seen no sign of either of them yet, nor the boy Gunnar, either. She would not be able to concentrate on any other victim, not properly, until she knew Ketil was safe. But even as they started their survey, she saw familiar figures standing further down the shore. It seemed they were also assessing the wounded.

Afi was all right, the big boat builder shocked but uninjured. Beside him Svart had been hit on his injured shoulder, and his head had started bleeding again. He was cursing quietly to himself.

'You're just unlucky,' said Sigrid, heartless in the face of his grumpiness. 'We'll be back to see to you.'

'I'll take him back up to the hall,' said Afi, shaking a little. It would be good for him to have something to do and somewhere warm to go, and Sigrid waved them away. She walked on with Bolla, sending a few others home, noting one or two who needed help but could wait a little longer, always keeping half an eye on Ketil up ahead. The women with them each dropped back to attend to someone more seriously wounded, but Sigrid and Bolla found only the lesser injured at this end of the shore, and when they reached Thorfinn and Ketil – with Gunnar and a pale-faced Alfarin – Sigrid was pleased to see that none of them seemed to have been hit by anything large or heavy. Thorfinn was staring at the ruins of his two beautiful warships, and Gunnar was crying. Sigrid met Ketil's eye, and backed away, back to the men she and Bolla could help.

Afterwards she gathered up her pack and belongings, and turned wearily towards home.

She arrived at last at her little longhouse, overlooking the north coast of the Brough and its landbridge, after the sun was past its height, though it had not shown its face all day. The door was closed and latched, but the cat, immediately appearing from nowhere and asking to go in, seemed sleek enough, and inside she sensed the warmth from the fire or its remains. It looked as if Gnup had actually been sleeping here, and maybe even heating food – presumably food he had begged from Helga. The place was tidy, the floor generally swept. All the wool was where she had left it, the loom still set, warped up, against the wall, her own bedspace made up and neat. No animals were in their section at the end of the house: it was too early yet for the cows to be indoors in the daytime, and it would not yet be milking time. A couple of hens followed her around, pecking optimistically at the floor. She inspected them critically but they seemed healthy and well-fed. Perhaps her faith in Gnup had been well enough placed. She wondered where he was.

It did not take long to collect up some of the gathered peats and kindling and coax a fire into life, then lower a pot of water over it to boil. Once that was done, though, she slumped to sit in her usual place beside it, the cat curled up next to her as if she had never been away. How long was it? Two weeks? Three? Her mind was a blank. She propped her head on her hands, careful not to press on her fingertips, and stared into the fire, lost.

How long she sat there, she was not sure. She was roused by a tap at the door, and noticed that the light around the inner curtain was much dimmer than it had been when she had arrived. At some point she must, absently, have moved the pot of water off the flames but it was still hot to the touch.

'Who is it?' she called out, before she could forget that there was anyone there. Her head felt empty.

'Ketil,' he called back, then pushed open the door. 'Are you all right?'

'Are you?' she responded. 'Did anything hit you?'

'A few pieces brushed past us,' he said, coming in and pushing the door half-closed, 'but we were too far away to be badly hurt.'

'Good, good.' She stared again at the fire for a moment, then remembered to pull the pot back over it. 'It's warm, shouldn't be long. I don't know what food there is.'

'Where's Gnup?'

'Don't know that either. Around, I think.' She gave herself a shake. 'He's looked after the place, as far as I can see.'

'He's done it before,' he said, and she thought of the weeks she had spent on Shapinsay.

'I haven't gone so far before. Anyway –' Reality hit her again. All that had happened that morning. 'What happened? What was that? Why – how did the ships burn so fast?'

'Have you heard of Greek fire?'

'Greek fire? No. What is it?'

'No one really knows. Fire that burns on water, they say, though others say not. Fire that can be thrown, shot the way Kolbein did it today, from the Sea Stag to Thorfinn's warships. Fire that sticks, that spreads, that keeps burning. There used to be stories from the east, stories of witches that made it, that sold it to men in exchange for their souls.'

She watched him, aghast.

'And that's what Kolbein used today?'

'It must be why the Sea Stag sailed the way it did. The weight of a stove, of metal tubes – Thorfinn had some idea of what it would need. He told me afterwards. Fuel to light it. And the concoction itself. No one knows – we thought no one knew – exactly what goes into it. Pine resin, maybe. Naphtha. Maybe something that smells spicy? Something he tried to mask with his trade?'

'The east, you say,' she said, feeling sick. 'His slaves, they're from the east, aren't they?'

'Only two survived, and neither of them speaks any language we know – not even Father Tosti understands them. Thorfinn has sent out messengers to Hamnavoe and Kirkuvagr in case any trader there might have some idea. That's if they're fit to speak. They're talking, but not even to each other – just babbling, I think.'

'And Kolbein?'

The corners of his mouth wrenched down.

'We found enough of him to know that he's dead.'

She crossed herself, something she did rarely, and he did the same. They sat in silence for a moment, until she realised the water was boiling. She scooped some into two cups, added herbs, and handed one to Ketil. The fragrance seemed deathly.

'So that was his secret, then? Is that why Thorgrim was killed?' Her voice sounded more assured than she felt.

'It must be, surely.'

She thought again. Kolbein and his toothy, malicious grin. It was easy enough to picture him killing someone, and this was a big secret to keep. What if the Sea Stag had not exploded? What other damage would he have gone on to do?

But why?

'Do we know anything more about Kolbein?' she asked.

'What do you mean? What do we need to know?' He sipped the herbal brew, then took a longer draught.

'Do we know where he came from? Do we know who might have sent him?'

'Interesting,' said Ketil. 'Thorfinn wondered if he was working alone. A man with a grudge. Only that Thorfinn knew nothing about him, so if it was an attack on Thorfinn he has no idea why.'

'How is Thorfinn?'

Ketil gave a small shrug.

'Uninjured, physically. Angry. Very, very angry.'

He would be, Sigrid thought. Angry at the waste – of life, and of resources. Of loyal, well-trained, men, and precious, scarce wood, and the months of weaving the sails and winding the ropes, and the years of experience and days of skilled working that went into that sweetly curved hull. Thorfinn had other ships, more men, but to lose any was enough to kindle his wrath.

'Did Gunnar have a chance to tell him about Alfarin?'

'He did, but not until after – everything that happened.'

'What did Thorfinn say?'

'He laughed. He said Harald would not think him much of a threat when two of his best ships were fired in his very harbour.'

'Unless Harald sent Kolbein.'

Ketil met her eye.

'Unless Harald sent Kolbein. Hm.' He thought for a moment. 'Why do that when Alfarin had not yet reported back to him? Why send them together?'

'There was no sign of them being together. Borgny even said they were not supposed to sail with Kolbein, but the ship they were due to sail on was damaged in a storm.'

'Alfarin was shocked to the core at what happened today. If they were working together, he was not expecting that.'

'Anyone would have been shocked to the core by what happened today,' she said. Ketil clearly was. Before she could change her mind, she stretched a hand out and laid it on his, trying to ignore her stupid bandages as she curled her fingers around his fingers. She could feel the strength there, the calluses from fighting and sailing, the warmth as, for a moment, his fingers responded, shifting to cup her hand in his.

This is not good, part of her head said. What if Thorfinn wants him to take on the hall and marry Borgny? How ridiculous will you look then?

This is very good, said another part, looking at the first part with contempt. How could it not be? This is where you belong. You've known that for a long time.

She heard him draw breath to speak, and her heart doubled speed. Then there was a clatter at the door, and the cat jumped up to investigate.

'Sigrid! You're back!' Gnup's surprised but grinning face appeared at the edge of the lamplight in the doorway. 'And Ketil! Sir!'

'Hallo, Gnup,' said Sigrid. Her hand slid from Ketil's and took up her cup again, but her heart was still manic. She swallowed. 'Everything looks well cared-for. Have there been any problems?'

'None at all, Sigrid. And look – here's supper! Straight from Helga's fire. And she's made me enough for a few days, so there's plenty for all of us!'

XLII

HE STAYED FOR a while after Gnup's appearance, elbows on his thighs by the fire as Gnup and Sigrid sorted out Helga's delicious food and Gnup demanded a full account of their voyage to Heithabyr and back. Gnup had never been away from Orkney, and had no notion of how long it might take to get anywhere, but even when Sigrid explained that they had turned back at Hjaltland he was impressed.

'Hjaltland! Where the soapstone comes from?' His eyes shone with wonder.

'You should go and see it some day,' said Ketil, and Gnup gasped at the possibility. Maybe he would, but Gnup liked his home.

'Will you stay and eat, sir? There's plenty – look!'

But Ketil was already standing to go.

'I should go back to the hall,' he said. 'I only came up here to bring Sigrid some news.' He looked down at her, with a rueful expression. 'Not very good news, either.'

'Was it about the ships down at the harbour?' asked Gnup, suddenly serious.

'To do with that, yes.'

'That was bad. Two warships. And all those men. Near a hundred, they're saying. Helga heard the bang. She was crying when I went to see her.'

There would be more than Helga crying tonight, Ketil thought. He raised a hand in farewell, but did not quite go.

255

'Shall I see you at the Brough tomorrow?' he asked Sigrid.

'I – I don't know,' she said. 'If all that – all the matter of Thorgrim and Vigdis – is settled, then I should probably stay here. There'll be plenty to do.'

'Of course. Yes, you'll be glad to be home.'

'Yes.'

He raised his hand again, felt stupid, and went briskly to the door.

'Good night!'

Outside it was dusk. The fine prospect he had grown to like so much at Sigrid's door, down to the landbridge and across to the Brough, was fading into grey and brown and black, a hint of mist blowing through the air. Did he really have to go back to the hall? But if he did not, what would he do here?

He walked slowly down to the landbridge, thoughts tumbling in his head. Exploding ships, burning ships, burned men. Sigrid. Alfarin and Gunnar, and what to do with them in their different ways – would Gunnar find work? Would Alfarin do them harm? Sigrid – he would talk to her about them. What was happening in Hjaltland? Was there trouble for Thorfinn? Would there be fighting? Or could he stay here, the place that was now home? Near Sigrid?

Almost without realising, he had crossed over to the Brough and was at the gate already. The gate guards emerged, saw who it was, and grinned. Then their expressions darkened.

'What a day, eh? Terrible, terrible.'

'They say it was Greek fire, is that a fact?'

'It looked like it,' said Ketil.

'Aye, like the stories you hear, aye. All those men – terrible.'

'Aye, and that fellow Kolbein – they say he did it? Before his ship blew up?'

'Yes. He seems to have brought it with him.'

'And slaves to use it, so they're saying,' the guard went on. 'From the east. Not that we saw any of them up here, mind. Kept themselves down on the shore, out the way.'

'Ach,' said the other guard, 'mind, he spent near all his time here down at the shore too. You'd think that ship of his was a new wife, the time he spent with her.'

'So I've heard,' said Ketil, wondering how much more talk

was in them. Not that he was in a hurry, but it was an effort to concentrate when Kolbein did not matter any more, except as a link to someone who wished Thorfinn harm – and Kolbein was no longer in a position to tell them who that might be.

'All yesterday he was down there, near enough,' the guard was saying, and something made Ketil waken up.

'Tell me,' he said, 'did you see the woman Vigdis yesterday? The one who was killed.'

'Black hair, aye? We saw her arrive, of course. And then later, she came out of the hall and round to the longhouse – maybe didna know about the side door, or maybe changed her mind when she came out, but it was the long way round she went.'

'Can you remember if that was before or after Kolbein went down to the harbour?'

The guards looked at each other, and in chorus at once said, 'After.'

'Aye,' one went on, 'for he'd not long gone through here, and I thought to myself Aye, here's another one coming, they'll be all over the place soon. But she stayed on the Brough.'

'And when did Kolbein come back again?'

'About this time of the night. Dusk, say.'

'Are you sure? Was he back in between?'

They both shook their heads.

'Definitely not,' said the first guard.

'And you never saw any of his slaves up here?'

'Nah,' said the guard. 'They must have had food down there, and all. Never saw them, only heard tell of them, until the two burned ones were brought up here today.'

'Thank you,' said Ketil faintly as he turned away.

If Kolbein had been down at the harbour before Vigdis died, and had not returned until after her body had been found, then, obviously, Kolbein had not killed Vigdis. And if he had not killed Vigdis, would he have killed Thorgrim? It seemed only reasonable that the same person had killed both. And if that were the case, then Kolbein was innocent – of that, anyway.

And for an instant he was almost happy. Sigrid would have more work to do.

'Then who in Odin's name did it?'

It might have been better to tell Thorfinn another time, when his eyes were not still burning with the flames of ships and men destroyed. But Ketil knew from experience that hiding things from Thorfinn produced even worse consequences. Once more they stood behind the high seat, in the shadows, out of the hearing of Ingibjorg and the honoured guests, Borgny and Alfarin. Nevertheless the hall was quiet. Everyone there had known the ships' crews, knew the survivors struggling with their wounds. Half the places were empty, vacated by the dead, the injured, and the grieving.

'Alfarin, Sibbi and Kjartan, or Gunnar,' Ketil said, taking Thorfinn's question literally. 'There has been no time to look more closely into where they were yesterday when Vigdis was killed. No doubt they were seen here and there. None of them, I believe, left the Brough.'

'Then how difficult can it be?' Fists on hips again, Thorfinn looked ferocious. Ketil kept quiet. 'How is it that every time you report to me these days, it's only bad news?' He looked past Ketil at the hall. 'Go on: you'd better make a start. See what you can find out. And don't talk to me again until you have something that I can take as a good sign.'

Ketil bowed his head, and went to pass the high table and find a place further down the hall, but a white hand pawed at his sleeve and stopped him. It was Ingibjorg.

'You know he's just upset, don't you?' she murmured, her fingers fixed into his arm. 'He's not angry with you. He'll come round.'

'Thank you, yes,' he said, wishing he could shake her off like an unwanted shawl. Ingibjorg smiled, and brushed her other hand down the arm of Borgny, next to her.

'You know Ketil, don't you, Borgny? One of my husband's best men – perhaps the best. I had hoped my own daughter would marry him, but she was snatched up by a man from the south – I miss her so!' She gave a breathy sigh. Ketil, who remembered her daughter very clearly, was sure neither he nor Ingibjorg missed her that much. He found he was gritting his teeth, and tried to stop. 'So now, of course, we must find him another wife, worthy of his position!'

'Not sure I'm quite ready for one yet, my lady,' he said stiffly. 'I'd like to give my full attention to my lord Thorfinn's business just now, though I thank you for your concern.' He bowed to her, and a little less formally to Borgny, whom he quite liked. Then he broke away and continued down the hall.

Skorri and Alf seemed to have been keeping an eye open for him.

'Problems?' asked Skorri.

'Thorfinn's angry - who wouldn't be? – and Kolbein didn't kill Vigdis. Which means he probably did not kill Thorgrim, either.'

They sat with their backs to the wall, watching the company in the hall, not too close to anyone else. That was easy enough, with the diminished numbers. Ketil could see Geirod, with his dog, sitting in silence with two or three men he recognised from the shore that morning.

'That doesn't leave us with many possibilities,' said Alf. 'Surely that makes it easier. I mean, that's one good thing about the whole … disaster.'

'Alfarin – and you don't like him as a killer,' said Skorri. 'And I see what you mean.'

'Gunnar,' said Alf, 'and you'd rather it wasn't him. And he seems a decent lad.'

'He could still have killed, and panicked,' said Ketil. He was not going to be accused of going easy on his family, if Gunnar could be guilty.

'He could. He was up looking at the pigs,' said Skorri, who was fond of pigs himself. 'The keeper saw him, and I took him there myself.'

'And left him,' said Ketil. 'Where is he, anyway?'

'He's somewhere out at the back where the food is,' said Skorri. 'Carving a cup for Bolla.'

'Good,' said Ketil. If he were not a killer, Gunnar needed to find some trade. Ketil had no idea how good he was at the family business. 'Alfarin?'

'Alfarin walked to the headland,' said Alf. 'I think the pigman saw him, too.'

'I'll have to talk to him again.'

'Then there's Sibbi, with Kjartan, or Kjartan, with Sibbi, or either of them on their own,' said Skorri.

'Surely not Kjartan!' said Alf, as shocked as if he had hit the wrong note in a song. 'Unless it was by accident.'

'That's possible,' said Ketil, thinking about it properly for the first time. 'He killed Thorgrim by accident, then told Sibbi what he had done, and Sibbi helped him to hide it.'

'But Sibbi would have known that he would be better telling Eyvind and paying a fine, wouldn't he?'

'Would he be better? They're looking for work,' said Ketil, 'for a position, trusted men. Where have they come from? Why did they leave? What if they were exiled for some reason – maybe even for a killing? They might not have wanted anyone even to think they were connected to another one.'

Skorri and Alf took their time to think it over, and neither looked convinced.

'I could see they might have been exiled,' Skorri conceded.

'All right, then,' said Ketil, wishing Sigrid were here, 'what about Sibbi on his own?'

'He could have,' said Alf kindly, 'but why?'

'He'd need to have taken him by surprise,' said Skorri. 'I couldn't see him beat a man in a fair fight. But he'd be clever enough to find a way.' He nodded confidently, a good judge of fighters. Then he shrugged. 'But as Alf says, why?'

'Maybe we need to get Kjartan on his own,' said Ketil slowly. 'Away from his clever friend.'

'Do you think he would say anything?' Alf asked dubiously. 'He'd be bright enough to keep his mouth shut, surely. If he had anything to hide, that is.'

But Ketil had a plan.

'Right, tomorrow – or tonight, if you see the right people in here, and they're up to talking – I want you two and Geirod to nail down as closely as possible where Alfarin, Borgny and Gunnar were yesterday when Vigdis was killed. As many details as possible, check and check again.'

'Sir,' said Skorri smartly. Ketil could see he was already considering his possible sources. Alf would have ideas, too. And Geirod was a good listener.

'Are you going to talk to Kjartan, then?' Alf asked, but Ketil shook his head.

'No,' he said. 'I think I'll make sure Sibbi is out of the way. I can think of a better person to talk to Kjartan.'

XLIII

SIGRID WAS PLAYING with nettles when Ketil arrived the next morning. At least, that was what it felt like.

'I'm trying to pull out the fibres,' she said. 'I thought I might be able to manage it by now, but I'm still clumsy.' She was sitting on the wall beside the nettle patch, a corner of the good arable infield. Fragments of the outer bark of the nettles littered her skirts, and she brushed them carefully off.

'That's a lot of nettles,' said Ketil, who knew very little of such things.

'Aye, well, they're useful in all kinds of ways – soup and beer and fibre and other things.'

'But isn't that field where you grow your beremeal? Wouldn't the nettles be better somewhere else?'

He must have been talking to farmers again. She did not want to discuss why this corner of her infield was so good for nettles.

'It can't be helped,' she said. 'That's where it is.'

Fortunately at that point Gnup came running round the corner of the longhouse, hair combed and face shining.

'That's me away!' he cried. 'Good day, Ketil!'

'Where are you off too?' Ketil asked, amused at the boy's excitement.

'I'm off to borrow the magic mule!' Gnup waved, with both arms, and shot off up the hill towards Helga's longhouse.

'It's not really magic,' said Sigrid kindly, seeing Ketil's

questioning look. 'It's just a mule. Helga's neighbour is allowing him to borrow it to carry the muck from the animals' stall out to the infield here.'

'Then why is it called magic?'

She laughed.

'It appeared from nowhere a few years ago. Just turned up at his door, and no one claimed it, though he asked all around Hrossey and some of the other islands, too. I think it fell off a boat, somewhere, and just swam to shore, but the old fellow swears it's a gift from the gods and just started its life outside his door.'

There was a pause. She did not want to ask him what he was there for: he could speak for himself. Or maybe, being Ketil, he could not. Either way, she picked on at the nettles.

'Kolbein didn't kill Vigdis,' he said. She blinked at him. That was not what she had expected. Then she took in properly what he had said.

'Are you sure?'

He nodded.

'Completely sure. The gate guards saw her after he had gone out and down to the harbour, and he didn't return until after her body was found. And I checked this morning down at the shore – Afi will swear Kolbein was at the Sea Stag all the time.'

'What about the slaves?'

'The gate guards are sure none of them had been on the Brough at all, not till the injured ones were brought up yesterday.'

'Well,' she said, looking down at the nettles on her lap. 'That's interesting.' She glanced up and met his eye. 'I'm sure Thorfinn's delighted at that news.'

'It's a long time since I've seen him so angry,' he said. He looked as if he would like to prop himself on the wall near where she was working, but was not going to. And again, that was up to him. Her muddled head hit on the thought that if Thorfinn were angry with Ketil, he would be unlikely to give him Buckquoy and Borgny, at least for now. She tried to concentrate instead on Kolbein's innocence, and thinking again about who might have killed Thorgrim and Vigdis.

'So we're back,' Ketil was saying, 'to Alfarin, Gunnar, and Sibbi and Kjartan.'

'And Thorir, surely.'

'And Thorir,' said Ketil quickly. 'Yes, Thorir too. I don't think Alfarin did it, as we've discussed. I'm not wholly sure Gunnar could have, either, but Skorri and Alf are going to check and see what they can find out about where both of them were when Vigdis was killed. We discussed this last night, and none of us can see Kjartan killing either of them, but we thought it was possible that if Sibbi had done it, Kjartan might know something about it.'

'Yes, that's possible,' she agreed. 'But surely they would have no reason to kill either Thorgrim or Vigdis? They would barely have known them.'

'I know,' he admitted. 'They seem the least likely to have a reason. But I wondered if, perhaps, you would have a talk with Kjartan? Just to find out a bit more about where they came from, maybe whether or not they are exiles?' He hesitated, and must have thought she was going to refuse. 'I thought if I distracted Sibbi – maybe offered him a game of hnefetafel, or pretended I was trying to find out some of his skills to see if they would benefit Thorfinn, you could talk with Kjartan. I don't imagine Sibbi would be reluctant to lie if he thought he could impress, but Kjartan is not so clever.'

'No, he's not, poor fellow,' said Sigrid. She could find out something, she was sure. And she did want to know if she had been right, and they were exiles. Another hard piece of nettle bark dug into her fingers, and she flung the stems down. 'And it's not as if I can do anything very useful here. Yes, I'll try. When do you want me to go to the Brough?'

'Come with me now, if you're ready,' said Ketil. 'Any progress would please Thorfinn.'

Come with him. Hm. She would not look too eager.

'I suppose I could. Gnup's busy, and the fire is tamped down.' She slid off the wall, brushed out her skirts, and paused as if considering. 'I'll get my other shawl.'

All Ketil talked about on the way back to the Brough was Kolbein and his activities. She had been right: any foolish hand-holding last night was best forgotten about. He had barely even said good night to her, too busy telling Gnup about all the places he could go. And since the matter of the murders was done with, Sigrid, of course, just wanted Ketil to get back to the hall so she could go to her bed. But today the matter of murders was no longer done with, and there was plenty to say.

Sibbi was a good deal better than he had been, and they found when they returned to the hall on the Brough that he and Kjartan had gone out for a walk. They caught up with them outside the little chapel.

'I know I fell over yesterday,' said Sibbi, 'but it made me realise I could get further than I had done for a bit. Kjartan looks after me too well!' He laughed, and Kjartan looked sheepish. Sigrid suspected he had only been doing what Sibbi told him to. 'So,' Sibbi went on, 'I said we should come and pay our respects to Vigdis, before the burial. I mean, she wasn't as lucky as me, was she? We both fell yesterday, but she fell a lot further.'

Sigrid wondered if he were trying to be poetic, or if he really did not know that Vigdis had been throttled.

'Anyway, she looks very peaceful now,' Sibbi went on. 'We've just been in. The priest is with her and all, so she's well looked after.'

'Poor Vigdis,' said Kjartan, and a sigh shuddered through his big frame. He wiped his bulging nose on the back of his hand, then pulled out a woollen cap from his belt and dragged it down over his balding head against the wind. Sibbi seemed impervious to it, though his lank red hair was almost as thin.

'I'm glad to have found you,' said Ketil to Sibbi. 'Perhaps we could walk on a little, to speak in private? Thorfinn asked me to find out something more about what you would be able to offer him in terms of service, if you were interested in staying here – and if you might be of use to him. I warn you, though: he is not an easy man to please.'

'I'd like that!' said Sibbi, and Sigrid could see that Ketil's careful flattery had hooked him at once. He stood up straight, and wiped his hair back across his head. 'I'm sure we could come to some kind of agreement, once he hears something of my skills.'

'Good, then let us talk,' said Ketil, and turned to lead the way through the cluster of buildings by the chapel, and out on to the open pasture of the headland, blotched with sheep.

'I don't think we're really part of this conversation!' said Sigrid cheerfully to Kjartan. 'Shall we just follow at a distance, in case we're needed?'

'I thought you were Svart's husband?' said Kjartan, looking puzzled from Ketil to Sigrid.

'Svart's busy with his poor old boat,' said Sigrid. 'Ketil and I have known each other all our lives – like brother and sister, really.'

'Oh, I see,' said Kjartan, though she hoped he did not.

'And what about you? You and Sibbi are kin, aren't you?'

'That's right,' said Kjartan, pleased to be on familiar territory. 'My mother and his mother are sisters.'

'So you've probably known each other all your lives, too!'

'We have, yes.'

'This would be a good place to work, you know, to settle, if Thorfinn likes you. Were you not happy where you were before?'

'I liked it,' said Kjartan. 'It was nice. Friendly. Sibbi liked it too, but he said we had to go on a journey. I hope we can go home soon. If it was Kolbein that killed Thorgrim, like Sibbi said, then we could go home.'

'Oh! I thought you were looking for a new place. So why did you go on your journey? I mean, sometimes it's just nice to see something new, isn't it? Was that it?'

'I don't think so,' said Kjartan, confused. 'That's not, um, not the reason.'

Exile, thought Sigrid. I was right.

'Oh, then maybe someone told you you had to go. That could be it, couldn't it?'

'That's right,' said Kjartan, much happier with this idea. 'Arinbjorn – I mean Atli, he told us we had to go. Not that he's our lord, but we had to do it, anyway. Sibbi said so. That's right. But still, I'd like to go home.'

'It's always nice to go home,' said Sigrid comfortably, wondering what they had done to offend this Atli that their own lord would not protect them from punishment. And she had thought that they had previously said that Atli was their lord. 'But you can make good friends when you travel, too. I can't remember if you said – did you know Thorgrim and Vigdis already? Or did you only meet them on the journey?'

'We hadn't met them, no,' said Kjartan. 'Sibbi and I had never seen them before.'

Sigrid frowned to herself. It was an odd way to put it. Almost as if they had heard of Thorgrim and Vigdis before they met them. But how could that happen?

Ahead, Sibbi and Ketil had reached the site where Thorfinn was planning his new bathhouse, to replace the one that had fallen off the crumbling cliff not long ago. No one was working at the site, and Sigrid had heard in the hall that they were waiting for wood to be brought from Ness for the next stage. That was why Sibbi had not been found for some time yesterday, when he had fallen into the foundations. Perhaps Sibbi was remembering his miserable stay, for the two men had stopped there, and Sibbi was gesturing as if telling a story. He turned from the site, and he and Ketil began to walk back towards the hall, the walk that would take them past the dairy and the brewhouse, then the blacksmith set apart, then the combmaker, and other small buildings. Thorfinn's Brough had everything one could wish for.

She was wondering what else she could ask Kjartan without arousing his suspicions, when she saw that Geirod was heading towards them, accompanied as always by his yellow dog, Friend. He made straight for Ketil, with a gait and face so purposeful that Sigrid broke into a trot to be as close as possible when he spoke. But still she almost missed his few words.

'It's your nephew Gunnar, sir. Skorri says can you come at once?'

XLIV

'THE NEXT TIME you bring me a message, Geirod, try to make it sound less as if someone has died,' said Ketil. 'Or someone might.'

'There's nothing wrong, Gunnar, is there?'

Sigrid had sat down beside the boy at once, backwards at the bench by the table. Gunnar had his feet under the table, a cup of ale, and a leather purse – a purse Ketil had seen before. Svart, across the table, was counting pieces of hacksilver and a few other objects.

'I'm not sure,' said Gunnar. 'But I've got my arm ring back! I'll wear it this time: it's safer.' He pushed up his sleeve to show a well-crafted silver band set with a piece of glowing amber. 'That's not one you'd break up to pay for something, now, is it?'

'Certainly not – it's lovely,' said Sigrid. Ketil remembered it, distantly: it had belonged to his grandfather. He was glad Gunnar had recovered it.

'So Thorfinn gave you back the purse?' he said.

'Got my silver back,' said Svart, gruffly, scooping it into his own purse. 'I can pay for my new boat now, I suppose, get myself home.'

'Was there much left?' Ketil asked.

'There's bits,' said Gunnar, pointing to the purse.

'And that's all? That's what you called me in here for?'

'Ah, no,' said Alf, lounging against the other side of the table. 'No, Gunnar found something else – something he recognised – in the purse. Go on, Gunnar, tell your uncle.' He smiled, the smile of one who knows he brings interesting news.

'It's this,' said Gunnar. He felt inside the purse again and brought out a small wooden box. Ketil leaned over for a better look. The box was about the length of a man's little finger, and the same in width and height. The wood was not polished, but there was a swirling pattern, like a ribbon, entwined on the lid, which was the kind you had to slide off. Ketil plucked it from Gunnar's hand and studied it more closely. The tangled pattern had a head and a long, forked tongue – a serpent.

'Have you looked inside?' he asked.

'Not yet: I wanted to show you, first.'

'Why?' asked Ketil. 'Where have you seen this before?'

Alf's grin widened.

'This is good,' he said.

'I saw Thorir give it to Eyvind,' said Gunnar.

'In Gulbervig? When?'

'After he fined me for hitting Thorgrim,' said Gunnar. 'I mean, I didn't know it was Thorir at the time, of course. Not until we saw him again at St. Ninian's Isle.'

Thoughts spun in Ketil's head. He looked at Sigrid, and could see the same behind her eyes. What now?

'He came into the hall when Eyvind was judging us – did you see him? And then later he came back and spoke to Eyvind privately. I saw him handing this over.'

'Then how does it come to be in Thorgrim's purse?' asked Skorri, a note of despair in his voice. Ketil knew how he felt.

'Eyvind didn't keep it,' said Gunnar. 'He opened it and took something out, then handed it back.'

Ketil shook the box gently, then slid open the lid. It was empty.

'Did you see what it was he took out?'

'People don't see me,' said Gunnar, 'and I like interesting things. It was a little clay pot with a clay lid to fit it.'

Suddenly something fell into place in Ketil's head.

'Round?'

'Yes. Nearly like a little clay ball.'

'What colour?'

'Blue,' said Gunnar. 'Not painted, I mean, but a kind of blue-black colour. As if it was burned, somehow.' He looked at Ketil, then around at all the other faces. Only Svart was paying little attention. Ketil's men, and Sigrid, were fixed on Gunnar. He swallowed, suddenly nervous. 'And Eyvind smiled, and gave him an arm ring. Not as nice as mine,' he added, pulling up his sleeve again to admire the amber band, 'but a good one.'

The honey for Ketil's wine, that Eyvind had poured so carefully. Had he taken any for himself? Ketil could not remember. After he had drunk what was in that little pot, he could not remember much.

'What do you think it was?' asked Skorri, watching Ketil's face now.

'It was honey,' said Ketil. 'And something else. And I think Eyvind bought it from Thorir, with the intention of poisoning me.'

'Let's find Thorir,' said Skorri.

Ketil sent his men to the gate to check whether or not Thorir had left the Brough: if he had they had instructions, just as they had their places to search and question if he had not. Gunnar, Svart and Sigrid stayed at the table. He hoped they did not expect orders, too, but they could still be useful.

'Svart, you're a Hjaltlander,' he began. 'Did you know Thorir before this journey?'

'I knew his face,' said Svart. 'And, you know, what he does. Medicines, salves, that kind of thing.'

'Good medicines, generally?' Ketil asked. 'Salves that heal?'

Svart shrugged, one-sided, and scowled.

'Never heard anything different. He's expensive, but good, that's what they say. Always keen to help. He's a bit odd that way, but I've never heard of him doing any harm to anyone. That's him. Kind, but a bit odd.' He clutched his purse in his good hand as he spoke, and his mind was clearly on the boat he would buy with his newly-recovered silver.

'What about Eyvind? Is poisoning something he does much?'

Svart looked up at him then, jaw sagging. He must have missed what Ketil had said earlier.

'Eyvind? Why would he poison anyone?'

'Your mother told me he likes to have control over the men

at his hall, play games with them,' said Sigrid suddenly.

'Yes, he plays one off against another, and if two of us argue he makes sure the quarrel grows. It's his way of ruling. I think it's – I don't like it much,' he finished, perhaps realising how disloyal he sounded.

'Are the men in the hall often sick?' asked Ketil.

'Sick? What, you mean drinking too much?'

'I mean as if they have drunk too much when they've drunk very little,' said Ketil darkly. Sigrid looked up quickly at him. She had caught up. 'I mean when they are like that for several days, stupid and dazed for a week, that kind of thing.'

Svart thought hard, then frowned.

'D'you know, that has happened a few times, just recently. Men who have questioned him, mostly. Maybe all of them. It was just thought they'd eaten bad shellfish, or something. It happens. But I suppose …' he went on, reluctantly, 'I suppose it's happened more recently, it's true.'

Ketil paused for a moment, and sat down softly on the bench opposite Svart, closer to his height.

'Interesting,' he said, and he made his voice gentle. 'Men who have questioned him. Does that happen much? Is he someone who comes up with plans that are difficult, or demands that are hard to fulfil? Or maybe,' he said, even more softly, 'ideas that might get him – and his men – into some kind of trouble?'

Svart's eyes flickered to Ketil's, then back to the table.

'I wasn't involved,' he said, surly.

'I don't expect you were,' said Ketil, who had no idea one way or the other, except that Svart seemed to have no objection to being here in Thorfinn's hall. 'But some men were working with Eyvind, weren't they? Some men thought it was time to push Thorfinn Sigurdarson aside, and look for a new leader?'

Svart, shoulders hunched, nodded slowly.

'Maybe working for King Harald, then?' Ketil tried.

'King Harald?' Svart glanced quickly around, but this part of the hall was quiet. 'Yes, some are for King Harald. I heard he wants to make sure of Thorfinn's loyalty. That's reasonable, I suppose.'

'It is,' said Ketil. 'What isn't reasonable is assuming, before looking, that Thorfinn's loyalty has faded, or does not exist. It would be polite, between such great rulers, to come and ask.'

Svart nodded more eagerly this time.

'That's right,' he said. 'I never had any problem with Thorfinn as the Earl. Why would I? But the idea of sending – well, you know …'

'Do you mean,' said Ketil, suddenly making another connexion, 'do you mean Kolbein and his Greek fire?'

'That was terrible,' said Svart at once. 'Terrible. No one should use such a thing. Burning those beautiful warships? That's wrong.'

'Did Eyvind send Kolbein?'

Svart looked him in the eye.

'Eyvind send Kolbein? He wouldn't have the idea, nor the power. No, I should say Kolbein had another master.'

Ice ran down Ketil's spine. It surely could not be, could it?

'Do you know who?' he asked, almost under his breath.

'I've heard a name,' said Svart, equally quiet. He glanced around again. Still no one was there but Sigrid and Gunnar, and no one was looking at them. Ketil held his breath. 'The name is Kalf Arnason.'

Ketil tried not to show his feelings. Kalf Arnason, Ingibjorg's kinsman, Thorfinn's constant enemy.

'How sure are you?'

The one-shouldered shrug again.

'It's a rumour. But I've heard it several different ways. And so has my mother.' A half-smile to Sigrid. 'Eyvind is a weak, stupid man. The hall is ripe for Kalf to take over, if he wants a stepping stone on his way to Orkney. That's what I've heard – and nothing I have seen at Gulbervig has made me doubt it.'

'I don't want to tell Thorfinn, not yet,' said Ketil. They had left Svart behind in the hall, and Sigrid and Gunnar followed him towards the gate. 'Not until I catch Thorir.'

'Wherever he's gone,' he heard Sigrid mutter.

'He won't have fled,' said Ketil. 'His silver is still with Thorfinn. Only Svart and Gunnar had theirs returned. And why should he suddenly have fled?' He was thinking aloud. 'He did not know that we found the wooden box. And even if he did, there is nothing in it to show what it contained.'

'And Thorgrim and Vigdis were not poisoned, either, remember,' said Sigrid. She and Gunnar stopped while he exchanged quick words with the gate guards, who pointed out and down. The harbour – and his men would be down there already. He led the way back down to the shore.

'Uncle,' came Gunnar's voice, 'if it's Thorir's box, and Svart's silver, how did the box end up in Thorgrim's purse?'

'I have no idea. And as to how Vigdis and Thorgrim died – would a man known for his medicines maybe kill another way, to deceive?' He could see Alf, his height making it easy to spot him between beached boats. 'By all accounts he held a grudge against his brother over the silver. If Vigdis had seen him kill Thorgrim, as we guess she would have, then he had double the reason to kill her – to keep her quiet and to collect the silver she had recovered.' It was all so obvious. How could he have overlooked Thorir when he and his men were talking over the business yesterday? The most likely killer of all.

Alf came to meet him.

'No sign of him, sir, but Afi swears no boat has gone out this morning beyond the bay – they've been bringing in the wreckage of the Sea Stag and the warships, where they can.'

Even broken wood was precious on islands with so few trees. There was always something to be salvaged.

'Has no one seen him go past?'

'They've been busy. Other things to think about.'

'Strange he didn't stop to help,' said Sigrid, catching up in time to hear this exchange. 'He always likes to help, doesn't he? Unless he had something more important … oh!'

'What?' Ketil turned to her at once. 'What is it?'

'I think I know where he's gone! What was he doing this morning?'

'Asking about all the men who were hurt yesterday,' said Gunnar. 'Making sure they had enough of his salve stuff. It smells nice,' he added.

'Then that's what he's doing,' said Sigrid. 'Not all the injured were taken up to the Brough. Some of them live down here, at the settlement beyond the harbour over there. He'll be making sure they're all right, won't he?'

And there, indeed, was where they found him, emerging

from a doorway with his usual cheery smile, and quite happy to return with them to Thorfinn's hall.

XLV

'POISON? I WOULDN'T poison anyone!'

'You'll sell poison to someone else and let them do it, though, wouldn't you?'

Sigrid thought Ketil was doing well at controlling his anger. He was more furious at the memory of that time of weakness than she had seen him at anything else, but to look at him now you would not think that Thorir's concoction had ended up affecting him directly.

The little wooden box, the serpent writhing on the lid, sat on the table, in the centre of the gathering.

'I don't understand,' said Thorir, wide-eyed and innocent.

'You were seen,' said Ketil heavily. 'You were seen with the box. You handed the pot of spiced honey from the box to Eyvind and were paid. Then Eyvind was seen emptying the same pot into someone's wine, and that man was sick for a week.'

'Oh,' said Thorir.

'And it seems that was not the first time, either, was it?'

'Well, no,' said Thorir, abashed. 'Seen, was I? That was careless of me. Eyvind won't like that.' He tapped his teeth thoughtfully. 'Yes, I admit it. Eyvind often buys a mixture that makes some of his men ill – they all recover, but he does like to humiliate them. He's not a very nice man, Eyvind, but I need the silver he pays me. Our farm is a poor one, and unaccountably all our family silver vanished.' He flashed a sardonic smile around the group at the table. 'And I've never killed anyone. After all, Vigdis and my brother weren't poisoned, were they?'

Just as Sigrid herself had said. But Ketil had said that might be part of Thorir's deception – if they had been poisoned he would have been the first to be suspected, no doubt. She watched Thorir from her place at the edge of the company around the table. Alf stood at apparent ease between them and the door, in case Thorir should try to escape – he showed no signs of wanting to – and Gunnar sat on the bench beyond Thorir, their backs to the wall. Ketil had glanced around, checking to see that Thorfinn was not there, trying to avoid bringing him another unfinished story. Whatever she thought about Ketil and Borgny and Buckquoy, Sigrid prayed Ketil could help solve Thorfinn's problems soon, settle Hjaltland, remove Eyvind, beat Kalf back once again. The very sound of Kalf's name chilled her. He had threatened Orkney more than once since she had come here, threatened their peaceful lives, done his best to break up Thorfinn's loyal following. King Harald testing Thorfinn's allegiance she could understand – no doubt Thorfinn did the same with his own local lords on his distant lands. But Kalf – Kalf was deception, and destruction, and division, and death.

But was Thorir complicit in that, or was he only guilty of supplying Eyvind with something nasty to keep his men – and passing representatives of Thorfinn – under control?

'You were quick to point out that Thorgrim and Vigdis weren't poisoned,' said Ketil. 'But someone who makes poison is not, surely, limited to using it. You could easily have killed your brother, or his wife.'

Thorir looked at him almost mildly.

'I did not kill Thorgrim, whom I had good reason to – dislike. It would have made more sense to make him tell me where our family silver was, rather than kill him and lose all hope of finding it. I was lucky, though: someone else killed him, and he must have told his wife where it was, so now I have the chance of recovering what is mine. Or it looks like luck,' he said suddenly, and grew sad. 'I should rather he was alive, and we were reconciled and sharing the silver as we were supposed to, and friends again. I had no wish to lose my only brother, never that.'

'Where were you that night that he was killed?' asked Ketil, apparently unmoved by his regrets. Sigrid was not sure: Thorir seemed truly sorrowful. And she almost believed him when he said he had not killed Thorgrim – but had he, maybe, taken advantage of that and killed Vigdis for the silver? She rubbed her forehead on the back of her hand and sighed. There should be a way to tell when people were lying.

'I didn't go anywhere near him,' said Thorir. 'Maybe if I had –'

'Where did you go, then?'

'Oh, off again. I think I went back to Skalavagr that night.' His eyes left Ketil for a moment. This did look like a lie. 'You know it's not a long walk.'

'And when did you miss this box?' Ketil's long finger tapped the serpent quickly, as if the creature might strike.

'I didn't, not for a good while. Where did you find it?'

'In Thorgrim's purse,' said Ketil, and something in his voice made them all stop still, silent. Thorir stared up at him, and for a long moment they were like a carving on a rock, no more. Then Thorir let out a long, narrow sigh.

'All right, I spoke to him, yes.'

'When was that?'

'It was after dark. I didn't go back to Skalavagr. I wanted to wait and speak to him. I stood outside the hall and waited – I knew he'd come out at least once, like everyone else. Some come out a lot more than once, don't they?' he asked, a sudden chuckle in his voice. 'You were out a few times, eh, Ketil? Making good use of Eyvind's wine!'

Sigrid winced, and looked at Ketil.

'I was poisoned by your spiced honey,' he said, and if the air could have turned colder around them, it did. Thorir's face fell.

'It was you? But why did he poison you? You're not one of his men.'

'Never mind that,' said Ketil. 'You were standing outside the door of Eyvind's hall while we were feasting. What did you see?'

'I – I don't know. I was just waiting for Thorgrim.'

'You'll have known the local men, no doubt. Their faces, anyway. So you'll have noted any strangers.'

'But then I wouldn't have known who they were, would I? How could I remember?'

'Try,' said Ketil, and his voice left no options. Thorir's eyes were panicky.

'I can't!'

'You probably can, Thorir,' said Sigrid hurriedly, with another glance at Ketil. 'It's just a matter of sorting things out, letting it all come back to you.'

'But it's not coming back!'

'Close your eyes.' She shuffled along the bench, supportive – closer to Ketil, but at the same time obstructing his way to Thorir just a little. 'Close your eyes, and imagine you're back there at the hall. What side of the door were you?'

'The right, looking from inside the hall. So people going out to the privy would be walking away from me.' His eyes opened briefly, with a look at Ketil, then closed again. 'I didn't really want anyone else to see me. They might have thought it was a bit odd.'

As it was, thought Sigrid. If he had just come into the hall – but then perhaps Eyvind did not want him seen too much around the place.

'Were you there for long?' she asked.

'I was there half the night!' he said. 'By the time I'd seen Thorgrim, it was too late to go anywhere else.'

'But surely he was out more than once?'

'Oh, he was. But the first time I could see he had his eyes on a woman, so I let him be. Thorgrim always liked a woman a bit above him, if he could find one.'

'So was that Borgny?' Sigrid asked.

'I didn't know that at the time,' he said, 'but yes, it was. I didn't know then, either, that he was married. Poor Vigdis! Women seemed to like him, but it never lasted.'

'Right, so you saw him follow Borgny out. Was anyone else nearby?'

'He was,' said Thorir reluctantly, opening his eyes again to point at Ketil. 'He went out before both of them, staggering around, and when they came back he was with them, sort of. The woman – Borgny – looked furious, and Thorgrim was cross, too. I thought maybe they'd been up to something and he –' Ketil again, 'had interrupted. So I didn't say anything. I mean, I should say that to start with I just wanted to make sure it was him. When I'd gone into the hall earlier, I'd heard the name Thorgrim mentioned but I didn't see who they were talking about, so I wasn't completely sure it was my brother they meant. And I hadn't seen him for … what, five years?'

'So he went back into the hall, and you waited again?'

'Yes.'

'Who else came out?'

'Oh,' said Thorir, closing his eyes again, 'everyone, in their turn. Kolbein came out – I knew his face and his name, for he called often at Gulbervig and traded, and I had bought spices from him once or twice. Very expensive – I couldn't really afford him. He went down to the beach to the Sea Stag and back, and back inside again.'

That was not the time, then, that Kolbein had told them about. Sigrid thought the hall ought to have had a guard on the door to account for everyone, if only they had known.

'Then I think it was Alfarin, maybe. Another one I didn't know till later, but he's the kind of man you notice. He stopped at the doorway, surveyed the bay, and headed off, and I thought he was a much more likely match for Borgny than my brother – of course, I didn't know he was *her* brother. I suppose you went out some time, Gunnar,' he added, relaxing a little more now as the evening came back to him, 'but I don't remember seeing you.'

Gunnar made a face.

'People don't see me,' he said.

'Then, I think, the hall started to quieten down. There's never much entertainment at Eyvind's hall, so I hear. I began to wonder if Thorgrim would come out again at all, but then he suddenly appeared, on his own. He looked sober enough, so I put a hand out and he jumped, and saw it was me. He was wary at first, but I said I just wanted to say good day to him – or good night, I suppose.

'So we stood and talked for a little. He told me he was married, and I said I was, too. I asked if he was still travelling and he said yes. Honestly, that's about all. I never even had the chance to bring up the subject of the silver. I think a few people came out past us while we stood there – you know, just one more visit to the privy before you settle down for the night, but we were just talking. Then someone staggered into us – him again,' he said, jerking his head at Ketil, 'and Thorgrim dropped a purse he was holding. Quite a big one, was the impression I had. I bent to pick it up for him –

and that must have been when I dropped that box, I think – but he was quick as lightning and swept it up out of my reach. He would have taken the box, too, in case it was worth anything. "I'd better go and put this in its place," he said, holding up the purse. "The wife's been wearing it, and she's complaining it's hurting her back." I nodded – I thought he meant he'd be back when he'd hidden it, but he wasn't.'

'And what about those people who came out while you were talking?' Sigrid asked gently. 'Who were they?'

'Kolbein was one, I'm sure,' said Thorir, after some thought and scrunched-closed eyes. 'He didn't go down to his ship, though he looked that way. He went round to the privy. And someone else … who was it? Let me think … After Kolbein – no, Kolbein didn't appear until after Thorgrim had left me. Then Vigdis came out – I was tucked back in, then, against the wall, sitting down on my pack. I thought she saw something, down on the shore, but from where I was sitting I couldn't see anything. She watched for a bit then went on round to the privy. I didn't know she was Thorgrim's wife, or I might have spoken to her, too, though to be honest I was tired enough after all that standing around. But …'

Something seemed to have struck him – a memory? Sigrid waited, praying everyone else would stay quiet, willing him to find what it was that lurked in his mind. She held her breath.

'But then Vigdis came back, and she didn't go into the hall.' The words came out sideways, as though he were straining to find them. 'She waited, like me, but on the other side of the door. And then two men came along.'

'Two men? Kolbein?' Skorri asked, and Sigrid shot him a glare. But Thorir had it now.

'Not Kolbein,' he said. 'He came later. No, it was Sibbi and Kjartan. And once they went into the hall, Vigdis followed them.'

XLVI

'DO YOU THINK he's telling the truth?'

Gunnar was the first to speak. Ketil was not sure that his nephew should be there – surely he should be off making cups and setting up his business? But he would need a workshop, and somewhere to live, and a means of buying wood to start himself off. How would he manage? He would need Ketil's help, no doubt – and would also need the murderer found so that no lingering suspicion hung over him like a sea fret. Ketil set the problem aside for now.

Thorir had gone, told to go and see to his patients up here on the Brough. Geirod was accompanying him in case he decided to wander further afield again. Even so, Skorri leaned in and looked around him before speaking.

'I think he's telling the truth,' he said, 'for that night. I still fancy Kolbein for killing Thorgrim. Then Thorir killed Vigdis to get the silver.'

Ketil nodded, not to show agreement but to acknowledge Skorri's contribution. He turned to Alf.

'I think he's lying,' said Alf, who had taken Thorir's vacated seat and was now leaning back luxuriously against the wall. 'He can't be as innocent as he pretends. If he's spent all these years hunting for the silver and blaming his brother for its loss, and then he's spent half the night standing in the dark waiting for a word with him, would they really just gossip about wives and travels? I think he followed Thorgrim down to the beach, maybe even believing his own silver was in that purse, and thumped him for it. When he saw it wasn't his silver, he left it – he's an honest man, at heart, but I reckon he killed his brother. And then I agree with Skorri – he killed Vigdis for the actual silver he wanted.'

Ketil nodded again. Gunnar looked confused.

'What do you think, then, Gunnar?' he asked, reluctantly encouraging. Gunnar swallowed hard.

'I think if he can poison people he could have killed them both. I thought he was a nice man until now! All he did for the people who were hurt when the ships were burned!'

'Very few men are consistently good or bad,' said Ketil. 'And hatred can grow inside families that never affects those outside them.'

This made Gunnar look even more confused, and he sat back, trying to work it out. Ketil turned to Sigrid.

'Go on, then,' he said with a smile.

'First,' she said, 'I think Thorir was telling the truth, mostly. When he told a lie he looked awkward, then corrected himself when he was challenged. I agree the conversation he had with Thorgrim was probably not as he told it, but otherwise I think he did expect Thorgrim to come back and carry on with whatever it was they were talking about – probably the silver. Because at some point he must have told Thorir that Vigdis knew where it was, so that Thorir followed Vigdis to St. Ninian's Isle and watched her dig it up. I don't think he followed Thorgrim down to the shore and killed him.'

'No, because it was Kolbein all along,' said Skorri, with a sigh of satisfaction. 'I told you. I'm with you, Sigrid!' He was close enough to lay an arm across her shoulders and draw her in for a quick sideways embrace of solidarity. Ketil frowned.

'You said "first",' he said. 'What's second?'

'Sorry,' she said to Skorri, 'I don't think Kolbein killed him, nor that Thorir killed Vigdis. I think Thorir was telling the truth. And what did he tell us? That after the moment we believe Thorgrim was killed – the event that Vigdis, standing in the shadows near the hall door, witnessed and the reason for her death later – Sibbi and Kjartan came back to the hall. We need to think about them.'

Skorri looked sorrowful, but joined in the general grunting of agreement.

'Where are they?' asked Ketil. There was no sign of them in the hall.

'Sibbi was saying his leg was much better,' said Gunnar. 'And he wanted fresh air.'

'Alf, go and find them and keep an eye on them. Let the gate guards know we're watching them – and Thorir.'

Alf rose from the bench like an otter off a rock, and left.

'Right,' said Ketil. 'What do we know about them? Previously we've dismissed them as having no reason to kill either Thorgrim or Vigdis. Gunnar, if you've overheard anything useful, now would be a good time to tell us.'

'I don't think I have,' said Gunnar. 'Sibbi's eyes are sharp. I think he probably notices a lot that's going on, even me.'

'We wondered if they were in exile,' Sigrid reminded him. Skorri raised his eyebrows.

'That might make sense,' he said. 'Aye, I could see that. They didn't care for Kolbein any more than I did – less, maybe.'

'They've mentioned being at a hall near Bergvin,' said Ketil. 'Does anyone remember the name of the lord? I think they've said it a couple of times.'

'Aye, Kjartan's always getting it wrong!' Gunnar laughed. 'You'd think he would know the name of his own leader! Not too bright, that one.' He shook his head, still grinning.

'Wait, though,' said Sigrid. 'He said it to me yesterday again. What was the name?'

'Isn't it Atli?' asked Ketil.

'That's what he corrected himself to. You were walking ahead with Sibbi, but Kjartan gave him a look as if he was scared Sibbi would have heard him getting it wrong again. But the name he gave first, the one he says is wrong, wasn't it Arinbjorn?'

'Was it?' said Gunnar. Skorri shrugged.

'I can't remember.'

'I'm sure it was,' said Sigrid, looking at Ketil.

'But – is that not the name of Alfarin's lord? Near Bergvin?' he said. 'Surely, if they were from the same hall one of them would have said something. There could well be two Arinbjorns.'

'Was there a father's name?' asked Skorri, but Sigrid shook her head.

'I don't think so. You could ask. Sibbi or Alfarin, either of them.'

'Or both – and see what they both say,' said Skorri, with a knowing smile. 'But surely, if Alfarin's lord exiled the pair of them, Sibbi and Kjartan, Alfarin would have known about it?'

'Hasn't Alfarin been away?' asked Sigrid. 'Borgny said she had been at King Harald's court, and Alfarin came to collect her. You heard about them there, didn't you, Gunnar? And if they were exiled, it was probably fairly recently. They were only just heading here from Bergvin.'

Ketil frowned, propping his chin on his hands and staring at the table. He tried to picture their progress, tried to fit what might have happened with what he knew of them. It was not much. Sibbi was confident to the point of arrogance, and Kjartan was his strong man. That was it.

'Alfarin didn't seem very happy at his lord's hall recently,' he said. 'If it's the same hall – what was it he said, Gunnar? A stranger had come in, some new man, and had his lord's ear?'

'That's right. That's what I heard in the King's court.'

'That might have led to disruption,' said Ketil. 'Falling out amongst the men. Maybe the new man had brought a hird of his own to add to Arinbjorn's – if it is Arinbjorn. Sibbi and Kjartan might have been involved somehow, made themselves unpopular. Or just not liked the way things were going.'

'I think we have to make sure of the name,' said Sigrid. 'Ketil, you'll have to talk to Alfarin. No one else can, unless it's Thorfinn.'

Skorri nodded agreement.

'I could speak to Sibbi when he comes back, sir,' he said. 'See if I can find out anything more from him.'

'I'm sure Kjartan said Arinbjorn,' said Sigrid. 'But whether Sibbi would confirm that or not, even if it is the truth, I'm not sure. Shall I speak to Borgny? She's quite friendly to me.' She met Ketil's eye again, and he knew she meant that Borgny had told her all about Thorgrim's attempted seduction. It was true, they seemed to be closer than Alfarin was with anyone here.

'Yes, do,' he said. 'She might not have been there in that hall so much recently, but Alfarin will have talked to her, and she'll know the general way things are, or were. She seems a sensible woman.'

Sigrid's lip twisted slightly, but she agreed.

'I'll do that as soon as may be,' she said. 'I think she's over in the longhouse again. I saw Alfarin go out with Thorfinn, I think.'

'So Alfarin is with Thorfinn,' said Ketil, 'Geirod is following Thorir, and Alf is on the trail of Sibbi and Kjartan – who are presumably together. Good. I'll see if I can find out where Thorfinn has taken his guest, and try for a little conversation with him.'

'What do you want me to do, sir?' asked Skorri. Ketil looked at him, and then at Gunnar. Another responsibility.

'Go with Gunnar and see if you can find some wood he can work, will you? Maybe down at the harbour. While you're there, see if anything interesting has washed in from the wreck of the Sea Stag.'

'Aye, sir,' said Skorri. Ketil did not have to explain to him that he wanted an eye kept on his nephew. Gunnar was still not clear of a murder accusation, but aside from that he seemed to have a knack for finding himself places to hear things – which was fine, as long as the people who were talking either did not mind, or did not know. Otherwise, Gunnar might find himself in danger. Having rediscovered him so recently, Ketil was surprised to find how reluctant he was to lose him again.

Skorri scrambled out over the bench and jerked his head at Gunnar, who seemed pleased enough to go with him. Ketil sat back from the table, rubbed his face, and looked at Sigrid.

'You really think it might be them, and not Thorir?' he asked.

'I think it's more than worth checking further. You know they were both out and around the place yesterday, when Vigdis was killed. Now we know – if Thorir is telling the truth – that they were out of the Gulbervig hall, too, at the right time to kill Thorgrim. I know they're not the only ones in that position, but they're the only ones we haven't properly considered.'

'Because they are the only ones with no obvious reason to kill Thorgrim or Vigdis.'

'That we know of.'

Ketil considered. Thorir, or Sibbi and Kjartan. Or Sibbi or Kjartan. Or, still, just maybe, Alfarin or Gunnar. There would be no consolation for Thorfinn in a list that vague. He would have to make some kind of progress, and soon.

'Right,' he said, and rose to step smoothly over the bench. 'Let's see what Borgny can tell you. And I'll go and look for her brother.'

XLVII

SIGRID WATCHED AS Ketil left the hall to find Alfarin, for a moment not really thinking about anything other than watching Ketil leaving the hall. He and Borgny would make a handsome couple, she told herself.

She continued to sit at the table after he had vanished, not wanting to rush into another conversation with Borgny without reflecting on all she had already learned about her, about Alfarin, and about their home and background before they boarded the Sea Stag. It was quiet in the hall at this time of the day: the women would be working in the longhouse, spinning and weaving, or in the brewhouse or dairy, while the men were in their workshops or the fields, or down at the harbour mending the boats damaged in the explosion. Or just talking about boats. She wondered briefly where Sibbi and Kjartan were, whether or not Alf would find them, what Alfarin and Thorfinn were up to, and where Thorir would lead Geirod and his dog. It felt as if she had been left behind, away from all the action. But she was probably the only one who could talk easily with Borgny, and Borgny was more likely to tell them about Alfarin's hall, in honesty, than Alfarin himself. Men tended to boast: Alfarin would want to show it and his lord in their best armour, weapons polished and ready.

What had Borgny already told her about herself and her home? Borgny had been away at the royal court, sent by Alfarin presumably to find a good husband – and she had succeeded, in

Bjorn Einarson. A very promising match, fit for someone of Borgny's beauty and intelligence. So Alfarin had come back to the court to take her to Orkney to marry Bjorn. Alfarin had been at his own hall up to then, and from what Gunnar had told Ketil, he had complained while he was at the King's court about some new man at his hall, someone who was too influential, and about his own lord's ambitions – was that right? Was she remembering correctly? She could make sure with Gunnar or Ketil later.

So Alfarin collected Borgny, and took her back home briefly before going to Bergvin to sail to Orkney. That diversion was what caused them to miss the news of Bjorn's death. Had Borgny said much about that? As far as Sigrid could remember, Borgny had barely mentioned her home and lord at all, except … Sigrid squeezed her eyes shut, picturing to herself that walk from Gulbervig to St. Ninian's Isle, when she and Borgny had started talking. Something had caused her some distress, made her sad. What was it?

She could feel the heather roots under her toes, smell the rich upland air, the gorse and the brambles, hear the birds above them. Borgny walked beside her, graceful even on that rough path. There was that ease of conversation that comes with walking, with not looking at one another, allowing the words to come out unimpeded by thoughts of interpreting the other person's expression. Borgny had told her about a friend – in fact, was it the lord's daughter? Granddaughter? There had been a seduction – there was a child, Sigrid thought, or that was her impression. And the father had left, gone before Borgny had seen him. Could it have been Sibbi?

Surely not. There was little charming about Sibbi. But maybe he and Kjartan had been complicit in some way? And exiled?

How would Borgny not have recognised them, though, if they belonged to her own hall? Sigrid tapped her fingers thoughtfully on the bench beside her, then squeaked at the tenderness. When would they heal?

The incomer, the new man that Alfarin resented – he could have brought his own hird with him. They had already mentioned that, hadn't they? The same way that Ketil had his three men, within Thorfinn's hird. Sibbi and Kjartan could have been amongst them. They could have arrived in Borgny's absence and been sent away before she returned. But surely Alfarin would have seen them?

Perhaps it depended on the size of the newcomer's following. Sibbi and Kjartan might not have been very prominent in it. Who was this newcomer, she wondered, with his bad influence on an ambitious lord? But that, at least, was surely a question they had no need to answer. Bergvin was a long way away from Birsay.

'Sorry! Forgot my bag!'

It was Gunnar, scuttling round to the other side of the table to root about under the bench where he had been sitting. He pulled out a sack with a shoulder strap and slung it over his head, beaming.

'I hope that's not your carving tools.'

He blushed.

'It is, actually. I was so excited to be off to see more around here I left them behind. It's all so interesting.' She smiled at one of his favourite phrases. 'And I keep wondering if I'll get word of my other uncle.'

'Your other uncle?' she asked in surprise.

'Yes. You maybe remember him. Thialfi? The youngest brother.'

'Yes, of course I remember Thialfi. He was a sweet child, though full of mischief. But Ketil told me he had gone to be a priest, gone to Rome. Have you heard from him? That will please Ketil.'

'We had word a year or so ago, maybe more,' said Gunnar, with a glance at the door. He was eager to be away. 'A trader came to Heithabyr with – not a message, really, only a bit of news. He had met Thialfi in Normandy, and Thialfi had said he was heading north. To here, to Orkney.' He spread his arms, as if to demonstrate where he meant. 'That's the other reason I came here. Both my uncles, in the same place! So I'm trying to find him.'

'Well, if he's still here, I'm sure you'll track him down,' said Sigrid. 'Priests don't tend to go unnoticed.'

'That's what I'm thinking,' said Gunnar happily. 'He's maybe on one of the other islands, though, not on Hrossey.'

'Exactly,' said Sigrid. 'He could be anywhere.'

Gunnar raised a hand in farewell, and made for the door. For a moment Sigrid sat motionless, lost in memories she had hoped never to revisit. Then she shook herself, stood, and went to find Borgny.

It only took a moment: Borgny had wandered into the hall as

if at a loose end, and was standing examining one of the newly completed woven hangings that Ingibjorg had commissioned for the walls. Extravagant they might look (and indeed Sigrid thought they were ridiculously grand, with their gold and silver thread brought from Francia), but they had certainly cut down the draughts at the top of the hall. So far they had remained undamaged and fairly clean, even on the rowdiest nights.

'Ketil says these are your work, too,' she said. 'They are beautiful. Is it your own design?'

'Yes, based on what Ingibjorg asked for,' said Sigrid. Very loosely based, in the end. When had Borgny and Ketil been discussing wall-hangings? 'She wanted ships, mostly, and eagles, things to indicate her royal ancestry.'

Borgny shot a look at Sigrid. It seemed that Ingibjorg had already brought her royal ancestry into the conversation, perhaps more than once.

'What skill!' said Borgny. 'If I ever had a hall – or even a longhouse – to adorn, I should love to have something like these. Would you undertake such a task again?'

'I won't be doing anything like them for a while yet, not until my fingers heal properly,' said Sigrid, wondering how soon Borgny might be looking for them. The hall at Buckquoy could certainly do with something against the draughts. But that would be a task demanding tact. Ingibjorg might be flattered that Borgny had chosen the same artist, but if she imagined even for a moment that Borgny's were better than Ingibjorg's, there would be trouble for Borgny and Sigrid. 'But I enjoyed doing these. I usually work on a smaller scale.'

'Your braids, of course.'

Sigrid smiled. She could not help liking the girl, despite everything. Which was just as well, if Borgny were going to be lady at Buckquoy.

'That's right. That's how I make a living.'

'It must be strange to live alone,' said Borgny, turning and surveying the empty hall. 'I don't think I've ever been alone. When our parents died, I went to live in Arinbjorn's household.'

'That's the lord of the hall where you come from, isn't it?' Sigrid's spine prickled, Buckquoy forgotten. It was the name that Kjartan had used, then corrected himself. She was positive.

'That's right. Alfarin says he's not a bad man, but he is ambitious.'

'Do you agree?'

'Hm, I think so. Alfarin sees him as his lord and his leader. I mostly see him as my friend's father, I suppose.'

Sigrid took a breath.

'That's your friend who had the – ah – misfortune you were telling me about?'

'That's right. I'm sorry I poured out all my woes that day.' Borgny propped herself against the nearest table, fair head hanging. 'I felt I should have stayed with her longer, but my brother was anxious to get away and make the final arrangements with Bjorn.' She could say his name now without that shadow passing so clearly over her face. Sigrid thought that if Alfarin could find her someone new, someone promising, she would be happy soon enough. But she needed to pay attention, and ask questions.

'There was a child, wasn't there?'

Borgny nodded sadly.

'There was a man she was intended to marry – I'm not sure if they had come to an actual betrothal, or whether it was just a plan. Of course he was furious.'

Furious enough to have Sibbi and Kjartan exiled?

'Someone in your father's hird?'

'Yes. I didn't like him, I have to say, but I barely knew him. She was pleased enough with the match, and so was her father. And maybe I was being unfair, for it was Alfarin who told me about this newcomer, setting the hall on its ears. I didn't like him before I ever met him.'

'But would he still take her?' That newcomer again. He seemed to have had an undue effect on events far away from Bergvin.

'It had not been decided when I left,' said Borgny. 'She could be married now, for all I know: they might have decided to make haste. Though everyone knew it was that other man's child.'

'Did you ever find out who this other man was? Who it was who seduced her?'

'She never named him to me,' said Borgny. 'She said she could not bear to. He had charmed her and seduced her and abandoned her – and she discovered later that he was married, too.

Well,' Borgny corrected herself. 'She said she discovered later. I wondered, when she was telling me, if she had had her suspicions at the time. He seemed to have cast a spell over her.'

'But if everyone knew that the child was his,' said Sigrid, puzzled, 'surely someone in the hall knew his name? Or talked about him?'

'Maybe they did,' said Borgny, 'but Alfarin has always counselled against listening to gossip. All I know is that the man was a merchant, and he and his wife came from somewhere in these islands. Oh!'

Sigrid looked at her. Borgny had her hand to her mouth, eyes wide in shock. Sigrid thought she might look much the same herself.

'What I told you - about what Thorgrim said to me – what he tried to persuade me to – oh, Sigrid! How stupid have I been? Do you think it was Thorgrim who seduced my friend?'

XLVIII

THORFINN HAD TAKEN Alfarin to see the chapel. Ketil found them there, which was lucky, as there was still not very much to see.

'As I travelled back from Rome I sought donations from various monasteries and churches to furnish it,' Thorfinn was explaining. 'Everyone was most generous, but nothing has yet arrived. Father Tosti here has written to some of the donors, but it seems that some treasure has gone astray.'

'It may be God's will,' said Father Tosti, a small, dark-haired man with a wide-eyed smile and a self-deprecating attitude. 'Sometimes God works in the gifts of others, and sometimes he might prefer it if we gave him our own works.'

Thorfinn smiled.

'Tosti can find the good in almost any situation,' he said, and turned to him. 'When are you planning the burial of that poor woman Vigdis?'

Vigdis' body lay covered on a trestle in the tiny chapel. There would be no room for her and the congregation on Sunday.

'Tomorrow, my lord, if Ketil is content too?' Tosti looked to Ketil, standing unobtrusively to one side of the doorway.

'I'm content,' said Ketil. 'I don't see any sense in delay.'

'Then if you'll excuse me I'll go and tell the women,' said Tosti. 'They can make preparations.' He bowed, and nodded to Ketil as he trotted off outside.

'It is nevertheless a beautiful place,' said Alfarin, turning slowly to take in the small squared building with its curving chancel at the east end. 'There is a sense of peace about it that not every church can quite capture, even the grandest I have seen.'

Thorfinn looked pleased. Ketil found Alfarin's words welcome, too: there was something about the chapel, a quietude even when the wind and rain lashed across the headland outside.

'That comes, no doubt, through Tosti. I should like very much to install a bishop here, but Tosti does not wish to be a bishop – he murmured something about Paul's letter to Timothy – and I could not in all conscience install a bishop to take charge over him. Though the accommodation for a larger community is all ready. We had a man from Colonia stay there not long ago.' Thorfinn hesitated slightly: that visit had not ended well. 'I should be happy to show you, if you are interested.'

'I should be delighted to see it. Such places interest me very much. But perhaps, just for a moment, we could pray here.'

Thorfinn looked to Ketil, a look of surprise. Alfarin seemed to be a like-minded guest. Ketil had seen it on St. Ninian's Isle, but it was new to Thorfinn. The three men knelt in silence, and Ketil wondered, as he often did, if Thorfinn's increasing adherence to the new religion – and rejection of the old gods – was at the base of King Harald's mistrust of him. Or maybe not: maybe King Harald was just being cautious.

Prayers over, Thorfinn rose and led them out of the chapel. Tosti had already returned, quietly, as they knelt: Vigdis would not be left alone.

'Had you something you wished to say to me, Ketil?' Thorfinn asked. Was he less angry than earlier, or was it just the effect of the little chapel?

'I was hoping to have a word or two with Alfarin, my lord,' said Ketil, 'if he has the time.'

'We could walk and talk at the same time?' Thorfinn suggested to Alfarin. Alfarin, with a look at Ketil, willingly agreed.

'Are these words to do with the deaths of Thorgrim and Vigdis?' Alfarin asked, keen to make sure he established the terms of their conversation before they started.

'Yes, they are, though at first they might not seem wholly relevant,' said Ketil, keeping his tone polite. Sigrid had told him once that he sounded severe when he was questioning people, and he knew that would not go down well with Alfarin.

'Curious,' said Alfarin. 'My lord Thorfinn, do you know what these irrelevant questions are?'

'Not yet,' said Thorfinn with a light laugh. 'I trust Ketil to know what he is doing.'

Well, that was something.

'Go on, then,' said Alfarin, just as they reached the doorway of the monastic quarters Thorfinn had had built near the chapel. Apart from Tosti, who did not always stay there, they were currently empty. Stone built, with several small rooms, they bore little relation to the longhouses and workshops around them. Alfarin was distracted.

'I can see you have travelled, Thorfinn! These could almost be in Rome!'

He explored, enthusing over each detail, with Thorfinn growing expansive in his description of what he had seen in the south, and how he had turned it to his account here at Birsay, and what he hoped it would become. Ketil gave up on any questioning until the three men were outside again, and Alfarin, delighted with all he had seen, turned again to Ketil.

'Now, then, I am ready.'

'Thank you. Can you tell me, please, about your home? The lord of your local hall, what he is like.'

Alfarin said nothing for a moment, staring at Ketil.

'You are quite right,' he said. 'I cannot see how that could possibly be relevant.'

There was another fractional pause. Then Thorfinn said,

'Well, you are a stranger here, and when strangers arrive in a place I think it is natural to want to know something of who they are and where they are from. You've asked lots of questions about Birsay and the Brough and my other lands. I should be delighted if you would give us some idea of – well, exactly what Ketil said. I'm sure it would be very interesting – your lord and I might have something to learn from each other.'

Thorfinn at his diplomatic best. Ketil almost smiled. Alfarin looked as if he might still refuse, then his shoulders relaxed.

'Well, of course. I only wondered what it might have to do with Thorgrim or Vigdis. As I understand it, Vigdis was from these islands, and Thorgrim from Hjaltland, was he not?'

Ketil did not answer, and Alfarin nodded.

'Arinbjorn Egilson is the lord of my hall, where my father was before me and his father before that,' he said. 'Arinbjorn is ten years older than me, and it has been an honour to serve him. He is skilled in everything that a lord should be.' The words came out stiffly.

'Near Bergvin, you said?' asked Thorfinn.

'To the north east,' said Alfarin. 'Two days' walk, or thereabouts. Bergvin is our nearest harbour of any size.'

'I gather you are in good standing with Arinbjorn,' said Ketil. He was sure that was the name Kjartan had given for their lord, then corrected himself.

'Of course.' But Alfarin looked up briefly as he said it, seeking guidance from somewhere.

'And Arinbjorn is in equally good standing with King Harald,' said Ketil, pushing on patiently.

'In very good standing,' said Alfarin, 'though he would always like to be better, of course.'

'What man is not ambitious?' asked Ketil lightly, and noted Alfarin's eyes tighten briefly. 'I had heard it said that someone at Arinbjorn's court was encouraging his ambition – perhaps helping him to find more favour in King Harald's eyes?'

'That sounds interesting,' said Thorfinn. 'Is that so, Alfarin? Because sometimes that can be a great move forward for a hird – someone new coming in with ideas and energy and willing to place them at the disposal of the lord. And sometimes,' he went on almost casually, 'sometimes, if the lord does not manage it well, it can cause division and strife. Old advisers feel themselves cut out – and quite rightly, too. Why should their counsel be ignored just because they have been there for years?'

'Exactly,' said Alfarin, unable to keep silent any longer. 'That's exactly what happened. This new fellow, with his hird of rough followers hardly fit to grace a hall of any quality – I saw he had his eye on Arinbjorn's daughter, a match I would have – well, anyway I was pleased enough to make an excuse to go and fetch Borgny from the royal court to bring her here. I could not have tolerated the man for much longer. It was as if he could see all Arinbjorn's dreams and ambitions, and turned them so that they could be achieved – yet in some way it seemed that that achievement was only really good for him, not for Arinbjorn – or anyone else in the hall. You could see that whatever credit Arinbjorn might get with the King, Kalf was going to get the glory.'

'Kalf?'

Thorfinn's question was so sharp it could have cut through stone.

'Yes, Kalf,' said Alfarin. 'That was the name of the newcomer. Kalf Arnason. A cunning, devious, divisive ... I am sorry, perhaps you know him? But if you do –'

'If I do, I would concur with all you say,' said Thorfinn. 'Kalf Arnason – I should have known.'

After that, Thorfinn decided they all needed a cup of strong wine, and a comfortable bench to sit on and hear more of Alfarin's story. The wind was angling around the chapel and the monastic buildings, catching the tails of their cloaks and chilling their fingers and faces.

'Did you know?' he asked Ketil as they walked back to the hall. His hand was approving on Ketil's shoulder.

'I knew there was something that would make it worth asking more,' said Ketil honestly. 'But take care: Alfarin might not be entirely friendly, even if he is hostile to Kalf.'

Thorfinn looked at him sideways, and nodded, frowning.

The hall was quiet. Ketil wondered if Sigrid was in the longhouse, talking with Borgny. His men must still be on their various errands. Thorfinn called for the wine, and ignoring his high seat he took a place near it at a table, gesturing Alfarin and Ketil to sit near him.

'Tell me, if you will, what clever ideas Kalf has had for furthering Arinbjorn's ambitions? I fear, knowing Kalf, that some of them might involve me.'

Alfarin pushed his cloak back over his shoulders, then propped his arms on the edge of the table, winding his fingers together. It seemed to give him time to think. Ketil reminded himself that Gunnar had heard Alfarin was supposed to be here spying on behalf of King Harald: he had not had the chance to warn Thorfinn, but all being well his few words to Thorfinn outside would be enough to make him cautious.

'Kalf is keen to encourage Arinbjorn in anything that might

please King Harald,' Alfarin began, keeping his voice quite low. 'He sent messages to the King with me when I went to collect Borgny. The principal thing,' and he stopped and drew a deep breath, 'the principal thing that Kalf was offering – in Arinbjorn's name – was a ... now, what was the word? A recovery, I think, of these islands, Hjaltland and Orkney. In the belief that their earl – you, my lord,' he explained to Thorfinn, as if it were not obvious – 'had turned traitor to King Harald, and given your allegiance instead to Scotland.'

'King Harald knows well the balance I must strike here,' said Thorfinn, growling a little. 'Half my kin are Scots. These islands lie closer to Ness than to Nordvegr, though Hjaltland is the other way around. I have, of course, visited his court and pledged my allegiance to Harald.'

An allegiance lightly held, Ketil thought. But still Thorfinn would not be hostile to Harald.

'You'll be pleased to know that the King was not wholly convinced,' said Alfarin. 'He sent a man to visit the islands, to visit this place, to see you and find out, for the King, what you were doing and how much of a threat you might be.'

'Did he, indeed?' said Thorfinn levelly, all his attention on Alfarin. 'Do you happen to know who this man is?'

'Oh, yes,' said Alfarin. He straightened his shoulders, and met Thorfinn's gaze, unflinching. 'I am that man.'

XLIX

'CAN WE GO outside?' Borgny asked with a shudder. 'I feel the need for some fresh air – clear that man out of my mind.'

They wrapped shawls about them, Borgny's a beautiful nailbinding concoction in several colours with embroidery along the edges, and Sigrid's a browny grey hotchpotch of wool not good enough for anything else, half-beaten, half-woven into place. It had spent the previous night as a layer on her bed. It was, however, proof against the wind, and she suspected that Borgny's was not quite so thick. Both folded their arms around themselves as they left the hall, holding their shawls down against the wind. The wet air soaked their faces at once.

'So you think Vigdis knew what Thorgrim was doing?' Sigrid asked, paying no attention to Borgny's desire to forget. 'With both you and your friend?'

'That's the thing,' said Borgny, stopping and looking about, wondering which way to go. Sigrid turned right, in the general direction of the gate but with the intention only of wandering around the settlement, not straying too far. At any moment, Ketil or one of his men might appear with news, or demanding to know what she herself had found out. Borgny followed. 'The thing,' she repeated, catching up to walk by Sigrid's side. 'I remember Ali, my friend, told me that the wife turned up just as she and the man – Thorgrim, if it was he – were about to leave. Before Ali realised she was expecting a child. The wife said she would not tell Arinbjorn what had happened if Ali paid her. Ali was terrified, of course. She gave the woman an arm ring and a pair of brooches, and prayed never to see her again.'

'But then of course everyone did find out, including presumably Arinbjorn?' said Sigrid.

'Yes, that's right. But the man and his wife were away.'

'They weren't deliberately exiled?'

'No, they'd gone before anyone but Ali knew what had happened.'

'There was no one else complicit? No one else they could blame?'

'No, not at all!' Borgny looked at her in surprise. 'Why would there be?'

'Just a thought,' said Sigrid. 'It's just, well ... Well, if Thorgrim did that, to your friend, and Vigdis was part of it – and that fits very nicely with what we think Vigdis might have been doing to get herself killed, too – then someone might indeed have wanted to kill them. Not even necessarily someone at Arinbjorn's hall. If Thorgrim and Vigdis did this to Ali, and to you, then who knows how many other well-born girls they might have tried it with? Did Vigdis try to get silver from you?'

'No, but then I think Thorgrim would have intended to go further before that point, only that of course someone killed him.' She frowned, and added suddenly, 'I hope you don't think I killed him!'

'I don't think I would have blamed you if you had,' said Sigrid with a grin. 'Nasty and greedy, the pair of them. If we're right.'

'Oh, I think we're right,' said Borgny. 'But who did kill them? I'm sure it wasn't Alfarin, either, before you ask,' she said. 'He would have told that lord at Gulbervig straight away. He's like that, my brother. A bit dull, but a good man.'

That had been Sigrid's general impression, so she said nothing. She had never had a brother to comment on. Ketil, though, had had two, Njal, Gunnar's father, and Thialfi, the priest. The priest who had been journeying to Orkney, and had not been seen since. She shook herself.

'Is there someone else who might have killed Thorgrim because of what he did to your friend?' she asked, forcing herself to concentrate on the matters at hand. 'Could Arinbjorn have sent anyone?'

'Surely they would have travelled with us, then,' said Borgny, 'and been on the Sea Stag, too. And we recognised no one there.'

'Would you know all of Arinbjorn's hird?'

'I think so. And any I wouldn't know, Alfarin would. And anyway, wouldn't Arinbjorn have told Alfarin to look out for them?'

'Then it must have been for something else he did,' said Sigrid, dismayed. 'We might never find out what, or who.'

'There's Ali's betrothed,' Borgny reminded her. 'We haven't considered him. He could have sent someone – he was furious!'

'And would you know his hird?' Sigrid was suddenly hopeful. She had forgotten that wretched nameless newcomer.

'No, not at all, for he arrived while I was away at the royal court. Alfarin might have known them, but I think he had as little to do with the man as possible.'

'So he could have sent someone, and they could be here now, and you would not know them?'

'No, indeed. But who could it be?'

'Let's start with who the newcomer was,' said Sigrid, admitting at last the necessity. 'What was his name and where was he from?'

'His name is Kalf,' said Borgny, 'Kalf Arnason. From Nordvegr, I believe. But what's the matter? Do you know him?'

'Not personally,' said Sigrid, when she could breathe again. 'No, not to meet. But I know the name. Everyone in these islands knows the name of Kalf Arnason.'

Borgny subjected her to a sharp look.

'And I should say he is as popular here as he is with my brother Alfarin. I had no idea he was so well-known. Well.' She was clearly curious, but prepared to wait for a better time for the story. 'But if Kalf sent someone, as I said, who did he send?'

Sigrid glanced around. They had been walking in a rough circle, had come round the back of the chapel and the monastic quarters, and were approaching the area where Thorfinn intended his replacement bathhouse to be – the place where Sibbi had been found, after Vigdis was killed. No one was close to them. They had spotted Thorir and Geirod amongst the longhouses on their way, and Skorri and Gunnar were over to their left, once more with the pig man.

'What do you say to the idea that he might have sent Sibbi and Kjartan?' she asked in a low voice.

Borgny, too, looked about her.

'I wondered about Kolbein,' she said.

'I think there was a connexion – he was doing something for Kalf. But Kolbein could not have killed Vigdis. And Sibbi and Kjartan could have.'

'Working together? Oh,' she said, 'I do not like to think of men we have travelled with for so long doing such a thing! I suppose we have known for a while that it was one of us – that it would make little sense otherwise. But to give them names, to say not this one, but that one – that is ice in my heart.'

'I know,' said Sigrid, 'but it has to be faced.'

'Not by us! Surely the men can deal with it – Ketil, and Thorfinn, and my brother …'

But Sigrid could see that she did not really mean it.

'A woman has been murdered, and we care as much as any man, don't we? So if we have ideas, or see things, or hear things, we must use them just as a man would. Though granted, if it comes to a fight,' she said with a grin, 'I'd rather Ketil dealt with it.'

'Are you and Ketil –'

'Just old friends,' said Sigrid smartly. 'I daresay Ingibjorg has told you all about him, and I daresay Thorfinn has his plans, too. He's a good man – though as he is almost like a brother to me I am loth to admit it!' Her smiled was a little more forced this time. Why was she saying this? Did she really want Borgny and Ketil to marry? Or was it just that she knew it was going to happen, and she was preparing herself to accept it?

And brothers again. She would rather not think about brothers.

'Anyway,' she said, 'the day Vigdis died, she was found away over there, where the cliff has fallen. Kjartan had us out looking for Sibbi, who was managing to walk further than he had before. And Sibbi was found just over there, where they're planning the new bathhouse.

'Why is there no one working there just now?'

'We're waiting for wood. Very few trees here.'

'Oh! I had seen that the houses were stone, but it had never occurred to me – of course. How strange.'

'He could have pushed Vigdis over the edge and then come here, I think,' said Sigrid, not interested in a lack of trees. 'It's muddy, and he could easily have fallen. But was there some other reason for distancing himself from where Vigdis was? I wonder.'

They were right at the edge of the shallow pit dug for the foundations of the bathhouse. She jumped down, leaving Borgny with her fine skirts and boots standing on the edge. The builders had already collected a quantity of the local flat stones for the walls, heaping them like so many stale flatbreads in one corner. She stepped closer to take a look. The heap was so irregular it had any number of hollows and holes between the stones. She crouched down.

Was there something there? And if so, was it what she was hoping for?

She reached in with her clumsy bandaged fingers, trying to loop them around a thin brown thing – a twig? A piece of string? No, a leather thong, just as she had thought. She grabbed it, and tugged gently. There was some resistance, as if whatever it was attached to was wedged in, shoved in hard, perhaps, amongst the stone. She leaned in further, trying to touch the thing itself. More leather, worn and soft, as far as she could judge through her bandages – she needed to be careful, or it might tear.

'Sigrid!' Borgny called. 'Sigrid, what are you doing?'

'Just a minute!' she called over her shoulder. She was going entirely by touch, but it seemed to help if she shut her eyes to concentrate. Could she grab a fold of the leather? It was difficult. If she folded it between her knuckles, rather than trying to use her fingertips, she might just ...

'Sigrid!' More urgent this time. 'Sigrid, you need to get up here!'

'I'm nearly there!'

'Sigrid!' Distantly she heard other voices, as if Borgny had turned to speak to someone else. The thing under the stones had all her attention. With the thong wrapped around her hand, and her fingers clamped around what was almost a handful of the leather, she eased the thing slowly towards the light, sliding it around a couple of sharp corners, then finally pulling it free. It landed on the earth in front of her, between the stones and her knees. It was a purse – Vigdis' purse.

'See?' She twisted round and called back up to Borgny. 'Oh.'

Beside Borgny, as if they had just fallen into conversation, were Sibbi and Kjartan. And if they had even thought of pretending their innocence, the look on Kjartan's face – and even Sibbi's – when they saw what Sigrid had found, was enough to say they knew exactly what it was, and how it had got there. And somehow each of the men had drawn a knife.

For a moment, nobody moved at the edge of the building pit. Over behind Sibbi and Kjartan, Sigrid was distantly aware of Alf, who had been following them, slipping towards the little gathering. But Borgny was very close to Sibbi: he had only to reach out, only to seize her arm, or the tail of that beautiful shawl … And what could Sigrid do, down here on her knees in the mud?

Then everything happened at once. Alf called out, and Kjartan turned. Sigrid heaved the heavy purse, and flung it at Sibbi's knees, as high as she could manage. Sibbi's hand flickered, and Borgny fell, landing heavily down beside Sigrid. Alf sprinted up, and Sibbi and Kjartan turned and ran.

L

THORFINN HAD NO chance to ask Alfarin what he meant, nor Ketil to admit that he already knew. There was a burst of shouting from outside, and Ketil recognised Alf's voice.

'Excuse me, my lord,' he said, already swinging over the bench. His axe was in his hand before he had reached the hall door.

Outside Kjartan shot past, panting, eyes fixed on the gate. Alf reached out an arm even as Ketil watched and seized Sibbi, pulling him off his feet and standing on his knife arm. Ketil went after Kjartan.

Kjartan evidently thought that with his weight all he would have to do was to charge at the guards like a battering-ram on legs to get through and out and free. But the guards had heard his heavy tread and were ready for him, braced with shields and axes. Kjartan stumbled against them, struggling, until Ketil came up behind him and twisted one hand behind his back.

'Calm down,' he said in Kjartan's ear. 'You're going nowhere. Not now.'

Thorfinn, already at the hall door, called to a few of his men to take Sibbi and Kjartan inside. As Ketil came closer with Kjartan, Thorfinn met his eye.

'A moment, my lord.'

'The lady Borgny is injured, sir,' said Alf, a long arm around the neck of a wriggling Sibbi.

'Get off, you great fool!' cried Sibbi. 'What are you grabbing me for? I've done nothing!'

'He was the one who injured her,' said Alf, pushing him away to his new captor.

'If you had done nothing, why were you running?' asked Ketil, but already he was following Alf to wherever Borgny was. Not another death, he prayed. Please, not another one.

'Sigrid is with her,' said Alf, and at once Ketil pictured Sigrid injured, too. How could he have let this happen?

Alf, at a jog, led him back to the building site where the new bathhouse was to be. In the pit sat Sigrid, and Borgny lay beside her, clutching her wrist.

'I think she's all right,' Sigrid called, as soon as they were close enough. 'He made a mess of her nice shawl, though.'

They were both pale, he thought, slowing as he reached the lip of the foundation pit. There was something lying on the ground.

'Isn't this where Sibbi was found, when he went missing?' Sigrid was asking. Ketil nudged the damp purse with his toe. 'I found that under the rocks here. I think it's Vigdis'.'

'You think he took it and hid it?' asked Ketil. He picked up the purse, and opened it carefully. Sigrid helped Borgny to her feet, and Borgny stepped forward for a closer look, rubbing her side. Sigrid picked out one object.

'A string of good amber beads,' she said. 'As mentioned by Alf. It's definitely Vigdis' purse.'

'I'm not absolutely sure,' said Borgny, 'but I think that arm ring there belongs to my friend Ali. Arinbjorn's daughter. Mother, we think, of Thorgrim's child.' She glanced around at Sigrid.

'Reluctant mother,' Sigrid added. 'Are you sure you're all right?'

'Just bruised,' Borgny smiled. 'He was in too much haste to be accurate.'

'Thorgrim's child?' Ketil reminded them. He was beginning to see the picture, he thought.

'Thorgrim seduced Ali, Borgny's friend,' said Sigrid. 'At least, we're fairly sure it was Thorgrim. And Vigdis, it appears, then got Ali to pay her some silver to keep quiet, and Vigdis and Thorgrim left the hall and travelled on – perhaps to try the same thing again elsewhere.'

'But you're not sure it was Thorgrim,' said Alf, helping

Borgny up out of the pit with a graceful hand.

'If it wasn't,' said Ketil, 'then Sibbi and Kjartan would not, presumably, have killed him.'

'Exactly,' said Sigrid. 'Ali was betrothed to that newcomer we keep hearing about, at Arinbjorn's hall. And guess who that is?'

'Kalf,' said Ketil, and smiled at her expression. 'Kalf sent Sibbi and Kjartan, and by chance Kolbein, too – no doubt he had no particular plan to send them all together, but he would have enjoyed the complications it caused, wouldn't he?' He put out a hand to help her, too. 'We'd better go and tell Thorfinn everything – though I think he knows most of it now.'

'We were just obeying Kalf's orders,' said Sibbi, somewhere between defiant and deferential. It was not pleasant to watch. 'Just like Kolbein was.'

'If you expect that to distract me,' said Thorfinn, 'it doesn't. We had worked out who had sent Kolbein.'

'Course you had, my lord. Kolbein was a fool. He wasn't supposed to go firing his new weapon just at anything, and not out in the open like that. He was too excited to be careful.'

'We're talking about you, and what you did,' said Thorfinn. 'You killed Thorgrim.'

'Kjartan did,' said Sibbi at once. Kjartan looked at him sadly.

'I doubt Kjartan worked it all out himself,' said Thorfinn. 'You said yourself that he is there for his strength, and you for the ideas. Surely you weren't just bragging?'

'Well. Kalf told us he wanted Thorgrim dead, because of what he did to a girl Kalf wants to marry. Vigdis saw us, but to be honest she needed killing anyway. She was in on all Thorgrim did: she got the women he seduced to pay her to keep quiet, you know? And then she tried that on us – told us we needed to pay her silver or she would tell you we had killed Thorgrim. That was stupid. You don't try that on men who have already killed, do you? But then Kjartan said he didn't want to kill a woman, so we had to wait until my leg was better. What a nuisance! We could have been long gone.'

'So you throttled her and pushed her off the cliff, then made off with her purse.'

'Only to get some silver back that Kalf reckoned she had

taken. The amount of silver those two had between them! When we killed Thorgrim – when Kjartan killed Thorgrim – he had a purse that weighed nearly as much as me, but the things we were looking for weren't in it. We're honest men,' he said, with a smug look that Ketil would happily have smacked. 'We left it with his body.'

'Which you had dragged over to the rocks.' Thorfinn glanced at Ketil, making sure he had the details right.

'We didn't want anyone interested in the Sea Stag, for Kalf's sake. Kolbein was busy enough talking about that old tub without us drawing attention to it.'

'Why didn't Kalf just kill Thorgrim in Nordvegr? He could have admitted it and paid a fine, and saved himself a lot of trouble.'

'Well, for one thing, my lord, Thorgrim and Vigdis were well away before Kalf found out what they'd done. And that didn't please him. And for another, that's not really the way Kalf works, is it?' He smiled a smile so slippery you could have used it instead of bear grease. 'Kalf likes to complicate things. It always causes more trouble that way, doesn't it, my lord?'

Thorfinn was still angry. You could see it in the economy of his movements, the fixed expression on his face. But he was not angry now with Ketil, or anyone on the Brough – not even with Sibbi and Kjartan, though they were going to be unwilling passengers on the next boat heading south, away from Birsay and away from any chance of reporting back to Kalf for a long time. With Kalf himself, though, Thorfinn was furious.

'I'll go back to King Harald, if you wish me to,' said Alfarin, 'and tell him all that Kalf has done.' He gave a wriggle of his usually steady shoulders. 'As your man, should you accept me.'

Thorfinn looked at him.

'You'd change your allegiance so readily?'

'My allegiance to Arinbjorn has been wilting for some time, since Kalf arrived. I cannot fight Kalf there, but I can here. If you'll have me.'

'I will. Thank you.' Ketil knew that Thorfinn would be keeping an eye on Alfarin, nevertheless, but for himself he thought that the man was sincere. He might go back to his hall when all this was done, where his grandfather and father had belonged before him, but for now he was Thorfinn's.

'I'll go with him,' Ketil heard Borgny tell Sigrid, in a low voice. 'Who knows what we might find out? And I hope, when I return, your hands will have healed and we can talk about braid!'

'I'd even stretch to wall hangings,' said Sigrid, 'if you needed them.'

Ketil wondered why Borgny might need wall hangings. Perhaps her brother had some other husband in mind already. He hoped the man would be good enough for her, for she was a lovely woman with a bright mind. Almost as good as Sigrid.

Sigrid ... he needed to speak to Thorfinn, now that he was in favour again. And preferably when Ingibjorg was not there to interfere. And then he would have to speak to Sigrid – that was a much more terrifying prospect.

He watched her for a moment, while Thorfinn issued his various instructions for the second little fleet of warships he intended to send, with more armaments than the first pair, up to Hjaltland. This time they would be more than ready for trouble, and have every eye open for anything they could discover about Kalf's intentions. The matter of the murders was done with, and he would have thought that Sigrid would be pleased, even with the threat of whatever Kalf was planning hanging over them. But she seemed far away, and unhappy. Was it her hands? Were they not healing fast enough? Was she worried about how she was going to live if they did not heal properly? There he could help her, though he knew that even if she were not worried about payments she would yearn to be making things. And she could cause a lot of bother if she were bored, he was well aware. He smiled to himself at the thought, at a wide range of memories.

She had disappeared in the direction of her longhouse before supper, carrying with her some sausage that Bolla the maid had saved for her from the evening's cooking. So surely she would be in a good mood, and even if Gnup were there, too, he might be able to persuade her outside for a few words. The evening was fine. If it all went wrong, he would at least have that consolation.

He joined his men for their preparatory wash and comb before they went in to supper.

'I'll see you later,' he said to Skorri. 'I just need a word with Sigrid.'

He thought his words sounded casual, but Skorri met his eye, and clapped him on the arm. Alf glanced back at them, paused, and raised his eyebrows. He had not said anything to either of them. How could they possibly know his intentions? Frowning, he brushed down his shirt, pulled his cloak around him, and set off.

The door of the longhouse was open, but Sigrid was already outside, standing at the wall overlooking the nettle patch where he had found her before. Wasn't there something about nettles growing where land had been disturbed? Her hands were wound tight into her shawl. Gnup, he could hear, was inside, presumably cooking the sausage. Was this his opportunity?

'Good evening,' he said. She turned at once, and nodded to him. Wordlessly she led the way back to the front of the house, perching on the stone where she normally did her weaving, when the weather was fine. He slid down to sit beside her as he often had before, legs stretched out, eyes on the view down and across to the Brough. He could see the lit doorway of the hall, torches flaring outside, shapes of men congregating. Some would be going to the chapel to watch by Vigdis' body: tomorrow they would bury her. Tonight ... well, what? What was he supposed to say?

'I had a word with Thorfinn this evening, before I came over here,' he said.

'I gather he's happy with you again,' she said. 'That's good. Everything will be settled.'

'In time to fight Kalf, by the sound of it,' he said, trying to make a kind of joke of it. He had discussed Kalf quite enough for one day. 'But never mind that – that wasn't what I was discussing with Thorfinn.'

He took a chance, and turned to see her face. She looked – panicky.

'What's the matter?' he asked. Whatever it was, maybe it could be cleared out of the way first.

'I have something I need to tell you,' she said.

'What?' Suddenly he had a feeling that it was going to be something he had no wish to know. 'I mean – can't it wait?'

'No. I need to tell you. I need to confess.'

'To confess?' He tried to laugh, but it came out like a choking sound. 'What on earth do you need to confess?'

She turned and faced him, so close – so close. She drew a deep breath.

'I think I know what happened to your brother. To the priest – Thialfi. I think – oh, Ketil, I'm sorry – I think he's dead.'

Outlandish words in *The Fate of the Sea Stag* (mostly place names)

Danmark – Denmark
Dunrostar hofdi – Jarlshof (this name, Norse though it sounds, was only given to the place by Sir Walter Scott)
Fritharey – Fairisle
Gulbervig – Gulberwick
Hamnavoe – Stromness (as re-used by George Mackay Brown)
Hjaltland – Shetland (as re-used by Northlink Ferries)
Hrossey – Orkney mainland (as above)
Irland – Ireland
Jorfhara – Orphir
Jorsalaheim – Jerusalem
Kirkuvagr – Kirkwall
Kittick – kittiwake
Knar – a kind of merchant ship
Mikligard – Constantinople / Istanbul
Nordvegr – Norway
Rinansey – North Ronaldsay
Skalavagr – Scalloway
Stone putter – turnstone (bird)

I've elected to continue rendering Orkney as Orkney and Birsay as Birsay, just to make you feel at home!

About the Author

LEXIE CONYNGHAM IS a historian living in the shadow of the Highlands. Her historical crime novels are born of a life amidst Scotland's old cities, ancient universities and hidden-away aristocratic estates, but she has written since the day she found out that people were allowed to do such a thing. Beyond teaching and research, her days are spent with wool, wild allotments and a wee bit of whisky.

We hope you've enjoyed this instalment. Reviews are important to authors, so it would be lovely if you could post a review where you bought it!

Visit our website at www.lexieconyngham.co.uk. There are several free Murray of Letho short stories, Murray's World Tour of Edinburgh, and the chance to follow Lexie Conyngham's meandering thoughts on writing, gardening and knitting, at www.murrayofletho.blogspot.co.uk. You can also follow Lexie, should such a thing appeal, on Facebook, Pinterest or Instagram.

Finally! If you'd like to be kept up to date with Lexie and her writing, please join our mailing list and claim your free copy of three novellas here:

Murray of Letho

WE FIRST MEET Charles Murray when he's a student at St. Andrews University in Fife in 1802, resisting his father's attempts to force him home to the family estate to learn how it's run. Pushed into involvement in the investigation of a professor's death, he solves his first murder before taking up a post as tutor to Lord Scoggie. This series takes us around Georgian Scotland as well as India, Italy and Norway (so far!), in the company of Murray, his manservant Robbins, his father's old friend Blair, the enigmatic Mary, and other members of his occasionally shambolic household.

Death in a Scarlet Gown

The Status of Murder (a novella)

Knowledge of Sins Past

Service of the Heir: An Edinburgh Murder

An Abandoned Woman

Fellowship with Demons

The Tender Herb: A Murder in Mughal India

Death of an Officer's Lady

Out of a Dark Reflection

A Dark Night at Midsummer (a novella)

Slow Death by Quicksilver

Thicker than Water

A Deficit of Bones

The Dead Chase

Shroud for a Sinner

Hippolyta Napier

HIPPOLYTA NAPIER IS only nineteen when she arrives in Ballater, on Deeside, in 1829, the new wife of the local doctor. Blessed with a love of animals, a talent for painting, a helpless instinct for hospitality, and insatiable curiosity, Hippolyta finds her feet in her new home and role in society, making friends and enemies as she goes. Ballater may be small but it attracts great numbers of visitors, so the issues of the time, politics, slavery, medical advances, all affect the locals. Hippolyta, despite her loving husband and their friend Durris, the sheriff's officer, manages to involve herself in all kinds of dangerous adventures in her efforts to solve every mystery that presents itself.

A Knife in Darkness

Death of a False Physician

A Murderous Game

The Thankless Child

A Lochgorm Lament

The Corrupted Blood

A Day for Death

Orkneyinga Murders

ORKNEY, C.1050 A.D.: THORFINN Sigurdarson, Earl of Orkney, rules from the Brough of Birsay on the western edges of these islands. Ketil Gunnarson is his man, representing his interests in any part of his extended realm. When Sigrid, a childhood friend of Ketil's, finds a dead man on her land, Ketil, despite his distrust of islands, is commissioned to investigate. Sigrid, though she has quite enough to do, decides he cannot manage on his own, and insists on helping – which Ketil might or might not appreciate.

Tomb for an Eagle

A Wolf at the Gate

Dragon in the Snow

The Bear at Midnight

The Fate of the Sea Stag

Alec Cattanach

HITLER MAY HAVE declared war, but police work continues in Aberdeen. Detective Inspector Alec Cattanach, torn between his work in the city and his love of the countryside beyond, has to deal with new crimes and old, regardless of the bombs and the blackout.

A Vengeful Harvest

The Gowden Wifie

The Journals of Dr. Robert Wilson

After Waterloo, and his service with the Honourable East India Company, Dr. Robert Wilson decides to travel east. He is accompanied by his secretary, Gil Archibald, who has his own reasons for the journey. With neither able to tell the truth to the other, how will they cope when faced with murder?

The Business in Blandyce

Other books by Lexie Conyngham:

Windhorse Burning

'I'm not mad, for a start, and I'm about as far from violent as you can get.'
When Toby's mother, Tibet activist Susan Hepplewhite, dies, he is determined to honour her memory. He finds her diaries and decides to have them translated into English. But his mother had a secret, and she was not the only one: Toby's decision will lead to obsession and murder.

The War, The Bones, and Dr. Cowie

Far from the London Blitz, Marian Cowie is reluctantly resting in rural Aberdeenshire when a German 'plane crashes nearby. An airman goes missing, and old bones are revealed. Marian is sure she could solve the mystery if only the villagers would stop telling her useless stories – but then the crisis comes, and Marian finds the stories may have a use after all.

Jail Fever

It's the year 2000, and millennium paranoia is everywhere.
Eliot is a bad-tempered merchant with a shady past, feeling under the weather.
Catriona is an archaeologist at a student dig, when she finds something unexpected.
Tom is a microbiologist, investigating a new and terrible disease with a stigma.
Together, they and their knowledge could save thousands of lives – but someone does not want them to …

The Slaughter of Leith Hall and *The Contentious Business of Samuel Seabury*

'See, Charlie, it might be near twenty years since Culloden, but there's plenty hard feelings still amongst the Jacobites, and no so far under the skin, ken?'
Charlie Rob has never thought of politics, nor strayed far from his Aberdeenshire birthplace. But when John Leith of Leith Hall takes him under his wing, his life changes completely. Soon he is far from home, dealing with conspiracy and murder, and lost in a desperate hunt for justice.

Thrawn Thoughts and Blithe Bits and *Quite Useful in Minor Emergencies*

Two collections of short stories, some featuring characters from the series, some not; some seen before, some not; some long, some very short. Find a whole new dimension to car theft, the life history of an unfortunate Victorian rebel, a problem with dragons and a problem with draugens, and what happens when you advertise that you've found somebody's leg.

Printed in Dunstable, United Kingdom